W9-BAL-797

She would drag the memory—hallucination?—of Veil with her for all her life, Allison realized unhappily. Although, she mused, maybe she just missed a possible place where she was called the Taliswoman and where a magical Cup won by accident could correct her own bad vision and heal the torn earth.

As she began to doze off, she heard a growl, soft and persistent. Alison sat up, groping for her flashlight. Even as she patted the ground, she heard the crackle—the rhythmic, deliberate crackle—of twigs. Something was exploring her campsite.

Something . . . wild.

"One of the most pleasing and resonant voices in fantasy fiction."

—R*A*V*E Reviews

Tor books by Carole Nelson Douglas

MYSTERY

Irene Adler Adventures:
Good Night, Mr. Holmes
Good Morning, Irene
Irene At Large

A Midnight Louie Mystery:
Catnap
Pussyfoot

HISTORICAL
*Amberleigh**
Lady Rogue

FANTASY

Sword and Circlet:
Keepers of Edanvant
Heir of Rengarth
Seven of Swords

Taliswoman:
Cup of Clay
Seed Upon the Wind

SCIENCE FICTION
*Probe**
*Counterprobe**

*also mystery

SEED UPON THE WIND

BOOK II
OF THE
TALISWOMAN

CAROLE NELSON DOUGLAS

TOR
fantasy

A TOM DOHERTY ASSOCIATES BOOK
NEW YORK

Note: If you purchased this book without a cover you should be aware that
this book is stolen property. It was reported as "unsold and destroyed" to the
publisher, and neither the author nor the publisher has received any payment
for this "stripped book."

This is a work of fiction. All the characters and events portrayed in this book
are fictitious, and any resemblance to real people or events is purely
coincidental.

SEED UPON THE WIND

Copyright © 1992 by Carole Nelson Douglas

All rights reserved, including the right to reproduce this book, or portions
thereof, in any form.

Cover art by Darrell K. Sweet
Maps by Darla Malone Tagrin

A Tor Book
Published by Tom Doherty Associates, Inc.
175 Fifth Avenue
New York, N.Y. 10010

Tor® is a registered trademark of Tom Doherty Associates, Inc.

ISBN: 0-812-51249-9
Library of Congress Catalog Card Number: 92-27469

First edition: December 1992
First mass market printing: January 1994

Printed in the United States of America

0 9 8 7 6 5 4 3 2 1

You throw the sand against the wind,
And the wind throws it back again.

—William Blake

QUEST SCAR

Axletree

Quarter of the Four Winds

PEOPLE OF THE HORIZON

ROOKERIES

Sylvin and Hammerhand Lands

ETHERION PIT

EARTH-EATERS CLIFFS

Desmeyne

MAP OF VEIL

© '92 D.M. TAGRIN

SEED UPON THE WIND

BOOK II
OF THE
TALISWOMAN

Prologue

DOG dreams.

Not the animal dreams that make the legs twitch in some phantom race, but the dreams made of human stuff, of memory and regret and rage, the dreams that make the heart race and sometimes break.

Dog sits before the Fire, the Single Fire that never burns out. He sits on his haunches, his long red tongue licking like flame from his sharp-toothed muzzle. He sits on his haunches, his long black hair forking like snake tongues over his naked brown shoulders. He sits, garbed in the pelt of his kind, of his mind.

He sees the five as reflections in a body of still water. Dog they are, like him, and not quite Dog, and not quite like himself. Brute intelligence looks back at him from under widow's peaks of fur, wiser than it is ever given credit for. Yellow eyes, so sage and wary, the flames dancing in the urine-colored irises. Leery canine smiles that show teeth as well as tongue. Coronas of fire-lit fur cloak their shoulders like royal capes.

Gray, black, and fawn, their temperaments name them in the way of wolves: Weatherwise, Quickfang and Cowlick, the males old and young; Featherstep and Moondrift, the young females, one dominant, the other dominated. The ways of the pack can be as cruel as the laws of humankind. No wonder wolf and human are enemies and, on occasion, allies.

Dog grunts. It is an almost human sound, but he is not all animal now. The fire is of his making. The circling wolves

11

gather around it despite their fear, for they fear his more-than-canine nature more than nature itself. They are no longer only wolves, but they do not know it, and will not know it. It is Dog's lot to know these things, to bear these things, to lead his kind beyond the boundaries of their senses and their selves.

He is bridge, is Dog, between brute and human, and which of the two best deserves the word "brute" is often debatable. He is humanimal, who is sometimes called Manitou when the world is soft and the trees bud, and who is named Wendigo when the world's heart wails and would break and humanity hates itself with good reason.

Sometimes, in very specific places, he is called Rambeau. In others as distant and as arbitrary, his name has been Eli. But this is Veil. Here he is Dog, and wolves attend him. Here she who is the Taliswoman is lost and has left. Here blue lightning sizzles in a bottomless black sky and the Heart of Earth fades to forgotten ash. Here the Wendigo blows the People of the Horizon to the far shreds of the sky, and the earth oozes pain.

The Cup is gone, and bitter ashes have nothing to fill.

SALT OF THE EARTH:
DIRT-EATING A "HARMLESS" PASTIME TO SOME

BY ALISON CARVER
STAFF WRITER

Pregnant women and poor folk—when it comes to the ancient but eccentric habit of dirt-eating, these are the prime practitioners. The habit is most common in the U.S. South and in West Africa.

This unusual topic arose at the annual meeting of the National Association of Nutrition and Health Workers, convening through Saturday at the St. Paul Civic Center.

While most of the six hundred attendees debate labeling issues and investigate new food products that manage to find substitutes for the four basically bad food groups—fat, salt, sugar, and cholesterol—medical anthropologists like Dr. Fred S. Farmer explore such borderline issues as dishing up dirt.

Connoisseurs of dirt-eating favor the clay-rich, deep-dug turf of southern hill country to the grittier "gumbo dirt" of the Mississippi Delta, says Farmer. His research shows no harm from the practice, and no benefits.

In past times, he said, observers thought that poor people and pregnant women used dirt to supplement minerals or metals missing from their borderline diets. Modern research does not bear out that theory.

"I just like the taste," Dr. Farmer's paper quotes confirmed dirt-eater Maridelle Oland of Mississippi. "A nice, sour flavor." She keeps a jar on her kitchen counter for snacking, and will sometimes bake a favorite clay with vinegar and salt.

The habit, known as "geophagy," is not so odd, Dr. Farmer insists. "Much of what we eat comes from the earth. And young children are notorious for cramming a bit of terra firma in their mouths. Dirt collected on the deeper levels that aficionados prefer is free of pesticides, contaminants and, er, insects."

Still, no one at the conference is betting that dirt will overtake Chee-tos on the most-wanted list at the grocery store, even if it is better for you. Kind of gives a new connotation to "Mississippi Mud," though.

1

"WELL." Mark McPherson stopped by Alison's desk, her morning food-section story folded open in his hand. "You sure taught 'em to stick you with a boring old nutrition convention. How'd you get on to Dr. Dirt?"

"He was listed among the usual convention presenters," Alison said with a grin. "All I did was actually read the press release."

"Innovative way of finding a story." Mark sat on the desk, or rather on the press releases and news clippings that papered it.

"Thanks, I think."

"How'd you get away with it?"

"It was a new angle, after all. Besides, the subject is fascinating, even if northerners don't have year-'round access to dirt."

Mark shook his bland blond head, the hair fine and straight as flax. "You never take a tried-and-true path if something radical beckons."

"It's called 'freshness'," she pointed out, a tiny edge to her voice. Mark McPherson had the environmental beat, while she was a Sunday feature writer. He could pick and choose his stories; Alison couldn't always, which was why she worked so hard to find a new angle on an assigned story. Besides, dirt-eating was a fascinating topic.

"Hear anything about your dog?" Mark asked.

Questions like that still hurt, although Mark had more right than most to ask them. Alison shook her head, hoping the gesture would disperse any tears predisposed to gather.

Mark nodded, awkwardly quiet for a moment. "I check in with your brother Peter up in Duluth every once in a while. He's a great source for what's going on up on the Iron Range. I'll ask if you want."

"Don't bother Peter about that," she said quickly. "He never was much of a dog lover."

"You two still don't get along, even after he and I 'rescued' you during that big storm last spring?"

"It's not even that." Alison shrugged. "We just don't see much of each other. Peter's still miffed about our folks leaving me the Island."

"Yeah, well, he's a developer. He probably thinks it's a shame for one person to keep a whole island to herself."

"It's Eli's island, too," she added.

"Eli? Oh, that Indian guy who disappeared at the same time your dog did. Nobody's heard anything about him either?"

Alison sighed and shook her head.

"How long has it been? A month?"

"Almost two."

"Maybe it's worth a story."

"The outstate reporter doesn't think so. I asked. I guess a missing old man and a lost dog don't count for much."

"You seem kind of down." Mark lowered his voice. "Why don't we take in a movie, *Terminator* Whatever, at the new downtown movie palace tomorrow night if you're off? Dinner at the Lex."

"Is this a date?" Alison lifted her eyebrows.

Mark shrugged easily. "It is if you say yes."

She said yes.

Some single women would find a Friday night date reason for celebration. Alison felt only a dull pang of interest as she came home to her condominium a few miles from downtown. Mark was right; she was depressed.

Without Rambeau's big white furry form lunging welcome at her, without the sound of his nails clicking across the bare wooden floors, without the kitchen water bowl needing a refill, and the huge rawhide chew-toy underfoot to trip her on her way to the upstairs bedrooms, the airy but compact rooms seemed painfully empty.

Okay, she'd been through quite an ordeal on the Island, and had come out of it. Hey, she'd even reaped a maybe-boyfriend. It was a good thing that Mark didn't know what had really happened up there that weekend. Weekend? Her two and a half days up there made Ray Milland's *Lost Weekend* look like a Cub Scout camp-out.

Alison paused in front of her great-aunt's breakfront in the dining area. Too small to be called a dining room, the space accommodated a four-seater dinette set and the massive piece of stately mahogany with pieces of family flotsam winking behind its glass doors: a Spode tea set too flowery for Alison's modern taste; the odd piece of Belleek, slightly chipped; her mother's delicate porcelain birds, forever perched on perfect petals of hand-tinted flowers.

And the Cup.

The Cup of Earth, from Veil, the land beyond the rainbow, just as near as her friendly family Island.

Alison stared at the object behind the glass. Formed of pale stone threaded with delicate veining, it looked like a prop from an Arthurian play. A metal filigree held precious stones of a half-dozen elusive colors that shone like star sapphires. That Cup had accompanied her across miles of Veil. At times it had felt heavy, at others it had weighed too little to be remembered. Its weight had become the most unbearable at the end, when a man-child had died to keep the Crux from claiming him . . . and the Cup.

Alison whirled away from the breakfront, imagining what Mark McPherson would make of all that. Veil . . . the Crux . . . a child-sized adult known as a Littlelost. And Rowan. What would Mark think of Rowan Firemayne?

She laughed. Like the Cup, Rowan himself was an escapee from medieval myth. She pictured him in her condo, sitting on the mushroom-colored leather sofa. No, not sitting . . . standing and glowering at it as if a simple seating piece were an alien life form. Rowan, with his lofty staff knocking into the light fixtures, his punk-red hair real and shoulder-length, his intensity that filled the out-of-doors suddenly snuffed by the cramped, trendy confines of Alison's so modern, so politically correct, so safe and sterile world.

But St. Paul wasn't really that safe. That was why she had kept Rambeau, a fiercely loyal, eighty-pound Samoyed. It tore her in two to think that she had left him behind in Veil, just as it disturbed her to sense the Cup sitting dormant in her breakfront, the Cup that she had seen work weird, undeniable wonders.

"Get it together, Carver," she told herself out loud. "You've got a date, girl, with a man decent enough to check on a fellow employee who might be stranded on an island during a bad storm."

She had never talked to herself before, just to Beau. Hungry, fella, huh? Pant, pant, yes, yes. Quick barks and playful lunges, and sometimes a sigh just before he laid his big black nose on his paws and went to sleep. Anyone who had never had the companionship of a dog could not understand her loss.

And no one who had never visited another world—who had never seen, tasted, smelled, or touched its reality, who had never left hostages to that reality—could understand how common and cold the real world was in its wake.

Alison turned again to the breakfront. One of the Cup's cabochon jewels winked at her as if catching a reflection. She had forgotten that she still carried the Cup when she'd run from the final horror beneath Veil, when she'd fled the Earth-Eaters' domain and a Littlelost's death. Mostly, she had fled the sight of Rowan Firemayne kneeling to gather his brother Lorn's ashes into his hands, his long fiery-red hair a veil obscuring his face, and his expression, as he bent to collect death like one who quested for his own.

Who would believe her, if she told? Told him. Mark? Or her brother Peter? Who would believe her but Rambeau, who was gone? Did she need so much to be believed? Or simply to be understood? Or did she need most of all only to believe?

She went to the breakfront, turned the tiny brass key, and took out the Cup.

* * *

Jenny leaned across the lunch table to squint at Alison. "You're not wearing your contact lenses anymore!"

"Goodness! How can you tell?" Alison laughed uneasily.

"I can always see the little white curved reflection when people wear contacts. What happened to yours?"

Alison shrugged and idly forked her salad. She wasn't used to lying to her friends, but telling the truth would be worse. "It's weird, but my vision just . . . got better. My mother always said I'd outgrow my myopia."

Jenny's open face squinched in amazement. "Not *that* much. Well, wow, it'll be nice not to have to mess with contacts. Wish I'd outgrow *my* myopia."

"Then you couldn't switch to knockout blue lenses for parties," Alison pointed out. Jenny had always loved extremes of fashion, even when they had been in high school together.

Jenny nodded. "True. I'm going to use them for the ceremony." Jenny's forthcoming June wedding was the reason for their lunch at Dayton's department store.

"Right," said Alison, not about to admit that contact lenses were the least of her worries.

"So what's new?" Jenny wondered.

"Not much. I still love my job, even though I have to fight to do good stories. Newspapers ain't what they used to be now that advertising is down. Management is more worried about declining circulation than about community responsibility."

"Maybe you're burnt out," Jenny said blithely.

"Maybe."

"Maybe you should get married."

"That's no solution to career burnout."

"No, but in the nineties, it's not a bad idea. Monogamy versus social Russian roulette. Got any hot candidates?"

Alison ate a bit of the salad her fork had been pitching like hay as she considered Jenny's question. "Another reporter asked me out. Mark McPherson. He seems nice."

"Then grab him! Nice; steady job; actually asked you out. What more do you want?"

"Jenny! This from a blushing bride-to-be? Whatever happened to romance and roses?"

"The nineties," she said direly, spearing the last shrimp on her plate. "Let's go look at the dress. I hope this is the last fitting."

Dayton's bridal department was a twilight zone to Alison. Since she'd first been brought downtown as a child, she had glimpsed the offset semicircle that led to it as a forbidden fairyland, like the fur department. It was not for little girls. One went there only when one intended to buy, on fairy-princess occasions that come seldom to a woman's life.

This forbidden world boasted a gatekeeper: a chic, middle-aged woman behind a delicate desk whose fingers glittered with nail lacquer and diamond rings.

Jenny was wafted into a fitting room the size of a racquet-ball court, Alison in tow. The saleswoman vanished like a gnome and soon reappeared bearing a cloud of silk organza and tulle. Jenny did not so much don the dress as allow the woman to guide its lavish yardage over her slim form. A white-sequined headdress spouting cataracts of tulle veiling was fitted onto her head like a crown. Then she mounted the two steps leading to a carpeted pedestal and faced the mirror. The saleswoman bent and fluffed and draped and smoothed the fragile cumulus of fabric.

"Well?" Jenny looked coyly at Alison over a puffed sleeve frothy with lace and opalescent sequins.

Alison's immediate and most honest reaction was that Jenny looked like a Loftlady of Veil, except that the Veilian ladies' attire was even more unearthly and glamorous than that of a wedding gown and was not to be found in the here, in St. Paul, and the now.

"Gorgeous, Jenny! It fits like a dream," Alison said. "You look like one." Yeah, mine. Only it wasn't a dream.

But now the saleswoman had to ensure that the proper alterations had been made, that the sleeves should not be taken up a smidge, or the hem let down another quarter inch. At last Jenny was divested of her gown and stood on her pedestal in her shocking-pink underwear, looking like an undressed Barbie doll. "Could my friend see the bridesmaid gown?" she asked the saleswoman.

19

Jenny dressed while they waited, and then the woman whisked back in, her arms bearing a full-length mass of pale-green *peau-de-soie*, which she hung from an empty hook with great panache.

Alison eyed the gown with its elbow-length puffed sleeves, full skirt, and scoop neck.

"Isn't it spectacular?" Jenny demanded. "Each bridesmaid picks her color, but the style stays the same." She looked at Alison's noncommittal face, then turned swiftly to the saleswoman. "And the maid-of-honor dress, the size ten!"

"I know what you're worrying about," Jenny said the instant they were alone. "But the maid-of-honor dress is always different. Don't worry. I thought of everything!" Her smile was encouraging, even smug.

Again the woman bore a gown into the room, this one of daffodil yellow. It bloomed on another hook.

"Fine," Jenny told the saleswoman. "I'll help her into it and call you if it needs alteration."

Alison saw at once that her gown had a high neck, a Victorian wedding-ring collar. Jenny waited impatiently for her to take off her knit skirt and jacket, the turtleneck sweater.

For a moment, the many mirrors surrounding them flashed back the straight, raw lines of the scars marking Alison's chest from collarbone to décolletage. Then the soft, enveloping gown was smothering her, Jenny's hands tugging it down past her raised arms and shoulders, at last zipping the back.

Jenny's reflection beamed at the Alison in the mirror.

"Isn't it great?" Jenny prompted.

Alison wasn't so sure. The yellow flattered her dark hair and slightly tanned skin; in the city, she jogged if weather permitted. The gown's design—a lace-edged, low yoke that cut across her shoulders, matching lace on the high neck, and semi-opaque organza bridging the skin between—cleverly camouflaged Alison's disfigurement while implying the kind of glamorous revelation that weddings and formal gowns require. Alison hated it so much that she was almost speechless.

In Veil, at least, her scars meant something. In Veil, they counted for something, as battle scars always did. Here, they were just a flaw to be hidden. What if she demanded a scoop-neck dress like the other attendants'? Would Jenny look away, try to talk her out of it? Jenny wouldn't say that it would ruin her wedding, but she would think it. And she would think Alison crazy to want to flaunt what she had felt necessary to conceal for most of her life.

Jenny was circling Alison, fussing with her hair. "Now that you're letting it grow out, you could put it up, with little tendrils hanging down. Well?"

"It's a great dress," Alison said, shaking her hair free of Jenny's gentle hand-styling and disliking the social lie.

"And it fits," Jenny added. "Step up. Mrs. Danbury will mark the hem, and that'll do it."

So Alison stood virtually motionless atop the carpeted pedestal for fifteen minutes, turning infinitesimally when the saleslady told her to, while pin after pin slid through the soft fabric at her feet. From every angle she saw herself, lovely on the surface but feeling trapped and diminished just beneath it.

She sighed with relief when she was allowed to step down and change back into her casual clothes. In a few more minutes, she and Jenny parted outside the bridal department. Alison took the escalator up to the china department; might as well get the wedding present while she was thinking about it.

The china department was another alien landscape. Alison was a pottery person. The remnants of her great-aunt's sets of china and glassware were her only truly fragile objects.

She roamed the aisles, dazzled by silver and crystal, at a loss for a suitable gift from a maid of honor. Something good, something bridal, something lasting.

She stopped before a pair of silver goblets. Traditionalist Jenny would treasure these. The price was beyond what Alison considered gift range, but you got married only once, especially these days, right? And Jenny had been a good friend, and only meant the best. She deserved the best.

Alison studied the embossed silver stems, her reflected face twisted into melancholy in the shining silver bowls. So like a chalice, she thought, touching one's cool, metallic surface. Modern life seldom called for anything more formal than a crystal champagne flute. In Desmeyne, in Veil, the very walls were fashioned from rock crystal. . . .

A bright flash of red streaked like a comet through the silver. Alison turned, startled. The only red in sight was on the head of the figure moving away in the main aisle, toward the escalator. A tall, fluid-moving man with spectacularly red hair worn long in back.

Alison's mouth dropped open. Think of Veil and see red? See Rowan-red hair? Rowan Firemayne himself? Incredible; she had never seen hair that violently red outside of Veil, outside of dreams.

She found herself moving after him, like a detective tailing a quarry in a movie, yet also drawn like a sleepwalker into a familiar dreamscape. She remembered only at the last display table to set down the silver goblet, where it rested among the china birds poised on their painted branches.

The crown of red hair was slipping below the notch-toothed horizon of the escalator stairs. She hurried, glad she had worn sensible shoes—Famolares—to her ladies' lunch with Jenny.

There he was, near the bottom of the constantly vanishing stairs and—Lord!—his hair really was that indescribable, unearthly color, part burnt-violet mahogany breakfront, part punk-fluorescent paint, part copper kettle and fresh blood and dying sunset.

She ran down the moving staircase, edged around shoppers content to ride, brushed past Dayton's bags and businessmen and ladies who lunched and had their hair done.

She reached the bottom. Her quarry had vanished. No, she glimpsed the red hair on the next down escalator. She leaped aboard with the pounce of a *taekwondo* expert, which she was. He was closer now. A tall man, with a springy step as he bounded off the escalator and turned tightly to board the next one down. She glimpsed a wedge of face before it blurred out of sight.

She was right behind him, but now he was walking down the escalator, a young man in a hurry. She hastened down the moving stairs herself, surefooted, determined. She had to get a good look at that hair. She had to see his face. Make sure. Catch up.

The extra-long escalator to Main displayed the crowds below—lunchtime shoppers milling among aisles laid out like an English garden maze, glittering with perfume bottles, jewelry and cosmetics. Alison was only five or six steps behind him now. Even as one of his long, blue-jeaned legs loped off the escalator, her feet stuttered across escalator steps that grew shallow before they disappeared.

He paused to turn and grin back at her, as if he knew she'd been following—chasing—him all along! The hair was ridiculously red, impossible to describe. But his face was . . . pleasant, ordinary. Not Rowan's face. His expression was unlike any she had seen on Rowan's face, too: a laughing, knowing, teasing look that stopped her in her tracks, which were . . . vanishing.

Forced to look down, Alison barely saved herself from tripping and falling at the escalator's treacherous end. She hadn't been gauche enough to do that since she was a kid. Her stomach gave a nasty leap as she caught the rubbery handrail she had spurned all the way down. Then her feet were on the terrazzo floor, and she stepped aside as the more demure riders funneled off the escalator, giving her scathing looks.

She gazed around. The tall red-haired young man was gone. She cruised the aisles, searching for his torchlike head. Gone. Just like Beau and Eli. Like Veil.

Mark McPherson's keyboard was clucking like a hyperactive chicken, chattering out some late-breaking story, when Alison got back to the office.

"Can I take a rain check on the movie?" she asked abruptly.

"Huh?" He looked up, lost in his story.

"Sorry. I have to go up to the Island this weekend."

"Sudden trip, isn't it?"

"I haven't been up there since Rambeau disappeared, since you and my brother came out to find me. I think I'd better confront some things."

Mark frowned, then nodded slowly. "Maybe it's a good

23

idea. You've been kind of . . . disconnected since you got back."

Alison nodded, too, not that she agreed with him, but because it was a good enough excuse as any. Maybe it was time to see if she could connect again with what had happened on Swan Lake, with the Island that had unfolded to become a strangely dangerous and endearing world, with Veil.

Jenny would say that she was crazy to walk out on a date, but maybe she had a date with destiny first. At five o'clock, Alison went back to her apartment, changed into T-shirt and jeans, and left for northern Minnesota. The last thing she stuffed into her well-outfitted backpack was the Cup of Earth from her great-aunt's breakfront.

2

THE Island never changed, and was always changing.

Now, in June, it was a peninsula. Gone were the high spring waters fed by melting snow that had made it a true island in April. Swan Lake glimmered blue in the distance, darkening as the sun withdrew behind the pine tops.

Alison eyed the old Carver family rowboat, stranded on solid land and looking more like a wooden sculpture than a water-worthy vessel. At least she wouldn't have to cross water to reach the family campground. Did she hate the water because as a child she had seen it swallow her older sister Demaris before her eyes? Or because it always reflected her helpless guilt? Alison touched the scarred place on her chest, remembering how an old Indian pot had cut her when she fell while running to seek help for her drowning sister. She had paid for her helplessness.

Or did she just hate the water because going near it might call for a bathing suit that would reveal her disfigurement?

Yet since her time in Veil, where she had bared her scars to prove her bizarre qualifications for winning the Cup of Earth, she had begun to resent hiding that childhood injury more than she dreaded revealing it. Since returning, if that was what she had done, she had even begun to resent life in the real world and to long for the cruel but unshirking certainties of Veil. At least she knew where she stood there, even if she did not often find the ground easy to hold.

She unloaded her backpack from the Blazer, parked under

25

its usual pine tree, and walked across the land bridge's grassy neck to the heart of the Island.

Everything was untouched: the concrete pad for the large family tent her parents had used; an old coffee can full of rocks; her sleeping bag in the storage shed, discolored near the foot where the wolf—a "Slinker" in Veil—had urinated to mark its territory, namely Alison herself.

Alison began her ritual inspection circuit of the Island, swatting mosquitoes and squirting on repellent as she pushed through woodsy underbrush. Ghostly birch trunks flitted past like silver needles impaling the rich tapestry of the forest's pine-green background. Squirrels stirred branches, making Alison look aloft for vagrant Littlelost. But only pine cones decorated the forest floor, not the ever-edible pomma of Veil, which the Littlelost had collected from the trees.

Eli's cabin also looked untouched. Alison approached its familiar log sides, her footsteps crunching fallen twigs. No signs or scents of life tinged the area. She pushed the wooden door open, tensed for signs of occupancy, even if only animal.

The only creature inside was the resident dogskin on the wall, its glass eyes without expression, its yellow-white coat lackluster.

It almost cheered her to see that Eli's bottle of Old Crow was empty, and his rifle gone. Maybe Peter had taken the rifle into safekeeping when Mark and he had rescued her in April. Alison couldn't remember. Maybe teenagers or other trespassers had finished off the whiskey.

That would be all right, just so the long-gone drinkers hadn't been Takers. Nothing in the cabin looked disturbed enough to have suffered the attention of those brutal taskmasters, though. No, only kids and raccoons had rustled through these woods since April. As for real-world vandals, give them time.

Alison returned to the central camping area as the sun set, not admitting to herself that she was disappointed to find no signs of alien occupation. Nor was the Island extending its square footage to encompass the mountains of Veil, as it had so seamlessly done before. Was she expecting to enter the not-so-merry land of Veil by simply setting foot on ground that had been remorselessly ordinary for generations? Did she think that she could click her heels together—not easy to do with sneakers instead of ruby slippers—and wish herself into an unreal world away from home?

She would drag the memory—hallucination?—of Veil with her for all her life, Alison realized unhappily, just as she did Demaris's death. Both had been accidents, but radical, life-altering accidents. And if anyone thought her crazy for taking her helplessness to save her sister so hard, they would really think her nuts to miss a place that had been, if strangely beautiful, cruelly real, a place that had rejected everything she was: a modern, working, single woman.

Maybe she missed a place where she was called the Talis-woman. Where a magical Cup won by accident could correct her own bad vision, heal the torn earth, and detect poison water.

Coming up to the Island had been a mistake, Alison decided as she ate cold beans. Eli was missing. Beau was no longer here. Now the Island harbored more than the ghost of her sister. The phantom-pale memory of Rambeau threaded the underbrush. Eli's firm but surprisingly soft step crackled under the pine boughs. Littlelost capered with squirrels, and the quick red flick of a male cardinal could be the lick of Rowan Firemayne's hair seen through a web of time, space, and trees.

You made your bed, now lie in it. Alison gingerly stretched out the sleeping bag for the night. A slight whiff of wolf whiz competed with the perfume of the pines. Mosquitoes droned inches away from the sickly sweet scent of the repellent she had smeared on. Now *that* was magic, an ointment that banished insects. . . . Tomorrow she would drive back to the Twin Cities, see if Mark would be game for the Saturday-night movie, and forget about all of the things that bothered her.

Tomorrow. An owl hooted mournfully in the distance. If she listened very, very hard, she could hear waves lapping like a water clock on the nearest shore. All was as it should be: she was on the Island, and no one, nothing, was on the Island with her that shouldn't be there. Maybe finding the place so properly abandoned would still her doubts, would set her mind at rest.

And then her thoughts sank into the dry waters of sleep.

Rambeau was tugging at her sleeping bag. And growling. Grrrr. Grrrr. *It's not a game, boy! Let go!* Teeth bared in a tenacious grin. Long, narrow white legs braced as he leaned back and pulled . . . pulled . . . pulled. Grrrrrrr.

It's not a game!

Alison awoke grasping the top of the sleeping bag, holding on for dear life. The night was as dark as it gets in the wilds, the stars random chinks in the entwined branches of the tall pines.

Despite the dark, she had expected to see the white blur of Rambeau, so strong had been the dog's presence in her dream.

Grrrrr, moaned the pine tops. Grrrr, agreed the underbrush. Grrrrr, she heard . . . soft and persistent. *Some*thing was growling! That had triggered her dream image.

Alison sat up, groping for the flashlight. Even as she patted the ground next to the sleeping bag, she heard the crackle—the rhythmic, deliberate crackle—of twigs. Then a snuffle as a nose perhaps tracked along the ground. Something was exploring her campsite. Something . . . wild.

She snapped on the light. It illuminated a needle-narrow shaft of landscape. She swept it around, spearing only dark-drenched trees, the corner of the concrete pad. Then something thunked on the ground near her head. She swung her only weapon, light, toward the sound.

Saw . . . gleaming amber irises. Saw . . . the dog from her dream. Saw . . . a piece of flesh at its feet.

"Aaayagh!" Alison scooted as upright as she could in her sleeping bag. "Rambeau!"

At the sound of the name, the figment of her dream sat on his haunches and tilted his white head, his tongue amiably draping a mini-mountain range of sharp white teeth.

"Rambeau?" she repeated softly, wonderingly.

The dog whimpered and inched his forelegs forward until he

lay in a sphinx position. His head ducked as his black nose nudged the object he had lain by her side.

The flashlight focused on it. Yugh. A piece of bloody meat, short-haired hide still hanging onto it. Alison trained the flashlight on the dog again, reached a tentative hand to the thick fur ruff at his neck.

A growl. She snatched her hand back. But the growl had not come from Rambeau!

The flashlight probed the underbrush again, this time striking the golden gleam of other irises. A wolfish face squinted into the spotlight. A Slinker. Then . . . oh, Lordy, maybe Rambeau hadn't come back to Alison and the Island; Alison and the Island had gone to Veil. Again. But—

Something mewed. A cat? Rambeau was consorting with a cat? A lot of cats, for the mew repeated and echoed itself. Her ears finally found the source. The flashlight revealed a knot of baby polar bears lumbering semi-blindly over each other. Even as she fixed them in the artificial light, the distant growling escalated to oncoming thunder.

A pale, lean form stood over the tumbling cubs, its muzzle wrinkled in fury, its slender, fur-feathered legs braced wide. Alison whisked the flashlight from the mother defending her cubs to Rambeau at her side with the dirty, greasy hunk of flesh.

"Family?" she asked the dog as if expecting an answer. "*Your* family? But, boy, you're fixed."

For answer, he nudged the awful meat closer to her. Alison shook her head. "No. No thanks." She pointed. "Them. Give it to them."

Beau looked puzzled, but he knew games of fetch and deliver. His big jaw closed on the offering and he dragged it over to the capering cubs.

His return with the meat sufficiently occupied the female so that Alison was able to catch the action in the flashlight beam. The light glanced off other hunks of meat on the ground. Apparently Rambeau had been dividing the catch for the family when he decided to share with Alison.

Family. The dog had been neutered! Yet the female certainly accepted him, and the cubs gamboled between both adults' big paws. Alison shook her head. Either this was the weirdest, most realistic dream she'd ever had, or she was back in the very odd land of Veil.

She blew out her breath as she switched off the flashlight. Better to let morning sort out fact from fancy. Meanwhile, if Beau and his cohorts were a dream, they couldn't hurt her. Even if they were real, she trusted Beau not to let anything harm her. After all, he'd brought her a gift. . . .

Morning awakened Alison gradually, with the subtle chatter of birds and the warming checkerboards of light latticing the ground. Bones lay in a littering heap where the Slinker and cubs had been. Nothing else was around.

Alison rose, glad she no longer had to bother with contact lenses in order to see, and stumbled over to the primitive but effective sanitary facilities her family had installed years ago. Something gnawed at her stomach: appetite, and the deeper hunger of curiosity. Had she crossed some invisible line into Veil again? Would Veil always be here for her? And if Rambeau wasn't really lost, was Eli somewhere out there, too? And . . . Rowan? Sage? The Littlelost? Maybe you couldn't go home again, but could you go *away* from home again?

She headed back to her sleeping bag, dug a packet of trail-mix from her backpack and gulped down a handful . . . though right now her biggest hunger was a ravenous need for answers.

She took the Cup from her pack. It looked as innocuous as it had while in her mahogany breakfront. She poured the springwater she had brought into the white stone bowl and drank from it. Did the slight cherry flavoring have a fuller taste, did the bubbles burst against her lips and teeth with a bolder zest? Or did she drink down her own imagination?

At any rate, the Cup was dry after she finished. She wrapped it in a soft flannel shirt and wedged it into the pack again. Time to go exploring. "Come on, Beau!" she called, as she used to do.

But all that came was the thought that she was pursuing an exceptionally vivid dream. A tramp through the same territory she had traveled last night showed only wilderness as overwhelming as a Loftlady: beautiful but empty. Perhaps she should be glad she hadn't crossed the Takers' barbaric traces that she had found in April. But without blemishes, was beauty really appreciated? And Veil had been beautiful.

In her search, she even ventured near the drop-off where Demaris had drowned at the age of fourteen. For once, the first sight of the water didn't clench Alison's stomach with regret, fear, and guilt; now the very fact that it was there disappointed her on some inner level. She had left Veil, rejected it, denied the land that had required the sacrifice of the Littlelost known as Pickle. Now she felt like a Cinderella who had told everyone at the ball how shallow and silly they were and then had run off without even the courtesy of leaving a glass slipper as a calling card. Now she wished she could go back and do it over again . . . differently.

Even as she thought this, the lake's gentle ripples skimmed toward the shore, toward her, a barrier to her not only on this world, but a barrier to the other world.

A raw bark interrupted her reverie. Beau! He *was* here!

She ran toward the sound. The bark was repeated, urgently: pure domestic dog crying a warning. She jogged along the shore, her backpack pounding against her spine, until she rounded a curve and saw the canines gathered by the water-line, cubs and all.

Alison stopped, seeing what caused Beau's barks. Two men stood in the tree shadows on the mainland seventy-five yards across the water. They ignored Beau's wild, hoarse barks, their eyes and arms straining upward, shotguns raised high.

Alison approached the canine family. Mrs. Rambeau, a fawn-coated wolf much slighter than the Samoyed, backed off, teeth bared. The cubs—some white and some tapioca-yellow, others gray, their little bodies too intertwined to count—milled at the water's edge. Their small ears were puppy-blunt, their snouts mere snubs, their eyes wet raisins.

Alison shaded her eyes against the bright morning to search for the hunters' prey. Nothing that she knew of was in season, but an ungainly silhouette was sawing through the sky-blue currents overhead. A Canadian goose? No, a wild swan, a bird once common enough to name the lake and now an endangered species.

"Hey!" Alison shouted at the men, cupping her hands around her mouth so her call would carry across the water. But her warning was drowned out by the bark of two shotguns in turn.

She stared up at the sky like the hunters, watching the swan hesitate as if hitting an invisible force field. Then it plummeted.

"Hey!" Alison yelled again at the top of her lungs. "Swans are protected!"

The hunters swiveled toward the sound of her voice. So did their shotguns. Somewhere she sensed the swan falling and slapping the water in a limp, mangled mass. Then she realized that these were real-time hunters in Frye boots and blue jeans, while she stood on the shore with hybrid pups of Veil and Minnesota milling at her feet.

The men aimed at her as mechanically, as thoughtlessly and as lethally, as they had followed the lone swan's sweeping course across the sky.

She doubted that they could hit such distant targets, but Alison dropped to her knees to gather squirming Slinker pups to her ankles like a mother duck assembling her flotilla of ducklings. The analogy was too apt; they were all sitting ducks for the shotgun barrels, especially the pale-coated animals. Still, the men would hardly shoot at them with a person in their midst. The gun muzzles lowered slightly to adjust to Alison's new squatting position—and as her mouth opened to shout a protest, she saw the hunters shrinking, drawing away like figures on a train-station platform.

The sparkling water between mainland and shore grew murky and dull. It stretched like overchewed bubble gum, the opposite shoreline dwindling into its own miniature, two barely visible mini-men poised to discharge their tiny guns.

Alison's vision blurred as her stomach lurched with motion sickness. She heard two pops, like muffled champagne corks releasing, and wondered if her hearing had suddenly shut down.

Then frenzied mewlings began at her feet. Beau's furry side brushed by as he bent to take his offspring one by one and drag them onto shore by the scruff of the neck . . . for the water's greasy, stretching surface had ensnared the pups. Their short legs flailed, their heads tilted back, and tiny-toothed muzzles strained to keep from sinking into the muck that engulfed them.

Their mother waded into the oily liquid to snatch a snow-white pup from the wet blackness. The once-broad ribbon of clean lakewater between Island and mainland was shriveling and thickening into a bottomless black puddle, spawning a vortex that drew the pups ever closer to its deadly center.

Alison eyed the adult animals' tarry forelegs, then stepped into the gooey mess and sank to her anklebones in cold, rubbery muck. She grabbed the scruff of a little neck and dumped the pup on the solid land behind her. In front of her, a small head that looked like a baby harp seal's floated toward the dark, swirling center.

Alison edged farther in, feeling the invisible slope underfoot grow steep. Who could see a drop-off in this obsidian ooze? The pup's face sank, then surfaced, sputtering what looked like coffee grounds. The poor thing wouldn't just drown, it would smother in this stuff. Alison took a backward look at the Samoyed-wolf family huddling behind her, the parents' brows wrinkled with puzzlement.

She didn't understand what was happening either, only that the last little pup was about to be swallowed up. Alison's feet moved forward for another eighteen inches, then dug down for purchase. At the same time, she shifted her balance as far forward as she dared, stretched out an arm. Fingers . . . brushed oil-slicked hair, slipped off the sinking head, reached under and grabbed a short leg. She pulled, letting her weight fall back. A yelp, a nasty sound like a suction cup jerking free, and Alison was falling backward into the animals.

Grinning wolf faces showed their teeth. Sharp, dirty claws clambered over her. Dizzy, she lay there watching the treetops play ring-around-a-rosy. A smell of burned tires and rancid bacon grease settled over her like an invisible blanket. When she sat up, there was no lakeshore, only a sunken, curdled pit of swampy earth the size of a hot tub.

Rambeau's mate was swabbing down her dirty offspring with true maternal devotion. Alison counted noses—three, four, five. She couldn't be sure that all were accounted for, except that neither adult was directing anxious glances toward the sinkhole.

Alison did it for them. The foul pit marked the otherwise green land like a suppurating wound. Her jean leg was caked with the blackish crud; its crude perfume overdosed them all. The backpack lay where she had dropped it. She grabbed it and rose, knowing that she had just seen Veil reach out and touch someone: herself.

"Let's go," she told Rambeau, not at all sure of where they would go. She was willing to let the dog lead her there, wherever it was.

3

ALISON felt an absurd sense of accomplishment.

Of course she was probably hallucinating—maybe from mud-sniffing—but still, everything around her felt like Veil, and she had Rambeau back, however altered.

She glanced at the dog trotting alongside her. "Altered" didn't seem the right word for him any longer. The tumbling puddle of pups weaving around his legs testified that Alison should return to St. Paul and slap a lawsuit on the vet for negligence in keeping Rambeau from conduct unbecoming an It.

The adult Slinker hovered at their rear, obviously intending to oversee Alison as well as her wandering brood. Every so often, the pale-coated wolf would melt soundlessly into the underbrush on a scouting expedition.

The woods looked the same as before, minus Takers, and so seemed almost safe. If Rambeau and family were serving as Veil's welcoming committee this time around, they were much more hospitable than the brutish Takers, who had forced Alison to shoot one of them in order to free the Littlelost.

Alison felt curiously lighthearted for one stranded again in a changed world. The inquiring reporter in her was eager to know what had happened here since she had been catapulted back to the real-world Island two months ago. Had the Littlelost and Rowan found their way back from Heart of Earth far below the Earth-Eaters' domain? How did Rowan's parents take the news of Pickle's demise, now that Rowan knew the Littlelost for his long-lost elder brother, Lorn? What of the

35

nameless red-haired female Earth-Eater, likely another abandoned Firemayne?

Affairs could not rest easy in the Firemayne family. All Desmeyne must be in an uproar at the revelations about the Earth-Eaters Rowan would have brought back. . . .

Alison stopped dead in her tracks. Suddenly she understood why her separation from Veil had rankled, and why she now welcomed her intrusion back into its strange and dangerous borders.

Veil and the Firemaynes were part of a story she had not yet finished reporting. Until she knew what made these people tick, what made Veil run, she couldn't rest content. She had been foolish to think she could outrun her curiosity.

She sensed the weight of the Cup in her pack again, as if it carried the whole world of Veil. The Cup did not belong to her; she was only its caretaker. It was a thing of Veil's that she had inadvertently removed. She remembered the paper's Pulitzer prize-winning reporter, who early in his ambitious career had snitched a family photo from a crime scene so the paper could print it. The managing editor had made him take it back. Alison had not meant to appropriate the Cup, but now, at least, she could return it—to Desmeyne, to Rowan.

Beau was leading the party down a narrow, twisted path veined with exposed tree roots. The animals shouldered past the whip-thin underbrush, but Alison had to duck the heavier branches higher up and angle sideways, her ground-bound eyes keeping her from tripping.

The forest thinned in the abrupt way it had of vanishing in Veil. She could see a vista of sky rimmed by clouds, and the world ahead of her plunged away into a sea of grass, down a sharply raked mountain meadow.

Holding her breath, she studied the deep valleys and far mountains of Veil, so at odds with the flat plains of Minnesota. Nearby, running water thundered into a waterfall. She felt as if she could fall off the ground she stood on and plunge endlessly into this stunning scenery. The same giddiness that had attacked her on the Island came rushing back.

Beau and company had gamboled over to the nearby waterfall, which meandered down a rocky wall to her left. The cubs' continually paddling short legs waddled toward the water; then Alison remembered—"Wait!" she called.

Only Beau paused at her voice. "Wait!" She rushed to the pool the waterfall made before thinning into a swift-rushing stream, and knelt by the water's edge. Even as she rooted through her backpack for the Cup, she had to pause to pluck first one, then another, water-eager cub from the poolside. With polite, mildly puzzled expressions, the adults watched her manhandle their offspring.

"Look." Alison produced the Cup and scooped up the glassy water. "Before you drink, we find out if it's wildwater."

The female—Alison eyed her pale gold coat and decided to call her Madonna—snuffled across the ground, then paused at the water's brink. Wriggling cubs swarmed around Madonna's feet, but she nosed them back from the liquid as if abetting Alison.

"Smart girl," Alison said. Wolf ears fanned forward, then back again to catch and weigh every intonation. Praise was not the usual tone this Slinker of Veil had heard in human voices.

Alison studied the Cup abrim with water, waiting for some phenomenon. At home in St. Paul, the vessel had shown only a stolid cupness. Here, she expected fireworks at the least.

Nothing happened.

"Must be mildwater," she concluded with a shrug of disappointment. Veil was addictive. Once you had seen its wonders, you wanted more, even if they were dangerous. "Okay, guys. Dive in."

At the word "okay," Rambeau sprang into the water and barked, wagging his tail. The knot of pups tumbled after him even as he leaped. Madonna, being wilder, was warier. She was also a native of this deceptive land. She minced to the water's edge, wet her nose and lips, then jerked back.

Alison submerged her hand to the wrist, finding the water temperature appropriately tepid for the gaggle of relative newborns. Good old Veil, with its hot and cold running water, living up to its reputation. What a vacation spot it would make, if they could only unload some unpleasant local residents, like Takers, Womb-bats and etherion coursers.

Alison gazed around, picturing the Veil she remembered as a potential theme park: on yonder mountain, ladies, gentlemen and kiddies, we have the sky-hung castle-city of Desmeyne. The Lost-Mine Ride will take you deep into the bowels of Earth-Eater land, where we have a revolving Caverna restaurant. See the rough Takers delving in the depths in their prison-mines. Watch the rescue of the Littlelost from their etherion pits, ending with a rousing aerial ballet as they are swooped high in the embrace of lighter-than-air metal monsters. . . .

Alison finally sipped from the Cup. She expected the same sizzling effervescence the Cup had conferred on its previous contents. Instead, the water was oddly still, flat. It tasted . . . stale. She spat out the liquid, rewrapped the Cup, and put it back in her pack.

Rambeau, undisturbed by her reaction, nipped at his litter's tiny heels to herd them from the water to their mother. Madonna had settled on her belly to tongue them dry—and to discourage any backsliders from attempting a helping of maternal milk. The cubs were obviously being weaned.

After first liberally shaking his wet coat onto her, Rambeau sat down beside Alison. It felt just like old times.

"At least the canine crew will be clean again," she said aloud, wishing she had access to a civilized bath. "But I wonder what else about Veil has changed. Maybe it's just this waterfall."

She looked up. The sun blazed overhead in motionless high noon. Her stomach growled, and Madonna looked up sharply from her pup-grooming. Alison reached into her pack for another fistful of trail mix. This time she had no nimble Littlelost along to scout for food. This time she had better find someplace, someone, pronto. She didn't relish making do on a menu of Rambeau offerings.

The pup-cubs had obviously never seen open meadow. Once washed, they toddled free of their parents and tumbled down the slope, half running, half falling. Amid the long, green grass bloomed Veil's surprising flowers. The pups charged them, only to see the blossoms take flight like butterflies. The runt of the litter, a snow-white pup with a golden blaze between his eyes, pounced to capture a scarlet bloom, then nuzzled it down to the crushed grasses.

Moments later he exploded upward in a leap that mimicked flight, only to plop down and drag his tiny black nose along the ground.

"Skunky-smelling, aren't they?" Alison went to pick up the wriggling creature. The damaged blossom skimmed away in the wind, brushing its petals over the grass-tops.

The cub was warm and soft. She scratched its ears and listened for low growls from the adults at her human meddling, but none came. These little critters would domesticate beautifully if they stayed around people. Sunlight warmed her head, bestowing an almost tangible benediction. Alison loved the wilderness, but Veil was beyond the pale of ordinary landscapes. Its beauty could hide beastliness.

She moved forward to get a better view of the opposing mountains. Her eyes widened, and her petting hand stilled. Then she smiled. She looked back at Beau, still sitting near his recumbent mate.

"Practically on Desmeyne's doorstep," she murmured. "Most efficient planning. I wonder what determines exactly where I enter Veil."

Still cradling the little cub, who was rubbing his nose roughly on her backpack's shoulder strap, Alison ambled over to the edge of the incline. Desmeyne had lost none of its magnificence. Across the valley, the castle-city lay suspended like a lacy drawbridge between the mountain pinnacles. Sunlight glittered off the sheer, cold expanse of its rock-crystal promenades, and the warm rays softened the striations of the golden and copper stone from which the city was carved. Desmeyne reminded her of a dazzling Christmas tree ornament that had fallen from some lofty height to wedge in a discreet notch, where its brilliance was protected.

Desmeyne and its people stirred mixed feelings in Alison,

but she could never quarrel with the glory of the city as seen from afar.

On the other hand, she could always quarrel with Desmeyne's designated heir and self-proclaimed hero, Rowan Firemayne. She sighed. Rowan would no doubt be furious at her defection of two months ago. So furious that he would probably overlook the fact that she was returning the Cup. Barely twenty years old, he was used to thinking only of himself, just as his entire self-sufficient city was totally self-absorbed. And he had been celibate in his quest-cause for more than a year, which was no guaranteeofgoodhumorinanymale.

Alison started down the incline, wishing she carried a staff like Rowan's instead of a wriggling wolf-Samoyed pup. Despite the music to be faced and the crow to be consumed in Desmeyne, she could hardly wait to find out what had transpired in Veil while she had been absent. It was as if she had picked up a favorite book of fairy tales, to discover a new, unread story among the long-familiar pages.

The animals accompanied her as the descent brought more of the valley into view. Alison was relieved to see smooth earth planted with a rickrack of crops below. The ugly gouges made by the Earth-Eaters' Harrow-worms were still gone—healed by the Cup's restoring powers in her hands. Desmeyne had never looked more idyllic, more peaceful. Maybe this place didn't need her or the Cup anymore. Maybe she had been dreaming to believe that she had "escaped" her own world with something vital, an item of great value wrested from the very essence of Veil.

The slope abruptly became a cliff. Had she been a waterfall and kept plunging on, she would have taken a quick turn straight down. Time to descend to the valley before toiling up again to the city gate, Alison told herself, not enjoying the prospect of her welcome there. The withdrawn Desmeynians did not make it easy for visitors, not even one from another world.

She sat down on the grassy verge of the cliff, releasing the pup. Rambeau's brood clustered around her, crawling over her legs and into her lap. Their father came close, leaning his big black nose against Alison's cheek. A touch, and he leaped back, ready for play or . . . farewell.

"I don't think these guys can climb down the cliff," Alison said regretfully. "Maybe you can wait here until I visit the city. Wait?" She emphasized the word, but it was not intoned as sharply as the everyday commands that Rambeau had once obeyed so well. He had his own world and responsibilities now, and his own place in it; he was no longer hers to command.

Rambeau tilted his head and wagged his white plume of a tail, looking so intelligently puzzled that Alison would have sworn he understood. His mate sank to her belly a few paces away, gravely reticent, like a foreign wife deferring to her in-law's odd practices.

" 'Bye, Beau." Alison laced her arms around the dog's thick-coated neck. It seemed so unfair to find Beau again and then to leave him, but she had to catch up on human events here, too. If the neutered Samoyed had sired puppies, imagine what the celibate Rowan might have been up to. The mind boggled.

A lingering, last look impressed the charming canine family into her mind like a Polaroid. She turned her back to Desmeyne and slid on her stomach over the edge of the cliff until her boot found the first toehold. Puzzled, sharp-nosed animal faces peered down at her for a long time after she began her descent.

The side of the cliff was exactly as she remembered it: a bumpy limestone surface ideal for descending . . . until she reached the sleeker sections farther down. Soon glassy bits of black rock winked at her in the rays of the midday sun. Her neck ached from craning over her shoulder to find footholds, and her eyes grew bleary from studying the dizzy depths below. She had last tackled this descent with vines linking her and the Littlelost to Rowan's sturdy staff. This solo enterprise was shakier, more dangerous. No one would stop her if she fell, or at least keep her company, or even tell anyone that she had passed this way again, however precipitously.

A shadow swept by, putting Alison into sudden, quelling

shade. She looked up for a cloud, but the sky was bald and blue, save for the fringe of horizon clouds ever present in Veil.

She twisted to look the other way without losing her grip on the stone, anxiously scanning for a sharklike, cruising Womb-bat, one of the huge, many-legged creatures that had kidnapped the Littlelost earlier.

No such monster glided above on smothering, velvet wings.

High overhead, resembling a kite that had slipped its moorings, a tiny dot glittered like windblown tinfoil. But anything that small, or that high, could hardly have put her in shadow, however fleeting.

Shrugging, Alison resumed her descent. She was tiring and would welcome crossing the level fields before having to climb the inhospitably steep road to Desmeyne. What these people need is an elevator, she grumbled to herself. She tried to imagine intemperate Rowan waiting meekly for such a device to fetch him, or a lavishly attired Loftlady catching her diaphanous trains in biting steel doors. . . .

A vague motion in front of her eyes brought Alison's mind abruptly back to the cliff. The stone had become more obsidian than anything else, as shiny black as licorice. Alison remembered that she was sliding down the thin stone skin covering the Earth-Eaters' domain; only this time she knew who—and what—the Earth-Eaters were. She shuddered in the sunlight, envisioning the dark, dank regions below, recalling those who shuffled and scuttled in those rocky corridors.

In her assertive, modern way, she had made a passionate case to the Desmeynians that the Earth-Eaters's condition was their doing, that therefore the Desmeynians should do something for the Earth-Eaters. Reporters often played the role of advocate for the unfortunate. Still, the Earth-Eaters were no longer fully . . . human. Alison secretly wished she wouldn't have to confront them or their murky underworld again.

A blurred fetus face floated into the oil-slick mirror the black rock provided. She jerked back, almost pulling loose of the cliff-face. During her first passage, she had mistaken such a glimpse for her reflection in the polished rock. Now she understood that this rock must be as thin as Desmeyne's rock-crystal window-walls and only as opaque as smoked Plexiglas. It could be seen through as well as it could reflect.

A cloudy assemblage of features bumped noses with Alison through the thin barrier of polished rock. One of the vague creatures spread webbed fingers that reached toward Alison. Behind the apparition bobbled the pale intimations of other formless faces.

Alison shook her head and hurried on down the cliff. Haste made her hands and feet slip, yet somehow she still clung to the cliff-face. A downward glance showed her only fifty yards from the bottom, where earthen waves of green stretched away toward the civilized fields of Desmeyne.

She continued swinging down the cliff with the agile bravado of a monkey, seeming to put no limb awry. Footholds sprang up to cup her feet like mossy stirrups. The art of zen regression. Her body met her need for swift descent with an easy, coordinated confidence. Performance under pressure was always a news reporter's long suit.

Then her left foot swung down to feel for another hold and found none. For a moment she balanced, before her backpack-laden weight began to pull her backward. Her free foot flailed wildly . . . kicked out for a purchase, any purchase, kicked through something smooth and brittle.

She heard the unmistakable crunch of thin ice cracking. Alison's foot swung toward the cliff, through the cliff, into someplace vacant beyond the surface—no doubt right into the faces framed in the obsidian windows.

She screamed as hands—chill, as soft as wet putty—grasped her bare leg between her low boot top and her hitched-up denim pants leg. The soft, imprisoning pressure pulled.

Far above Alison, Beau barked hoarsely, the sound reaching her as though through pillows. His mate remained silent. Did wolves bark? she wondered. A silly question, and one she'd not answer right now. She continued to be drawn down and inward, her upper body steadily sucked from its grip upon the rock-face, her shoulders and backpack scraping over a ragged edge of broken black stone as daylight collapsed into a porthole behind her.

The dark was warm and still, yet somehow cold at its heart. Like moths, the Earth-Eaters' pallid faces and hands fluttered over her, brushing her clothes, her hair. A constant chirping murmured from their midst.

These are merely the deserted children of Desmeyne, Alison told herself, struggling upright. She occupied a niche hollowed from rock and once covered with a glasslike sheet of obsidian.

Like inarticulate ghouls, the Earth-Eaters seemed to be dead and buried, yet they were still moving, still touching, testing, fondling her. She felt like the girl in the Brothers Grimm fairy tale who was sent to hell and draped with myriad spiderwebs— in this case, the Earth-Eaters' gentle, trespassing touches. Now they were tugging her along a low passage.

Stooped and confused, and ashamed of her natural revulsion, Alison went where their brushes prodded her, down into the dark, away from the fist of daylight still clenched at her back, her feet stumbling over a rough, rocky floor she never saw. The walls bled a dim fluorescence, the only light. Their path led down, into claustrophobic despair; then at last, it turned upward again. Always the air was stuffy and stale. Always the voices crooned (or perhaps cursed). Always Alison was pulled and tugged and touched.

She wished that she could stop to dig out the Cup from her backpack; perhaps the talisman would manifest some power that would awe the Earth-Eaters. But the cramped tunnels allowed her no room to turn, or even to struggle. The creatures surrounded her like so many formless midwives, urging her body through a tortuous birth canal into a world she did not wish to enter.

Finally the tunnel widened into a cave. Here the inherent luminescence swelled into actual light, however dim. Within this lurid little grotto stood a draped figure.

"Hurry," it whispered, the walls magnifying the word into a chorus.

Alison paused, wanting to question this figure who was not only in command, but who could speak. The hood of its robe fell back at the prodding of its deformed hands. Alison braced herself, then recognized the strands of thin red hair dangling from the balding head.

"You are the Firemayne heiress—" she began.

"You are the Taliswoman," the creature retorted before Alison could finish. "We take you to them, to your Firemaynes. Hurry. The Crux is cruel."

"The Crux?" Dismayed, Alison watched the Earth-Eaters' speaker join the massed figures. They all shuffled onward into another narrow tunnel, bearing her with them. "You are allies with the Crux," she called. "Why keep me from them?"

A hood just ahead of her turned, and the same voice issued from it. "Earth-Eaters have no true allies but themselves and what they pry from the hard ground. Hurry."

The spokeswoman's voice was almost as murky as the coos trilling around Alison from the deeper darkness.

"Why would you aid me?" she asked, no longer sure that the speaker bobbled along before her.

"This is not aid," came the bitter answer, from her right now. "We wish to be rid of you, to speed you away from us. Your last journey here has angered the Crux."

"What of Desmeyne?"

"Ask the Desmeynians."

"I will when I get there."

"You will get there sooner, and safer, if you let us guide you."

"How can I not?"

A gurgling laugh came from the crooning darkness on her left. "You have powers. If you stopped to think, you might use them."

Alison squinted to see in the demi-dark. It was unnerving not to know which shapeless hood addressed her, which hunched form both rescued and reviled her. She had no powers but those of her brain and body, and no idea of how she could use either of them in this encompassing custody. She was caught up in a gelatinous tide of not-quite humanity, and helpless for the moment.

4

INTO that ill-lit darkness seeped a corona of light, an electric blue that gleamed on the rock walls' most prominent surfaces.

Ordinarily, Alison would have welcomed any light in these dungeonlike caverns. This neon-blue light—the mere sight of it—sliced into her eyes like a razor.

A united tremor shook the small forms crowded around her. After a shocked, silent pause, they rushed onward, sweeping her with them. Their constant cooing had ended abruptly, as if a communal garrote had clutched their shrouded throats.

All sound ceased except for the rasp of feet over rock, the distant drip of liquid stone in the stalagmite gardens, and the fizzing hiss of blue lightning rods. Alison had no desire to confront a Crux-master before she had her feet on Desmeynian ground. She pushed forward among the Earth-Eaters, a prisoner become cohort.

"Here," came the speaker's voice.

A small offshoot tunnel beckoned like Alice's rabbit hole: narrow, mysterious, and unpredictable. Earth-Eaters clogged the tunnel entrance, waiting to funnel through. Alison had to swing the pack off and carry it behind her, fighting her dislike of dark, confined, unknown places. She looked back.

Blue light hissed like a snake through the serpentine tunnels they had passed, casting a halo around corners. It spread like air, or airborne toxins made visible. The sizzle reminded Alison of flesh-eating acids, of frying fat, of numerous unpleasantnesses. She hadn't yet seen one of the vertical bars of blue light that announced a Crux-master's presence, but the amount of illumination consuming the passages signaled an entire company of Crux-masters.

She bent from the waist, ducked, and followed—pushed, rather—the last of the Earth-Eaters into the intimidating tunnel.

A rising, hissing tide of blue light pursued them. Ahead lay only deepest darkness and the urgent sound of scuttling feet. Once all of the Earth-Eaters went single file into the tunnel, the pace picked up. Apparently they were used to burrowing speedily in the dark. Alison wasn't. She kept straightening unconsciously to ease her aching back, bumping her head on the low ceiling when she wasn't rubbing her elbows raw on the claustrophobically close tunnel sides.

She ping-ponged along the rough surface, regretting that she had somehow become last in line. If the Earth-Eaters intended to shield her from the Crux-masters, their making her into a sitting duck—duck tail, rather—wouldn't do the job. She couldn't turn to check on the oncoming light, but the smaller tunnel magnified its hiss into the shrill drone of millions of insect wings.

She stumbled forward, wishing she could free her hands and clap them to her suffering ears. The drone became the shrieking whir of a dentist's drill, a noise so intense that she expected to see exploding novas of multicolored lights ahead, like those that migraine-headache sufferers experience. Her teeth hurt. She was tempted to drop the backpack, cover her ears, shut her eyes, and just freeze in place.

Exactly what the Crux wanted, she thought, tightening her grip on the pack. The lights ahead winked like tiny fireworks. Then they steadied. Alison stopped, stunned. Alien constellations of light painted the opaque face of the dark, strange phosphorescent flecks embedded in the walls of the Deeps below Desmeyne.

A touch from the darkness in front of her tugged on her jeans. She sprang forward ahead of a wave of blue light that momentarily tinted the pale backs of her hands. She was tugged right and then left, following her escorts with bruising consequences. The tunnel narrowed into a shaft, and then into a slit. She shimmied forward as far as she could, glancing over one hunched shoulder to see a wall of blue light pouring down the larger tunnel. None of the light leaked into this cul-de-sac. Odd, Alison thought. Light is not a solid. Light expands like gas to fill all visible crevices. Yet this light thrust ahead in the manner of the very Harrow-worms that had drilled the passages, all the while hissing like a steam train.

Something disgustingly flaccid touched her hand. Alison shook off the touch but followed its instruction and moved into a last narrow alleyway of dark. Hot sparks of red, green, and gold glittered ahead. Moving rock revealed another cavern, then began to grind shut behind her.

"Wait!" She implored the emptiness. "My pack!"

The pack was jammed in the crevice that Alison had squeezed through. She thrust her hands into the diminishing space to lift and flatten the pack's contents, which immediately assumed a new, unwieldly formation.

"Hurry!" came the speaker's familiar rasp. "The Crux—"

"I can't!" Alison gasped, punching the pack into yet another shape. She could feel the utter dark pinching shut on her fingers, and jerked the pack forward so hard that she teetered back on her heels. The rock wall ground shut with a final thud. Panting, Alison found herself clutching the freed pack to her bosom like an infant.

"That wasn't there before." She nodded at the impressive wall gate.

No one answered. She turned to confront the one figure whose voice she knew. The cavern was empty. Alison blinked, trying to adjust to the spangled darkness. The place reminded her of a trendy disco, truly "underground." She explored the cave, stepping carefully to avoid a woundlike trickle of viscous liquid that glimmered on the floor.

Above her, like so many pierced bells, still hung the vacant cages that had been used to imprison the Littlelost . . . and others. She jerked back when she saw a small figure dangling from the open door of one of them.

"The mechanism is meant for Desmeynians to operate," the

lone Earth-Eater said. Her voice grated like the cages that swung on rusty chains, their doors that creaked on corroded hinges. "My lesser weight will not draw me to the ground again."

Alison set down the pack after a last glance at the securely shut rock wall. Apparently this device served as a formal gate between Desmeyne and the cavern realms. She looked up. The Earth-Eater swung softly, like the clapper of a bell.

"I'll have to jump up. Then you let go, and I'll break your fall."

"How?" the Earth-Eater asked a bit dubiously. It was refreshing to hear one of this downtrodden breed express concern for its safety.

Alison's empty hands indicated her own chest. "When you fall, you'll land on me. I hope you weigh as little as you seem to."

When there was no answer, Alison said, "Ready? Here I come."

She leaped up, something she had not done in a long time, starting in a deep crouch and straightening as if to aim a basketball at a hoop. Her upstretched hand touched the coarse burlap robe. Then the Earth-Eater dropped on Alison. She braced herself for the encounter with an alien form as well as with an unknown weight . . . and found herself clutching what seemed only a load of laundry.

She collapsed into her crouch again, her knees taking the impact, then let herself and her burden tumble backward. The Earth-Eater sprang away with remarkable speed.

"You're lighter than a waffle!" Alison marveled. She had not expected an adult's weight, but the creature was barely half of Rambeau's poundage. Yet Rowan's older . . . sister . . . must be fully adult, as fully adult as one's life in the darkness beneath Desmeyne would permit.

"What is this waffle?" the creature asked, shaking out its crumpled robes.

"A kind of cake," Alison said, "with great volume but little heft."

"Volume?"

49

Although Alison had learned to translate the languages of Veil at the Wellsunging on the night she had won the Cup, she still seemed able to produce alien words, or at least alien concepts, in it. How odd, but she was neither a physics teacher nor a linguist. She was just a reporter, and she had her own questions: who, what, when, where, and why.

"I recognize the Deeps beneath Desmeyne; why have you brought me here?" Alison believed in getting to the heart of the issue in an interview.

The little figure straightened. "I have a meeting with the Firemayne. Your unexpected presence will be a quaint surprise for him," the Earth-Eater said with relish.

I? Only two months ago, the Earth-Eaters had seemed too beaten down to accept the concept of individuality. Now this spokeswoman flourished the first person singular, and with some pride.

"You don't think the Firemayne will be pleasantly surprised?" Alison asked with a grin.

"No." The hooded form approached Alison to look her over more closely.

"And why," Alison asked, "is the link between your . . . lands now sealed by this movable wall of rock?"

"Earth-Eaters and Desmeynians talk, but they do not trust."

"Who erected the wall mechanism?"

"Desmeyne," the spokeswoman returned.

"So the Desmeynians don't trust you."

"Rightly so. The Crux still comes and goes within our corridors whether we will it or not."

"What of the others of your kind, that we left behind?"

The robes shrugged. "The Crux has no argument with Earth-Eaters. We have traded with the Crux for generations, just as we have, although less happily, with the Desmeynians."

"But the giant worm of blue light—"

"—will not harm us. It is meant to purge the tunnels of intruders. A service, say the Crux-masters, to us."

"Such services can turn lethal."

"Not as long as the Crux needs the things of Desmeyne."

"What things?"

"Yourself. The Cup."

Alison bent to pull the backpack over one shoulder. "Then things have not changed since I left."

"Oh, no, Taliswoman. Things have changed immensely."

Did a hint of sly humor coat that rough voice? Alison decided not to comment on that and asked her final question: "When are you expected to meet with the Firemayne?"

"When I arrive."

"But not here?"

"No."

The Earth-Eater speaker made a terrible interview subject. Answers came forth like reluctantly pulled teeth.

"Where, then?" Alison asked.

The hood jerked almost imperceptibly, indicating above.

Alison shrugged. Two could play at that game.

The Earth-Eater bustled up the gentle grade that led to more tunnels, then to stairs hewn out of solid rock, then to risers of rock crystal that glimmered like step pyramids sheathed in running water.

Alison—what else?—followed.

If Alison's entry into Earth-Eater land had been cramped, claustrophobic, and eerily threatening, her return to Desmeyne should have been a cakewalk. Still, she moved into the city's airy, exotic environs with a curious internal mix of excitement and dread mixed with a dash of bravado.

Bravado was for people who were afraid of something, and what did Alison have to fear in Desmeyne? She was returning the Cup the Firemaynes craved. Apparently the Desmeynians had taken her parting advice to explore a treaty with their little-known traditional enemies below-ground. Alison should be received with open arms, not the edged variety.

Guards bracketed the door leading to the lower arcade that bridged the sprawling city. The men's impassive faces ignored the Earth-Eater as if she were indeed dirty laundry, an improvement in the Desmeynian attitude; once they would have slain an Earth-Eater on sight.

The guards' eyes tightened at the sight of Alison, however. She doubted they recognized her from her previous brief sojourn. Their hands slapped sword pommels. She stopped, automatically primed for challenge. Someone whose tae kwon do moves had brought their Firemayne to his knees was not about to buckle to hired muscle.

"She is with me," the Earth-Eater said.

Glowering, the guards retreated to their posts.

Alison was impressed. "You have much liberty here, for a once-hated Earth-Eater."

"It does not hurt that I am related to the ruling family."

"They accept that?"

"No, but they cannot deny it, since the Taliswoman herself raised the suggestion. The young Firemayne will not let the issue rest, for any of us."

Mention of Rowan quickened Alison's pulse. So he *had* returned from Heart of Earth. She kept telling herself that he shouldn't object to *her* return, but instinct told her differently. A woman winning the Cup was anathema to the men of Veil.

The two now followed the broad walkway that linked the Lofts in which Desmeynian girls and women dwelled with the Men's Quarters on the opposite side. Like most Desmeynian streets, this one was covered by a rock-crystal vault on which the sun showered its bright bounty. Alison spied gray-clad servants moving down on Desmeyne's internal avenues like toothless sharks among the lavishly caparisoned Desmeynian men. Other than the servants, the women, of course, were sequestered, even the wedded ones.

"Your face grows sour, Taliswoman," the Earth-Eater beside her noted. "Perhaps you are as pleased by this forthcoming reunion as the Firemayne will be."

"Perhaps I merely remember the bland, unpleasant food served here. And I cannot see *your* face."

"Consider yourself spared."

Alison found herself before the familiar carved-bone gate to the Firemayne's quarters before she was quite ready to encounter it. Rowan had accompanied her the first time she had broached this barrier. Now what would she say? Hello again?

It occurred to her that Rowan might not attend this meeting, although the Earth-Eater had said that he had insisted on such talks. Surely he would be present? Alison's hands turned clammy, as they had not when she confronted the sword-rattling guards. Honestly, one staff-armed Desmeynian was nothing to worry about, she told herself.

Then she remembered the knowing, mocking smile on the face of the red-haired man as he had vanished down the escalator in Dayton's department store. Maybe she didn't want to know where he went, where he had come from, why he had such unearthly red hair. . . .

Too late. The Earth-Eater's robes brushed the Harrow-worm bone as she waddled through the gate. Alison hurried after her.

Inside, nothing had changed: the great cartwheel of buffed wood still served as a tabletop; the backdrop of draperies was the same; and the Firemayne, Rowan's father, was there.

What changed the moment Alison stepped into the firelight was the Firemayne's face. For stunned moments, they regarded each other in silence. He had aged far more than mere months would warrant. The last flicker of Firemayne red in his graying hair had dulled to a rust color. He had not lost the thickening weight of middle age, but his flesh had sagged unhealthily, even in small pockets surrounding his eyes. Alison was shocked. She had expected Veil—and Desmeyne and its inhabitants—to remain embedded in the amber matrix of that world's strangeness, like a time-frozen Brigadoon.

"Taliswoman!" was the Firemayne's first word, and it was not intoned like the curse Alison had expected. "Rowan said you had run down a throat of fog and been swallowed."

"I have been coughed back into Veil," she answered, walking farther into the room. "I am pleased to see that you speak, at least, with the Earth-Eaters."

He glanced down at the squat but imperious form watching them from the noncommittal shadow of her hood.

"I speak only with this particular Earth-Eater, on Rowan's insistence."

"Since when do you pursue any course on your son's insistence?"

The husky, Earth-Eater voice answered. "Since his son and the Littlelost returned from the hot Heart of Earth, bearing a vessel of ashes."

"Then they, too, returned safely from that horror below?" Alison's relief knotted at last into a lump in her throat. If Pickle—Rowan's Littlelost brother—had died, at least Twist, Rime, Faun, and Camay had survived. "Where are they?"

The Firemayne looked away.

"You haven't imprisoned them again?" Alison demanded. "Do you never learn?"

"I had no opportunity," the Firemayne said shortly. Whether his lost opportunity involved imprisonment or learning was not clear. He paced before the low-burning hearth, then paused. "Why have *you* returned?"

"I'm not sure," Alison answered honestly. "It can't be that I missed Desmeyne. Something reminded me of it, though, and I found my world shaping itself to this." She lifted her pack to the glossy tabletop and delved until she found the Cup. She held it out for the Firemayne's inspection. "At least I remembered to bring the Cup. I thought that it would be better in its natural place. And I didn't want to be remembered as a thief, however unthinking."

He stepped toward it, hope illuminating his face but quickly fading to worry. "You have brought it in scant time, Taliswoman. The Wellsunging comes in two days."

"Two days! But the competition is held every year and a day."

"Two days," the Firemayne repeated stonily. Then he sighed. "Perhaps when you return it, you can again win it."

"Why should you want me to? It was my winning the Cup in the first place that upset all of Desmeyne."

He sighed again. "In the past, you have lent the Cup to our needs. Perhaps you would do so again."

"But what of Rowan? Surely he has not given up his determination to win the Cup for Desmeyne? Unless he has disqualified himself—oh."

She put a hand over her mouth. Had the likely happened and Rowan's youthful, hot blood overruled his vow to remain celibate—and thus he was eligible to compete for the Cup? She smiled. Nature would not be denied forever.

The Firemayne hadn't noticed the direction of her thoughts. He was not a subtle man. He shifted his shoulders under his brocade cloak as if even its weight were too ponderous for him now.

"Rowan is gone," he said.

"*Gone?*" She should have expected this, but not the feeling of disappointment that accompanied the news. Of course Rowan would not linger in sheltered Desmeyne. All of Rowan's energy, his every thought, had been to win the quests that would ensure Desmeyne's safety against a disturbing array of noxious happenings. Alison had a sudden thought. "And the Littlelost who also returned from Heart of Earth?"

"Rowan took them with him, far across the mountains."

"Some sort of quest, no doubt."

"No."

"Then it makes no sense."

The Firemayne offered a pallid smile. "That is exactly what I told him."

A throat cleared. The Earth-Eater spoke. "I have grown accustomed to chairs when within the chill, sharp air of Upper Desmeyne."

The Firemayne drew a small, tapestry-upholstered bench from near the hearth and offered it to the small figure as if to a child. "Sit, then."

Alison claimed another such bench, taking the Cup with her. The Firemayne stirred and looked around.

"No servant will abide in the same chamber as an Earth-Eater. There is water—"

"I prefer the wines of inner earth." Even though the bench was low, the small figure's feet didn't reach the floor.

"Char," Alison said decidedly.

The Firemayne started and seemed about to argue. Only the men of Desmeyne consumed the heady liquor. But Alison had faced hard going to get here, and a shock or two on arrival.

After a moment, it seemed to occur to The Firemayne that no one was present to object to trampled customs. He poured two goblets of Char and presented one to Alison.

"Thank you."

He looked surprised, as if gratitude were unknown to Desmeynians. Perhaps he had never done anything for anyone to earn such a response. He then took his Char to a high-backed chair angled to catch the fire's heat. "Much has changed," he said.

"In two months?" Alison asked.

He shook his grizzled head. "You are an alien woman and count the hours differently. It is almost a year since you last saw my face. I cannot explain your confusion."

She sipped Char and considered. A year! Was it possible? Had the red-haired man in the department store been a kind of White Rabbit crying "I'm late!" to lure her back to Wonderland? If so, the ruse had worked.

"Why do you two meet?" she asked her companions at last.

"Rowan insisted up on it," the Firemayne said.

"Rowan insisted? Firemayne, the last time I was in Desmeyne, whenever it was, you were the one who insisted and Rowan who obeyed, or at least he thought about it."

"He has changed," the Firemayne said. "He came from beyond the Deeps with a furrowed brow and thunder in his voice. He was not content to keep himself safe for the next Wellsunging. He always had a most unDesmeynian will to wander, but after he went heedless into the Heart of Earth, he came back wounded. Now he hazards his very life in enterprises he will not discuss, and barks orders when once he sat and listened. He regards his elders with contempt."

Alison could hardly quote Dr. Freud to the Firemayne, but obviously Rowan's guilt at his older brother's death had spurred him to undertake risky quests. She sipped Char, savoring the smoky, coffee taste, and studied the hooded face on the adjacent bench.

"I can understand that the Firemayne might feel impelled by Rowan's rage," she said, "but why do the Earth-Eaters

bother to meet with Desmeynians after all this time of aliena-
tion?"

For answer, the creature lifted its hands. They were covered
with bleached-muslin mittens. Alison blanched to think of
what might lie beneath the fabric. The rough burlap hood fell
back, revealing the wasted features and scant red hair of the
Earth-Eater spokeswoman.

"Rowan ordered us as well to this course, although we do
not heed any Firemayne's commands. But I was curious to see
if what the Taliswoman had said of the world above was true.
And the Crux has taken the Earth-Eaters for granted. All allies
should suffer some uncertainty; it strengthens the association."

The Earth-Eater then regarded the Firemayne, observing
his nervous glance away from her ravaged features.

Alison wondered whether Rowan or the Earth-Eater had
told any Desmeynian of her own suspicions—no, of her accu-
sations—that Desmeynians abandoned imperfect or inconve-
niently female infants to the Deeps and the Earth-Eaters.

"So what do you talk of?" Alison asked innocently. She
looked at the stunted Earth-Eater. "Does the Firemayne negotiate for the return of the abandoned babies the Earth-Eaters
have taken?"

"No," the Earth-Eater said.

The Firemayne looked away. "There are no Desmeynians
below."

"But your wife admits that such unwanted children were left
in the deepest caverns. Where did they go?"

"They do not survive," he said. "They were eaten."

"By what?"

He was silent.

"Harrow-worms?" Alison suggested. "Womb-bats? Earth-
Eaters themselves?"

"One of those," he said uneasily.

"If Rowan's older brother, Lorn, was living among the Littlelost, no larger than when he vanished at the age of nine, why
shouldn't other missing Desmeynian children live among the
Earth-Eaters?"

"Because it is not so!" the Firemayne said angrily.

Alison glanced at the putty-soft features of the spokes-woman, seeing the aged face of an abandoned infant. "Is this why your talks reach no understanding?"

The creature nodded.

"Maybe we should start with a name," Alison suggested. "What do they call you below-ground?"

"We do not need names!" the Earth-Eater answered with sharp vehemence. "We are Earth-Eaters all, and thankful that we are not Desmeynians. On that we agree, Firemayne."

Alison sipped her Char, then suddenly lifted the Cup from where she had set it on the lapis lazuli apron before the hearth. She poured what was left of her Char into the Cup and extended it to the Earth-Eater.

"Then I will name you. How can you treat when you have not so much as a word in common to call yourself?"

"I do not wish a name!" was the furious answer, but interest dawned in the Earth-Eater's ash-pale eyes. Alison thought she detected a faint tinge of blue there, like the sky at the very rim of sunrise. "You would let me sip from your Cup of Earth?"

"It is *the* Cup of Earth," Alison said. "And who more fit to use it than an Earth-Eater?"

The eyes lifted to peer over the Cup's cool stone edge into the oil-dark liquid within. "Char is one product of Desmeyne we might wish to add to our trading."

Alison tilted the Cup, let the syrupy liquid roll and coat the inner surface with its glistening sheen as rich as dark, wet earth. "A name is not a tether, merely a convenience."

The Earth-Eater seemed mesmerized by the Cup, by the slow, rolling motion of its untasted contents. The head nodded suddenly. "Name your name, but I will answer to it only here, not below."

Agreement caught Alison off guard. Names like Eurydice and Persephone caromed through her mind, but classical allusions were alien to Veil. Besides, lengthy words overwhelmed such a small person.

"Dusk," said Alison out of the blue.

A pause while the Earth-Eater considered. "Dusk," she repeated, the word suiting her husky voice. She reached for the vessel.

The Firemayne winced. For generations, those below Desmeyne had been a faceless, nameless enemy, known simply as the Earth-Eaters. To see one named, and drinking from the Cup of Earth—meant to redeem the land-dwellers of Veil, not its underlings—went against the grain his kind had polished to an impervious gloss for centuries.

Alison was not done with him. "And you, Firemayne, must have a first name, as Rowan does."

"It has not been used, save by my wife, since I became the Firemayne."

"The word 'Firemayne' is as hateful to those below as the name 'Earth-Eater' is to you. If you cannot share your true name, I can give you another one to use here in this room, when you parley with Dusk."

"It was from you that Rowan contracted his lunacy!" the Firemayne charged. "And you cannot tempt me with a draught from the Cup of Earth. I will not touch that which an Earth-Eater has besmirched."

Dusk, smacking her pale lips over the generous swallow of Char, let her eyes glitter but said nothing.

"Drink from your own goblet, then." Alison lifted the Cup to her lips, suddenly wondering if some communicable disease might be caught from the malformed creatures below. "I will name you—"

"—Callan," he said, the risk of allowing her to choose too great to take. "I am called Callan."

Alison nodded solemnly and extended her vessel toward him in toast. The stone stem tingled in her fingers. The Cup was beginning to manifest its powers now that it was back in Desmeyne, or at least her bond with the Cup's uncertain magic was reviving.

The Firemayne begrudgingly toasted the Cup, lifting his own to down a gulp of Char. *A spoonful of Char makes the medicine go down, even in a Desmeynian way,* Alison thought.

She sipped her Char, then said, "Now that you two can call each other by name, I can leave Desmeyne. I must return the

Cup to the Valley of Voices and find Rowan, if I can, in time for the Wellsunging."

"You cannot!" The Firemayne's voice was firm now. "There is barely time to reach the Valley, much less to hunt for my wayward son."

"And," said a woman's cool, sad voice from the doorway, "she cannot leave without first visiting the Ladylofts."

5

ONCE Alison would not have regarded the luxurious hot-house that was Desmeyne's Ladylofts as a refuge. Rather, it had seemed a well-upholstered prison.

Yet after her perilous subterranean approach to Desmeyne and the uneasy meeting between the Firemayne and his unacknowledged daughter, whom she had just named Dusk, entering the Lofts was like falling into the cotton batting of a department-store jewelry box.

In fact, the thick, silver-threaded white samite that carpeted the floors reminded her of glitter-dusted Christmas cotton batting from years ago. Her boots crushed the nap as the Loft's barefooted residents could never do, leaving tracks as if through fresh snow.

Inside, the high, illuminated niches furnished in shades of white reminded her of banks of vigil lights in a church, or of roosting places in a dovecote.

"What of Sage?" she asked her escort.

Zormond, Rowan's eerily youthful mother, appeared impassive behind the translucent veils that covered her upper face. "The old woman is gone."

"When did she leave?"

"After Rowan returned from the underworld."

"Then Sage didn't accompany Rowan on his . . . enterprises?"

Zormond was silent for a moment. "Who is to say who, or what, accompanies my son these days? Sometimes I feel that I do not know him."

"Perhaps you never did."

Zormond's airy robes quivered indignantly as she paused to confront Alison. "You know so much of us after so short a stay?"

"Maybe not, but I know a thing or two about my own world. Rowan's long-cherished illusions about Desmeyne crumpled too swiftly. He will not soon forgive the illusionists, simply because he can't forgive himself for believing them."

"And who is responsible for breaking Rowan's faith?"

"I am," Alison admitted. She had little fondness for illusions, especially those that perpetuated social blindness. "And you are as well, for having a conscience that never forgot the girl-child abandoned to the Earth-Eaters." Alison began walking again. "Why don't you join your husband and the spokeswoman Earth-Eater at their talks?"

"Women do not just 'talk' with men, especially not with the Firemayne!"

"Your daughter does."

Zormond's painted palms shimmered as she lifted her hands to her temples to more firmly anchor the veils there. "Do not call this Earth-Eater by that term. There is no proof."

"I named her today," Alison said thoughtfully. "Dusk. It was agreeable to both parties, her and her father." She ignored the angry twitch of Zormond's long, trailing sleeves. "It's easier to yield something that is never named, never claimed. In my world, we don't call them the Littlelost or the Earth-Eaters. We call them the homeless."

"The Earth-Eaters have a home! Too much of a home: all the riddled earth beneath our feet and as deep into the mountains as they can delve."

"Did they choose it?"

"No, but it is rich in rare minerals. They trade with our enemies, the Crux-masters, and hold Desmeyne hostage."

Alison eyed the luxurious, pallid surroundings. The hushed, soft-lit atmosphere had a soothing, almost narcotic effect.

"You hold *yourselves* prisoners," she said. "I'm not sure I want to meet with Darnellyne. My views have been formed elsewhere. She won't convince me to change them, any more than I could convert both of you to blue jeans and boots."

From behind the diaphanous glitter of her veils, Zormond eyed Alison's attire, her mouth set in a line of polite distaste.

Alison laughed. "We are so hopelessly different; our worlds are so hopelessly different. At least I have returned the Cup. It's what Desmeyne wants, what Rowan wants and needs. I'll find him, tell him to be a good boy and come home to tend the family quests. Perhaps if Rowan returns to what he would have been had I never come here the first time, your world will revert to normal."

"Normal?" Zormond queried.

"To its usual state."

For once the woman's limp attire did not flutter with alarm or other emotion. "I fear not. I fear none of us can ever claim our usual state again. Come."

Alison mounted the suspended stairs that spiraled up to the glittering niches. The torpid air felt oppressive now. Flickering lamplight ebbed and flowed to a migraine throb.

Reclining in their niches, Loftladies nodded as she passed. A new fashion had altered some of their veils: gemstones masked the eye area, their weight pulling the fragile fabric still and stiff. The old, undecorated veils had riffled at the women's every breath for a fluid, sensual effect. These motionless, glittering facades were sinister, inhuman.

Zormond paused on a landing, then crossed a fur-draped catwalk. A niche glimmered beyond it like the mysterious interior of a Faberge egg. Alison clunked across behind her, the backpack hitched over one shoulder banging against her hip. The Ladylofts made her feel like a barbarian. No wonder male Desmeynians kept manhood-mates in the surrounding villages, she thought. They would always have to walk on eggshells in the presence of these exquisitely tended women. And no wonder they wanted their wives and daughters kept apart and only occasionally available.

The three-foot-long arched passage to Darnellyne's chambers was intersected by a series of variously hued veils, so that one entered by brushing through a silken rainbow.

On the other side waited a richly attired girl-child of about five. She was a Loftlady in living miniature, except that her face was not veiled.

Although Alison had once shared Loft quarters with Sage, she had never visited a Loftlady in her niche. The furnishings were similar: low, fabric-draped lounges; etherion lamps tethered on hammered metal chains floating at varying heights; a hundred and one shades of white agleam with metallic threads and gemstones. Such richness of setting would make it hard to pick the human being from the background into which she was meant to blend with such studied subtlety.

Silks seethed, and gems clicked like hail. A hand sheathed in ivory-enameled metal talons pulled back a curtain, and then another veiled, white-draped lady stood in the room.

Zormond backed away like one eager to escape. "Your information was correct," she told the figure poised against the pale curtain, which trembled delicately. "She is back. I have brought her straight from the Firemayne's rooms in the Men's Quarters."

"Zormond! You did not go there yourself? You could have waited outside."

"But *you* cannot wait, Darnellyne."

Zormond stepped backward and retired through the gentle gantlet of veils. Alison and Darnellyne stared at each other, finding conversation a squeaky wheel that would not turn.

At last Darnellyne spoke. "I wish to show you something." She beckoned Alison through the shrouded opening.

Alison went, feeling that she trod upon a soul; none of these luxe, furred carpets and gossamer curtains invited walking upon, or even brushing past.

Darnellyne paused beside a curtained niche as gossamer-swathed as an infant princess's cradle in a fairy tale. Alison almost felt impelled to offer the Cup as a christening gift. Then Darnellyne's taloned fingers drew back the layers of chiffon one by one to reveal the slumberer within.

"Camay!" Alison said, too loudly.

The youngest Littlelost stirred like a three-year-old awakening from a nap, her cheeks rosy, her yellow hair silky and tangled.

"I would not let her go to the Webbings," Darnellyne said, referring to the net-hung quarters in a cavern below Desmeyne where young children were reared by Grayladies in communal fashion. "And I persuaded Sage Wintergreen to let her remain here for safety."

"Desmeyne has not been a citadel of safety of late," Alison noted.

The child, for so Alison still thought of her despite knowing that the Littlelost quickly aged in spirit and knowledge of the world, if not in outside form, stirred. Then her eyes flared fully open, her mouth soon following suit.

"Alison!" she cried with what could only be interpreted as joy. She sprang up from her fussy bed and flung her little arms around Alison's neck. "Where is Beau?"

Alison hesitated. News of the dog's adorable new family might make Camay unhappy with her safe haven here. No wonder adults so often told children well-meaning fairy tales.

"Beau is in the woods," Alison answered finally. "He's happy. Are you?"

Camay, more wakeful now, shrugged and eyed Darnellyne. "I am happy to be out of the Webbings, but I wish I had gone with Sage and the others. She would not take me. No one would take me."

"Darnellyne took you," Alison reminded the child.

Camay regarded that veiled, glittering figure. "But Darnellyne does not do anything, or go anywhere."

If anything, Darnellyne stood more still. Then she extended a hand to assist Camay down the shallow steps from her luxurious nest. The smallest Littlelost's hand curled around the Loftlady's mandarin-nailed forefinger.

"You may go now, to the Arcade. I will ask the young Loftlady to take you."

Camay's floor-length shift of some supple, shiny material fell in unwrinkled folds. Darnellyne held back the flimsy draperies to let Camay precede herself and Alison. She addressed the stiff figure of the girl-child in the outer room.

"Take Camay to see the mountains through the Arcade crystal," Darnellyne told her. "Leave us."

Darnellyne unnerved Alison, especially now that the Loftlady's outermost veil bore the same harsh, glittering mask of jewels that Alison had seen on the other Loftladies. Only one difference showed her higher status as Cup-maiden, the woman born to marry the Desmeynian man who won the Cup of Earth and brought it to Desmeyne: her face veils fell past her chin. Now Alison could see absolutely nothing of Darnellyne's naked face, nothing but the sheer opacity of her many-layered, glamorous mask.

"Alison," the other woman said on a sigh, as if both sad and glad to see the Taliswoman again. Her voice was as soft and supple as ever. Alison suddenly wished she could see Darnellyne's eyes, but that was impossible. No Loftlady was known but to her mirror, before which she applied the glimmering face powders that sparkled like a snow phantom behind the teasing curtain of her veils. With the new fashion, Alison couldn't even detect these fabulous makeups, their ingredients gained in trade with the despised Earth-Eaters.

Those glittering eye and cheek powders were one artifice of Desmeyne that Alison could have happily exported to St. Paul.

"The Taliswoman," Darnellyne said, as though speaking to herself. Some terrible inner tension entered the room like a breath. "Do you still bear the Cup?" she asked intently.

Alison nodded. "But it's not mine to keep. I'll go to the Valley of Voices in time for the Wellsunging, and I'll not be tricked into competing this year."

"Is that how you won the Cup? By a trick?"

Alison nodded unhappily. "I didn't know what the competition meant, or what the prize represented. And I especially didn't know that women were barred from competing . . . or that I had not been taken for one."

A smile touched Darnellyne's voice, at least Alison thought so. "You do not look like a Loftlady."

Alison glanced down at her woodsy attire and smiled in turn. "No. But I didn't know that before I came to Desmeyne. I told

66

the Firemayne that I would try to find Rowan. Perhaps you know better where he's gone, and why.".

Darnellyne paced away in a swaying shimmer of silky albino glamour. "No. I do not. Why should I?"

"You two are childhood friends. You are the prize he would claim by winning the Cup. I thought that he might confide in you—"

"No. Rowan is not the same as when you left. None of us are."

"You look the same."

Darnellyne's laugh came sharp and bitter, surprising Alison. On her last visit, she had liked Darnellyne despite her web of feminine artifice.

"Darnellyne," Alison began thoughtfully. It was the first time she had used the other woman's name. She had spoken truly in the Firemayne's rooms, more truly than she herself suspected. To even speak a person's name makes that person more real. Now she heard an all-too-real distress in the Cup-maiden's laugh. Only something dire could have unbalanced the Loft's inbred equilibrium. Something unthinkable. "Is Rowan gone because he's angry with himself rather than with Desmeyne?"

"Yes." Darnellyne ran her long, artificial nails along the frost-pattern brocade covering a divan.

"Is Rowan angry with himself because he . . . violated the conditions necessary to compete for this year's Cup?"

Darnellyne turned into Carrara marble exquisitely carved by Michelangelo, the folds of her gown so fluid you could touch them, except that they might burn like dry ice.

Then she spun and stalked toward Alison with more energy than Alison would have believed. "No, Taliswoman. Rowan has not—would not—break faith."

"Would you know?" Alison asked.

"Yes." The furious tone brooked no argument.

Alison was not a reporter for nothing. The most adamant answer sometimes hid the greatest self-deception. "Celibacy for a man of Rowan's youth and expectations is a grave limitation," she said carefully, and clinically. "Celibacy enduring for more than a year, for almost two, in a culture where men are not restrained but women are . . . believe me, I've been there, and know it would be the most natural thing in the world—"

"No. These quests are Rowan's heart-blood. I have never doubted his ability to bear whatever burden is demanded. There is no wrong on Rowan's part, there is nothing wrong with Rowan." Darnellyne turned away fiercely, a core of hot emotion contained only by the icy sarcophagus of her gown. "I wish that he *had* done as you suspect! How much worse that his sacrifice is—"

A silence lasted because Alison did not know what to say, or even to ask. She glanced around the chamber, noticing milky ovals of polished pewter mirrors inset between sweeping draperies. The Cup-maiden so matched her anemic surroundings that she was nearly invisible in her own mirrors. Alison, on the other hand, reflected back as an unavoidable clump of navy cotton knit and blue denim.

Darnellyne finally lifted her head. She slowly drove her long-nailed fingers up under her face veil to her temples. Alison winced to see a Loftlady touch her so ritually guarded features, and asked gently, "What is it that disturbs you?"

"Surely you have seen that Desmeyne is much changed since your departure."

"I see uncertainty, perhaps, but not change . . . not really."

"Change is not always visible," Darnellyne said tightly.

"Amen."

"You have ever spoken as if change were always good."

"No . . . but adapting to changed circumstances is."

"Adapting?"

"Another word from my world. Growing accustomed to change."

"That is a contradiction."

Alison smiled. Contradictions were not permitted in Desmeyne. "Yes, I guess that it is. We'd call it a paradox. We must get used to change, use it, or it will use us . . . and badly."

"Some changes are not possible to . . . accommodate."

"Can you be sure? You have seen so little of the world."

"And this world has seen so little of me."

"That's true, but it doesn't have to remain so. Not only Rowan can change your world. You can, too. If he wins the Cup this year, wins you, he will have great force among the Desmeynians. You can persuade him to allow you, and all the women, greater presence beyond the Lofts. Rowan is stubborn, and shortsighted, but he is reachable."

"Oh, yes," Darnellyne said listlessly. "Rowan could change. Rowan could be persuaded, by the right person at the right time. Desmeyne could change . . . Desmeyne is changing, Taliswoman, and not for the better! Look."

Beneath her veil, Darnellyne's hands moved. With the shriek of sheer fabric ripping, Darnellyne's veils began to tear away.

Alison stepped back before she thought, lifting her forearms as if to shield herself from a fire's searing heat. Darnellyne's act, utterly violating the customs she honored, was as drastic as if Rowan had publicly forsaken his sworn celibacy in Desmeyne's great Arcade. Darnellyne was stripping her soul bare. Alison did not want to witness this self-mutilation. She had been longing to see Darnellyne, but not this way.

She leaped forward, grasped the frail wrists. "Wait! You must think—"

"No," came the anguished answer. "You are the only one, Taliswoman, who can see my face and tell me the truth. Release my hands!"

"You aren't thinking of the cost—not to me, but to yourself!"

Alison manacled Darnellyne's wrists with the disciplined hands that could split wood. But that apparent advantage was matched by the surprising strength of the deeply stressed. The torn veils trembled before the Loftlady's face; then her hands, stubbornly pushing against Alison's resistance, reached to tear at her own eyes.

"Oh, my God!" Alison cried.

But Darnellyne was not attacking herself. Her mandarin-like fingernails were blindly combing away strands of shredded veil, wrenching the material from its anchor in her headdress. And she was sobbing.

The sight of a self-contained Loftlady unraveling shocked Alison deeply. She backed off, calmed herself. Clearly, Darnellyne's action purged some virulent emotion.

"Can you see yet?" Darnellyne asked between sobs, plucking the glamorous webbing from her eyes. "So many layers, so many became necessary . . . is it obvious yet? Can you see?"

Alison shook her head mutely. She saw Darnellyne's distress, but no reason for it.

"Look!" Darnellyne moaned.

Alison could glimpse eyes glimmering through the veil remnants, glimmering through a veil of tears that shone like snail tracks on Darnellyne's cheeks and chin.

The Loftlady's wild grief had made the luminescent powders of Desmeynian beautification into a mockery of their former powers. The luscious colors—lavender and silver, copper and gold, twilight blue and sunset magenta, grass green—had run into a horrid melange, like the long, multicolored balloons sold at state fairs. From behind this melted mask, Darnellyne's eyes stared out, as dark as Char, rimmed in bloodshot crimson instead of kohl, the eye sockets an angry maroon, her cheeks splotched with the vivid colors dripping over them.

"You're fine," Alison said gently. "Except that you've not only ruined your veils, but your face powders have run into a mess. You'll have to wash your face with a cool cloth and calm down."

Darnellyne shook her crowned head, strands of her ashen hair whipping against her garish face. "No, I do not have to do any of that, wash or calm down. Alison, I am wearing no skinsilk. No powders."

Alison stared. If she was not viewing a heavily made-up woman who had been caught in a rain of her own making, what was she seeing? Flesh reshaped by acid? Certainly skin raddled and stained to a lurid parody of a fine complexion. Alison had thought she herself had some special insight on scars, until Darnellyne unveiled herself.

"How long?" Alison asked, a sick sadness in her stomach. No matter the crisis, the reporter's reflex was to ask questions.

To maybe find answers. To change things. To help somehow.

"I do not know." Darnellyne had calmed now that the damage was revealed, now that Alison was accepting the fact. "We Loftladies are seldom without our skinsilk powders and our veils, even in our own quarters. And the powders are virtually priceless. We never wash them off unnecessarily."

"You apply them over the previous layer?"

Darnellyne nodded and moved wearily toward one of the pewter ovals. Polished metal did not have the crisp reflecting properties of silvered glass. It was just as well. She regarded her image, the hideous face. "I regret most that no one saw me before, that *you* did not see me before."

"Does no one else know?"

Darnellyne shook her head, and the atrocity in the mirror mimicked her. She sighed. "Some of the Loftladies complain of 'blemishes.' That is why the fashion for more concealing veil jewels came about."

"You must tell them! Warn them to stop using the powders."

"They would as soon not breathe. Besides, I cannot swear that it is the skinsilk. I cannot swear that this is not some specific evil visited upon me."

"Or upon the Cup-maiden."

"I do not understand."

"The Crux. I know little about this . . . force, but I do know that it wishes to stop Rowan's quests. It killed a Littlelost. You are the human reward for Rowan's attaining his first quest. If you are attacked, he may stop everything else."

The Loftlady's ruined head nodded slowly. "That is why no one must know. Last of all, Rowan. I will not have him abandon a quest that could save us all."

"Then why tell me? I don't live well with deadly secrets. My whole personal . . . quest . . . is to tell the truth."

Darnellyne's talon-tipped hands clutched the delicate fabric over her knee. "You are the Taliswoman. You too have been marked, and live with that condition. You will understand."

"What if I don't want to?" Alison cried out. Frustration pressed her ordinary, yet sharp, nails into her palms . . . and

71

reminded her of something. "That's right! Your palms! Loftladies also powder designs onto their palms."

Darnellyne uncurled one hand to reveal the gaudy skin. "Nothing yet. But this is a more recent fashion."

"You must stop using the powders even there."

"Someone will notice, and ask."

"Then answer them that you are starting a new fashion. You are . . . in mourning over Rowan's absence. They would honor his quest by following suit. Tell them . . . tell them you have forsaken all powders until his return! That way, you at least buy some time."

"Buy time? In your world, that is possible?"

"In my world, it is attempted, anyway. Veil offers far more possibilities; I don't know it well enough to tell you what. But above all, you must protect the others. You'd do it best by being frank about your difficulty."

"No! I cannot. I would rather strip my face off first."

Alison was quiet, thinking. She had often urged people to bare their secrets and their souls so that others could learn from their heartbreak. Unwed mothers, AIDS and rape victims, abused children. A reporter argued that they must testify to stir compassion and understanding. They must rip open their own wounds so others would care enough to stanch them and prevent new wounds in potential victims.

Alison's hand had unconsciously traced her collarbones. Why? To protect her scars? To hide them? Or to remind herself of them? Hadn't she worn an invisible "veil" all through her adolescent and adult years, her clothes bought to conceal the flaw, the ugliness, the thing that set her apart? Did that help her to understand Darnellyne? Was a sheltered Loftlady of Veil not so different from a modern woman, from herself in particular? Oh, Lord . . .

"The Cup," Alison said suddenly. "We must treat you with the Cup. It heals cracked earth. Human beings are all of earth at bottom."

"I had not thought of that. Do you think—?"

Alison smiled. "I once was blind and now I see. Because of the Cup. Ask Rowan. He saw. I had to . . . use magic drops of

72

water on my eyes to see well. After I drank from the Cup, I realized that I saw perfectly. We can try."

"Should the Cup be used for such a personal cause?"

"If it helps you, it can help others beset by the same plague. And, Darnellyne, there *will* be others, until the Crux no longer troubles Veil."

"Call me 'Dar,' " she answered.

Alison could not help but look confused. Why this interjection of a trivial social distinction into so dire a situation? The Loftlady's ghastly face shifted, attaining a kind of serenity. Alison recognized it as an attempted smile.

" 'Dar' is easier," she said. "When I was a child, that is what my friends called me."

Alison realized that Dar's notion had not been trivial at all.

The Cup rested upright on Alison's palm, supported by her other hand, as if presented for admiration or for auction, yet weighing as heavy as a millstone.

She wanted to throttle the smooth, cold stem, to choke it into producing some phenomenon. Whenever she glanced up, Darnellyne's ruined face stared at her, a lurid, distorted portrait from a museum of modern art. The Loftlady's now-naked eyes of soft azure radiated a poignant, gemstone-sharp clarity, twin blue topazes set in a mottled mockery of flesh. They read Alison's disappointment in the too-frank mirror of her expression, but Darnellyne said nothing.

"Perhaps I expect miracles." Alison turned the Cup in a slack, helpless gesture. "Instant gratification."

"Miracles?" Darnellyne's lips, swollen shapeless, repeated. "Instant?" Her voice rang clear, untouched by the ruin around it.

"Immediate results." Alison peered down into her reflection—eyes and forehead only—in the clear liquid filling the Cup. "Perhaps the water is wrong. Are you satisfied that it's untainted?"

"We have always drunk from the wells deep below Desmeyne."

That, Alison thought to herself, doesn't answer my question. Desmeynians had long used Earth-Eater cosmetic powders also—apparently far too long. She set aside the damp cloth she had used to bathe Darnellyne's face. Her initial horror of touching her, of contamination, had faded. Still the Cup offered no balm.

"It no longer . . . scintillates," Alison complained.

"Sin-till-ates?" Darnellyne repeated.

"Ah . . . sizzles. Effervesces. Tingles. I can't explain it, but when I handled the Cup before, I felt its power. Now the Cup is empty. Dormant."

Darnellyne bowed her head for a moment. "Perhaps I am the flaw, made visible."

"No, not you. Me." Alison forced a grin. "Listen to us wallow in self-accusation, when we could be blaming someone who's not here."

"Who?" Darnellyne asked quite seriously.

"Rowan, of course. Born to be blamed. So sure he can do no wrong—"

"I cannot blame Rowan for my condition, only for my fear of it. If he should find out—"

"He won't. Although he'll have to when you, if you—"

Darnellyne's fluid face froze. "We will not wed," she said firmly. "A flawed Cup-maiden is unthinkable."

"No more than a flawed quest-heir, and Rowan's already got you beat there."

Darnellyne frowned. "Why are you so angry with him?"

"Because . . . he always thinks he's right."

"And you do not think the same of yourself?"

"Well, yes, but I *am* right. There's a big difference. What irritates me about Rowan is that he thinks ignorance is right."

"I do not know that word either."

"Oh, Dar, I'm sorry. I'm not really angry with Rowan, I'm angry with myself and with the Cup. It's easier to blame the absent."

"You feel anger for the Cup?" Darnellyne sounded shocked. "Why?"

"Because it won't work, Dar! It won't fix you."

"Perhaps I am not meant to be fixed."

"No." Alison refused to accept that. She sighed and wrapped the Cup in its lowly flannel shirt again. "Perhaps it needs recharging," she muttered. "I have to get it to the Valley of Voices in time for the Wellsunging." Her features lightened. "Rowan will win this time. I wouldn't sing if my life depended on it. Maybe in Rowan's hands, fresh from the Wellsunging, the Cup will take on new power and heal you."

"Rowan must not know of my difficulty," Darnellyne said stiffly.

"Not now, of course, but once the Cup is officially in Desmeyne's corner . . . you wouldn't let him see you even to heal you?"

"No Cup-maiden may reveal her face save to the quest-heir she marries. I would have to wed him to reveal my secret, and I will not wed him to . . . this!" She caught hold of the golden, waist-hung leash from which floated an etherion-framed circle of pewter and raised the small mirror to her face.

Alison could not see the reflection, but she winced as Darnellyne studied herself. The Cup-maiden did not cower, but looked long and soberly, as if awed by the alteration in her features. Alison tucked the Cup in her pack and rose from the low divan, her knees protesting their lengthy jackknifed position.

"I really think," she told Darnellyne, "that the only cure for this ill is for me to reach the Valley of Voices before the Wellsunging. I must allow Rowan a chance to win the Cup of Earth for his own world, on his own terms. Then both of you may do as you will. I'll have done what I can, and—hopefully—will find my way home again."

Darnellyne rose also, drawing fresh veils from a small chest down over her face one by one so that her horrific visage first softened, then vanished.

"You must not blame yourself," she said, holding out a limp, warm hand.

"I don't have to, Dar," Alison assured her. "Remember, there's always Rowan."

6

ROWAN lay belly-down on a bed of rotted leaves, hanging over the edge of a rise.

He had never before seen the like of this forest: thick, rank, and darker than the inside of a decaying log. Putrid scents seared his nostrils; by comparison, the foul-smelling flowers that dotted Veil's meadows seemed sweet.

Yet beings moved in the noxious muck below, swarming over the black heart of this putrification. He wondered that the stench did not strike them senseless.

"You become used to it," a hoarse voice whispered at his elbow.

He twisted his long body to view the Littlelost beside him: clever Twist, who had proven his name a dozen times on the long journey to this dread place that Rowan would have never believed shared the skies of Veil.

He grunted, unnerved that the Littlelost had read his thoughts. This was Rowan's quest, though outwardly it benefitted the Littlelost. Most of the tiny figures toiling in the sludge below were of that kind. Yet each distant, tattered figure haunted Rowan, who both hoped and feared to see an unlikely blaze of red hair beneath the filthy scarf covering each head. He had lost one of the Littlelost before even knowing what they—and he—were. Now the ghost of Lorn, known among the Littlelost as Pickle, inhabited every diminutive form Rowan saw, until he freed it and knew better.

Rowan's grip on his hardwood staff tightened, his knuckles slimy from the disintegrating leaves.

"Five Takers," he said, flickering his eyes to either side so the contingent of Littlelost accompanying him—three small, intently bitter faces—would know that he was outlining an attack plan. Why else had they all journeyed so far? "Why so few?" Rowan went on. "I count at least fifteen Littlelost to guard."

"The Takers expect no trouble," said one. "The Littlelosts' ankles are bound to one another with vine, so they cannot escape, not even by grabbing fistfuls of etherion scales and floating aloft." Contempt for Rowan's ignorance touched Faun's voice.

Rowan bit back a retort. This was Littlelost terrain now, where they had labored long: enslaved, abused, and no one's concern. He began to understand the hint of contempt as he studied the scene below. How such a pit of denigration differed from Desmeyne, whose people were safely embraced by a mountainous notch and their own willful ignorance of evil!

Evil exhaled almost tangibly from the ooze-filled crater below that the Littlelost called an etherion pit. Evil entered on every rancid breath of the fetid, humid air. Evil burdened the bent heads and backs of the Littlelost as they shuffled, shackled, onto woven willow mats that floated atop the scum-ridden slime filling the pit. He watched them bend, dipping their long-handled tongs into the scummed surface to retrieve the gleaming scales of airy metal that coated the liquid.

Etherion, a beautiful, lighter-than-air metal, worth its weightlessness in trade. Littlelost lives and freedom were worth nothing to the Crux, which commissioned the Takers to gather the rare metal. Even the light, an eternal twilight that filtered vision as if through a smoky tavern, had a heavy, vile feel.

Rowan's hand tightened on his damp, slippery staff. Five Takers. Brutish hulks, their minds no larger than the pommels of their oversized knives, cruel axes thrust into their belts. And he himself was forbidden to carry edged steel by the terms of his quest.

The Littlelost were not thus restrained. Rowan's mouth tightened in grim amusement at what the Taliswoman would say to see her precious foundlings armed with short swords, long knives, and expressions as ferocious as their weapons. Even often mute, flaxen-haired Rime, one of two females in their odd band, wore a lethal grimace.

He felt a stab of guilt for accepting their aid, but he had needed guides to this sinkhole. And the Littlelost were not about to forgo the pleasure of revenge, no matter the risk. The Taliswoman had underestimated her charges, as she had underestimated much in Veil and Desmeyne. Including himself.

Rowan frowned. It did no good to think of her—or of the missing Cup of Earth. A year had nearly passed. Though the annual Wellsunging loomed, this year there would be no object to win, thanks to the so-called Taliswoman. Her flight from Veil had brought only one good: the absence of herself. He would never see her again . . . more's the pity, because he had some serious bones to pick with her.

He returned to the plan of attack. "We will encircle them stealthily, like Slinkers." Eager little faces smiled approval. "We will rush in at once, you when I first show myself. Rime, use your knife to sever the vines that tie the workers. Faun and Twist, hide behind those large, empty wagons, then join me in disarming the Takers."

All three nodded, as serious as Desmeynian guardsmen despite their childlike size.

"A last word," Rowan said a bit gruffly. "We aim to free the Littlelost. We do not wish to lose any of them, even among our company."

Twist's face screwed derisively. "What we may lose now cannot equal a hundredth of last year's losses in the pits."

That said, he wiggled away on his belly, blending into the soft leaves through which he crawled molelike. Once Faun had helped Rime tie a brown rag over her candlewax-pale hair, she and Rime wriggled off in the opposite direction.

Rowan eased out a long breath, though he thought it must perfume this putrid air much like the odd pink soap the Taliswoman carried in her bag of many artifacts. Her again! He had counted every day of the past year, and none of them good, yet the better for her absence. He was free once more, free of an unwanted, unworthy rival for the Cup-quest. Why was she haunting his mind like a bad dream? Because the time of Wellsunging had come again? He was tempted not to go, yet felt a wrench at the idea.

Then he forced all disruptive thoughts aside. His allies were making their furtive way to opposite sides of the clearing that circled the pit. Their slow progress down the slopes that edged the rise did not disturb him; he was used to waiting. It had taken him almost three months to recover from the events below the Earth-Eaters' caverns and to decide what to do. By then, the old wisewoman Sage had shepherded the Littlelost away, save for Camay, who had been left behind for safety's sake. For seven months Rowan had sought them, and spent yet another month convincing the Littlelost to lead him to the site of their enslavement. Here his brother Lorn had labored, until carted to another part of the woods. There the Taliswoman had freed the five Littlelost by slaying a Taker with her foreign artifact that spat smoke.

Had Rowan come here a year ago, on this quest instead of on his own quest for the Cup, he could have freed Lorn with the others. Lorn might not now be dead, mourned only by those Littlelost comrades who had called him Pickle. And by himself.

Such thoughts rekindled his ever-simmering rage, as he had wanted them to do. Rage is the best ally when one fights against odds. He dug his staff into the mushy ground, then sprang up and forward over the rise.

His boots thudded on the soggy carpet of leaves below as if pounding hollow earth. A distant Taker turned, slack-jawed, dull-eyed. Apathetic Littlelost trekked back and forth from the mats over the pit to the pondside as if sleepwalking. Another Taker turned. By now, Rowan was close enough to see the un-kempt hair covering head, hands, and brutish faces. The first Taker reached for his ax. Rowan ran at him, swinging the wooden staff in a half-circle, slicing its gnarled and carved pommel into the side of the Taker's neck. The barbed carv-ings, not mere decorations, slashed a line amid the snarled hairs that bloomed, then fountained blood.

Two Takers were charging, pulling wicked ax blades from

their belts as they came. His staff cut a lower swath. One Taker, legs knocked from under him, vanished from Rowan's sight as if drowning in the rank air.

Rowan's neck felt the whistle of an oncoming blow. He leaped aside to avoid a fourth Taker even as he thrust his staff lancelike into the oncomer's belly.

At the edges of his vision, small figures darted inward to harry the fallen Takers while the brutes struggled to rise. Rowan ducked. Two unfallen Takers converged on him. The breeze from an ax stroke caressed his ear, and a lock of red hair drifted like a feather to the ground. He whirled, driving up with his legs and his staff, and struck a Taker under the chin. The creature's strangled groan was answered by a gurgle of rage at Rowan's rear. He rammed the staff back without looking, then turned in time to knock a doubled-over Taker in the temple. The Taker crumpled.

Rowan spun. The five Takers were down and disabled. Faun and Twist were stripping them of weapons. Still the ground thrummed with footsteps. Rowan frowned, nearly retching from the gulps of vile air his exertions forced him to breathe. His heart and his ears pounded in tune. He turned in a full circle, trying to orient himself. Why was he hearing things?

The carts! The covered wooden wagons! Pouring from them now were Takers, screeching, running, reaching for belt-hung weapons . . . two, four, even more.

Rowan bellowed at his three Littlelost, who had seen and were leaping up, brandishing the Takers' own axes. There was no time to consider retreat. Too many Takers were arriving too fast.

He managed to back away from the site of the first encounter; injured Takers could still seize legs and cut hamstrings. The Littlelost had multiplied into a substantial knot. He spied a flaxen head of hair bare of its scarf. Rime had released some of the rescued Littlelost. Now all of them claimed Taker weapons with angry faces. Still, what were a few fighters of child size against these monsters?

An ax flew through the air, hurtling toward him. The last of the first five Takers was alive and kicking. Rowan dodged, parrying the spinning haft with the length of his staff and diverting the aim. More Takers converged on him. He crouched low, staff smacking oncoming Taker ankles and knees, then jumped back to whack the falling creatures in the heads and shoulders. More came.

Sweat greased his face, stung his eyes to tears that blurred his vision. Movement eddied all around. He felt and saw Takers fall like rotted leaves, but not enough of them. His arms and legs seemed to have turned to wood; they felt as impervious as his staff to mortal weakness. But they were not proof against ax cuts, no more than were the tallest and strongest trees.

A quick, blurry appraisal showed that canny Twist had gathered the freed Littlelost into a prickly circle, a sharp-edged shield of weapons around them. Still, the four Takers that harried them loomed much taller; one good head-knock would shatter a Littlelost forever.

Rowan went for them, remembering his older brother's small figure trembling under the strikes of the Crux-masters' blue lightning. Beating, jabbing, thrusting, clubbing—he could no longer see; instinct guided his weapon to his enemies. It was not an undignified way for a quest-heir of Desmeyne to die.

A hot slice of steel whispered and then settled into his shoulder. His shoulder-length hair had loosened from its ties. Red strands flailed into his vision like threads of airborne blood. Moths of light flickered in the dim distance, a ring that neared as Rowan turned and struck, advanced and retreated, gave and got. Like sparks accompanying a blaze, they circled closer. He blinked, wanting to retreat from the tiny tunnels of searing heat, small yellow sparks of death in the dark. His staff crossed the haft of an ax shaped like a spinning wheel and slipped off. He went down on one knee, the staff anchored in the ground beside him, half cane now, hardly weapon.

The lights converged, growling, and Takers screamed.

Rowan swayed on his knees. Hot breath fanned his cheek. Breath that reeked of raw flesh and death, but not of the particular rot of an etherion pit. A hairy form brushed his wounded shoulder. Not an unkempt Taker, but—Slinkers! Rowan levered himself upright on his staff, watching the animals hurl themselves on the remaining Takers with outstretched claws and teeth as white and sharp as ice needles. And their eyes gleamed red and yellow like embers, darkening as they neared.

The huddled Littlelost . . . laughed.

Rowan followed the Slinkers back into battle, his staff hungry again, striking down those the Slinkers had not knocked over and bitten. In moments, the battle ended. Any Takers not lying senseless on the ground turned Slinker themselves and vanished into the dark woods.

The Littlelost wasted no moments. Rowan's three had seized knives, and now they knelt before those of their fellows still tied, sawing through the tough vines linking the prisoners' ankles.

The Slinkers, too, assembled—gray, black, and fawn of coat—and sat on their haunches panting, their tongues hanging out like that of the Taliswoman's white-haired Slinker. Rowan groaned for the first time in the fierce, wordless battle. Why must he continually think of her, bad omen that she was, ill-made woman that she was?

He eyed the Slinkers. How could their timely aid be intentional? They were surely mad beasts, who knew no side but their own bellies. They would as likely devour him as well as the Takers, though they seemed disinclined to do so now. Instead, they watched the Littlelosts' liberation with amiable curiosity, almost as if possessing an intelligent understanding of that act, this scene.

Rowan frowned. And counted. Four Slinkers. Before, a year before, when *she* had been here, there had been five. The Slinkers were missing a member, as the original Littlelost were missing two members. At least Camay was safe in Desmeyne with Darnellyne. Had the Slinkers also left their youngest member behind for safety? Rowan remembered a slight, pale-furred creature that was almost as comely as the Taliswoman's Beau, if one could learn to admire Slinkers, a bad breed to begin with. Where was the fifth Slinker?

THE fawn-colored wolf lies panting, long rose-colored tongue sagging between her bottom incisors. Cubs crowd against her, their sides heaving in rhythm, extended tongues red with exertion.

Rambeau regards them with worried dark eyes. Much grass has bent beneath their paws since they left Alison on the brink of Desmeyne; many stones have sheened their footpads, rubbing the black skin rosy.

More miles must be trod, for game is scarce in these empty meadows and deserted woods and vacant mountains.

Fatherhood has reinstated Rambeau's earthly instincts. The few months before the Taliswoman's return, he lived an idyllic canine existence. Now undoglike thoughts nudge his simpler instincts aside. Now voices other than Alison's urge him with commands half-heard, like game half-scented or dreams half-seen.

He whimpers and lays his belly on the cool grass. He has pushed his family as far and as fast as it can go, given the cubs' tender age and their mother's sapped condition.

Yet some instinct other than hunger nips at Beau's heels. Haste must be made. An event is about to occur, one with no significance to wolves or to dogs, yet it is a hunt of a kind.

For this he must be swift beyond the ways of dogs and wolves. He must again tread the unseen paths and find the sage within himself—half human, all spirit.

His nose lifts to sniff the air. Earth smells explode: the rich, wet scent of loam, traces of life leaving spirit trails on the wind.

Some odors that might repel a human greet Beau's sensitive nostrils like old friends: decaying leaves and the distant smudge pot of fire; water in many forms and states of purity; blood both fresh and ancient, equally tempting.

He growls at the fleeting odor of an enemy so old he is almost forgotten, save that Dog forgets no man or woman's scent. And then he comes across the spoor he has sought without knowing until he finds it: the irresistible reek of raw fish that dominates underscents of wet wool, tobacco, and a specific human perfume.

Beau leaps up, his family forgotten. A pure, icy tang rides on the wind. He trots after it, lifted nose leading his flashing legs. He crashes into the nearby woods, his feet churning up leaf dust and evicting dozens of tiny insects from their humus homes. Such small sacrifices barely register in his nostrils.

He sniffs the spirit wind and follows its invisible whorls. He chases the course of the Great Milk River where it flows like an invisible veil through air and earth and fire.

He seeks the bodiless ground where the Bone Buffalo's hooves thunder at the head of a countless herd. If he is thirsty, he can drink the breath of the mountains. If he hungers, the white hart will cast itself upon its ghostly knees before him. If he feels pain, the trembling hand of time itself will stroke his brow.

He will bathe in white water and snow showers. He will swallow stars and tread on comets' tails. And when he has seen the face he seeks, and finds it in himself, he will return to earth and tend to homely things.

Rambeau runs, and in running, outwits time. He runs faster than any clock, faster than the Great Milk River. He runs all the way back to the Island, almost pausing to revel in familiar, long-lost scents but driven on like water, like wind, until he comes to a cabin in the woods.

Inside, an old man with weathered skin sits under a dogskin on the wall.

Fishhook eyes wink from glassy rows of bottles, and a fresh-caught pike gleams like a silver rainbow on the tabletop.

Rambeau comes to sit before the old man, who is as still as

a mountain of dusty flesh frozen onto a straight chair. Yet a hand reaches out, rests on Rambeau's head as he waits panting.

"Dog has come a long way," Eli says, without praise or blame. "Dog has longer to go, but the time comes."

The icy wind dies like a snuffed candle. Rambeau is alone in the woods, his nose rich with the scents of cubs and female. At his feet, a two-foot-long pike lies like a silver trophy. He picks it up, the smell nagging at his appetite, and trots to the forest's edge. He crosses the swaying grasses until he reaches the waiting wolf and her cubs.

Then he drops the food to the ground and rends it for allotment. He eats last. He has more to chew on than flesh.

7

DESMEYNE did not mourn Alison's abrupt departure. Even Camay kept a stiff upper lip, although she made Alison promise to "bring everybody back."

The Firemayne impassively provided her with what food and water she would need for the trip: packets of Desmeyne's rubbery dried vegetables, the turkey jerky she had first seen Rowan chewing in the wilderness, and fresh spring water from the deepest well.

Before she left, she had filled the Cup with spring water, which she poured into a glass decanter in Darnellyne's niche, instructing her to wash her face with it daily.

Alison felt silly about leaving the Desmeynian equivalent of holy water behind, but she hoped it would do some good for the Cup-maiden, who deserved better than her present lot.

The Ladylofts were dim-lit and cheerless when she left Darnellyne. Loftladies had dutifully set aside their powders and painted palms, but now pouted behind their veil-hung niches, certain that all beauty had flown with the skinsilk they so prized, the same skinsilk that might cause that very tragedy.

This time Alison avoided the Earth-Eaters' underground. She hiked down the winding road from the cleft-hung city, tramped carefully across the fields and scaled the creepy cliffs again. Pale faces still glimmered at her through the shiny black portholes in the cliff-face, as if veiled like a Loftlady's. Their unfocused distortions now reminded her of Darnellyne, and she shuddered as she passed, climbing faster.

She dragged herself atop the grassy verge, hoping for a wet

canine welcome, or at least for something more appetizing than a hunk of raw carcass. She found neither.

For the first time in Desmeyne, Alison felt lonely rather than alone. Before, Rambeau had accompanied her, then the Littlelost, Sage, and finally Rowan. Now everyone she knew had scattered to the wild ends of Veil. She drank Desmeynian well water from her canteen, adjusted her backpack, and started across a high mountain meadow she vaguely remembered, heading toward a valley she could never forget.

Alison walked for some hours, her eyes filled with the near and far beauty of the surrounding mountains. Distance bruised the harsh stone peaks to shades of hazy blue and magenta. At her feet, the grasses shimmered in arpeggios of wind-tossed greens—jade, emerald, chartreuse—and flights of flowers skimmed over the grass like bees in search of nectar. Unclouded sunlight warmed her shoulders. The very pleasantness of the terrain—and Veil was wondrously welcoming to the eye—lulled her to a subtle alteration in the world around her.

Intending to rest, Alison eased off the backpack and let it lie on a bed of bent grasses. Unburdened, undistracted, she forced herself to do something she had unconsciously been avoiding. She inhaled deeply of the Veilian air, wincing against the anticipated whiff of the foul-scented flowers.

But a different scent invaded her nostrils, teased through her head, defying definition. A . . . sublime scent. Sweet and elusive, like jasmine or gardenia or certain expensive Rodeo Drive perfumes. A scent that made her hasten to exhale so she could draw it in again, long and deeply. Spicy, too. And warm, like fresh-baked bread with crisp, golden crusts.

Such a scent broke every rule of the Veil she had encountered before. She picked up her pack and stepped cautiously ahead to find the aroma, afraid that so delicate a smell would withdraw at her approach, like a wild thing.

Grasses bowed before her, hissing slightly in the wind. Every step was hushed by their breaking stems, but the scent grew stronger as she moved down the meadow, away from the mountain pass she aimed for.

A vision of Dorothy's dangerous poppy field snicked into the

87

moviola of her mind. But this smell invigorated rather than enervated. She felt ready to stride over mountains, as indeed she needed to do. More, she felt jubilant that Veil had added the heady attraction of sweet smell to its eye-pleasing landscape. Maybe there was hope for Darnellyne, for Rowan, for—

The ground gave before her, dropping down for at least a foot. Alison caught herself, her stomach twisting anxiously. The scent surged up at her, so overwhelming that it almost blinded her. Then she gagged and struggled backward, falling to her knees and clawing her way back up to higher ground as a drowning person thrashes to regain dry land.

Beyond the tall grasses and the sudden drop-off lay a revolting pit of blackened, oozing earth. Despite the overpowering scent still swelling around her like an angel chorus of addiction, Alison knew that such a pockmark could waft no odor but decay. She pinched her nose shut with one hand and scrambled farther back even as she detected the faint toxic mist wreathing the pit like steam from a big, fresh bowl of battery-acid soup.

Drifting on the putrid surface were flotillas of open-petaled blue sunflowers.

Too weak to rise, Alison remained sitting on the ground, dug her heels in, and skittered farther backward, dragging the pack with her. The burden seemed too hideously heavy to bear. Perhaps if she lightened it by discarding the Cup? Didn't the cursed thing's weight wax and wane simply to inconvenience her?

Maybe the Cup could "cure" the hideous outbreak if she threw it into the muck from a distance. . . .

Horrified, Alison recognized her thoughts for delusion, not reason. She gasped a huge swallow of air, then struggled backward, and farther backward, until she could no longer see that grim, dark wound in the earth. Back and back, until surely she could no longer smell the alluring scent that emanated from it. Sweet, sweet decay, fit to perfume an empress—a dead one.

Inch by inch, she shinnied across the ground on the seat of her jeans, her path slicked by crushed grasses. The pack came with her by bump and by golly; the weight on her lungs lifted, and the sky no longer seemed tinted electric blue at the edges of her vision.

Finally she rose to her knees, the grasses grazing her cheeks, and sniffed experimentally, like an animal. Only the faintest trace of the heavenly scent remained, as imperceptible as the last notes of a fading song.

She stood, sweaty and shaky, and slung the pack over one shoulder. Perverse Veil, to clothe beauty in stink and corruption in aromas that would make an angel weep. She walked on toward the mountains, less confident now, wondering what other surprises this outwardly lovely land hid beneath its rocks and rills.

The sun was declining before Alison found the stomach to consider eating. Desmeyne was long beyond sight; she had climbed over the broad, grassy shoulder of one mountain. Below her glittered the plummeting contrails of the twin waterfalls that marked the passage through the mountains she and her party had taken before.

She had not sought the underground entrance, unwilling to encounter the crude, humanlike beasts that had attacked them in those caverns. She inhaled experimentally again, and drew in only chill mountain air tinged by the distant reek of those lovely-to-look-at blossoms that flew like birds. Ah, normalcy.

Light left the mountains in long, slow stages, dimming as artfully as theatrical lights at the end of an act. It seemed only that the colors of the grass and the sky and distant mountains dimmed and darkened slightly.

Alison knew, though, that in an hour or two, it would suddenly become so dark that it was no longer safe to step ahead, and she would have to stop where she was. Better to seek shelter now.

Below her, the treeline bristled like a brush made of Christmas-tree needles. The pines would hide her, but they would also hide whoever shared them with her: Slinkers, or worse.

Instead, she headed across the meadow toward the narrow streams feeding the waterfalls that plunged below. Raw hummocks of rock thrust up here and there from the grasslands. A protected niche among them would settle her nicely for the night, and fresh water would be at hand—if it wasn't the poisonous wildwater that Rowan had feared in every streambed and waterfall.

Alison circled an outcropping until she found a welcoming arrangement of turf and rock. Here the morning sun would hit her eyes and awaken her, and she would be invisible to anyone but an overhead bird, of which she had seen none in Veil.

With almost domestic contentment, she began to unpack her bag and contemplate which of the uninspiring foodstuffs she would eat. She enjoyed camping out after the deadline-enhanced rush of urban life. She had done the right thing, going back to the Island. Why else would she have so readily come here again? It was only proper to give Rowan another chance at the Cup, proper that someone of Veil possess it.

Alison frowned as she laid out a selection of turkey jerky and dried veggies, with trail mix for dessert, on the open backpack flap. The Desmeynian reports indicated that Rowan had gone off the rails since he had knelt deep within the earth to gather his brother Lorn's ashes. Rowan was off on errands of a peculiar nature. What if he didn't return to the Valley of Voices for the Wellsunging? Could a designated hero do that? Well, so what? Someone else would win the Cup of Earth then, as Rowan had felt himself fated to do. But Rowan had always been so convinced that this world would not win through without him; he wouldn't simply abandon his quests. Would he?

Certainly any obligation she might owe Veil was over when she returned the Cup, no matter who vied for it. Or who won it. That person would not be her. She knew better now than to be led to the wisewoman Sage's ends.

Alison gnawed what she had named turkey jerky, but it was tougher and more tasteless than turkey. Her jaws cracked as she chewed, the sound almost obliterating the drowsy buzz of a bee. But no flowers dotted the nearby meadow; she had picked a place untainted by their noxious odor.

Still, the air vibrated with a distant hum; maybe it was more of a sibilant *whoosh*. She glanced up at the sky, still light and bright although the sun had dipped behind the mountains and the circlet of horizon-level clouds shone crimson and copper, like red hair, like flagrantly red hair. Like a bloody noose throttling the limits of Veil.

Two specks wheeled, far silhouettes in the brightly pallid sky. The whistling sound spun with them. Alison stopped chewing and shaded her eyes with one hand. She leaped up, dropping the tough jerky, wishing for binoculars.

Planes! Two airplanes swooped high above, the unseen sun glinting off gleaming metal bodies and outstretched wings. The high-pitched drone must be from their engines. As she watched, they circled like lazy, mating dragonflies.

She could only think she had been catapulted back to the Island again, back into real-time northern Minnesota. A moment's relief flashed through her, along with an irritation that she was once more responsible for a displaced talisman. At least she was no longer a displaced Taliswoman in Veil. So be it.

The two forms collided with the audible grinding of blade meeting whetstone. Blue sparks sprayed to earth like fallout from a spectacular fireworks display.

One flyer sheered off from the other, looping swiftly toward the ground, mobile wings sweeping, the entire nose portion wobbling as if disconnected. The second craft slashed downward on a red-gold glint, like a giant sparkler. Their paths crossed, more blue sparks exploding against the dimming alabaster sky.

Alison looked again. "That's no insect dance," she muttered aloud. "That's a dogfight!"

Indeed it was, for all those air-show swirls and dives, the distant ballet of thin air and heavy metal. Yet now that she saw them more closely, now that they plummeted nearer the earth, she noted that the aircraft were bizarrely formed. Each one had the jointed, biomechanical look of a monstrous insect. Humankind had been blending the totems of monster and machine ever since prows were carved into figureheads and automobiles were named after wild beasts. But did Veilians do such things as well?

The two craft waltzed through the empty air, tilting their

wide, brazen wings to joust at each other. Which one should she root for? Or for neither? What were they? How did they fly?

She gasped as one glided to a full stop in midair. The other sped directly toward it. Then the stalled craft's wings *folded* down. It dropped like a stone; the oncoming craft sped on—toward the hard ground hundreds of feet below. The first craft spread its wings and flipped like a gymnast, gaining height against all likelihood. The charger had no such flexibility. Wind whistled against the cutting edge of its scaled wings, against the thin, spinning circle of its invisible propeller blades. It angled to earth like a sun-dagger flung over a mountain. In seconds, it had plowed into an ocean of pine-green waves on the opposite mountain and was still.

A faint keening came on the cutting edge of twilight. Alison looked up again. The first craft was spinning awkwardly about in the sky—clumsily, off balance—yet it was heading inevitably toward her camp, as if something large and sentient had decided to land near her.

She shook her head, not wanting to meet the personage, the . . . pilot? . . . of such a lethal and indescribable artifact. The last light played on mottled metal. Was this another ruin of Veil's, like Darnellyne's face?

The closer the object came, the larger it loomed. She remembered the Littlelost pointing up at an etherion . . . courser, they had called it, shuddering. Flight from this air-beast, they had insisted, was of no use.

Flight was of no use for Alison on this barren hill, where she had camped at the only protected spot. The whistling increased to a high-pitched drone as the twitching wings and body, tail and head, wobbled to within thirty feet above her.

Suddenly a length of rope, or wire, or chain, snaked down from the hovering shadow, a whipping tail of shade. She ducked among the rocks to avoid its lash.

A sound fluted from within the whirlwind of whine: perhaps it was a song, as birdsong is melody and meaning. In those haunting tones, Alison heard no threat, only plea.

She straightened, wondering if she were crazy. The sound rose high with appeal and urgency. The trailing length wavered, an umbilical cord to earth. Was she to climb it? No way. An etherion courser, close up. Etherion, the lighter-than-air metal that the Littlelost were forced to harvest from the woodlands' rotting pits, where the Takers kept them prisoner. A metal that flew, like a balloon filled with helium. Again the fluted request, demand. An etherion courser that, like a dirigible, like a Desmeynian pewter mirror framed in etherion, needed anchoring! Of course.

She reached up for the strand. Her hands fastened on braided metal wire as flexible as a hair, yet as thick as her wrist. She drew it around the rocks; through and around and under a jutting ledge, again and again, until she ended with a huge knot that seemed likely to hold.

Before she looked up again, she burrowed in her pack and pulled out a flashlight. Batteries worked just fine in the land of Veil, as she knew from her previous visit. The sky reflected the last light of sunset, pale and bald at its top, broodily dark halfway up the horizon. Alison aimed the flashlight at the juncture of gently bobbing craft and umbilical. Something moved, then came clambering down the line to earth as nimbly as a monkey.

As it touched down, Alison froze it in her flashlight beam. Rowan would have thought the phenomenon magic; perhaps this inhabitant of Veil would think so, too.

The cozy golden beam illuminated the form of a tiny woman as pretty as a fairy in a picture book, attired in artful wisps of cloth like so many aviator scarves.

The creature came swooping down toward her, fluting eagerly.

8

ALISON awoke to the sight of a beaten-metal ceiling drifting amiably in the wind.

She sat up, disoriented, reaching for the backpack. It lay beside her, exactly where she had placed it last night. Then she remembered the etherion courser and its alien pilot. The elfin woman crouched atop a rock, awake and watching the fragile craft rock at its moorings. For a panicky moment, Alison had the oddest feeling that she was breathing underwater, breathing *in* water, and that the tethered etherion courser was a boat floating above her.

Certainly it seemed to be seen through the wavering depths of clear water. Even in daylight, it was an ungainly thing: a gigantic mechanical dragonfly bouncing on a blade of grass, a visionary World's Fair construction from the early years of flight, a gossamer tin can cut into an animal totem.

The little woman regarded it with steadfast concentration, ignoring Alison's stirrings even when she left to take care of her sanitary needs and returned to delve noisily in the backpack for food and water. The creature had seemed eager to share her spot for the night; indeed, Alison would have had to leave had she wanted some privacy. She had decided to accept the company and see what happened. Overnight, nothing had. Shaky, Alison poured canteen water into the Cup. Maybe drinking from the magical vessel would clear her vision; it had before. Maybe woman and whazzit would vanish, like the phantoms they must be.

Maybe she had not seen another alien flyer crash and burn, or simply crash and vanish.

The water braced her like iced Aquavit, clear and potent.

The woman turned her head, saw the Cup, then lifted delicate eyebrows more feather-down than hair. Her voice fluted into the air, as clear as water. Midway through the pleasant sounds, Alison recognized a word, then another. She swallowed wrong and sputtered for several seconds.

"Yaooodel fulee fulee Valley ah vree." The visitor smiled.

Alison smiled back. It was hard to suspect this dainty creature of any ill will, though her aerial maneuvers had presumably sent another pilot to a crash landing on the opposite mountain.

"Sylvin." The woman gestured at herself.

"Alison."

The woman cocked her head. "Ah vree? Alison choa Valley ah vree? Choa ree Desmeyne?"

Alison nodded slowly, a gesture of bewilderment, not of agreement.

The woman stood. "Wellsunging," she said. "Soon." Her large, pale-lavender eyes flicked to the mountain behind which the sun had set and on which her enemy had fallen. She eyed the Cup, her expression growing serious, even accusing. "See you win last time. Alison late."

Alison examined the Cup with some resurgence of awe. Not a drop of water remained in it. Though it had done nothing for Darnellyne, it still dried itself, and apparently it still acted as an instant translator. She packed the Cup and rose. Obviously she must get going, now that her new friend had told her in plain English that she was late.

The woman's feathery brows met in a frown. She pointed skyward. "No Valley. Crux."

That made Alison pause. She eyed the opposite mountain and indicated the pale scar of splintered wood among the bunched pines. "Crux?"

The pilot nodded soberly. Her fine white hair was cut into a cloche around her face. Wind would barely ruffle it. She pointed upward to the bobbling etherion monstrosity. "We will take you to the Valley."

"You understand me now?"

"Now that you speak the tongue of Desmeyne. We Sylvins soar everywhere and hear all manner of tongues."

"But you didn't understand me at first."

"Of course not." Her voice was modulated and musical, but it no longer fluted. "At first you spoke only strange sounds, but now you speak sense."

"Are you saying that you will . . . fly me to the Valley of Voices?"

A brisk nod. "You must mount first. I will untie and come up after." She eyed Alison's body critically. "Did you weigh any more, it would not be possible. At least you will wallow my corsair down while I climb. We Sylvins seldom take passengers. It is a courtesy to the Cup."

"Corsair?" The term was close to courser, but it had more disturbing roots in Alison's own world. "An etherion corsair?"

"Certainly. Mount."

"I don't know where."

"It will become obvious."

"I don't know if I want to."

The light violet eyes shut and opened slowly. In that long, shuttered motion, Alison read an impatience refined to contempt. She walked meekly to the tether.

"I may be too heavy to climb this."

"We will see."

Above her, the belly of the beast swung idly, its sheet-metal scales glittering. She remembered approaching amusement-park rides with similar dread and excitement. Sunlight had warmed the metal cord pleasantly. Backpack strapped over both shoulders, she leaped, grasping the tether firmly.

"Ooooh!" The moment she touched the cord, her body lifted of itself, as if water-buoyed. She "swam" upward, hand over hand, giggling like a child at the sensation. She had not felt so free in . . . ever.

She drew near the thing above, its form warmed by the sun. It seemed to have no more substance than tinfoil sheathing a melting chocolate bar. Though it was metal, it was not cold and stiff, but pliant. Though it was inanimate, Alison felt she clambered up to the many-jointed form of a sleeping dragon. Though it was in a sense machine, in a deeper way, it was sentient. The weightless metal swayed to the tease of the air, to every nudge of her clumsy body.

There was no entrance on the belly. If this beast had a back, it lay between the wings. Alison crawled carefully onto the softly bucking surface. It reminded her too much of a boat adrift on the constant slow clap of waves. Her stomach tightened, and when she looked down . . .

Swags of fine metal wire drooped everywhere, like reins. Her entangled limbs extracted themselves painstakingly. From above, the construction seemed more web than body. She paused, suspended on the warm back belly-down, like a swimmer floating on the surface and eyeing the fish far below.

The Sylvin woman flashed up the tether, her tattered attire whipping in the breeze. *She* walked upright atop the bulk, ducking daintily through the wire rigging. She prodded Alison's legs, an arm, the backpack. Alison now clung to the metal like a jockey stretched along a horse's neck and withers, or a bug clinging to a can about to be hurled into a trash bin.

The corsair floated up, trailing its loosened tether. The Sylvin woman hung from a thread of wire, pulling up the tether until the end weight reached her tiny hand. When she removed the weight, the tail of wire snapped straight upward before she wound it around a portion of the wing and tied it off.

Alison looked down again. Veil's windblown meadows shifted from light to dark green, like shoals of shallow sand seen through shoreline waves. The snowless mountaintops glittered, their red-and-white stone surfaces embedded with rock crystal. Marshaled pine tops marched up incline and down valley. The waterfalls shot downward, trailing sprays of diamond drops.

Around Alison, the etherion corsair came to eerie life. The Sylvin woman cast herself facedown on her network of wires, plucking them like a harp, shifting parts of the airy framework to work the wind. The wind itself curled through the corsair,

stroking the thin metal, vibrating the web until the entire construct crooned a melody of flight and sail and motion and time.

Over the naked land, which Alison always saw as deserted
from ground level, small groups of hikers headed for the Valley
of Voices. She was not too late, whatever the Sylvin had said.
She strained to see at least one walking form clearly, to see
what sort it was: man or woman, Desmeynian, local villager, or
some other inhabitant of Veil. None seemed small enough to
be Littlelost. None sported a crest of long red hair, although on
her previous visit, Rowan had hidden his hallmark until his
arrival at the Wellsunging.

The Sylvin's high voice crooned a set of syllables Alison
could not translate even now. The fragile framework shuddered, then suddenly soared like a kite. Alison's stomach remained fifteen hundred feet below. Around her, the metal
body, its wings flapping, screeched in the wind. The people
walking below were now scarcely visible dots, and the mountaintops crowded around them as if begrudging their unwanted ascent.

Alison gasped, barely able to inhale against the rush of chill
wind. Her fingers curled desperately into the available hand-
holds: thin bicycle spokes of alien metal trailing the tendrils the
Sylvin played into a rippling mass of sound and motion.

The shrill cacophony tempted Alison to release her grip on
the corsair and cover her ears—but her hands were busy holding on. The Sylvin's close-cropped hair was blown back, and
Alison was not surprised to see that her ears were almost
nonexistent. Obviously, sharp hearing was a detriment to
the job.

Luckily, the etherion corsair was as swift as its name. Alison
saw the deep green vee of the Valley appear ahead with the
sudden familiarity of a carnival viewed midway from atop a
Ferris wheel. Descent was as abrupt as takeoff: the corsair
slashed to the ground at an angle Alison swore would toss her
off backwards. Instead, the wind glued her breathless to the
shrieking metal. Then the Sylvin snarled her hands and feet in
the wires, the great creaking wings rose up around them like

sheet-metal sails, and they lofted down in a meadow as neatly as a butterfly on a chrysanthemum.

"Hurry," the Sylvin said, the construction bucking under her slight body. "Your weight is all that holds us down. Leap off."

"You are not coming to the Wellsunging?" Alison stiffly slid along the now wind-chilled metal, eyeing an eight-foot drop to a meadow that looked to be down-soft but was hard dirt at bottom.

"We Sylvin flyers watch above. Hurry."

Alison slid over a side that was definitely not aerodynamically smooth, her denim snagging on rough metal joints, and thumped to the ground in a crouch that cushioned the shock. Some.

Like a steed too high-tempered to pause long, the corsair jerked free of earth once Alison's weight was gone. Up it soared, wheeling at the top of its arc to glide over the neighboring mountains and vanish.

Rubbing her rear, Alison turned toward the Valley, noticing that people were converging here from all directions, as they had a year ago. That was encouraging. Veil showed a certain real-world predictability in this respect.

She joined the flow to the Valley, drawing nearer to people and recognizing villager garb, noting some of the Sylvin's sisters in the slight, scarf-clad figures who, surprisingly, sat with huge, heavyset men. No children accompanied the attendees, as they had not on the previous year. Alison smiled to remember her arrival with the five Littlelost; what a breach of etiquette, had she only known it. And yet she, the innocent flouter of Veilian custom, had won the prized Cup of Earth. For all the good it did anyone, especially poor little Pickle—no, she wouldn't think of that. Next, she would dwell on her lost Samoyed. Seen again, but a different dog now. Not hers. As the Cup was not hers, not really. It belonged here, in Veil.

She crested the brow of the familiar hill and joined the dozens of folk stuttering down the steep slope of grass and scentless flowers. Her morning journey had brought her here early for the twilight ceremony. She would have a long day of waiting. Of waiting—she looked around for a familiar shock of red hair—and wondering whether Rowan would come.

The day wore on slowly. Though she settled near the Valley floor, where the stones formed a natural stage, no one addressed her. She ate when hungry, drank scrupulously from her canteen—no use in flashing the Cup as a common drinking vessel among this crowd—and strained to watch the continual flow of figures over the Valley rim.

No one whom she knew came. Every time an energetic figure crested the Valley height alone, a staff clutched in his hand or the neck of a musical instrument across his back, she watched his approach. These young men, the celibate contenders for the Cup and forbidden to carry edged steel, strode straight for the small arena of rocks from whence they would vie, shedding cloaks and readying instruments even as they came. Though some were tall and slight, some lean and sturdy, others dark or light of hair, none bore the rare red hair common only to the Firemayne family.

As the afternoon sun slanted behind the mountaintops and the light cooled and thinned, the Valley's voices began a silken rustling. Speculation buzzed over word that the Cup-bearer, alien as she was, had returned. Eyes hot with conjecture stabbed Alison repeatedly. Amid a gaggle of younger escorts, the circle of elders arrived, their steps feeble, their long, thin beards dripping from their chins, their heavy-lidded eyes watery with yellowed whites.

The elders' glances in her direction were those of relief, if not of welcome. If she had alleviated their anxiety, her own remained rampant. Would Rowan come? Of course he would, she told herself. He had been a positive fanatic about following every rule of Veil, about meeting every expectation of him.

The dimming light was now icing the daylight warmth lingering on the meadow grasses. The scentless pale flowers showed a feeble glow that would intensify into light as true twilight fell and the singing competition began. Alison found herself anticipating the outpouring of song that would well from the Valley's throat. She almost wished she would take her place among the contenders, though to risk winning the Cup again would destroy everything she hoped to gain by her return.

How could Rowan, a true son of Veil, refuse the ritual call when she, an alien, had been drawn from another world to answer it?

She craned her neck to see the Valley rim again. It cut sharp and dark against the lighter backdrop of the adjacent mountain. No more figures poured over the horizon line like ants heading for a pile of sugar. Everyone was here, and the games were about to begin.

The elders stood. One of them made the ritual speeches, his quavering voice amplified by the magic of the site into a loud call to trial by music. Alison rummaged in her bag for the Cup, but when she withdrew it, an elder shook his head at her. Apparently they didn't need it yet. Apparently she was to present it to the winner.

An elder nodded, and a young man stepped forward cradling an instrument of polished wood like Rowan's. She had christened it a mandotar in honor of its hybrid resemblance to both mandolin and guitar.

A liquid strum riveted her attention. The rocks at the performer's feet radiated soft light, creating a warm niche in the spreading dimness. Song came suddenly in a voice of deep sweetness, in words like none Alison had ever heard, in melody that touches the wellspring of emotion in any land.

Again, each performer seemed possessed of an individual magic—the specific attributes of lyric or melody or voice—that elevated the act of music to a sublime peak of perfection. Caught up in the wonder once more, Alison forgot that she was alone here, that she did not belong here. Like any member of an attentive audience, she was transported to a unique and private realm of time and space.

A rustle among the audience came first as an irritation. She frowned, hers not the only face illuminated by her particular patch of luminous petals that did. She shifted position, cranky, and concentrated harder on the current song.

A soft *whoosh* at the far edge of the Valley tumbled down the hillside like running water, both fluid and implacable. The

101

performer faltered and stared into the twilight. Rustles and grumbles came closer, as contagious as a brush fire.

Alison, lost in the music, turned, ready to hiss *"Shhhh"* at the interruption. Her eyes narrowed at the hillside dotted with ambient blossoms as tiny as stars and a corona of light drawn along the edge of the Valley. Cresting the ridge, silhouetted as if cut from black construction paper, was a canine form.

"Slinker!" came the whispered, fearful diagnosis of the audience. "Slinkers," others said. Now Alison could see the trail opening through the seated people, who crawled away, crushing vigil lights of flowers, to avoid the newcomers. The dark forms came straight down the hill, an entire line of them. The flowery footlights showed now and again a sweep of Slinker tail, a muzzled profile. Slinkers indeed. The parade came on, and now most of its members were no longer canine, but squat, like Earth-Eaters, or merely short, like the Littlelost.

Despite the angry whispers around her, Alison stood and saw there were more than four Littlelost; dozens of Littlelost were coming. The muttering among the onlookers had become a sullen growl. Song had fallen silent. The current singer stood gaping, watching the descending ribbon of darkness unroll toward Alison, and the Cup.

She recognized the human leader with amazed relief.

"Rime!"

The Littlelost's fair head shone like a light-bearing bud in the reflected blossom-glow. Twist and Faun came close behind, then a tarry, tattered array who carried the stink of Veil's loveliest flowers with none of their beauty. The audience members scrabbled away from this onslaught to sight and smell. Something slapped Alison's thigh: the wagging tail of a black-eyed, gray-coated Slinker, as glad as a domesticated dog to see her. She laughed at this surprising welcome. This was a place of sound; after such long, shocked silence, her sudden laughter floated up as pure as a prayer.

That simple, human sound quieted the onlookers' grumbles. And in that silence, the last, looming figure to come down the hill came close enough for Alison to see.

"Rowan!" Again Alison's spontaneous sound was amplified, every nuance of that word, that name, was plucked and spun into a separate thread, then echoed into a round of itself. Her own uncensored emotions mocked her: surprise, vindication, curiosity, an undercurrent of challenge.

Rowan passed her without a word and stepped to the rear of the silent Cup-rivals, who were standing stupefied. A startled elder waved him to the fore, but he shook his shocking red head and remained behind the others.

Alison was pulled down to sit amid a happy tangle of re-united Littlelost and their guardian Slinkers. The other Littlelost settled around the central core in a malodorous ring, given a wide berth by the audience.

The interrupted performer, a plump young man with curly brown hair and a chin dimple, cleared his throat and resumed his song. His magic had evaporated, and he knew it. He stopped and bowed himself off the rocky platform, defeated, as the next candidate stepped forward. The Valley seized this one's vibrato tenor and wove it into a pulsing paean of tone and color. Softly, the singing tightened its grip on every ear but Alison's.

Quite the dramatic entrance, she thought, eyeing the late-comer. And that humble fade to the background and last place. Rowan, the red-haired fox, had seen her surprise final inning a year before and realized that performing last can be an advantage. And where had he acquired these ripe new Littlelost? Refusing to be seduced by the other singers, she watched him. He still had his staff; it now leaned against the ring of rocks.

But his hair, his face . . . good Lord, a beard. With that shoulder-length hair, he looked like a wild man. Certainly he would not simply repeat last year's performance. This, she told herself, ignoring the press of offensive smells around her, should be interesting.

The previous year, the Valley's exquisite acoustics, the exotic instruments, and the fresh singers had hypnotized Alison. This year, the Wellsunging had lost its electricity. Perhaps she was simply jaded, no longer the dazzled newcomer not knowing what to expect. The audience struck her as listless, the music uninspired, the performers tired. She waited impatiently for Rowan to reveal himself through his song. Had he changed in more than surface ways? If so, surely the change would sing out loud and clear, in this of all places.

Yet the Valley of Voices seemed like the Cup, its power muted and muffled. She took out the vessel. The cold stone sucked the heat from her flesh, made her wrist bones ache arthritically. She was tempted to set the vessel aside.

Others shared her immunity to the singing's old magic, she realized. The radiant flowers had turned sinister; the light they cast up made the Littlelost faces look worn and bitter rather than wondering and innocent. A lethargy spread through the Valley. All around her, heads drooped on insupportably weary necks. The audience's silence was not respectful or awed, but bored.

Finally no one was left to sing but Rowan. He stepped forward into the eerie light cast by the rocks, shaking his head at the offer of an instrument. Silent long past the point of beginning, he eyed the crowd, seeking to raise those drooping eyelids.

His silence became a tangible thing, almost a slap in the face. Murmurs stirred the flowers into vibrating fireflies as grumbling breaths left slumped bodies. Now all the people of Veil who were gathered in the Valley of Voices thought Rowan Firemayne was exactly what Alison had thought him on meeting him a year before: arrogant and self-concerned.

She sat up straighter, held the Cup closer. More than arrogance motivated his erect but casual stance, one leg slightly bent at the knee. His clothes were not the shapeless, disguising pilgrim garb he had worn a year before. They were fresh from the halls of Desmeyne, or rather, had been fresh a few months ago. Hard use had made the full, open-necked velvet shirt look faded and shabby. Its roughened nap reflected the light in a two-tone pattern of blood-dark burgundy and pale pink. One full sleeve was rent above the wrist, revealing a glimpse of arm as white as bone. Once-sleek tights bagged at the knees; the boots had been wet and untended for weeks.

The shirtfront's deep vee neck revealed an inverted triangle of pale skin and wiry red body hair. At Rowan's collarbones lay the talismanic scars inscribed into his skin at the age of eleven. He did nothing to hide these dangerous marks or his equally dangerous profusion of red hair. His eyebrows—like his face, no longer shaved daily by rubrock—glinted ruddily in the rock-light.

Alison leaned forward to squint at the alien object partially covering but in no way disguising his chest scars. A pouch. A small pouch on a leather thong. Her hand tightened on the Cup stem even as her heart constricted. Ashes. Rowan carried the ashes of his elder brother, the Littlelost known as Pickle, virtually in plain sight.

She sank back on her heels, repulsed. He might mean to honor the brother he had known as Lorn, but he no doubt also meant to use those ashes as a stepping-stone toward the accomplishment of some arcane pattern of quests.

By now, Rowan's potent silence had sanded the audience's patience to a rough edge. At the very moment when rebellion was about to grow tangible, at the instant the rustlings and throat clearings increased to a wavelike sussuration, Rowan raised a hand for silence.

He got it. Then he sang. The first words and notes came so abruptly that his voice cracked as it broke the ice of silence. This rough beginning only intensified the effect. Alison recognized the melody of the ballad that he had sung last year, but the words poured out of his throat as if torn free, each one cauterized in pain and loss, each rinsed in the acid rain of unceasing anger.

Such scalding intensity of emotion held the song in thrall so that even the translation abilities of the Cup failed utterly. Alison clutched the vessel to her breast, hearing only meaningless syllables that spoke more strongly than any words she knew to the death of her sister Demaris by drowning, to the absence of the old Island Indian Eli, to Rambeau's painful loss and transformation, to the moment when brave little Pickle defied the Crux and was lightning-struck into the oblivion of instant ashes.

Her throat clogged shut with choking emotion. Now she

loathed her front-row seat of crushed grasses; it was too searingly close. She looked for a path away from this accusing storm of lightning and thunder. Everyone else sat motionless, too attacked, too rapt in horror, to escape. Even twilight had not dared to steal away into night's dark, concealing skirts. Light as anemic and as blue as skim milk still washed the sky. The mountains were semi-silhouettes in the distance, stabbed by the rare white lightning of faraway waterfalls.

Against the beaten pewter sky something flashed: real lightning, Alison thought, summoned by Rowan's song.

On the song went, as heedless of the discomfort it brought as a raging river is of the banks it scours raw. Rowan's voice sought no beauty, merely the most apt expression, and found a terrible power that held each listener in place to be pounded senseless by the melodic fury that reached beyond the range of human vocal chords.

The end came as brusquely as the beginning. One moment Alison was cowering under a rain of heartbreaking sounds, the next moment the evening was empty and as still as a desiccated pond.

Soundless, remote lightning sizzled above the mountains. The air had a stricken, frantic weight, as if the notes of Rowan's song lay heavy on it. Alison stood, finally freed to retreat as she had wished to, needed to, but first she had a duty to fulfill. Others around her stood, too, except for the Slinkers, who sat in a circle and sniffed the air and whimpered uncertainly.

She took one step toward the performance circle, starting to hold out the Cup, to offer it to the overwhelmingly clear winner.

The movement caught Rowan's attention. His head turned toward the Cup as if he owned it, as indeed he did in a sense. His eyes met Alison's, rejecting and recognizing her in the same instant.

It's over, she told him in the empty corridors of her mind. The Cup is yours now. I have nothing more to do with Veil.

His eyes moved from hers to the Cup, pausing on the place where her own accidental scars made the same pattern as any quest-heir's. She was veiled there now, with navy knit. Hidden. Under cover. Incognito. The Cup was all his, as was the quest, the land of Veil. Her thoughts faltered. Darnellyne was all his now, too. She thrust the Cup toward him, not wanting to hold a thing of such ashes and agony and expectancy any longer.

But the distant lightning flickers assembled into a bright blue lance of Crux-light and struck down the Valley to the rocks. The Valley of Voices echoed with the sounds of senseless screams and the clatter of stones kicked by fleeing feet. The circle of self-lit rocks shattered into shards as a thin rod of blue light reared among the dazed quest-heirs.

The Crux had come to claim the Cup.

9

ABOVE them in the dim, milky sky, lightning and thunder clashed together at the same instant, like cymbals.

Alison looked up from the dreadful blue rod; she hadn't heard thunder, but several etherion coursers colliding against one another like wind-tossed kites whose lines had tangled. More than half of the craft radiated a neon-blue aura, bright against the twilight sky—boxy, hybrid flyers with none of the Sylvin corsair's innate grace. Crux-craft! Mutual destruction could be the only outcome.

Those who had gathered for the Wellsunging scattered and fled up the incline, hoping to outrun the aerial attack. Airy, unarmed Sylvin corsairs flew like paper planes into the face of the Crux's bitter blue power, striving to maneuver the coursers into suicidal dives. Alison froze, her eyes glued to the battle overhead. Some of those huge, graceful sky-skimmers must bear living pilots. Sylvins.

A pull on her sleeve drew her attention back to earth.

"Hide it!" Twist shouted into the joint howl of clashing metal and screeching mob.

Alison didn't know what good that would do, but she pulled the backpack around and jammed the Cup inside. Looking down at the rocks, she saw a lurking piece of the night—a Crux-master—materialize into a shadow puppet to wield the blue rod against the elders, scattering them.

The neon lightning from the enemy craft above further split the surrounding rocks. They tumbled asunder to reveal polished black throats as high as doorways, from which gargled out massive human forms growling gibberish.

Alison, recognizing the Crux's two-pronged attack from above- and below-ground, rejoiced that she had hidden the Cup. Rowan's staff was in his hands. Along with the other quest-heirs, he was fiercely repelling this outpouring of over-sized enemies so suddenly among them.

The three Slinkers and the Littlelost charged, harrying the backs and heels of the massive attackers, yet more giants lunged forward from the rended rocks as their comrades fell.

Alison, surprised, found Twist, Faun, and Rime still at her side, like a guard. They four were momentarily safe in the eye of the storm, overlooked by both the enemy aloft and that on the rocks below. Eyeing the gruesomely vague figure threatening the elders with blue ruin, Alison shuddered to remember the dance she had shared with Dearth, that utter emptiness on the edge of time and space. In a moment, the falling elders would no longer command the Crux-master's attention. Then Alison's turn would come.

Retreat seemed wisest. So Rowan apparently thought, too; he had fought his way toward their group.

"You have the Cup?" was his intently single-minded greeting.

Alison nodded, watching his glance flick away. Seconds later, his staff cracked the ribs and then the head of the man perhaps seven feet tall who had been rushing at them. The giant toppled like a tree. Alison searched its somehow familiar face for a clue. Even a battle grimace could not obscure a refined, almost Oriental cast of feature. These creatures, though large and fierce, were not the half-beast Takers.

Rowan grabbed Alison's arm to hurry her—and doubtless the Cup she carried—over to the hill. Then he looked up, noticing the air battle for the first time, and paused. Anyone reared on black-and-white World War Two TV movies would recognize the action. Rowan, innocent of such phenomena, stood and gawked.

Faun and Rime pulled at his sleeves, chirping terse advice. "Etherion coursers." "Must run and hide." "Hurry!"

Good idea. Alison started up the hill again, but Rowan's grip still held, and he didn't move with her.

"Stop staring at the sky," she told him impatiently, "before the Crux hurls a lightning strike down your throat."

"They could . . . send their foul power that far afield?"

"If they're using what I think they are, they can." She looked behind him. "Ooops!"

Rowan turned. The Crux-master had vanished, rod and all, but another oversized rock-borne figure was hurtling toward them. Toward him. He released Alison to spin the staff crosswise in his hands, ready to parry the oncoming ax-wielder either vertically or horizontally—until, just as the two were about to knock heads, Rowan abruptly sidestepped, yanking his staff away from the onrushing figure.

Momentum carried the attacker past them to a frame-shaking fall to the ground.

"You had won!" Alison demanded. "Why give way?"

Rowan turned, confused. "It is . . . female."

She eyed the fallen giant. "Barely."

"Women do not fight," he said. A familiar statement, now repeated with an air of dazed doubt.

"This one is getting up to fight again," she pointed out.

Again the creature charged Rowan. Again he feinted, though its wicked blade came within a whisker's breadth of his shoulder.

In the broken glow of the shattered rocks, the performance area was littered with fallen elders, attackers, and quest-heirs. Only this last enemy was harassing their group, but in moments the others pouring from the sundered rocks below and harrying the fleeing crowd could regroup, capture and kill them all, and waltz off with the Cup.

Meanwhile, Rowan was doing some wierd Apache dance with this hefty female berserker! Alison had to do something.

She shrugged off the backpack and handed it to Twist. "You know enough to get away from here before it's too late. I suggest now."

The Littlelost's wise-weary face wrinkled in uncertainty.

At that instant, Rowan catapulted into Alison, almost

knocking her over. He landed like an overturned turtle on the ground beside her, staring with astonished horror at the amazon looming over him.

Alison couldn't blame him. Seven feet of attacker was awesome, no matter the sex. Such height was even more overwhelming when she herself stepped between its ax blade and Rowan. Littlelost wailed at her back.

Female this creature might be, but in its blank and brutish face, its eyes were corroded with hatred. Its ax lifted high as it charged Alison, bringing the blade down in a berserk arc that would have sliced arm from body had Alison not moved.

The ultimate test. Alison donned her *taekwondo* patterns like her practice robes. The world withdrew as drastically as it did when she had unknowingly danced with Dearth, but here she was both center and boundaries. She was the one who acted, if only to avoid—

The attacker thundered past her, its very weight, so deadly when met head-on, drawing it beyond her and offering its undefended back. Alison twisted, her right foot kicking out, and her right arm executed a chop to the conveniently extended neck as it sailed by.

She had rebalanced herself and stood waiting for the creature's maddened return. Was this how matadors saw the bull? Alison fiercely disapproved of bullfighting, but it provided a model. She must be the thin, fixed pin around which the greater force is compelled to spiral until it collapses of its own bulk. Her hands and feet, legs and arms, struck out like snakes, swiftly, and with only enough force to sting. In two more charges, the strange creature lay unconscious at Alison's feet, having literally knocked itself out.

Rowan had risen but remained immobile, horrified by the unconscious female at their feet, perhaps more horrified by the conscious one at his side.

Despite the danger, Alison couldn't help but smile. He hadn't changed completely, after all.

"We have no time for Desmeynian courtesies," she jibed rather unfairly, since he had not been about to offer any. "Let's get away and then stop to think about it." She took her pack from Twist.

Rowan shook off his shock and started forward, the jabs of his staff punctuating a zigzag path up the incline. Alison approved the unpredictable path and followed in his footsteps, or rather in his staff gouges, the three Littlelost alongside her.

By now, the sky battle continued in pitch dark. Blue sparks carved arcs against the blackness and lit the metal-monster limbs that soared and clashed like huge fan blades. Breathless, the party at last crested the Valley.

"Anywhere nearby where we can be safe?" Alison asked.

"I am not returning to Desmeyne," Rowan said.

"Neither am I. But what about a convenient cave close by, some sheltering woods where we can go to ground?"

"You would willingly go into the ground?" he demanded. "After what we have seen lives there, seen what has poured from the very rocks at the center of the Valley of Voices?"

"Not deep, just a little."

"And forest," he added. "If you had seen the abominations that I have seen under the shadows of trees—"

"All right, a depression in the meadow, a single tree to shelter us. Anyplace like that."

A small hand tugged at her shirt hem. "Follow Slinkers," suggested Faun.

"They're here?"

Then Alison sensed the Slinkers milling around them in the dark, almost close enough to touch. If only Rambeau—

A tiny hand curled around three of her fingers, all it could hold. "We touch the Slinkers' shoulders. Follow us, and we will follow them."

Animal instinct. Not a bad trailblazer in a world gone dark and dangerous. What had they to lose?

Rowan, too, had apparently been taken in gentle tow, for he stumbled forward, then matched his long strides to the cautious steps of beasts and Littlelost.

By the lightning still flashing, Alison glimpsed lurid snatches of her companions: a Slinker tooth gleaming neon blue;

Rime's fair head shining with a sickly azure aura; the long, thin bone of Rowan's staff in his blue-knuckled grip.

They stumbled blindly down the mountain until the metallic thunder dimmed and they seemed to be lost amid the treacherous tiers of a black amphitheater, looking for a seat on the edge of an unknown drop-off.

"Oof!" Rowan's protest meant contact with something unexpected.

Alison reached out, surprised to find fragile saplings brush her groping hands. Keeping her arms before her face to ward off their whip-sharp backlash, she felt her way forward. The warm little hand had slipped from her fingers. She could hear the others breathing softly now that the air was clear of the hideous sounds of conflict.

Sighing, Alison sank down.

"We must wait until light." Rowan announced the obvious from somewhere above her. His tone was bewildered.

What a dislocation it must have been, Alison suddenly realized. One moment Rowan had been delivering that impassioned song; the next instant, the serene, even sacred, Valley of Voices had erupted in Crux-fire.

"Sit down," she suggested. "I have travel food—"

"I as well," he said stiffly, even as she heard the twigs and his knees creaking as he followed her advice.

Something was thrust into her hand, something dry, stringy. More turkey jerky. "Thanks, but I have some. I took it from Desmeyne when I left." She dug the trail mix out of her pack. "Try some of this."

"You have seen Desmeyne?"

Actually, the dark made it easier for her to read Rowan's often-controlled underlying emotions. His last question had been touched with surprise, and a dollop of envy.

"First thing when I arrived."

"How are . . . matters there?"

She felt the Littlelost settling between them, heard the rustle of reclining Slinkers; if the Slinkers were anything like Rambeau, they would turn around several times before setting belly to ground in exactly the right position.

"Desmeyne is unsettled," she said. "And agog with talk of how Rowan Firemayne has changed."

That remark kept him silent for a time. "The difficulty is not that I have changed, but that they have not."

"Don't be too sure." In the obsidian mirror of the dark, she could picture Darnellyne's distorted face staring at her in unveiled white anguish.

This time the pause was so long she thought he had finished speaking. "What is . . . this foodstuff?" he asked at last.

"Trail mix? Raisins, nuts, cereal and, best of all, bits of chocolate."

"I have heard of none of these foods." Suspicion again salted his tone.

"They are not native to Veil."

"They taste . . . foreign. They burn and make my tongue curl."

"Perhaps it's the salt on the peanuts, the sugar in the chocolate."

"It is not poison?"

"Only if you eat too much of it."

Silence.

"Salt and sugar aren't instant death like wildwater. You'd have to eat half a mountain of them over a lifetime to harm yourself. Don't worry."

"Try," begged a greedy little voice.

Alison felt a cupped hand in the dark and filled it with trail mix. Another nudged it away. Soon Littlelost were munching in audible harmony.

"Good," Twist pronounced, "but not pomma."

"You'll have to find us pomma in the daylight," Alison told him. "We're not packed for a long journey, and Rowan doesn't wish to go back to Desmeyne."

"Why are you here?" he asked from the dark, his tone gloomy.

"To return the Cup."

"Then you have failed."

"Why? I have found you. You obviously won the Cup. Here, do you want it?" She reached into her pack.

"No!" He sounded as repulsed as he had been by her offer of trail mix. "We will talk in the morning, when I can see your face."

"Aw, I didn't know you had missed me."

"I did not miss you," he said with great dignity. "But it is easier to see a lie in daylight."

"Sometimes," she answered, "it is also easier to hear the truth in the darkness."

"More," put in a Littlelost.

Alison laughed and closed an eager cupped hand on itself. "Enough sweets. Rest now." She sighed, remembering the destruction that lay around them. "I hope we will like what we see in the morning."

She curled onto her side, her head nudging something—a Littlelost, or even a Slinker—and tried to sleep.

After the pyrotechnics over the Valley of Voices, the silence was eerie. Why had the stars and the moon not come out this evening? Did even the heavenly bodies shut their eyes at the clash of Sylvin flyers and Crux-coursers? Or was an unlit night just another phenomenon of Veil, perverse and lovely land that it was?

Alison slept despite these misgivings. The presence of the Littlelost and Slinkers was strangely comforting, like nap-mates at rug time in kindergarten. Besides, they were the perfect chaperones when sleeping with a strange man, and Rowan certainly qualified for that description.

She awoke to dense darkness. A sound had disturbed her. She lay quiet, waiting. At a short distance, something mewed. Something wild and small. Twigs snapped. Something snuffled. She kept herself motionless, imagining a bestiary of unlikely creatures sneaking up on them. Odd that the Slinkers had not stirred, hadn't warned them—

Ohhh. Something snuffled along her jeans, up under her shirt. A cold and wet finger prodded her bare midriff. Her breath collapsed within her ribcage, though she wanted to scream. The intruder burrowed farther, a short-shorn warm fuzzy the size of a stuffed bear. Her hands reached to stop it, and she almost giggled aloud. A baby Slinker! Another bumbled against her side. And then she heard the unmistakable sigh of a large dog settling down beside her, laying his long nose patiently on his paws and deciding to rest despite the wriggling escapades of his offspring.

"Beau!" she whispered, reaching out to bury her hands in the coarse luxury of his neck ruff.

10

ALISON awoke to dawn light and a litter of warm puppies sleeping in the curve of her body. Her eyes moved farther afield. Oops. A litter of warm wolf pups. Mrs. Rambeau lay two feet away, the narrow, wolfish snout cradled on her paws. Her wide-open dark eyes announced that she had not slept a wink while her babies explored foreign territory.

"Nice Madonna, sweet Madonna," Alison crooned, carefully easing herself up. She nudged the drowsy pups toward their mother.

Hah. Mean Mama Madonna, the dubious yellow glint behind the unnatural black answered mutely.

Other Slinkers stirred, growling softly. Rambeau and his bride were newcomers; now the proper pecking order had to be asserted. Although the dark female seemed dominant, Alison guessed that Madonna would never again take a subservient role in the pack. She had become the Slinker equivalent of a Loftlady, married and with children. Any who would relegate her to last in line would answer to Rambeau's teeth.

Remembering that wolves mate for life, Alison felt a pang of loss. Rambeau was no longer her pet by any definition, even if she had the papers to prove her ownership in a kitchen drawer at home. As if he knew she was thinking of him, Rambeau sat up and smiled the same genial, black-lipped grin that had won Alison's heart when he was a blunt-pawed pup in another litter.

She jiggled her backpack. "I've got my own grub, boy. Just concentrate on feeding your family."

Madonna whimpered. More likely she was the family hunter. Alison could not imagine her dog running down live prey, even now.

The Littlelost were awaking, poking sleep-swollen faces from their own litterlike pile. Alison eyed them fondly. Even knowing them for adults in child guise, even knowing that they had experienced a harsher life than that of most adults, she felt fiercely protective of them. She must stop thinking of them as abused children from her world; they were not quite the same.

"Have you been all right while I was gone?" she asked them.

"Of course." Faun disdained Alison's latent maternalism. "We were with Rowan."

"Oh, it was fun," Twist added with a rogue grin.

"With Rowan? Fun?" Alison looked around. The man in question was gone. She hoped not permanently. Not that she cared, she told herself, but he was the reason she had returned the Cup. Once he accepted it, she would be free of Veil and its problems forever. Outa here. How, she wasn't quite sure.

"We returned to the pits," Twist added fiercely.

"How could he do that to you? Take you back to those awful places."

"Easily. We came rushing in on the Takers, and we hit them left and right and they fell and Littlelost laughed . . . we came away ten times stronger. All came away, all Littlelost. We laughed and laughed like the wild Littlelost in the Rookeries."

Alison studied his ferocious expression, reflected in Faun's and even shy Rime's faces.

"Rowan freed other Littlelost from the Takers? Did he say why a Desmeynian should care about a kind his people despise?"

A silence. Was it so obvious?

"Rowan hates Takers," Faun boasted. "Now Takers have reason to hate Rowan."

"It figures. But . . . what about Rowan's quests for Desmeyne?"

Their combative joy faded. "We do not like Desmeyne," Rime said, snuggling against Alison's side. "We are sorry, Alison, but we do not like Desmeyne."

"Desmeyne does not like us," Faun announced.

"Desmeyne does not understand," Alison said. She was about to say more but the Slinkers backed away growling, and the Littlelost grew suddenly silent.

Rowan returned from wherever he had been, looking grim. "I cannot find the other Littlelost."

"Perhaps they have gone in search of the Rookeries," Faun suggested.

"The Rookeries!" Rowan looked distracted and drove weary fingers into the thick, incredibly red hair at his temples.

He sat down and ran his palm over his mouth, over the red luxuriance of his mustache and beard. He looked older so accessorized, and fiercer, like a Viking. Alison felt a new unease with him, different from the one she had known before.

Except for the tumbling cubs, the Slinkers had quietly withdrawn into the woods. Littlelost followed them. Alison and Rowan regarded one another with the wariness of Slinkers meeting strangers.

"Can I see it?" he asked grudgingly.

She stiffened, for a moment thinking he meant the scars cut into her chest.

"Oh. The Cup. Of course."

She dug it out from her pack and unveiled it rather shamefacedly. Her old plaid-flannel shirt was soft, but it seemed a shabby wrapping for a magical talisman.

He looked at the Cup of Earth with bitter, hungry eyes.

"It's yours now," she told him. "You won it."

"Who has said this? Which elder bestowed it upon me?"

"None could. They came under instant attack. But obviously you had won. You sang . . . incredibly well. Besides, I was not competing."

"And if you had been?"

She only shrugged. "I would never knowingly compete for this Cup, this burden. It is yours. I give it to you gladly." She thrust it toward him.

"I will not take it."

"You came to the Wellsunging. Late, but you came. Why, if you won't take the Cup?"

119

"Not from your hands."

She rose to her knees to match his seated height. "Why not? I am Cup-bearer. I won it. I can relinquish it."

"Perhaps. But I need not take it."

"It's important to Desmeyne."

"Perhaps Desmeyne is no longer important to me."

"Rowan, what has happened to you? You are a Firemayne of Desmeyne. You are a quest-heir. I may think it's all a delusion, but Veil is your world. You have to believe in it and its customs, even if I don't."

He eyed her levelly. "You believe in it enough to want to return the Cup."

"I believe in leaving the things of Desmeyne to Desmeyne, of Veil to Veil, and of myself . . . to myself. This Cup is yours. Take it."

His eyes, the ruddy brown eyes that sat so strangely in a tanned face framed by an aura of violently red hair, regarded the Cup with a chill distaste alien to him, to her.

"Once I would have killed for this Cup," Rowan said slowly, "died for this Cup. Now . . . I bear a more potent talisman." His fingers touched the soft pouch resting on his collarbones.

"Freeing the Littlelost will not bring back Lorn, Rowan."

"Nor will my claiming the Cup," he answered. His fist swallowed the pouch, and the red-leather thong from which it hung grew as tight as reins around his neck.

Not leather, Alison saw, but a braided length of his own hair.

"This is my quest," he was saying. "I must complete the amulet that Lorn died to protect—and to produce—the talisman that holds his heart, which was truer and braver than mine and wiser than yours, Taliswoman. I would not trade his ashes for any other artifact, however ensorceled."

"But you don't have to trade anything. I give you the Cup. I declare my possession ended. I declare you the fair winner of the Wellsunging. Rowan, I heard you sing; it was magnificent. Your song shattered the edges of the Valley. Had you sung like that a year ago, I would never have won the Cup. Only I can tell you that honestly, because I *did* win. I know why I did, and I know why you won this year. Besides"—she hunted a closing argument that would clinch it—"if you accept the Cup, you've also won your own personal freedom. You can live as a man again. Your long celibacy is over."

Her words brought him up to his knees in fury. "Can any of Desmeyne live as a man while outcast infants and children of our kind and others live in slavery, live twisted under our own earth? Keep your Cup. Keep your title, Taliswoman. I have more pressing quests to fulfill."

Alison drew back, wounded. Winning the Cup had cost her much. Though she had mocked its purported powers at first, she had finally felt them. Now her and Rowan's roles had reversed; he spurned the Cup she found herself defending.

"I brought the Cup back because it belongs here. I can't keep it, and perhaps I'll never find my way home again."

He regarded her without pity. "You always said that we Veilians had much to do to mend our world. You can see to it now." Rowan rose. "I go to seek more Littlelost, the ones freed on the last raid, others still toiling. Beyond that, there is something else I seek: the Quarter of the Four Winds. There I will offer my amulet to yet another force, which will test both it and myself."

Alison stood also. "What of problems closer to home? What of the halfhearted negotiations between the Earth-Eaters and the Firemayne?"

"That is for them to settle." He turned toward the rolling meadow of windblown grasses and walked away.

"What of the problem closest of all?" Alison cried out after him. "What of Darnellyne?"

He stopped, the grasses lashing gently at his cinnamon-colored boot tops. "What of Darnellyne?" he repeated, his featureless back turned to her.

Alison could hardly reveal Darnellyne's plight. That was privileged information. Besides, it would only increase the Cup-maiden's agony.

"You should at least bring the Cup to Desmeyne before you leave again," Alison said lamely. "She has waited for so long—"

Rowan turned, angered by her implication of neglect. "Desmeyne needs more than the Cup; Veil needs more. I have seen that much on my travels. You think I free Littlelost because of Lorn, because he was one of them? No, Taliswoman. I free Littlelost because Veil needs an army, and I recruit it."

"And the Cup needs a proper bearer. I'm afraid it has lost potency. Perhaps in your hands—"

Those hands lifted in a gesture of rejection. "I have burdens enough of my own, Taliswoman; I will not carry yours."

"You wanted this Cup so much. Sometimes I thought you would kill me for it. What has happened to your faith and commitment?"

"And you wanted me to see the truth in Veil and in Desmeyne. I have seen more truth than even you want to admit to. What has happened to your certitude?"

He turned and left in his old, abrupt way, the staff in one hand, a pack upon his back, a chip upon his shoulder.

Alison loosed a strangled scream of frustration. She could either go traipsing after Rowan on his newest quest, or— She turned to the woods and whistled. In moments a white, wolfish form appeared amid the tree trunks, then came the rest of the Slinkers.

The three Littlelost came running, too, their hands, pockets and cheeks full of the nourishing pomma.

"Great. Put what you can't eat into my pack. We're taking the Cup back to Desmeyne."

The Littlelost paused in stuffing their harvest into the knapsack.

"You won't have to stay," she promised. "Camay's there. You can bring her away to these Rookeries you talk of."

"You will leave Veil again?" Twist asked, his eyes clouded.

"I hope to go home eventually, just as you hope to reach the Rookeries. But I won't leave so suddenly, and the Cup will await Rowan in Desmeyne. It will be there for him when he is willing to admit that he won it."

Twist silently consulted Rime and Faun. All three nodded their agreement. They would accompany her to Desmeyne. Good. She had better things to do than traipse along in

Rowan's almighty and mysterious wake, even if he was up to good.

They started over the meadow, Littlelost, Slinkers, and Rambeau. Alison was recalling the path they had previously taken from the Valley of Voices to Desmeyne. Aha, right through that quaint little village where the toothsome tavern wench Triss held sway. Odd that Rowan hadn't grabbed the Cup and headed straight there to relieve himself of his celibacy . . . but Rowan had always been stubborn, and now he was even worse. He was committed.

She could see the torch of his red hair whipping at the horizon's edge. Fine. Let him stalk off by himself. She knew her way around this place now. The Littlelost could find plenty of pomma in the tall trees bordering the meadows. Who needed him?

But their paths, though separate, remained parallel. The Woody Woodpecker crest of Rowan's hair bobbed in the distance. Alison angled farther to her right, even though her travel sense told her the village was dead ahead and over the next mountain.

Then she saw a strange brownish wilt on the grasses far ahead—one that wriggled! She stopped dead.

"What?" Twist demanded.

"Something odd." Alison lifted Rime, the lightest, until they shared an eye level. "Does Veil have . . . hordes of earthworms?"

"Littlelost," Faun trilled in excitement. "From the last raid." In her excitement, she struggled out of Alison's grasp and thumped to the ground.

"Why would Littlelost mill around like that?" Alison asked. "That's strange—"

But the three Littlelost were bounding through the grasses that tickled their hands, Slinkers chasing their sudden motion. Alison felt a sudden fear: Slinkers ran down prey. Their dark eyes flashed as shiny as ebony beads. Their white teeth, like diamond-studded saw blades, sharpened themselves on a bright whetstone of sunlight. Were their open, tongue-lolling mouths anticipating play—or fresh prey?

123

Far to her left, Rowan had broken into a trot and was also converging on the seething spot of brown amid the green grasses.

Alison ran anxiously, the backpack pounding between her shoulder blades with every stride, the Cup hitting as hard as a stone pendulum.

As they converged on the phenomenon, Alison began to see the "worms" for what they indeed were: the dirty brown and gray, rag-clad limbs of dozens of Littlelost. All those who had accompanied Rowan down into the Valley of Voices must have fled during the chaos, fled here . . . and stopped. Why?

She moved close enough to make out grubby individual faces. Soon the forerunner of these Littlelost would announce itself: bad odor. She held her breath, even though it made it harder to run, then she was forced to expel a lungful in one burst and immediately suck air inward again. An inhalation of scent nearly knocked her off her feet—not stink, but fragrance so fair it could have made a linebacker swoon.

Ahead of her, the Littlelost and Slinkers slowed their steps in common confusion, as if to prolong their contact with the sublimely scented air. Alison glanced sideways. Even Rowan had virtually halted and was looking about him with the vacant air of a tourist.

Such an addictively pleasant scent meant only one thing: a loathsome pit that brought forth the pale blue flowers of pure perfume.

"No!" she shouted to anyone who would listen, but she couldn't keep even herself from continuing forward; the others were oblivious to her warning.

As they neared, Alison could see the black, oozing sore upon the earth. The recently freed Littlelost were wading into the edges of this obscenity, reaching for the fallen stars of the blue flowers.

Even the Slinkers were prancing forward eagerly, their fierce noses lifted to consume the breeze. Some leaped up as if chasing invisible butterflies. All hurtled toward the abominable quagmire.

Not all. Beau stopped, his profile alert. He dropped back to rail at Alison, his barks shouting "do something!" She shook her head as if to keep the seductive scent from clouding her actions. Beau charged forward, planting himself before the oncoming Slinkers and barking them back. Confused, they milled before him; only his frantic nips herded them from the deadly sinkhole.

"No!" Alison shouted at Rowan, who was striding through the long grass like a blind man promised sight.

Her own Littlelost were mingling with the outer members of their kind, merging into the grubby mass boiling at the edges of the waiting blackness.

What could stop this lemming-like rush? Alison, used to smell as a seductive sense, guessed that she could restrain herself. Beau had the Slinkers cowed, even though—oh, no, an advancing tunnel through the grass showed that the pups had escaped him.

Alison hurtled forward, lifting Littlelost by the arms and thrusting them behind her like sacks of sand. She drove her hands into the wavering grasses and brought up two pups, hurling them several feet back. Their protesting yips were lost amid the ecstatic croons of the bewitched Littlelost. As fast as she pulled the small forms back, they crawled past her boots and made for the noxious stew of fair scent and foul ooze.

Rowan was reaching the opposite edge of the mire, still moving in hypnotic stateliness, stepping around and over the crowding Littlelost as he headed straight for the heart of the pit.

By now, the heady scent was working its baneful magic on Alison. If she wasn't inclined to rush knee-deep into putrefaction, she was no longer clearheaded enough to keep her directions straight; the energy required to redirect anyone or anything seemed too vast.

The Cup. She should throw the Cup into the greasy quagmire: it might purify its environs even as it sank from sight.

A lumpy brown figure at the mire's very verge suddenly straightened to adult height. An ally, who was fruitlessly pushing back the Littlelost. Even better, Alison recognized . . .

"Sage!" she shouted, not believing her eyes.

The stout brown figure never glanced in her direction, but drew something from one of the capacious pockets that rumpled her already crumpled robes. The oily liquid of the pit had soaked into the hem of her robe, climbing the fabric in peaks like a foul decoration. A chubby hand lifted something green and leafy to her mouth.

Then she stood taller, grew taller and straighter, grew slimmer, grew lighter. In the accelerated, time-lapse photography manner of a flower blooming, Sage became a Loftlady of Desmeyne.

The oil clinging to her hem hardened and fell from the gown's sparkling, snowy magnificence. Veiled in sheer cloths as reflective as ice, Sage dazzled the scent-blinded eyes around her long enough to make the group pause. She shone bright at their center, Disney fairy godmother in the flesh, then reached into her still-homely sack and sprayed a handful of opalescent green glitter—it looked to Alison like the very skinsilk that had pitted Darnellyne's complexion—over the dark and noxious mire.

Sage's act seeded the wind with scent: a crisp, medicinal, frosty smell, neither putrid nor pleasant, that drove all memory of the previous seductive perfume from mind and nostrils. Alison was reminded of the eucalyptus oils used in health-club steam rooms, of Vick's steam inhalers given her for her childhood colds. Of spearmint chewing gum. Of a dozen ordinary earthly odors, and of none of them at all.

Whatever the substance, it scrubbed the air free of the blue flowers' insidious perfume. The blossoms themselves shriveled, petals slowly curling to show oozing black undersides, and sank. So strong was the scent Sage cast upon the wind that everyone stepped back at once, as from a blast of arctic air. The quagmire hardened, pockmarks the only traces of where the flowers had been, the wind's gentle waves frozen into its surface.

"The black surface of Dearth's dancing floor!" Alison exclaimed as she recognized it.

Across the throng of Littlelost heads, her glance met Rowan Firemayne's. His sober eyes reflected the same recognition.

He moved toward her thoughtfully, as though to consult an ally after a demoralizing sneak attack.

Sage waded toward them through an adoring circle of Littlelost, sprinkling her green fairy-dust on their matted and tangled heads.

"At least," Alison greeted her, "they will smell better now."

"Who is this?" Rowan asked. Respectfully.

Alison couldn't resist teasing him. "Don't you know? You only traveled these mountains with her for several days."

"I traveled with no one of my choosing," he answered pointedly, "and certainly not with a lady as lovely as this, who should never set sandal to the cruel and naked ground." He bowed.

Alison lifted her eyebrows. Even given Desmeyne's elaborate and ultimately imprisoning courtesies accorded women, this was a bit much. Perhaps Rowan was beginning to consider his celibacy past, after all. She grinned at Sage, who accepted his flattery with a sweet, simpleminded simper.

"What was that quagmire?" Alison wanted to know. "It's the second such abomination I've encountered recently."

Sage turned lissomely, the fragile tissues of her gown and veils seeming to vibrate aura-like around her rather than to move.

"Earthgall," she said in a voice so light and sad that everyone leaned nearer to hear it, even the Slinkers. Her pristine white hands touched the Littlelosts' unappetizing pates. "The scent attracts children, and those who breathe it long enough wander from their homes. They never grow an inch after that encounter."

"This . . . makes . . . Littlelost?" Rowan asked, aghast.

Sage nodded. "So I have finally learned. Once earthgall mires were rare, no more than puddles with a flower or two to entrance the occasional child. Now there are many, and they grow and spread."

"And the green stuff you sprinkled over it?" Alison asked.

"I have spent months walking this world to find an antidote." She held up fingertips dusted green. "It took a combination of several."

Rowan was indignant. "You have loosed foul weeds into our presence?"

"Had I not, Rowan Firemayne, you might have breathed in an eternal weakness, even walked into the mire and sunk from sight as easily as you walked from the Arcade of Desmeyne into Dearth's dire realm."

"How do you know of that, Lady?"

Sage gave a slight smile. "I tended you both afterward, in the Lofts."

Rowan stepped back, repelled. "I recognize you now. You gave us Char . . . from the Cup. I grew confused." He looked at Alison and suddenly reddened. With shame came anger. "You are the infernal hag who dogged our footsteps through Veil!"

Sage nodded serenely. "Perhaps you recall my name?"

"I cannot say that I do."

"A pity. You might have guessed my double identity. Sage Wintergreen."

"And this guise—"

"—is as I was once in Desmeyne. Yes, young Firemayne. I could be a distant relative. There are more like me in Veil than you know."

While Rowan stuttered with shock, Sage tucked her herb bag into a slit in her diaphanous gown. The very act of depositing such a homely item in such an exquisite shroud shattered the illusion, if that's all it was, and her figure shrank, fattened, grew squat and brown-robed.

"Whatever your guise," Alison said fervently, "I am very glad to see you again, Sage. Perhaps you can explain what is going wrong with Veil."

"I cannot," Sage said. Her stubby finger pointed up at the sky.

They stared upward to see the glitter of a silent etherion corsair coasting on the upper draughts. "But she can."

Rowan looked as if he had eaten a Harrow-worm whole.

11

LITTLELOST gamboled across the mountain meadows like grubby brown sheep, going where whim would take them. Freedom's addictive flavor was also dangerous. Only the Slinkers circling the party kept them loosely herded together.

Those in the group whom Alison regarded as "adults," though the category was inadequate—herself, Sage, and Rowan—kept up the rear. For one thing, Rowan was not sufficiently adult, to her mind. For another, most of the Littlelost were as adult as they would ever be; they would never grow beyond their current size of four- to twelve-year-olds. As exuberant as the rescued Littlelost were, mystery still surrounded them: where exactly they came from, where they went, and what their world would make of them when it truly acknowledged them.

Perhaps "Big People" best described the unlikely trio at the rear, she decided. Alison herself was reminded of "The Three Bears": tall Rowan was Papa Bear, medium-tall Alison was an unwilling Mama Bear, and squat Sage was an overage Baby Bear. Not so strange that fairy-tale images should populate her mind in this Brothers Grimm land.

Of all the Slinkers, only Madonna and the litter ambled at the rear with the Big People. Alison eyed the adult animal's lean, golden form, flanks and shoulders sharp from the privations of bearing and nursing. Madonna struck her as a kind of peroxided shark prowling the buoyant sea-green meadows. Slinker or wolf, in any world Madonna must kill to eat. She must provide for her young, yet what prey fed her? Except for

129

faint, anonymous rustlings in the woods, Veil seemed bereft of birds and beasts, even and especially of squirrels and deer.

She recalled Rambeau's welcome-back present: the hunk of meat. She had avoided looking at it too hard, but it resembled part of a deer. Where did the Slinkers find such prey? And when? Their current docility was unnatural.

As if sensing Alison's attention, Madonna's head turned toward her. Alison shivered inwardly at the dark eyes so alien to wolves in her world. At night the irises glowed yellow, even if by day every Slinker wore the faithful brown gaze of the tamest spaniel. They hadn't always been dog-eyed. She remembered their amber surveillance of her on the Island. When had the color of their eyes changed? And why?

Rowan, walking on her left, sighed pointedly. "This Sage is ever determined to drag us to unlikely destinations," he grumbled. "What did she mean by speaking of that etherion abomination as a 'she'?"

"Just that," Alison answered. "That 'abomination' is a craft of the air. As such, it requires someone to guide it. In my world, such persons are called 'pilots.' The pilot of that particular corsair is no doubt a woman."

"Impossible!" He snorted. "No person can defy nature and fly, and especially no woman. Unless," he added direly, "she is an unnatural construct of the Crux."

"The only unnatural constructs of the Crux we've seen lately have been the blue-light-spitting etherion aircraft above the Wellsunging."

"What say you? That was lightning."

Alison shifted her shoulders so the backpack rubbed at different points. "You were rather occupied with fighting off those brutes spilling through the rocks from below-ground. What were they? Some Earth-Eater kin?"

Real worry creased Rowan's face. "I have never seen such folk before. The men are not fast upon their feet, but they possess a stubborn power that resembles—" He shrugged, unable to describe it.

"Unstoppable stupidity," Alison prompted. "They're big,

ugly customers, none too bright but nothing to underestimate."

Rowan nodded with slow surprise. "It is as if they are only half human, but the nonhuman part provides a strength we can never match."

"And the women?" she asked mischievously.

"Those!" Outrage rang in his voice. "As formidable as the men, with no restraint."

"All women are not as well constrained as the Loftladies of Desmeyne."

"No," he agreed sadly, missing her sarcasm. He nodded at Sage, who trudged before them, surrounded by a mob of Littlelost, several of them carrying Madonna's pups. "Why would such a one abandon her gentle guise for this rude appearance?"

"So she can be what she really is. Sage is a wisewoman, interested in matters deeper than show on the surface . . . on the surface of anything, even of herself."

"But she could be—she is—as lovely as any Loftlady. Can she not be wise in that guise?"

"Not if she wishes to search Veil for forbidden herbs and to answer questions no one of Desmeyne has yet thought to ask. Could you imagine . . . Darnellyne walking these woods and meadows?"

"No. But Dar is—" He tightened his lips, then stared ahead as if facing an unseen enemy. "You have seen Desmeyne more recently than I. Darnellyne is well?"

Alison hesitated, not knowing what to say.

Luckily, Rowan anxiously qualified his question. "She is not angry at my absence?"

"No. If anything, she is relieved."

His head snapped about to regard her, the action alone a powerful challenge for clarification. Alison went on, treading a thin line between the truth and the Cup-maiden's right to reveal herself to those she chose.

"Darnellyne, too, feels the pressure of her position, and yours. Matters remain uneasy in Desmeyne. The Firemayne is not pleased about having to negotiate with the Earth-Eaters in person. Nor is the Earth-Eater spokeswoman I have named Dusk pleased."

"Dusk." Rowan tasted the word. "Earth-Eaters live in an eternal twilight. There is something female about the name, as there is about that Earth-Eater." His russet glance softened. "You named her well."

Alison basked suspiciously in his praise, but it was a shower rather than a long soak. His tone grew brusque again.

"I am not yet certain that Desmeyne's advantage lies in treating with the Earth-Eaters, or that these depth-dwellers are what they—and you—claim: our long-lost kin. Yet the Littlelost are more than I thought, as you also claimed. Have you noticed the oddities among the new batch?"

"No, life's been too exciting since we crossed paths again. I haven't had a chance to get acquainted with them."

Rowan pointed into the distance ahead. "I see the spray of a waterfall. You can test the water with the Cup. If it is safe, we can wash the stink of the etherion pits off the new Littlelost so you can see them better. Many curiosities abound, among the Littlelost and within the reason for their enslavement." His lips tightened again. "I will have no more Lorns in Veil, if I can help it."

"A commendable resolve," said Alison, meaning it.

Rowan eyed her suspiciously, as leery of her approval as she was of his. "Do you mean the promise of a cleansing, or the further freeing of the Littlelost?"

"Both," she said, smiling. "And we could use the cleansing ourselves."

By midday they had reached the misty curtain of waterfall Rowan had indicated: a short, broad plunge of water that pooled before meandering into a stone-strewn stream farther down the mountain.

"Wait," Alison sharply ordered Beau. He broke from the pack to stand guard before the waterfall, stiff legs planted, ready to drive back any human or canine who might crowd to the water's eddying caldron.

Though she would never admit it, Alison's heart sank at the notion of taking out the Cup to test the water for such a thing.

The Cup had seemed anemic since she had been back in Veil. She no longer trusted its potency, not after seeing how helpless it had been to heal the skinsilk lesions that corroded Darnell-lyne's face. The more magical Veil's beauty, the more that bounty seemed able to turn on those who used it.

She lifted the vessel into the strong sunlight. The Cup of Earth's pallid surface could either blush or pale, reflecting reactions as fragile as the emotions painting a human face. It wore its own skinsilk.

She offered it wordlessly to Rowan. He shook his head, his arms remaining firmly folded across his chest. Perhaps the Cup no longer answered her usage, since she truly believed Rowan had won it. But if he hadn't, the Cup would likely not perform for him either.

She dipped the bowl in the motion-simmered pool water and lifted it brimming from the foam. Rowan, Sage, and Madonna pressed forward to watch. Squirming pups in Littlelost arms raised dry black noses toward the tempting water. They were thirsty, dirty, and tired. She hoped the water was worthy of their needs; bypassing it would be hard on them.

Nothing happened within the Cup; clear water stilled as the last agitated bubbles burst. Alison peered in cautiously and saw only the reflection of her seeking eyes and a wavering bit of nose and cheeks.

Then the bottom of the Cup grew dark, like a pit. The clear water was only a lacquer over another, thicker, blacker liquid. The eyes that gazed back at her suddenly were not her own watery blue-green, but as opaque as midnight, changed as the Slinkers' had been by some unknown transformation.

They were not her own. She jerked her head away.

"What is it?" Rowan asked.

Sage frowned and bent toward the Cup.

But it was Rambeau's intruding muzzle that nudged the wisewoman's face away. The dog sniffed the water deeply, nostrils flaring as if to inhale knowledge as well as scent. Then he looked into Alison's eyes, nothing doglike in his glance—no pleading, no aggression. Just flat, unweighted regard, an impassive, unsettling, Eli Ravenhare kind of look.

Before Alison could decide what that meant, Rambeau's snout dipped into the Cup. He began noisily lapping water.

"Sacrilege!" Rowan reached to push the dog away. Teeth as white as the Cup gleamed wetly near his hand.

"Sacrifice," Sage answered, staying Rowan's hand. "The animal tests the water's purity."

Alison pulled the Cup away from Rambeau. Only water filled it—clear, clean water. She hated thinking that Beau had drunk down the distorted visage in the water: that reflection of herself that was so very different, very altered, even evil. Yet she didn't fear it was wildwater; Beau drank it to show her that it wasn't. Alison shivered to think that the phenomenon didn't reflect the condition of the water or of the Cup, but of the current Cup-bearer.

Beau left the Cup and Alison, walked to the poolside and bent to drink further.

"It must be safe," Sage declared.

Slinkers followed Rambeau's suit, then Littlelost. Alison wrapped the Cup in flannel and put it away, unable to link her misgivings about the vision she'd had to anything solid.

"Is it warm enough?" Sage asked eagerly.

Alison pulled free of an unhappy reverie; water always unsettled her, but this was absurdly shallow. She could see the bottom stones two hand's-breadths away through the crystal water. "I don't know. The pooling water is cool; perhaps the falling water is warm. If we're lucky."

The Littlelost had crowded on all fours to push their faces into the water like animals and drink. They seemed disinclined to any further immersion, but Alison sat down, pulled off her boots and socks, rolled up her jeans and waded in.

The pool-bed was cool, solid rock. She waded near the falling sheets of water that roared and sizzled, and a fine, warm spray misted her face and clothing. Veil's famous "hot" running water.

"Everybody in," she ordered. "I haven't enough soap to go around, so you'll just have to rub your clothes and yourselves clean."

"I have something." Sage stepped to the water's edge. From

134

a pocket she pulled featherlike flakes colored a bright magenta.

But Littlelost fresh from the etherion pits weren't ready to enter a liquid of any kind. Beau rounded up Slinkers to herd them in, and Twist, Faun, and Rime led the way, coaxing the others to follow. Every Littlelost who crossed into water received a pinch of Sage's flakes. Once wet, these fragments swelled into bright bubbles. Soon, with instructions from Twist and Alison, lurid suds bloomed on the dull-colored Littlelost like a disease.

Sage placed a double pinch in Rowan's hand as he stood on the bank. An onrush of Littlelost pushed him in, boots and all, as his staff and pack fell aside on the ground. Alison laughed, but then a canine nose nudged her into the spilling water.

The waterfall poured noisily on suds-crowned, hot-pink little heads, and laughter floated up to meet the falling water. The Littlelost tussled for more of Sage's flakes, while Slinkers waded at the fringe, getting wet only up to the delicate feathering on their lower legs. Beau barked in warning as his pups waddled in a swirling foam of magenta bubbles up to their black patent-leather noses.

Rowan got to his feet, sopping, only to slip and fall. He went down spectacularly amid a gaggle of Littlelost. Alison put her hand to her mouth, half-unnerved by the fall, half feeling like laughing. Rowan beat her to it as his head emerged from bubbles, Littlelost, and paddling pups.

Only Sage and Madonna remained on the bank, one looking benign, the other wary. Motherhood had no doubt made Madonna dubious of all things magical and mundane. Alison saluted the blond Slinker; somebody had to keep a cool head in this bizarre world where water could either warm and wash you or poison you.

Then several of the Littlelost surged past, and her own feet slipped. She plopped down in the tepid water, warm bubbles foaming around her shoulders. She lifted her hands to her face, to her hair. The world dripped past in a rose-colored haze. Soapy water ran into her eyes, but didn't sting.

She stood, giddy, her sides aching as if she had inhaled a king-size dose of laughing gas. Above the bathers' sopping

heads, pink bubbles reflecting rainbow shades wafted up—
some as large as croquet balls, some the size of marbles—
taking their flagrant color with them, lifting dirt and fatigue
away on a gleaming flotilla.

Alison studied the swirling water, foaming white and pure.
The Littlelost, considerably cleaner, bore no pink residue on
their wet clothing or faces. Rowan had risen dripping plain
water, the only vestige of Sage's exotic soap the magenta glint
in his lank, wet, red hair.

Above them, sunlight siphoned the rising bubbles into
bright, evaporating glory, a sort of airborne city drifting high
and away until it burst.

"That," Rowan said to Sage in classic Desmeynian understatement, "is the most remarkable bubblebath."

Alison giggled. She couldn't get over the fact that soap was
called "bubblebath" in this world, as if it came from the nearest K-Mart in a recyclable container.

Sage smiled mysteriously. "Much may be found in the farther reaches of Veil, and much of it good. Only lately have we
seen so much evidence of the bad."

That sobered Rowan and Alison. Disappearing soap was
one thing; earthgall and etherion pits were quite another. The
party assembled on the banks, shaking off water like dogs.

"These boots will never dry," Rowan complained.

"Wait and see," said Sage. "The greatest magic of all is the
sun, and it is plainly visible almost every day."

Alison inhaled mightily. "We all smell like air-dried sheets.
That's worth a little dampness."

She looked up again, cleansed from the dark, reflected vision
in the Cup. Faint bubbles twinkled far above. An etherion
corsair stabbed the bright-blue distance.

"Will we find them, Sage? The airborne people?"

"Perhaps not. But they will find us when they are ready."

They marched on that afternoon, their clothes drying as they
walked.

Granted that they all wanted to put the Valley of Voices and
the shock of the Crux-attack behind them, Alison still couldn't

understand Rowan's docile accompaniment. Where had the brash young questor gone?

He walked beside her, his staff rhythmically jabbing the turf. Shepherding Littlelost seemed a meek occupation for one born to pursue exotic quests.

"Why stay with us?" she finally asked. "Now that this lot of Littlelost is free and the Crux has receded for the time being, isn't there something heroic you should be doing?"

He eyed her without the flare of self-justification she had come to expect. "If all goes well, these freed Littlelost will lead me to my next goal." His fingers absently touched the pouch at his chest.

Grisly token, Alison thought. Cremation was a common form of dealing with the dead in her world, but survivors didn't carry the ashes about with them.

"Just exactly what is your next goal?" she asked.

He nodded at the mob of Littlelost preceding them. "The Rookeries, where the wild Littlelost dwell, lie at a legendary distance. Near there, from the innocent tales the Littlelost tell, grows the Axletree, the object of my next quest, at the Quarter of the Four Winds."

"Then your great desire to free the Littlelost is nothing more than enlightened self-interest?"

The staff pummeled the earth and stuck. Rowan stopped. Alison did so as well.

"No. You twist everything I say and do. First you charge that I free the Littlelost for Lorn's sake. When I say that freed Littlelost can fight for Veil and lead me to my next quest-goal, you say I use them." Anger seemed to set Rowan's beard afire. Or was it merely the slanting rays of a waning sun? In these mountains, sunset was a long, slow, pale-orange melting. "All the mysteries of Veil link one to another," he said more patiently. "Earth-Eaters. Littlelost. Crux. Quest. This is what you said. Do you no longer believe in your own words?"

She shrugged, the pack itchy and heavy against her back. "Maybe not."

He shook his red head, so oddly the precise match of his beard. "You have changed." He resumed walking.

"I? I have changed?" She caught up with him, not used to the note of judgment in his tone. Distrust, yes; not judgment.

"You have lost faith," he said.

"What of you? You won't accept the Cup, despite the fact that you won it in every way but formal presentation."

That made him stop again, eyes considering the turf at their feet. "The Cup demands a worthy bearer."

Such heretofore unheard-of humility! Alison wondered anew whether Rowan had violated his self-imposed celibacy. If so, it would sadden her, although she believed that celibacy— or any kind of imposed self-denial—was a rotten way to show commitment to anything, even to virtue. Usually men practiced it in service to some vague "good," which reduced women and sex to no more than an evil to be avoided.

"Rowan . . . is there some reason you don't want to return to Desmeyne as Cup-bearer? Is there something in Desmeyne that you don't want to confront?"

He mutely weighed her words.

"Dusk?" she suggested.

He bridled finally. "Dusk. My so-called 'sister.' No, I do not fully accept that notion of yours, but I fear no Earth-Eater. We Desmeynians must learn to deal with the Earth-Eaters. You may be right that they are *of* us, as well as beneath us."

"Most . . . open-minded. Is it your father, then? You follow the quests, but not on the paths he thinks best. Do you fear seeing him again?"

"I fear no man," Rowan barked, so intensely that Alison backed up a step.

But she had her answer in the emphasis he had put on "man." "Your mother?" No reaction. Then, "Darnellyne?"

He spun away, using his implanted staff as a pivot.

Oh. Oh, my. Alison studied his impassive back, bearing a pack much like her own. And Darnellyne horribly defaced on top of it . . . oh, poor lass. Poor lad. Rowan the heroic would probably march straight for Desmeyne if he knew of his would-be betrothed's distress, rush headlong into strict compliance with his father's wishes. Neither Darnellyne nor Alison could tolerate that. Alison sighed. She hated the secret she carried almost as much as she had hated bearing the Cup at first.

"Rowan—" she began carefully.

He turned back to confront her. "Say nothing," he said, unwittingly urging her own intentions on her. "Last year, in my youthful enthusiasm, I saw no good but to free Dar from her position as prize to anyone who could win the Cup. So long as you keep the accursed thing, she is safe from that. But I . . . I see now that there is more in Veil to protect than the Cup-maiden and the customs of Desmeyne."

"You don't want Darnellyne," Alison breathed. By their own conventions, Rowan and the Loftlady were fated for each other, whether they wished to be or not. Poor lass. Poor lad.

Rowan's lifted hand brushed her words away. "I do not want Darnellyne sacrificed to her position. Yet now I have glimpsed greater dangers. . . ."

He frowned into the distance. Alison saw—with horror—that part of the change in his understanding was due to her influence, to her interference in matters she knew nothing about.

"Oh, Rowan!"

He did not seem to hear the pity, the horror, in her voice. His fingers again caressed the object of her pity and horror, the ashes at his throat. Pickle, the ludicrous name made so terribly tragic. Lorn, the true name, the one that better fit the emotions they both felt at his loss. Lorn.

"You've carried his ashes since the—" She could not name what had taken place and her flight.

Eyes the warm brown of fresh-turned earth regarded her unflinchingly. His fist tightened on the pouch, a gesture of claiming, not of anger. "These are no mere ashes," he said. "A change occurred. Even as you ran from the Heart of Earth, as you vanished into the mist-ridden tunnel, the clay pot into which I brushed Lorn's ashes cracked and broke."

"The pot . . . broke?" Alison put a hand to her chest, to her scars. Rowan had forgotten that a broken Indian pot from the Island—a twin to the one she had found near the underground lava river in Desmeyne—had etched the Veilian quest-scars into her flesh, that only accident had brought her to this land to usurp his right to the Cup.

He nodded. "Fearing that I would lose what little remained of Lorn, I swept the ashes between my fingers from the hot hearth of inner earth and held them there until my own flesh burned. Between my fingertips, this formed."

Rowan reached into the pouch to withdraw an object.

Alison lifted her head to see it better: an elongated oval of hardened red clay, slightly sheened, shaped like an Egyptian cartouche.

"Ashes?" she asked.

"Ashes, and what heated clay I intermixed with them as I clawed at the earth to contain my brother," he answered. "My fingers shaped this tablet; they hurt, but did not burn." He murmured the ancient rime.

> "The heart that is human, born to Dearth
> Will beat for all time in an armor of earth."

"What will this Axletree that you seek do?"

Rowan held the small, blank clay tablet in the cradle of his palm. "The winds of the world will scribe the quest-marks onto this surface. Lorn will be quest-heir, as he was meant to be."

"And you? What will you gain when you transform your dead brother into a talisman?"

"I will empower Veil and foil the Crux. And perhaps—" His eyes lightened with the vision of a more personal quest.

"What?"

"Nothing. I have my suspicions, that is all."

His lack of frankness stung her. "You have always had your suspicions."

He nodded, refusing to be drawn into an argument. Such restraint on Rowan's part was even more unsettling than his beard or his recent passion to free the Littlelost.

A voice lifted from the hikers ahead. "I told you! There! There!"

Alison and Rowan looked beyond them at shadowed meadows as empty as yesterday's mailbox, then at each other.

"There!" Sage trilled again, one sleeve-draped arm pointing upward.

Around the nearest peak, crowning it like a swarm of gilt bees, veered the brassy, wide-winged bodies of a dozen etherion corsairs.

"Crux-craft!" Rowan muttered even as he gawked.

"You've got it half right," Alison congratulated him.

12

IN the long, soft twilight, the etherion corsairs swooped one by one to earth.

Only Alison understood the nature of the dangling chains the craft trailed over the meadows. She leaped up to snag one as it passed above her head. But the wind kept the corsair gliding, and she was lifted off the ground, to the screams of the Littlelost.

Alison enjoyed the ride, dangling four feet above the earth, but a pounding noise on the turf was followed by a jab from below. Rowan's staff was at her hip.

"Catch on, before you drift away!" he urged.

"No, you catch me!" At that moment a breeze swooped up the corsair until Alison's stomach did a swan dive. Even as the wind slackened and the craft eased toward earth again, she was enveloped by a pair of arms and pulled down.

"Release the leash of the beast!" Rowan ordered.

She did no such thing. Her feet now on the ground, she turned to him. "Quickly! Help me fasten this chain around . . . those rocks!"

By then, rings of excess chain had coiled to earth behind her. Alison and Rowan tethered the corsair to the nearest rocks. Then Alison looked up for the dismounting pilot. Around them, the imitative Littlelost had caught hold of other trailing chains and of each other, forming clusters that dragged the sweeping corsairs toward the ground.

In minutes the entire flotilla was shading them like a latticed roof. Pilots were dancing down the tethers, lithe high-wire

142

artists with airy garments whipping like pennants around their tiny bodies.

All of them were women, and barely a head taller than the tallest of the Littlelost, but there was nothing childlike in their forms, only a wiry delicacy as fragile-seeming as their crafts' metal-sheathed wings.

Sage, stretched into her youthful guise to greet them, glimmered in the waning daylight. The pilots flocked to her, apparently familiar with her.

"What are these creatures?" Rowan demanded.

"I'm not sure, but they know Sage," Alison answered, aware that this fact would not reassure him. "I saw women of this kind among the listeners at the Wellsunging, didn't you?"

"No." He seemed confused, then embarrassed. "I did not study the audience."

Rowan's single-mindedness again amazed her. "Surely you came across these folk if you have traveled widely in search of Littlelost?"

"No." He absently rubbed his bearded chin. "I have not. They do not look like creatures of the Crux."

"What do such creatures look like?"

"You know well enough. Brutish and large, cruel and vicious. These are . . . little women."

"Indeed. Most petite and pretty." Alison smiled. Poor Rowan, so enamored of chivalrous stereotypes. "That one there, I think, brought me on her corsair to return me to you."

"You flew atop one of those?" He looked up, astonished.

"Yes, but I have flown before. It was no great feat." Of course she had never flown by clinging to the outside of a wing, though.

"The Crux. You say such . . . machines served the Crux in the battle of the Wellsunging?" he asked.

"I didn't glimpse them well enough to say if Crux-coursers were exactly like these, but Sylvin corsairs like these were definitely there. Given the blue-lightning firepower of the Crux-fighters, I'm amazed that any corsairs survived to fly at all."

Three of the tiny women broke away from Sage and came

toward Alison and Rowan, their windblown scarves fluttering.

Rowan retreated. "I will have words with the Littlelost; they have grown unruly."

With this understatement, he left before the trio arrived. Alison regarded them with interest. Sylvin was with the two other women, who had equally pale hair and equally feathered eyebrows and lashes.

She was sorry that Rowan had fled, although she could understand how shocking it was for a Desmeynian to meet another race—and liberated women, at that. She was lucky he hadn't cried "Crux!" and gone wading among them flailing his staff. Rowan was actually becoming reasonable, now that he knew the eternal verities of Desmeyne were true only as far as Desmeynians went, which was seldom past the fields that lay between their city and the world.

Sage drifted over after the newcomers, the setting sun painting her pale robes a luminous rose. Among such a fragile and glamorous company, Alison felt clumsy, big and rough.

"He has left," Alison's pilot greeted her in a trilling voice full of disappointment, "the tall, handsome man. Sage Wintergreen says that he is a Desmeynian. We have never seen one . . . close up."

Her two sisters twittered. There was no denying the interest that kindled their pale eyes.

"I have," Alison assured them. "Desmeynians are much overrated."

They understood the last word perfectly but seemed not to take her word for it, continuing to crane their long, dainty necks for a further glimpse of Rowan among the milling Littlelost.

All three of the voluptuous little creatures had narrow faces, minuscule noses, almost Oriental eyes, and brows that tilted up at the corners. They sported the same skull-hugging pixie haircut; perhaps that was as long and as thick as genetics would allow their hair to grow. Genetics, or magic? Here in Veil, that question was more valid than Alison liked to think.

It struck her that the women's very physiognomy was geared for flight, as though sculpted with the wind forcing their garb, their hair, their features back. They were as sleek and seductive as the spritely hood ornament on a Rolls Royce.

The women turned to Sage. "You insist that this is a female?" one asked uncertainly.

Sage nodded graciously.

"She is not Desmeynian."

"Hardly," said Sage.

"Nor Sylvin."

"No."

"And dressed most roughly, like a man."

"Yes."

The pilot who had given Alison a ride stepped nearer. "She is large, but not for one of non-Sylvin race. She cannot be a Hammerhand, and she is no Halfling. We are perplexed. We have overflown almost all of Veil, most often undetected, yet we have seen nothing like her, save perhaps in the villages. Is she a peasant?"

"Probably," Sage said.

Alison considered her Old World ancestry and had to agree: no nobility there, unless it was of character, and anonymous to the end. At least she had learned that "Sylvin" was not an individual's name, but that of an entire kind.

A Sylvin's porcelain hand tugged at Alison's knit sleeve. "Heavy, immobile stuff."

"I wonder," another Sylvin confided to Alison's former pilot, "that she did not sink your corsair like a Hammerhand."

All three laughed, a bell-like sound that made heads lift in the twilight, looking for the source.

Sage intervened. "I did not arrange this meeting for you to marvel at an outlander. Alison carries the Cup."

"The Cup." Whichever one spoke silenced the others.

The woman she had flown with smiled. "So I, Lenaree, have carried the Cup in my corsair. That should render the craft safe in the next encounter with the Crux-coursers, at least."

"What is a Crux-courser?" Alison asked.

"Vile." Her pilot's delicate face puckered with distaste.

"Deadly," added another. "We have no weapons but our

skill in the air. Crux-coursers are cumbersome, magic-lofted machines. They spit blue death."

"Aren't your corsairs also machines?" Alison asked.

"No." The word seemed an outrage. "They are . . . creations."

"So are machines," Alison began, but Sage interrupted her. "We will discuss the difference later," the wisewoman said. "The others must hear what the Sylvins have to report. They have been the oft-unseen eyes of Veil for generations. Do you know how rare it is that they touch earth? Much less engage in a contest with alien vessels above a Wellsunging! We must secure ourselves for the night; then we will have a Welltelling."

"A . . . Welltelling?"

"Tales, not song," Sage explained. "And the tales to be told will give none of us aught to sing about."

Dark cloaked the land by the time everyone had gathered into a circle and shared food. With her kindling moss, Sage had started a central fire that consumed only a little grass. The evening rang with the vibration of the wind on tethered, agile metal, producing a constant, almost undetectable, whine.

In the night's veiled darkness, a dozen etherion corsairs trembled at air-anchor, eager to be off and up. Holding them earthbound desecrated their essence. So, Alison thought, did bringing the Sylvin women down to the ground.

Sage had shrunk back into her everyday persona; Alison wondered if she meant to avoid competing with their guests' glamorous presence. The fire's cool pink flame lit the surrounding faces and figures without illuminating the tethered corsairs. This precaution's subtlety gave Alison Crux-chills. Above, no stars winked in the blue, cold rhythm they had displayed over the Island. A perfect night for an air raid.

Rowan occupied the crushed grasses only a few paces from her. Although Littlelost and pups gamboled around her, he sat apart from the rest, as if reserving not only judgment, but himself. The more human he became, the more puzzlingly aloof.

Alison shredded the last of her dinner pomma. Though

nourishing and readily available, it was also bland and taste-less. She hungered for a spicy taco salad, or a pizza. Her backpack lay before her, an impromptu dinner table.

Seated twenty feet away and across from her, near the rosy grass-glow, the Sylvin women seemed enchanted creatures, as rare as Belleek china, almost transparent in their pale perfec-tion. If only for their feminine fragility, Rowan would at least listen to them, although women were not much listened to in Desmeyne. But they more resembled the Desmeynian women than Alison did, and wind currents only polished their smooth complexions.

Sage stood, an undistinguished hummock in the flattering firelight. "We gather for a Welltelling. Unlike a Wellsunging, it is a ceremony of women. We only will speak, but all may listen. We gather here to win nothing but news of each other. Among us number several Sylvin flyers. We also include Lit-tlelost, Slinkers, a stranger, and one man of Desmeyne. We know much of ourselves and little of each other, and in that is our weakness. We are here to speak and to grow stronger together.

"I have walked much of this world unnoticed, but not un-noticing. What I have seen has troubled me. Sometimes I have grown very afraid. All of us know the heavy hand of the Crux, but only in fractured forms, in separate fears. Now the Crux shows its power more fully; it pours from the earth below; it walks the air above. Perhaps it poisons our water and eats at our earth. We must discover who and what the Crux is, and what of us it wants. But first we must discover these very things about ourselves. I will let Ystar of the Sylvin women speak, because her kind are the unseen eyes of Veil. Tell us now."

Sage did not so much sit as vanish from everyone's atten-tion. Ystar stood to murmurs of approval from her Sylvin sisters, the grass fire illuminating her diminutive form.

Alison must have been tired. If she didn't listen closely, Ystar's words became confusing trills and nonsense syllables. The Sylvin's soft, chirping voice was an unlikely instrument for a grim subject.

Still, between the alien sounds, the true tale came through.

"The world of Veil," she said solemnly, "erupts with random foulnesses. Dark water that cannot be seen through spreads like spilled ink, blotting the edge of the inhabited lands, hemorrhaging inward. Pits of black earthgall corrupt the grasslands. New etherion pits come to their rank simmer in a hundred shaded dells, yet for all that, we Sylvins are hard put to get etherion even to repair our corsairs, much less to replace them as needed.

"Now alien coursers slice through the upper airs—churning, clumsy flyers, cobbled from alien substances and etherion. They drone as they fly, as if moaning. These blue-haloed flyers bear the infamous blue bolts of fire and destruction we all have seen. Many a Sylvin corsair has come back crippled from an encounter with such a monster. Foreign Slinkers ravage the deepest forests. When we fly to our farthest borders of upper air, the People of the Horizon can be seen massing in huge thunderheads beyond the rim of the last lands."

"Why?" Alison asked when Ystar's voice had fallen silent.

"We do not know," Lenaree answered. "Takers are said to menace even the Rookeries, finding the wandering Littlelost insufficient to harvest etherion from the decaying pits."

Rowan's voice raised next in question. "Where does the Axletree grow at the top of the world? Surely the eyes of Veil would know."

"These do not." Lenaree spoke for the Sylvin flyers present.

"I have encountered," a Sylvin named Mesula revealed abruptly, much surprising her sisters, "a patch of air so belabored with opposing winds that no etherion corsair can enter it, not even Crux-coursers, I would think."

"Where?" Rowan asked eagerly.

"Beyond the Rookeries of the wild Littlelost," Mesula said, "above the spreading black blot of the tainted lake, almost to the rim of the world, where the People of the Horizon stir so restlessly. I cannot recommend that anyone of wisdom seek such a fell place."

Rowan asked no more questions, but Alison was not deceived.

13

IN the morning, Rowan moved among the sleeping Littlelost, bending to examine their peaceful faces. He carefully avoided the place where Alison slept near the Slinkers.

At last he grunted his satisfaction and lifted up a drowsy form: a very young female the size of Camay. She stirred in panic, fearing Takers, but then her wide, pale-lavender eyes recognized her rescuer's unmistakable red hair.

She grinned, pulled his beard, and allowed him to carry her to Sage and the Sylvin women, who were sharing their common foodstuffs in a morning repast.

"Rowan Firemayne." Sage's acknowledgment both greeted him and questioned his intent.

He crouched next to the seated women, still bearing the Littlelost in the crook of his arm, a shepherd returning a lost lamb to the fold. Sage eyed him curiously. Rowan did not show great sentimentality toward any of the Littlelost he had rescued.

"Wisewoman." He addressed her as brusquely as she had hailed him. "No one has said why the Crux employed their corrupted coursers to attack the Wellsunging, or why the Sylvin corsairs arrived in time to counter them."

"The Cup." She offered him a common clay mug filled with hot pomma soup.

He took it and sipped absently, the sleepy Littlelost still drooping on his shoulder. "The Cup may be compromised. The Taliswoman says it has lost power since its sojourn in her land."

"Perhaps the Cup is simply between bearers."

He frowned, but did not comment. "I bear my own talisman in the making," he said finally, his eyes flicking down to his chest. Several Sylvin women followed the look with appreciation. Rowan did not care: he felt only the weight of the pouch against his breastbone, how it swayed when he moved and polished his quest-scars like some fateful pendulum. "I put my trust in that."

"Your privilege," Sage answered, stirring her own cup of soup with one stubby finger.

"I must find this place where the Four Winds collide."

"It hangs above the highest peak," Lenaree said. "Even we Sylvins can barely breathe in those heights, and we are used to thin air. Only an etherion corsair could take you high enough, and you are too big of bone and heavy of muscle for such a flight."

"What can I pay you to take me to the heart of your land, and thence to the place where the winds debate each other?"

"No pay," she said adamantly. "Only the foolhardy would consider such a journey, and we Sylvins do not reveal our nests. With the Crux now airborne, we are especially loath to do so."

"What of the traffic in Littlelost among the allies of the Crux? Does such enslavement not trouble you? If I achieve the next quest, I will empower my talisman further. I can bring a new force into play to end such evil."

"We have seen your commendable efforts to attack the Takers and free the Littlelost. We admit we could well use the etherion you also liberate, for we Sylvins can also harvest the etherion, if we must. But your 'if' is a word that ever lingers beyond the next rainbow."

In answer, he swung the Littlelost onto his bent knee, an exhibit. "Because I found my lost brother among the Littlelost, I assumed that all of them were as he: lost or abandoned children from Desmeyne and the surrounding villages. Then I began to range afar, seeking to free whatever Littlelost I could—" Rowan stroked the fine, light-brown hair from the Littlelost's brow. The gesture caused the childlike face to lift to the warm morning light, feathery brows tilting up above slanted eyes.

The Sylvin flyers stood in a body, scant taller than the Littlelost themselves but possessed of a rare authority, now turned to shock and outrage. Their mugs thumped to the grass, undamaged, leaking thin soup on the bent blades.

"This is not Halfling!" Ystar said in hushed wonder. "Only Halflings have been born to us for decades. That is why we dare not risk our whereabouts becoming known. For every flyer who falls, there is none to take her place, for only Halflings can we bear, who will never fly. Even most of those births are fatal to the bearer. What is this . . . child? Where did you get her? What is her name?"

"Plume," the girl said shyly.

Rowan studied her innocent Sylvin face. She looked no older than Camay, who herself looked no older than a normal child of four. He shook his head sadly.

"I found her among the Takers, but now I realize that she is obviously Sylvin. The other Littlelost are small, but none so dainty. And the eyes, of course. I had never seen a Sylvin before, so I did not understand. Perhaps Sage can tell you."

"First," the wisewoman suggested, "you must tell us of the Halflings. What are they?"

Rowan gave Sage an appreciative look. She was wise indeed to question the Sylvins while they were held hostage to the wonder of finding one of their own among the Littlelost.

The women's luminous lavender eyes exchanged glances softer than shot silk. They were a lofty kind, and did not discuss their ways with down-to-earth ease. The Sylvin flyers sat again, sighing, their fluid garb curling around them while Sage refilled a fallen cup from her brewing pot and offered it to the small sylph in Rowan's custody.

"We have for generations forged an alliance with the Hammerhands," Lenaree said. "They spring from a race of large, strong men able to bend and beat the etherion into the shape of our corsairs. We fly the results."

"The arrangement has pleased both sides," Ystar said in a voice like breaking glass. "The Hammerhands, with their gross

151

weight and ponderous bone, could never rise above the bonds of earth. We, in turn, could never fashion the metal into as apt a means for flight."

Sage nodded. "Such an alliance uses the strengths and weaknesses of both parties to advantage. Why, then, did you mix mutual cooperation with intermarriage?"

A faint flush touched the speaking Sylvin's cheeks. "To work together required knowledge of one another. Each kind admired the other's talents: we, the earthbound strength of the Hammerhands; they, the fragility of our kind that makes flight possible. Marriage was not the difficulty."

Sage nodded again, but Rowan felt puzzled. He knew the Littlelost he held was Sylvin. Why was Sage making it so complicated? In this tendency, she had much in common with the Taliswoman.

"And when you Sylvin women became fruitful?" Sage went on.

"That was no problem. In those days, Hammerhand women were smiths like the men, and Sylvin men flew the corsairs like the women. Happily, as we married amongst our kinds, our offspring matched the mother."

"So," Sage put in, "a delicate Sylvin would bear a dainty child, and a Hammerhand woman would birth a big, hearty infant?"

Lenaree nodded. "At first the maternal strain dominated. We bore mostly Sylvin children, most of them female. With time, the heritage of the Hammerhands made itself manifest. Our newborns became larger, and were more often male. Even some of the females grew ungainly before birth, and after. We hardly noticed when Hammerhand women began bearing only boys, and Sylvin women only girls."

"But," Alison prodded, "eventually you would have only male Hammerhands mating with female Sylvins!"

Lenaree nodded. "With the number of Hammerhand females declining, and Sylvins bearing only females, both our kinds were doomed to ultimate extinction. And then Sylvins began bearing large and cumbersome babes of either gender."

"Halflings!" Alison intoned.

"What," Rowan asked with considerable patience, "exactly are Halflings?"

Lenaree's delicate Sylvin face grew troubled. "They are our offspring, half of each kind—Hammerhand and Sylvin—and bereft of the virtues of either. To bear such a one risks the mother's life. They grow large and, in time, ill-tempered. Too big to pilot the corsairs, they are yet too weak to work the metal as we require. Hence, they grow up hating both sides of their houses, being barred from either. Thus were the Halflings born before we even understood. It took decades to see what a disaster their existence would be to all concerned. We Sylvin women dwindle, with none light enough to take our places. Idle Hammerhands lose spirit. And now etherion has grown scant."

"And these Halflings? What becomes of them as they mature?"

Lenaree shrugged. "They wander off, bitter and betrayed by their own heritage. We have nothing to offer them, or they us. That is why"—her arms reached for the childlike creature perched on Rowan's knee—"we must know how a Sylvin child came to be among the Littlelost. This lovely girl could grow up to become our first new flyer in a generation."

"No." Rowan set the small Sylvin down on her own two dainty feet. "She will not grow up to become anything. She is fully grown; in fact, she is likely older than any of you."

"But she could fly!" one Sylvin burst out, indifferent to the implications of Rowan's announcement.

Lenaree came close to study the tiny figure, an exercise that was mutual. Plume seemed awed as she looked Lenaree up and down.

"Yes, her hair would have paled as she grew, had she grown instead of aging. How," Lenaree demanded, "has this happened?"

Sage spoke thoughtfully. "She no doubt became Littlelost as Rowan's elder brother became Littlelost. She wandered away from home, fell under the spell of an earthgall pit long enough to become forgetful, to inhale the bitter venom that prevents further growth and aging, though not adulthood. At last she

153

encountered others of her outcast kind. In joining with the Littlelost, she became prey to the Takers and other servants of the Crux."

"The Crux!" Rowan stood, frowning. "Are these Halflings brutish folk, larger than I, at least in girth? Slow-moving and thinking, but strong and angry? Men and women both?"

The Sylvin women nodded slowly.

"Then those were Halflings on the ground at the Wellsunging! Halflings fought on the side of the Crux! Is it possible?"

"Anything is possible." Ystar stared numbly at the Sylvin Littlelost. "Are others of her kind among the Littlelost?"

Rowan waved a hand to the sleeping ranks of small figures. "Several. I begin to see that the Littlelost are not simply the outcasts of Desmeyne, but beguiled children of all kinds. They served the Takers, unwillingly, and some in ways that are ugly to know. They are small, but they are not children, and will not behave as children. Are you still willing to claim them?"

As his words struck home, Sylvin eyes changed shade, becoming deep purple before they cleared. Lenaree smiled.

"Some village folk who glimpse us mistake us for children, because of our smallness. We are used to shocking others merely by being ourselves. That is why we stay aloft and apart. Yet we have created a half-race that hates itself and its origins. We are none to judge the actions or the innocence of others. If these . . . so well-preserved . . . once-children of our more able youth wish to become flyers, we welcome them, whatever time and fate has made of them. At least they are alive."

Rowan lifted his sun-bleached red brows. The Sylvins accepted with such ease the conclusion that the Taliswoman urged upon the Desmeynians and that his people still resisted. Another thought crossed his mind. "What will the Hammerhands think of this?" He nodded to the shy but alert Sylvin Littlelost watching the discussion.

Lenaree's delicate hands rested firmly on Plume's shoulders. Her fey lavender eyes sparkled with vitality, joy . . . and gratitude. "You—and we—may soon see, Rowan Firemayne. You and all the Sylvin Littlelost must accompany us to our

ancient nests. We will help you find the Quarter of the Four
Winds, because you have given us a gift beyond counting."

Rowan's hand flew to his talismanic pouch without knowing it.

In minutes, the Sylvin women were bending and stooping
among the drowsing litter of Littlelost as he had been, seeking
their own lost ones.

Rowan watched them, surprised by their generosity and
quick reversal. "For shy creatures, they know what they
want," he said.

Sage came and stood beside him. "They seek to continue
the tradition of their kind. They are grateful that you have
shown them a way."

"But they cannot yet guess how unlike them these so-like
Littlelost are. Or—" He had already thought of this, but now
it seemed vital. "Can the Littlelost reproduce?"

Sage shook her white-haired head, coarse and yellowed in
the sunlight. "I have never seen an infant Littlelost. Perhaps
the earthgall pits prevent that."

"And how long does a Littlelost live?"

"No one knows, for no one has paid them any attention
before. I think they may survive as long as an Earth-Eater. You
are the expert on that kind. What age do they reach?"

Rowan considered the question. "I have no notion, and
there is no way to tell, although . . . Dusk hinted that their
span is for generations. But then—" he smiled grimly "—she
is a hard negotiator. Perhaps she exaggerated in order to impress us."

"You think creatures as foul as Earth-Eaters might be vulnerable to such a vanity?"

"I think that all creatures are both more and less than I once
thought of them."

"No doubt you owe such insight to the Taliswoman."

He eyed Sage, then abruptly changed the subject. "This talk
of Halflings is most disturbing. Do you see what is happening,
wisewoman? The Crux causes the discontented folk of Veil to
do its bidding. It has even enlisted the cooperation of the
Earth-Eaters below Desmeyne's very halls. The Takers may be

part-magic, part-beast, but they are not wise enough to establish their own ways. But these Halflings, they could be many, and they are strong. And—" He hesitated, troubled.

"And they number women warriors among them." Rowan chafed to realize that Alison had mentioned his humiliating encounter with the female Halfling to the wisewoman. Sage smiled until a mass of fine wrinkles masked her features like a veil. "Do not worry. We begin to form our own alliance. The Sylvin flyers are our warriors of the air. Let us hope that your father is not foolish enough to spurn the aid of the Earth-Eaters. And we have also the Taliswoman."

"And the Cup." His hand again clasped the pouch hanging beneath his throat. "We have spent too long not knowing what folk dwell at our borders, and what concerns them. What good can one venturing Desmeynian do in a world full of such wonders, and such ill?"

"What good can one Taliswoman do in a world full of talismen?" Sage asked.

He turned to find that Alison had at last arisen and now assisted the Sylvin women in claiming their own.

"And the Littlelost!" he said. "The Littlelost are an ally now that I have freed them. They may be small, but they are numerous. Now I see that many kinds dwell among them. Free, they may act as a bridge between our shattered kinds, just as the captive Littlelost became a human bridge between the Crux-masters' greed and the etherion floating on the pits."

He turned to survey the party, as if numbering the very blades of grass as newfound friends. "And the Slinkers! Why do they tamely accompany us and offer no harm? The Taliswoman brought her own ice-haired Slinker among us, whom she loves better than she does some people, and he has . . . interbred with our world. She told me those . . . pups are his. Are Slinkers allies as well, Sage?"

For the first time, he called the old woman by her name, as if she were not an ugly and insufficient female past all use, but simply another person. Rowan was shocked to find past hurt hidden beneath the triumph in the wisewoman's pale eyes. And the triumph was for him, not for herself. He looked away.

His world shook beneath his feet, but he felt a dawning strength that had nothing to do with personal power: the strength of the new value he was finding in others.

"I must talk with the Taliswoman," he mumbled, leaving Sage to pick up the fallen mugs, to wash them, and to smile at these important tasks that looked so humble until someone failed to do them.

Alison sensed his approach and turned from the new Sylvin Littlelost she had just found and awakened. Her face shone with excitement.

"Lenaree said you discovered that Sylvin Littlelost were among the band you freed. Look! Here's another."

He nodded, stunned by Alison's enthusiasm, by the Sylvin women's bubbling happiness, and by the Littlelosts' wonder as they saw some of their own claimed by those who resembled them. They had never known they had belonged anywhere, he saw, and thus had never believed they had a right to.

They remain Littlelost! he wanted to shout. They will never be the unhurt, innocent children they still resemble. But it did not matter, this fact. What mattered was that the contours of their shattered world were dovetailing with the specific curves of other peoples' knowledge. They had belonged somewhere once, and they could again. He felt a stab of regret that Lorn had never known such fulfillment. Or had he?

"It's wonderful," Alison said, ignoring the two Slinkers that wound around her legs: the tame white Spirit Slinker she called Rambeau, the golden wild Slinker called nothing that he knew of.

Pups gamboled under Rowan's feet, and he dared not move, but the grasses swayed and Littlelost sprang up at a common touch as the Sylvin women moved among them in search of their own. Confused, Rowan felt the alien in his own world— his own world that he had never known.

And danger threatened all this: the people, the creatures, the wind, even the very grass. Danger charged, wearing a dozen faces. One might be his father's, one his own. He saw the sunlight shining down on a multiplicity of heads: ice-fair Sylvin and particolored Slinker; Alison's earth-brown hair, crowned with a rainbow circlet; Sage pale in the distance. Tousled brown and black and yellow and white-gold Littlelost heads lifted from the long grasses like unscented blossoms . . . and nowhere among them was there a trace of red, except for that upon the balding head of the Earth-Eater Alison had named Dusk.

How was he to walk through this world that had become so crowded with strangers and strangeness? He thought he saw a shimmer in the distance that might have been his mother—or Darnellyne—walking toward him. He turned. Not back. He could never go back. His vision darkened; at its center stood the small, red-haired Littlelost defying the Crux-masters' animated blue wands of pain and death. He turned again, and the colors leaked back into his sight, the sounds returned, even the soft smell of crushed grass.

He must save this somehow, this confusion and this ignorance always on the brink of knowledge. The world of Veil was wide enough for all of them: Sylvins and Hammerhands, Littlelost and Earth-Eaters, Slinkers and Sage, each capable of good and evil. Veil could not encompass the outright evil of the Crux.

"Taliswoman," he said, and she turned from her pleasant task of rousing Sylvin Littlelost, her face still radiating unguarded joy. "I will accept the Cup."

14

"YOU changed your tune in a hurry," she said.

They had removed themselves to a distance from the camp. She had brought her pack, carrying it by the straps, and now it bobbled against her ankles as she walked.

He winced and tried not to show it, having become excruciatingly conscious of the Cup. She studied his features as if to learn more than a face should ever betray.

"Why?" she asked.

"You were all too eager to concede the Cup to me. Now that I request it, you resist. Why?"

Alison smiled. He saw for the first time that her smiles, while frequent, were often self-mocking. "It's . . . not easy to let go of. Or maybe it won't let go of me. I have to be sure that you're . . . serious. That you're worthy."

When he had said the same to her more than a year before, she had dismissed him.

"I am of Veil," he reminded her. "As is the Cup. You admit that my song won this Wellsunging."

"But I was not the judge."

"You are now, it seems." He waited. She said nothing. "Then ignore my claim. I need nothing that you have."

He turned to go, not wanting to abandon the Cup or the argument, but pride left no other avenue.

"Oh, yes you do."

He whirled at the challenge in her voice. Oddly, she seemed most sure of his right to the Cup when he was willing to give it up.

"What is this need?" His tone sounded touchy even to himself.

She released the pack, letting it fall the two inches it dangled from the ground. "You're impaired in your ability to protect it. I'll let you have it on one condition."

"I do not need your conditions; I do not need your Cup." Having declared himself, there was nothing to do but glare at her.

She stood with her legs braced, as if challenging him. He had come to accept her odd garb; her leg-wear was not as sleek as Desmeynian tights, but it emphasized the long, strong line of limbs no Loftlady would reveal except in the marriage bed.

She laughed. "Oh, yes you do. For the first time, you realize how much you do need them both. It rubs you raw, but there it is. For the first time, you see that your mission is big enough for Veil, not just for Desmeyne. Welcome to the real world, Rowan Firemayne. Now fight me for the Cup."

"I will not!"

She shrugged. "If you had at first, perhaps Veil would not have had to suffer as it has in the past year. Perhaps the Littlelost would not have languished in another full year of hideous servitude; Darnellyne would not still be waiting and wondering, and you would certainly not be wasting your energy maintaining a foolish celibacy—"

"*You* are foolish!" he charged, following up his words with a literal charge . . . even as he realized that she had deliberately taunted him for other ends.

She stepped aside like mist. "Rowan Firemayne would not hurt a woman. He thinks too little of women to waste any energy on them, be it in combat or . . . in conjunction."

"That is not true."

The grasses swayed, his senses followed suit. She no longer stood where she had. He turned to find her behind him, like a shadow that had turned on its owner.

How jaunty she was, with her weight on one leg, her opposite hip jutted out, as if he were not a serious enough threat to worry about. Still, she had moved the pack so that the Cup was behind her.

"If you are afraid to fight a woman," she told him, "you are afraid to love one. Both actions require the passion of commitment; both require you to respect the woman as an equal."

"You are not of Veil," he pointed out. "I need neither honor you nor despise you."

"That's true, and unfortunately those are the poles of your reaction toward women—to honor or to despise them—when we want love and respect. At least you respect my magical fighting ability; you keep your distance."

Her words drew him in, enraged and frustrated, unsure of what he would do. Seize the Cup, perhaps; leave her untouched, yet capture the Cup.

He lunged as he would for a Taker, then swerved in another direction, eyes on the pack, and . . . went flying like a Sylvin corsair, over the grasses, aware of a swift thump at his hip, of the world spinning until he sprawled grass-side down.

She stood ahead of him, when he had outrun her. How? The pack huddled at her feet, as docile as a Slinker pup. She moved like water around rock, liquid where he was lumpish. Perhaps he could be liquid, too.

He gathered his strength and came rushing up, intending to pull her feet out from under her, as cowardly as such a move would be. She would fall, as he had, but she would not hurt more than her pride. Then he would snatch the pack, claim the Cup, and—

She crouched, straightened, sprang. A foot caught him on the chest, spun him in some direction he did not wish to take. The earth met him with another resounding thud. Through the grasses he could see the pack hunkering beside her legs that were swathed in those absurd trousers of faded blue cloth.

His head swam and his frame ached like that of a Hammerhand's who had fallen to earth. He dug his palms into the clotted soil and prepared to thrust himself up again. She squatted near him, the pack tantalizingly within view, but behind her.

"Rowan, Desmeynian outrage will never win the Cup against *taekwondo*. I can *teach* you how to fight without a staff, how to fight a woman even, even a Halfling woman, and win."

His anger boiled at his position. For a quest-heir to have to humbly learn from an alien usurper! Yet one part of him—that new part that had defied his father and rescued Littlelost and been grateful for a wisewoman's understanding—realized that he was being as foolish as a Halfling, those ungainly half-breeds that fit in no one world. This *taakquandoe* was a talisman as potent as a Cup or as the clay tablet that that lay on his chest; at least it was for this particular Taliswoman. He who will not change will *be* changed, and not to his liking, he thought grimly.

He measured her face. She was amused, but not condescending; or even worse, smugly sympathetic.

He pushed himself semi-upright. "There is a trick to it," he complained.

"Yes," she admitted blithely, "a lot of tricks."

He stood, and she sighed. Perhaps she did not really wish to deal with him in this way, but felt that she must. Much as it seared his pride, he recognized truth, even necessity.

She began to speak in a more serious tone.

"You must learn to use an opponent's—any opponent's, even one you do not wish to hurt—an opponent's own strength against him, or her."

He nodded. The words were not unreasonable. The Cup no longer beckoned, although he intended to bear it. She was right that it was his; so, too, should be this alien knowledge.

"You mustn't charge like a wounded bull; be patient," she was saying, "and wait. Regard it as exercising a kind of celibacy for a good cause."

For the first time, the word "celibacy" struck him as a lack rather than an honor. Her words implied that he must give up cherished notions; one of the first was the idea that he needed to protect her. She was the Taliswoman, after all, and had defeated him at the Wellsunging a year ago, had never sought his personal protection. He owed her nothing but to use her advice to defeat her, as she seemed to want him to do.

So he practiced the uneasy skills she taught him, engaging her in a dance that even Dearth had not imagined, holding his ground and giving way only when she had committed to an attack, using his feet and legs as more than foundation, as weapons, like his arms. Still, the ground remained a drum upon which his bones beat. Again and again he fell. He lay looking up at a cloudless sky, watching an etherion corsair float into his sight.

She bent over, extended a hand to help him rise as if he were a Littlelost. Maybe he was.

"There are no practice mats in Veil; sorry," she said. "You almost had me that time."

He rose again, lunged at her again, waited again. Patience, and tricks, and letting her defeat herself.

Rowan forgot sunlight and sweat, forgot falling and rising. He strove to learn another's ways, and by learning, to better himself.

The hardest part was to strike at her with the intention of bringing her down. Even if he summoned all of his old anger and confusion, some barrier remained. Sweat was running down his cheeks and chest. His knees creaked, his muscles ached, and his jaw throbbed from the clench of his teeth, from how they jarred each time he kissed the ground.

The frustration made him angry, even as Alison's voice echoed in his head with new recommendations, new precautions. There was no graceful way to retreat, even though only she witnessed his humiliating failures. And he vowed that the knowledge she grasped so easily should not elude him. He rose again.

They moved together. Apart. The wary measures of it seemed like a dance on the great Arcade floor. This method of combat was indeed as structured as a dance, except for the sudden, surprising moves.

Together. Apart. And then Alison lunged, he did something, she veered as he twisted . . . and she went flying, until she hit the ground, rolling, and was up again.

"Very good," she said. "Do you know what you did?"

He shook his head.

She grinned. "You will." And she was at him again, forcing him to stand firm, to dodge and to lunge, to take blows, escape blows, to give blows.

Many times he glimpsed the sky: always cloudless, always blue, but he learned to roll up to his feet again as she did. The next time he tripped her, he continued moving, as did she. Her hair darkened with sweat and clung more closely to her face. Where she was always talking, always explaining, suggesting, sometimes encouraging, often criticizing, he was mute, shifting his stance and his opinion like a tongue-tied dullard, like one too exhausted or too angry to speak.

There came a moment when he glanced down to see her pack between his feet, and he was defender, not taker. The earth beat like a heart to the thumps of their feet and their bodies, and finally he was so weary and so eager to end it all that he stepped fluidly in her way, deflected her body even as it leaped through the air and pounced upon her as she hit the earth, using arms, legs, and old-fashioned Desmeynian brute force to pin her down.

"All right," she said. A drop of his sweat hit her cheek and rolled sideways like a tear. "The Cup is yours. Satisfied?"

Despite her light tone, he now knew her well enough from the dance to know that her eyes held a trace of alarm.

He released her, swept with sudden shame at his superior strength and his intense awareness of it. He reached for the backpack, fumbling for the Cup and for words. He also felt a certain shy sense of achievement that he had not known since a child, a hopeful suspicion that he had done well at something new and difficult.

She took the pack from under his hand and extracted the Cup in its ugly patterned wrapping. "You seem to be getting the idea," she said. Her eyes held his, even as her hands withheld the Cup. "You didn't have me down, you know. I just thought it was time to finish."

He was not about to let her belittle his hard-won victory. "You fought long and well, but my strength is superior. You could not have freed yourself."

"No force is superior as long as you continue to fight it." At the doubt in his eyes, she added, "And I haven't taught you everything."

She handed him the Cup. Petty discussions of strength and

superiority faded as the chill stone bowl filled his cupped palms like the pommel of a well-loved sword.

He thought he detected a throbbing in the stone, so faint and so fast that it was a mere thrum of vibration, as when Desmeyne's rock-crystal walls trembled almost imperceptibly to the chords of dinner music.

No unmistakable surge of certainty or power accompanied the Cup's possession. Rowan's questioning gaze had told the Taliswoman that before he thought to hide his surprise. Yet a still center of peace pooled within him like mildwater, somewhere between where the clay tablet lay and his hands. An odd thought came to him: stone sang to human clay entombed in its own dust, but only the dead or the deaf might truly hear that melody.

15

ENDLESS meadows ended at last in eternal vistas of peaked white clouds and snow-crowned mountains. Only the occasional skirl of an etherion flyer through the blue dome of the sky relieved the scenic monotony and the temperate weather.

On the ground, the journey toward the Sylvin mists and the Rookeries beyond was proceeding without incident save for the sudden discovery of a waterfall or of a pomma-bearing pine stand. The party avoided the rank black rash of earthgall that pitted the lower slopes like soot.

Still, the earthgall blight fascinated Alison. Perhaps housewifely urges made her want to erase that blatant dirt from Veil's fair surface, to scrub the galls loose with ammonia and detergent, then hose away the residue in a flood of fresh water.

Without the Cup, she felt oddly redundant, as if she might as well retrace her steps and look for Island signs. But then she wouldn't find where the Sylvin women dwelled, would never meet a Hammerhand, never see the wild Littlelost in their far Rookeries, or watch Rowan set out for the Quarter of the Four Winds. And she had a feeling that Veil wasn't done with her yet.

Whenever the party paused at a waterfall, Alison beckoned Rowan for a round of *taekwondo* instruction. Teaching him much of the elaborate Oriental philosophy that underlay the ancient discipline was difficult, but at least he understood discipline. Two-some years of heroic celibacy had seen to that.

Alison wouldn't be around forever; she might as well show the designated hero some off-world tricks. At least the waterfalls provided a good shower after a workout.

Rowan improved rapidly; the more adept he became at martial arts, the more he distrusted her motives in sharing such a potent skill. He no longer mistook *taekwondo* throws for magic, which took some of the fun out of it for Alison. No Cup, no bewildering moves; she felt bereft of her edge. She felt misplaced, even a bit *re*placed. Still, if she wanted to leave this world better than when she found it, Rowan had to be taught. She must sensitize him far beyond the horizon line of his hopes.

After one such workout, they sat on the thick grasses their bodies had flattened, knees up, arms linked loosely around their legs. The shower etiquette would be, as always, implacable. Alison would bathe in the waterfall first, with Rowan standing guard. Then she would leave and he would take his turn. Apparently a designated hero needed no guard for his privacy. Certainly he never threatened to violate hers. His self-control would have been remarkable, Alison thought, had he not found her so personally distasteful. She began to wonder if his celibacy could disguise a lack of passion. Yet, on Alison's previous visit to Veil, the behavior of his manhood-mate Trissellyn testified that Rowan had not been renowned for self-restraint until his quest began.

"The Cup," he said now.

She caught her breath. "What of it?"

"I saw it respond to you, outlander though you are. It does not do the same for me."

Alison nodded. "I'm afraid I'm coming to an ugly conclusion."

"How can something as immaterial as a conclusion be ugly?"

"It can be unwelcome, at least." She bit her lip. There was much she could say that she might regret, such as revealing the fact of Darnellyne's disfigurement. Why did she tell him only things that were to her own discredit?

"There's no sidestepping the question," he said.

She smiled wryly. "Sidestepping" was an expression he had heard from her during *taekwondo* lessons, and she wondered if he realized that he had contracted his subject and verb.

"No, Rowan, there isn't. When I took the Cup from Veil, when I turned tail and ran back to my home island, I think that I weakened the Cup's power. This new outbreak of visible evil—open sores of earthgall springing from below, the Crux's lethal etherion coursers busy aloft—may result from the Cup's absence."

He nodded, not surprised. "It has languished in another world. You have much to answer for."

She said nothing. If her suspicions were right, his accusation was all too true.

"What else," he mused, "has turned tainted that might have waxed well had the Cup stayed in Veil?"

Bite your lip, she told herself. He would have to discover Darnellyne's secret on his own.

"It's not only the Cup," she said. "I wonder sometimes about your vow."

"You have never understood."

"In my world, some people are forced into celibacy by the social . . . plague I told you about."

He frowned. "Yes, this plague that makes your people fear to take pleasure with one another. At least my abstinence is by my own will, not from fear."

"I for one don't find abstinence for its own sake worth much."

"What do you mean? It is a long tradition—"

"So is almost everything that doesn't work in any world, Rowan. What does relinquishing intimacy with women gain you? A sense of self-control? The Cup you hold is a Cup of Earth; earth's fruition is not denial. It's offensive, this notion that you can't save your world unless you renounce intimacy with women, as if we were all pits of earthgall to enmesh you in our filthy toils. Is your mother such a one? Sage? Triss of the raven hair? Darnellyne?"

"No!" He had risen to his knees. "Such a forgoing would not matter if it were not a sacrifice."

"But why women? Why not sacrifice your long red locks, Rowan Firemayne? Go bald in the world; announce your mission with your own humiliation. Instead, your celibacy announces that women aren't worthy of participating in your quest. Great!"

He scowled. "It is that *I* am not worthy of satisfying my small gratifications when I am engaged upon important work."

"Oh, even better. Women are minor gratifications that might distract men from vital things? How self-defeating this celibacy notion is! You'd value your sexual freedom more if you lived in my world, where every contact—casual or a planned commitment of long standing—may bring a mortal taint."

"I cannot help what is wrong with your world."

"That's where we differ," Alison returned. "I still believe that I can help your world."

"Then remove yourself!" he said. "That alone would do much to improve Veil. You are no longer needed. I have the Cup and the quest-scars."

"And a smattering of *taekwondo*," she added ruefully.

"What is . . . smattering?"

"Good enough for you. My lessons are over. You have always known more than was good for you, or thought you did."

"I will wait while you bathe."

Alison stood, brushing at the grass stains on her jeans. "I don't think so. I don't trust you."

He looked stunned. "I would not violate your privacy if my life depended on it."

"That's just why I don't trust you. What is renunciation, Rowan, if you don't want what you give up? Maybe Dar could answer that question."

Alison stomped off, already regretting that his self-sufficient superiority had annoyed her. But what else had he ever been taught? Just a few *taekwondo* moves.

A hand caught her upper arm abruptly and whirled her around. She freed herself and would have retaliated, except that Rowan's face was white-masked with shock as if by flour.

"What do you mean about Darnellyne? Why do you call her 'Dar' now? That was a child-name between us. Why do you always behave as if you know more than anybody else?"

Because, she thought wryly, Veil is at least one place where I do, about some things anyway. Yet the dread freezing Rowan's features made her pause. His massive male indifference just now had miffed her, especially when he had actually said that she was beneath his notice, and she had loosed a few random arrows before leaving: the approved twentieth-century arguing technique. She saw that her verbal aim had been all too accurate. Now she would have to lie to him to avoid the ugly answer hidden among his welter of questions.

"I mean that last year all you wanted was to win the Cup for Desmeyne, and to free Darnellyne of the possibility of an unwelcome suitor by winning her as well. Now you avoid the Cup, or complain about its lack of power, and Desmeyne is farther from here than the Littlelost's Rookeries."

His expression melted to reveal a patchwork of shifting doubt. "You are right. I have glimpsed a greater evil and a greater cause than those that center in Desmeyne." He looked away to the far peaks. "In part, perhaps, I have discovered these things because of what you said. Yet the loss of Lorn, so soon after discovering that one of Desmeyne—a Firemayne, the first quest-heir—could live among the Littlelost . . ."

"You have lost faith in your quest, then?"

"No!" His eyes returned to her, flashing dark fire. "No, Taliswoman." Their anger moderated as his glance flicked down to her chest, acknowledging the common scars they shared, though hers hid behind her shirt.

This sudden reminder made her uneasy about concealing the disfigurement in a land where such was honored, albeit with attacks on occasion. She had grown impatient with camouflage at home, yet once here, she reverted to her old, discreet ways.

"I have seen that a broader quest awaits," he said, his hand lifting his pouch. "The Cup has its purpose and its wonders, but this rough-made talisman touches me more. If I follow the

170

Quest to the Four Quarters, I will forge a talisman for all of Veil."

Alison eyed the pouch containing Lorn's ashes. It repelled her as much as her own scars had, but now it covered Rowan's identical scars, whose pattern she had come to take for granted, like the random swirl of glinting red-gold hairs on his chest.

"Perhaps I was wrong." She ignored the way his brows lifted at this admission. "I championed Pickle and the Littlelost far earlier than you. To me, they were simply abandoned children, and so they are, in part, though much more complicated than that. After your initial disdain for the Littlelost, your acceptance of Pickle's death as something to be turned to your quest's advantage seemed cruel."

"How did he know enough to resist the Crux?" Rowan demanded. "Lorn had never suffered the Cutting of the quest-heirs. He had vanished before that day came, unmarked. But at the Heart of Earth beneath Desmeyne, he underwent his own Cutting by the Crux-masters' blue rods—and he defeated them! He was not turned into a false quest-heir for their use. Why should he object to serving as a talisman for his own kin and kind?"

Alison's eyes blurred with sudden tears. Was it so awful to find sense in senseless deaths? Perhaps her world was too removed from self-sacrifice. Yet she still saw Pickle's forlorn little face under its dirty scarf and wondered why he had been fated to die.

"I have no right to accuse you of callousness," she said, her voice unsteady. "I'm estranged from my own brother, and while my sister's drowning was a terrible shock, I really didn't like her very well."

"I did not give Pickle much opportunity to like me," Rowan answered quietly.

Alison looked up from the pouch and the scars upon which she had focused her traitorous, teary eyes. Was Rowan offering consolation? Were his eyes sympathetic?

"Demaris was older than I," she went on, needing to explain

for some reason, "and at that awful age between child and adult when she could be such a snot."

"Snot?"

The words that came naturally to Alison wouldn't work with Rowan, words like stuck-up, bullying, mean in a sneaky, sneering way that made Alison feel guilty when she remembered her sister. After all, Demaris was dead; the dead should be esteemed, shouldn't they? Maybe not, the thought came. Maybe Rowan's way was more honest. He truly mourned the brother he might have known. Maybe that's what Alison should do as well.

"Snot?" he repeated.

"Full of herself. Inconsiderate of others."

"Ah," he said, "as you found me."

Was he . . . laughing at her? She eyed him suspiciously.

"At first," he added solemnly.

"And at last," she riposted with relish. Her tears were gone, despite a sudden new spasm of seriousness. "Don't underestimate the Cup, Rowan. I've felt it at full power, and it's nothing to sneeze at."

"To sneeze at?"

"What you do with snot."

It took a moment for him to make the connection, but when he did, he laughed like a baritone in an opera, long and richly.

"Your world has its rough edges as well," he finally said.

"Yes. Very rough. I never claimed otherwise. Perhaps the ills of my world tainted the Cup, and the longer it resides again in Veil, the stronger it will become."

He nodded, not rejecting her suggestion.

"About Dar," she added. "She and I had a . . . good talk when I returned to Desmeyne. She asked me to call her that, and it seemed natural. I like her, Rowan. I don't want to see her hurt."

"Nor do I!" he said in some bewilderment. "But Dar is safe in Desmeyne now. I hold the Cup, and even before this, your possession of it kept her from unwanted claims."

"Then you intend to claim her when you fulfill your quests?"

He didn't speak immediately; this was another change in impulsive, always-certain Rowan Firemayne. Alison found herself waiting anxiously for the answer.

"I will return, if I can, if I live," he said finally. "If the Crux permits," he added. "I will bring back the Cup. I would have won it had you not been at the Wellsunging a year ago. I won it this year. But—"

"But" was another new word for Rowan. Alison listened with some uneasiness. She had told him not to underestimate the Cup. Had she underestimated him?

"You were right," he said in a rush of unconsidered truth, of thoughts that had occurred to him for the first time. "Some customs are pointlessly confining. When I bring the Cup home to Dar, it will be for her keeping. I cannot stand between her and her fate forever. She will be free to do as she wills, and if any man—including my father—should challenge my decision, he will have to enforce his will."

Alison caught her breath. Poor Darnellyne. Freedom from mandatory marriage was a boon, but would she see Rowan's generosity as rejection?

"And if any *woman* should challenge it?" She was thinking especially of Rowan's imperious, yet obedient mother, Zormond.

"Then such a woman will have to enforce her will," he said evenly, admitting for the first time that a woman might be as able to do that as a man.

Alison only nodded. Rowan believed she meant herself, she realized, and indeed, what other woman in Veil had ever challenged him? They walked in silence back toward the others.

Her thoughts were churning. He had learned, this youth of twenty, a lot more from her than some *taekwondo* moves, and much of it unintended. Maybe she—and Veil—had been better off when he had been naive, ignorant, and hampered by quaint and chivalrous notions.

16

SLOWLY, with tidelike tenacity, the forest crept up from the valleys below and lapped at the mountain meadows. The trees' advance forced the party to push higher into thin air and cooler temperatures.

The guiding etherion corsair that showed itself from time to time loomed larger against the vast bowl of the sky. Even the ever-present, horizon-ringing clouds were often hidden at this height by the mountains' hunched shoulders of shale and scrub.

Snow dust in distant crevices sparkled icily.

Lenaree, unable to tether her corsair when the ground tilted at such a sharp angle, still could glide down into their midst. Today, as usual, hordes of Littlelost swung onto the chain she lowered, weighing down the corsair while her high, piping voice lifted to make itself understood.

"Takers in the passes!" she called. "We will have to find another route."

"We are many," Rowan shouted back. "What care we for a few Takers on the march?"

Lenaree's feathery head shook mournfully. "Many, many Takers. And Halflings. Too many. Flyers will find a way."

With that, she shook the trailing line. Littlelost dropped off as the corsair soared almost straight up between the rugged peaks.

"How many Takers and Halflings can there be?" Rowan grumbled.

"Ready to demonstrate your *taekwondo* on them?" Alison needled.

He refused to be goaded. "Yes."

The need for food forced the party lower, closer to the treeline. The Littlelost fanned through the forest, hunting pomma and berries. But Lenaree's airborne anxiety found an earthbound echo.

Only minutes after they had scampered past the underbrush, flocks of panicked Littlelost came exploding through the irregular fence of trees. Twist, at their fore, made straight for Alison.

"Etherion pit! B-b-bigger than, than—" his short arms stretched to their fullest "—all Desmeyne!"

"Nonsense," Rowan interrupted to reassure the frightened faces congealing around the three Big People. "Surely the Littlelost exaggerates," he told the wisewoman, who had hobbled over, brushing thick yellow-white strands of hair behind her ears as if to hear better. "Can it be?" he asked Sage in a confidential tone, so as not to further frighten the Littlelost.

"I have never seen such a thing."

"The Littlelost are the experts on etherion pits," Alison put in, smiling at Twist.

Petite Plume spoke next. "Such terrible . . . things fill the pit! Dead coursers." Her tiny voice was strained.

Alison's hand buttressed Plume's frail shoulder. "Dead coursers can't help us, but they can't hurt us." Still, if the fallen flyers were Sylvin corsairs rather than Crux-craft, any pilots would have plunged with their craft into the noxious stew-pit, perhaps still alive as they slowly sank. . . .

"We must see for ourselves," Rowan declared. "Perhaps you Littlelost have found a rare, Taker-untouched pit that the Sylvins can cultivate."

Alison consulted Sage, who nodded surreptitiously.

Distant thunder growled. Alison turned to find Rambeau sitting on the group's outskirts, his ruff fur raised in distrust.

"Watch here," she ordered him. "Only a few of us will go to the pit. Rowan and—"

He continued for her. "—Sage, Twist, and Plume, because

175

it is good to see that dead monsters are dead. Rime, Faun, you there—"

"Thump," answered the burliest of the new-freed Littlelost.

"—and the Taliswoman," Rowan finished without looking at Alison.

"Last but not least," she murmured.

"What?" Rowan turned.

"A saying in my world."

"Hurry!" said Twist. "The giant pit . . . swallowed Boulder, Littlelost of the Hammerhands."

"Boulder was caught fast by the feet," Plume added. "All of us together couldn't free her."

"Why did you not say so?" Rowan roared, turning to hurry the designated rescue party and don his pack, which he kept with him constantly now.

Alison felt an unexpected pang to think that the Cup of Earth rode in his knapsack, not hers. Still, they might need the contents of hers more. She fetched it and ran to catch up with the backs and heels already disappearing into the deep green fringe of forest. Surely Twist exaggerated. Boulder was not "swallowed," merely mired. And an etherion pit as big as Desmeyne would be awesome, not to mention worth a lot of wooden knots, if communities in Veil other than Desmeyne counted such things as currency.

Alison brought up the rear, whip-thin saplings lashing at her from between the pines. She was reminded of the narrow path to Eli's cabin on the Island. For a wild moment, she thought of how wonderful it would be to find that very cabin at the trek's end, with Eli in it. If Rambeau had vanished from the Island but remained in Veil, couldn't Eli have come here, too? But wishful thinking would not bring the old man back, or even reveal what had happened to him.

And Veil was not the Island.

The others had paused in a line curved like a parenthesis. Alison broke into their semicircle to see what had stopped them. A chasm of darkness lay below, glimmering like a wet eel. No mere pit, it was as large as a lake: vast, black, and still. Velvet slime.

"Where is Boulder?" she asked.

Twist pointed down the brush-choked incline.

"What on earth would possess anyone to go down there?" Alison wondered aloud.

"Coursers," Plume trilled in the ponderous silence. Even words grew heavy here after being spoken, and sank slowly toward the black morass below. Plume's dainty arm pointed, too.

Alison saw some sharp black objects protruding from the muck, like semi-submerged grasshoppers as big as dinosaurs.

As Rowan started down the slope, Alison finally spied, far below, a small, flailing figure, pale against the fat black slug of oily water and floating etherion.

"Wait!" Her hand caught Rowan on the bare chest. Her palm could feel his heart's accelerating beat, the warm skin and hair, a few ridged scars. The pouch, as soft as suede, brushed her fingertips.

He waited impatiently; to Rowan, every endangered Littlelost was Pickle at the Heart of Earth, was Lorn his brother.

"Rowan, this pit is too . . . rich to be deserted. We should all be cautious."

He nodded, then swung past her, heading down the incline alone.

"Good advice," Sage said, but she began easing her lumpish form down the same incline anyway.

"No bridges." Soft-spoken Rime glanced up from under wings of frost-white hair. "Safe from Takers."

"But are we safe from those?" Alison indicated the black carcasses that could be Crux-coursers shining dully in the forest shadows. "Stay well behind me," she instructed, and hurtled down the hill at a dangerous speed to catch up with the others.

She arrived to find that Boulder was not seriously mired in the tarlike scum that edged the pit. Rowan had grasped the Littlelost under the arms. He now gave a few mighty tugs and pulled Boulder free with an enormous sucking sound.

"It hurts," the chubby Littlelost cried, staring dolefully at her tar-coated feet and legs.

177

Kneeling, Sage pulled an assortment of bags and vials from her pockets. She selected a purple vial and dusted a fine gray powder—like pumice, or ashes—over the Littlelost's legs.

"Wait," Sage said, as she peeled powder and black substance back like dough. Boulder writhed under Rowan's hands, which both restrained and comforted her. Her coarse trouser fabric pulled away with the substance, and her tough hide boots as well.

Boulder moaned. Her bare legs and feet looked red and angry. Alison guessed that the Littlelost had just suffered the equivalent of a crude depilatory wax job. Yet it was more than that.

"Burns," Rowan muttered in amazement.

Sage nodded, digging among her ointments even as Alison ransacked her own pack for a tube of cortisone cream.

In the end, both potions—Alison's antibiotic cream and Sage's anonymous herbal salve—were gently patted onto Boulder's raw legs.

"Why did you rush down to such an Earth-Eaters' hole?" Rowan demanded, anger edging his voice.

Twist answered for Boulder. "We had never seen such a pit. So large, so still. And though the p-p-pits we harvested contained sunken . . . things, we never really saw them, only felt them stirring beneath the passage of our s-s-skimming tongs. I have never seen so much etherion," he added wistfully, as if challenged to harvest such a rich crop.

Alison kicked at the now-caked mire fragments torn from Boulder's legs. "Caustic. The black stuff is caustic. That's why the Takers need the lightweight Littlelost to risk the surface and skim off the etherion."

"What is 'caustic'?" Rowan asked.

"You've seen what it does: burns on contact, on touch. Like acid." Even that word fell unrecognized among them. "Like a Crux-master's rod," she added.

Rowan nodded soberly, then eyed the expansive sable lake curdling before them. "A Crux-place, for certain. The Littlelost are right. I have never seen the like of those . . . foreign machines in the pit."

Boulder squirmed and squealed at their feet as Sage applied a second layer of salve.

"Rowan." Alison phrased her words carefully. "You mentioned seeing foreign artifacts when I was in Veil before, when I first met you. Machines, you said. Were they like these? How do you know the word 'machine'?"

"I have traveled Veil beyond the ken of any Desmeynian, even a Firemayne. In wild, far places, I have glimpsed fragments of things made and animated, things that are not of flesh and blood. Even the Sylvins' alien corsairs seem clean and alive compared to such dark remnants. I know enough of what is natural to Veil to recognize such differences."

"And those submerged forms out there in the pit remind you of them?"

"Yes."

"Do you still keep the . . . artifact I left behind?"

"You left nothing behind but questions," he answered with sudden vehemence, "and us to find our own way out of the deepest earth."

"How *did* you do that?" she asked, so curious that she dropped her first question.

The answer was not as scathing as she expected. "Followed your pathway through the tunnel," he admitted.

"And you came out above-ground in Veil. Interesting. But not as intriguing as these artifacts." Alison edged nearer to the slick black verge of thickened water.

The dappled surface reflected myriad faint, flickering colors, the thin skin of etherion that sealed this pesthole.

"You urged caution," Rowan reminded her, taking her arm so she shouldn't slip in.

"Caution, I'm afraid, won't be enough against this," she said, surveying the pit's mired constructions.

"What are they?" Sage moved closer to look. "I have seen the like far and wide, in fragments. They always instill me with terror, and a sick tightness in my throat, like an earthgall."

"So they should." Alison did not know how to say it. She watched the apparent sharks' fins—tilted barrel ends?—lying motionless in the midnight muck. Did they float, or touch

179

bottom? A vital question. As for the great broken limblike shapes thrusting up into the soft, shadowed forest air . . .

"I'm not an expert, but I recognize the . . . refuse . . . of my world. Waste cans. Toxic waste cans. Years' and years' worth. And those 'monsters' of the Littlelost. They scared my people, too, years ago. Gave them chills in the night, and fiery death that burned the skin and lungs and brain. Death in the water. This is insane! Is Veil simply a cosmic landfill?"

Her own words made her want to deny them, made her mind ache to blank out what it saw.

"She is not speaking sensibly," Rowan remarked over her head to Sage.

"She hails from a place alien to us," the wisewoman answered. "Perhaps these words mean more there than here. I know only that I have seen the pieces of such monstrosities before, in deserted etherion pits of Veil, which are becoming more common."

"No," Alison dully answered herself. "It can't be that simple. That . . . deadly. But the Earth-Eater taint . . . from below ground. Is it seeping through? Is Veil our underside, and are we its?"

She stumbled back from the noxious edge of the pit that was so still, so potent, like black-widow-spider soup. Back from the long, disjointed legs and wings of metal mutating here in Veil into weightless etherion. Rotting in an obsidian acid bath. Peeling flesh from bones, a metal skin seasoned with rotting flesh, perhaps. Someone had flown those earthly flyers.

Veil. She could accept this world, with all of its flaws, its problems, as its own weird little corner of the imagination. But if it only reflected her world in a dark mirror, then the reflections within reflections became unthinkable.

Alison put her hands to her scars, as though to hold her appalled heart in her chest. Words echoed around her like static. Sight and sound diminished down a long black tunnel.

"I'll take her," one string of syllables said. "You take the Littlelost."

She was lifted, as she had once been lifted onto an emergency-room table, borne away from the rancid, tarry smell, from the stilled propellers, the shifting bones sinking into the slime. She was lifted away from the dark water to some other place, and she didn't care where it was. Demaris drowning, planes plummeting into water generations ago; vegetation chewing its own rotten cud like a worm orouboros, a mechanical mouse with a bomb timer eating at the heart of the world; Earth-Eaters in solemn procession, a graven grail in their pale, distorted hands, borne on a pedestal of plastique.

Veil. Not only Rowan's people, Rowan's place, Rowan's quest. But hers.

She could feel the pot breaking again under her falling eleven-year-old body, its shards engraving slashes into her flesh. Could see the identical, yet alien, pot shatter after she left Veil last year, scattering Pickle's ashes into Rowan's waiting hands. Could see the Minnesota woodland scene fly past as her child-self fell again, and could smell raw earth packing her nostrils, her eyes, her wounds. Could see Demaris drowned again. And Lorn burned to ash again. Could see shadowy Crux-masters wielding blue lightning as they conducted a symphony of hidden corruption—greed, despair, and death—on dual worlds.

Dearth's hooded head lifted from beneath the dark, hidden under-earth and under-water, from beneath thick, metal-slicked mud, a coal-black cobra whose scales were diamonds and dust. Dearth Stared at her, at Rowan, at Veil. And at her home of Island-Not. Earth.

Alison shuddered as scenes of times past and places distant shuttered her senses. Something, someone, was reaching out of the dark water for her. No wonder she hated water. Had always hated water. Water was the link between the worlds that would ensure their mutual destruction.

17

ALISON came back to herself—or, more accurately, her self returned to her body—and to the sound of wind chimes. Their pleasant, random tinkling soothed her ruffled anxieties. She breathed deeply, only slowly becoming aware that what she heard was not wind chimes, but more like the chink of breaking glass.

Until she sat up abruptly, she did not know that she had been lying down, or that her eyes were closed. The darkness behind her lids was total. In the safety of that interior darkness, her mind opened slowly to memory.

She groaned softly. She had been catapulted onto a sort of mental merry-go-round, torn between dual times and places: the Island, where she had seen Demaris drown, had fallen on the Indian pot and scarred herself; and Veil, which she had fled last year after Pickle's terrible death via the Crux-masters' blue wands. A pot, twin to that on the Island, had broken after she left. Had that coincidence sealed some long-time link between herself and Veil?

She opened her eyes, not sure of where she would find herself.

First she turned toward the mysterious noise. The source was a narrow waterfall plinking—the sound like the very highest piano keys—over a naturally artistic arrangement of rocks.

Such clean, running water could not be evil, she reassured herself. Still water, stagnant water—lakes and ponds and swamps—disturbed her, not honest, moving freshwater that spewed out of faucets and hurtled off the tops of deserted mountains.

The late-afternoon sun warmed her. She felt lazy, immobile, unwilling to stir, as if she had been sick but was now well and was going to enjoy the sensation.

Her eyes roamed the sky for signs of corsairs, but it was as bare and as lucid as a cabochon jewel airbrushed onto the empyrean. Then her glance dropped to the foaming pool at the waterfall's foot.

Oh.

Rowan hunkered there, sanding rubrock over what had been his beard.

Rowan. Alison's eyes shut in hopeful denial. Surely she had not been carted here from the etherion pit like a swooning southern belle? By Rowan! It was to die.

She reached out as if to push the possibility, the unwanted memory, away, and her hand brushed a cool, curved surface.

The Cup lay beside her. She snatched her fingers back and pressed them to her scars. Not to the shirt covering her scars, but to the bare skin itself.

She found herself eyeing Rowan so accusingly that he looked up from his task, sensing her unspoken questions at once.

"You were stricken by a vicious fever beside the etherion pit," he explained. "You no longer saw or heard us, but wrenched the top of your garment open as if strangling."

Alison listened to the words, horrified. She had never dropped out of consciousness like that before, yet remembered a churning confusion.

Rowan went on as if relieved. Or embarrassed. "Your . . . quest-scars raged as angry red as poor little Boulder's legs, as if they, too, had been scalded by the deadly pit."

"But—" Alison's exploring fingertips felt no burns, no pain. Only the familiar ridges of the scars.

"Sage and I and the Littlelost carried you and Boulder away from there. Boulder was comfortable, but none of Sage's ointments, nor even the one you carry in the yellow . . . container, would rouse you from your senselessness. Not even the gray powder she used on Boulder."

"But I'm fine now, aren't I?"

Rowan's eyes lowered to the neck of her shirt, then looked quickly away. "I brought you here, away from the others, so the Littlelost should not be distressed by your strange state. Then I used the Cup to fetch water to wash your wounds."

Alison winced. No wonder she had awakened from dreams of drowning. Still . . . her fingers played over the familiar cicatrix. No heat, no hurt.

"The Cup washed away the crimson color at once," Rowan said. "Your . . . sleep seemed less troubled."

"Then the Cup still holds power! And you used it. It holds power for you!"

He frowned. "Perhaps." Turning back to the pool, he resumed the monotonous rub of rock on his cheeks and chin.

Alison pushed herself up on her knees. She felt shaky when she moved, as though her head—or the world—still spun. "Perhaps nothing, Rowan! The Cup banished a Crux-dream. Lucky for me that you thought of using it."

He glanced over at her, abashed. "I had no choice. It was like watching Lorn in the sway of the Crux again. I saw you writhing as if encompassed by a fire-agony, and watched you reveal what you always hide. And the scars that match mine grew so red, searing your skin like flames—" He shook his head, unable to speak further.

Something in his words surprised her more than the description of what had happened to her. "You . . . identified with me?"

"What does this 'identified' mean? I know who you are. I even admit *what* you are."

"It means that you shared my distress."

How often she had accused him of having no fellow-feeling, no compassion. But he had transcended that, perhaps because he had seen more than most Desmeynians.

His gaze was intent, even concerned. Alison felt a sudden awkwardness. "And, by the way, I don't always cover the marks," she added briskly. "In fact, at home in . . . Island-Not, I was growing impatient with hiding them. But when I came to

Veil again, it seemed that you were doing enough flaunting of scars for the two of us."

"Why should what I do affect what you do?"

"I don't know, and it shouldn't. Why are you shaving off your beard?"

"Shaving?"

"Removing."

The rubrock in his hand paused in its methodical circles. "After I saw you bare your scars, it struck me that I was hiding also—perhaps from the Crux, more likely from Desmeyne."

Alison absorbed this rather sophisticated insight in silence, studying his now-naked face. Rubrock was a marvel: no razor burn, no nicks. The only sign that Rowan had worn a beard at all was a slightly darker mask of suntanned skin around his eyes.

Alison touched again the open throat of her shirt, felt the familiar ridges her fingertips knew by heart. "I'll tell you what," she offered. "I'll forget buttoning up my quest-scars from now on if you'll ditch the beard."

"Ditch?"

"Leave it off."

"You didn't like it?" Rowan rocked back on his heels and sat down in surprise.

"No. I didn't."

"Why should what I look like matter to you?"

"We're Corsican twins, remember?" When he looked even more perplexed, she did not try to explain the old story about the separated Siamese twins who felt each other's pain; she simply laughed. "I have to look at you; you don't."

"I still don't understand—"

"Rowan, I don't know why I prefer you one way or another. Maybe with a beard and long hair you remind me of certain predictable types from my world—bikers, or hippies, I don't know! Besides, you look younger without it, and I always did like younger men," she added in mock-Mae West tones.

"Why?" he asked solemnly.

Alison rolled her eyes. Even if she had meant to flirt with this guy, he was as dense as Schwarzenegger in one of his alienbeefcake movies. She tried the truth. "They're supposed to have more stamina—*if* they're not celibate."

For a moment his eyes and face were blank. Then red slowly suffused his beardless cheeks, the soft flush of embarrassment. "Why should you care about these things in your world if such contact between men and women can be fatal?" he demanded.

"That's another reason I find celibacy such a stupid waste here in Veil, where you face no such threat. I told you: I don't think that keeping yourself apart from—and by implication, superior to—other people, of whatever sex, makes one better or wiser. Only lonelier."

The flush did not fade. Alison realized that Rowan had been set apart, lonely and tacitly superior to other human beings, since the age of eleven. He just hadn't known it until she had pointed it out.

"I'm sorry," she said quickly. "My point of view isn't valid for you. What does my opinion count?"

"You are the Taliswoman," he said slowly. "It must mean something."

She swallowed a smile at this painful acknowledgement of her perplexing value. He had conceded a lot for a Firemayne.

Rowan reached across the distance separating them, bridging the gap with his lean length, his shirt falling open to fully reveal the eerily identical pattern of his ritual scars—and more—then picked up the Cup.

Alison swallowed. Her throat was desert-dry. Must be the aftermath of Crux-fever.

He reclined on an elbow, turning the Cup slowly in one long-fingered hand. "I did feel something when I pulled it from your pack. And when I dipped the bowl into the mildwater, there came an invisible . . . sharpness snapping at my hand."

"Electricity," she murmured, having also felt it, that benign effervescence, that life force lapping at her fingertips.

"Then I . . . poured the water on your wound. Too much. It ran down into your garment—"

Alison was suddenly aware of damp cotton-polyester clinging to her skin, to her breasts. A flush began in her chest and surged up across the scar, a languid, warm, invisible blush, not the mystic fire that had apparently possessed the site earlier.

He continued, sounding as though he were caught in his own confusing fugue of feeling and memory, fear and wonder. "I had to drip the water upon my fingers, apply it like one of Sage's salves. I felt the heat of your searing, but before the fire could travel from my fingertips to my hand, the water cooled it. The fire-crimson died along the lines of your quest-scars. I felt as I did when I had the second-seeing in Desmeyne, the time you were endangered by Dearth. In two places at once."

"As I felt by the pit!"

"Both under assault and yet exalted."

"Yes, Rowan."

"Both weak and strong."

"Yes!"

"And not . . . alone any longer."

His fingers reached out to her, mimicking the action that had transported him to the portals of power, to the brink of the magic contained in the Cup.

Alison felt the lightest of touches along the pattern of her scars, softer than the brush of a butterfly wing. She caught her breath. No one had touched her there, not ever. Even a lover would diplomatically, exquisitely, ignore the disfigurement— in word and in deed.

Rowan touched her with wonder, with fellowship, with common confusion.

The flush on her chest rose into her cheeks. Her throat was a parched column in quest of the Cup and a stream of chill liquid flowing from it. Desire seized her like an old, once-snubbed friend.

He had not yet seen where his words and actions were leading; his own particular portions of strength and vulnerability blinded him. She reached up to push him away—there was still time—but her fingers moved unerringly toward his identical scars, brushing the swaying talismanic pouch aside.

Her touch ignited a similar conflagration; she saw desire flare in the earthy brown of his eyes.

"I don't know how men in your world—" he managed to mutter.

Their faces neared like suicidal ships in the night. Rowan's red hair expanded into an aura she could not see beyond. She felt him fumble to remove the pouch, and then her hands and mouth took its place. He fumbled further, this time at her clothing, as she did at his.

Alison again could feel the drumming throb of Heart of Earth beneath and within her body. The Cup, ignored, lay in the scant space between them. Rowan's long-denied hunger, vague and indiscriminatory, seared to a devouring flame when joined to his sudden, bewildering, specific appetite for her.

She felt it in his kiss. He was as enamored as she, flying in the face of all reason, all past history, all sense. The thought flickered once through her mind: how did the women of Desmeyne make love? And it spiraled away, irrelevant. She made love as the Taliswoman did, with courage and fear, tenderness and terrible power. Rowan met her in that intimate duel, until they crested like crashing waves and melded together. And apart. And quieted. Sobered. Began to search for ways to explain. To hunt for and don lost clothing while still tied in the knots of their abruptly ludicrous shyness. To say something to each other.

The barking of a dog intruded into the awkward silence of aftermath. Rambeau danced only feet away, forefeet braced, head lifted to howl. Even as Alison's mouth dropped open, the creature's thick white ruff of fur lifted. Blue lightning snapped at its fringes. Rowan looked away from the animal, toward where it stared. The Samoyed howled in paroxysms of sound. Of warning.

Rowan spoke first. "My . . . Lorn's . . . pouch!"

She saw the danger at once: an unimpressive lump upon the ground a few feet away. A mere toadstool of fabric, glowing now in a faint aura of blue.

"My God!" Alison scrambled toward it, while Rowan struggled to realize what was happening.

She cast herself full length, but missed the pouch even as the aura became a searing vertical rod. It widened to reveal the dark form of a Crux-master leering from the lurid, X-ray light as from a doorway, the pouch dangling from a skeletal hand.

The vision snapped shut, like a book, like a seam in the twilight.

For dusk had fallen, which was the only reason the blue light had become even briefly visible. Alison sobbed once.

"My fault," Rowan said in a dead voice.

She did not argue, although she should have, but merely pounded futile fists into the cooling earth. "No!" she muttered. "No. No."

18

"WE will get it back," the Taliswoman said.

She sounded calm and certain now, but Rowan did not look at her. He could not look himself in the face; why should hers be any easier to confront?

Distant blue flashed in the dimming mountain peaks—lightning, or Crux-strikes?

"We weren't attacked," she added. "All they wanted was the amulet."

"The Crux wanted Lorn a year ago; now they have him."

"Or," she added after a moment, "they have prevented you from using the amulet as the keystone of the next quest."

" 'They' have not. I have," he said ferociously. He meant to berate only himself, but the words hung in the air like a whip that had not quite descended on a chosen victim.

Alison lowered her head, then bent to the ground. Wings of short hair veiled her face. Rowan found her clothes plain to the point of ugliness, even for the dress of a man of Desmeyne. Her motions were always purposeful, sometimes strong, or even threatening. Not for her the Loftladies' exquisite trailing encumbrances or the hundred hesitant mannerisms they had developed to manipulate their finery and their veils—and their bedazzled male relatives and suitors—to best advantage.

Yet Rowan knew that sometime over the months and weeks of the past year, they had lost their power to enchant him. And she, the Taliswoman, had gained it.

"It is my fault," Rowan burst out. "I have broken my vow,

destroyed my quest before it has fairly started, given Veil over to the Crux-masters."

"No." She said the word calmly, and rose, holding something. "It was both our faults. And I'm still not so sure it was a fault."

"You had no vow."

"But I had—have—responsibility for my actions."

Rowan shook his head. "A man starts such things; a woman only sways to his greater needs. He must stop such things as well."

She came toward him. He would have recoiled had it not been cowardly. He was the cause of this calamity. She had done nothing seductive. Could it be that it was her very disdain for such things that attracted him? He could not understand his sudden hunger for the Taliswoman, but it was there. Still.

"Rowan. If you don't permit me to say 'yes,' you deprive me of the right to say 'no,' and I won't give that up for anything. I said 'yes.' I am as responsible as you for the loss of the amulet."

He was almost glad that they had this cursed theft to discuss; otherwise, he might blurt out his questions: why did their coming together create an intensity of feeling he had never felt before; why had she met him almost as a partner in her strange *taekwondo* rather than with the teasing, limp acquiescence of a manhood-mate? Why had she laughed softly after she had cried out and he had frozen, certain that his foreign ways had injured her?

She lifted the object she had picked up, holding it like a barrier between them, as well as a link. "The Cup. The Crux-master left the Cup."

"It no longer is empowered, as you suspected," he said bitterly. "The Crux-masters know our every motion and motivation, it seems."

She shook her head slowly. "But the Cup is warm all of a sudden, and the glow of more than twilight fills it. Look for yourself."

She thrust the object into his hands before he could object. A bone-warming heat suffused his chill fingers. His muscles loosened; his emotion-snarled thoughts quieted. The Cup's subtle circle of light radiated toward their faces, softening the self-doubt and pain. Rowan almost reached to touch her again, but mastered the impulse by reminding himself of his massive guilt: Lorn, lost again, because his faithless brother Rowan had dallied to break a vow that had withstood all temptations for more than two years. . . .

She spoke serenely, as if drugged by the subtle light. "The Cup is stone, but you are not. The Crux could have come in your sleep and taken the pouch."

"I was not asleep," he said tightly.

"No," she admitted in a tone that was almost amused.

"I will see that you are not outcast if you become—"

"I won't," she said quickly.

"How can you be sure?"

She lifted one arm, put the fingers of her other hand on a place halfway between elbow and shoulder. "Feel here."

He hesitated, fearful of doing anything that might ignite his feelings for her.

"Just here," she insisted, guiding his fingers to the spot.

He detected a welt in the skin, like a scar the size of his first finger joint. His hand recoiled.

"It doesn't hurt, but it does prevent me from becoming pregnant."

He winced at the word. "You are certain?"

"As certain as sunrise. Such devices are common in my world."

"Yet you cannot prevent this terrible plague you speak of, that makes people ill from . . . what we did?"

"Not yet. But we've always had plagues of one sort or another, and we keep trying to cure all of them."

"We must tell no one," he said suddenly.

"About what?"

"About . . . anything. Either thing."

"The others will notice your missing pouch."

"I will fashion another."

"But—"

"It is not to save face, but to maintain their faith in my quest."

"I don't think all is lost," she said. "The Cup feels heavy again, full. For some reason, it gains strength."

"I would give a thousand Cups for the tablet of clay containing Lorn's ashes. That the Crux should have it, hold it, perhaps destroy it—!"

"Shhh." Her hands were warmer than the Cup-heat as they closed over his. "Don't despise what you have while longing for what is lost. If the Crux has the amulet, we'll need every means possible to reclaim it."

"You truly believe that this is possible?"

"I believe that everything is possible. Haven't we just seen that?"

The reminder made him wrench away from the truth, from her, from his own impulses. Her hands fell as he moved; he was left holding the Cup alone. Heavy indeed, as she had said, yet its warmth offered a certain energy, if little comfort. He turned to hunt for his pack in the half-dark, at last finding it beside the waterfall.

His fingers continually worried his quest-scars, unshielded now. Already he missed the small, comforting weight of Lorn's remains, of the hope it embodied.

"Don't put the Cup away." Alison spoke across the dimming distance. "We can use it as a lantern to guide us back to the others." She was, as always, practical.

A fire surrounded by familiar faces greeted them.

"She is better now?" an anxious Littlelost voice spoke out.

Rowan was startled. Of course. They last remembered Alison gripped by a strange swoon.

"Yes," she said cheerily, "I'm better. And hungry. What magic has Sage performed for our dinner?"

With relief, Rowan watched Alison join the others. He felt a stiff tension in her presence. Though she did not accuse him of anything, he felt that she might do so at any moment. Women took such events as this seriously: in Desmeyne, if it did not follow marriage, it would quickly lead to it, were the girl of good lineage. He wondered how Darnellyne would react to this turn of events, then flushed in the dark for thinking of her in such a context.

He was passed a mug filled with a thick, spiced stew of pomma and jerky. Sage employed a free hand with her herbal potions nowadays. The high seasoning made him cough, but he ate the food despite it, eventually enjoying the warmth that coursed through his chilled frame. Fear and misery receded a bit.

Beside his foot, his pack lay pregnant with possibility, holding the Cup again. Was the Taliswoman right? Did the vessel respond to him? He would investigate the question on his own. He dare trust no one with the burden of his problems, especially not her. Not now.

She sat across the fire, smiling amid a circle of Littlelost as if nothing had happened. How could she forget so soon? Or behave as if she had? Was it so common an occurrence in her world? If she bore a device to prevent the consequences of such acts, then surely the acts must be not unusual. Casual. Like himself with Triss before he had taken his vow. The notion was . . . irritating. If he must pay so high a price for the act—the loss of his self-respect, his reputation as quest-heir if news of his vow-breaking should spread—how unfair that it meant so little to her, that she should lose so little by it! Indeed, Triss in the village would no doubt have considered it a triumph to tease a sworn quest-heir from his celibacy. Perhaps Alison had some similar notion.

Sage rose, a lumpish silhouette against the flames of their fire, burning high to warm those gathered around.

"The Sylvin women left us this." She flourished a flask. "First taste to the Taliswoman, who fell so ill."

"No, really," Alison demurred. "I feel fine—now."

Rowan understood her embarrassed protest; she had hardly behaved in the least ill not an hour before.

Sage bent to pour the libation into Alison's cup anyway. The Taliswoman drank, then lowered the cup from her lips. "Whew. Headier stuff than Char. No wonder the Sylvins fly."

"Stronger than Char?" Sage turned to face Rowan in the

dark beyond the firelight as if she saw him perfectly well, knew everything about him. "We will test it on a Desmeynian."

His mug was still half full of Sage's stew. His appetite was uncertain tonight, but he could use the bracing effect of Char. He dug in his pack, knuckles brushing the cold, alien metal of the Taliswoman's weapon—he had forgotten he had it—before his fingers closed on the Cup's tepid stem, still vaguely warm.

He lifted the vessel to Sage. It shone in the firelight, cabochon jewels winking like stars through Desmeyne's rock-crystal roof. As Sage poured, something pale like liquid starlight streamed into the bowl.

Rowan tasted it, and his limbs tingled all the way to the extremities. A profound peace swathed his senses. He quaffed deeper and felt the night wind warm even as the fire sank lower.

Across from him, the fading flames painted vivid highlights in the midnight of Alison's hair. He remembered drowning in her eyes, as ambiguously blue-green as pooling mildwater. He wondered what color the Sylvins' libation was in daylight. Blue perhaps, like the sky they soared upon.

Sage offered the Littlelost some of the Sylvin brew, but they shook their ragged heads. They had never developed a taste for such diversions. The fire finally blurred to a red-gold aura. The Littlelost stole away to sleep, perhaps to engage in the same unthinkable things he had. He frowned. Something wrong with his world. All not what it seemed, had never been what it seemed. The Cup's smooth stone rim soothed him. Sylvin liquor softened his panic. He remembered feeling the full weight of his pain, then shifting it onto another. He remembered most distinctly not being alone.

"Potent." Sage nodded at Rowan's slumped form just visible across the dying embers. Alison, who had been lost in her own musings, looked over. The Cup lay beside him, its glow illuminating him like a night-light.

She nodded in turn. "He needed a cup of forgetfulness.

Nepenthe, we call it in my world. What do the Sylvins name this?"

"Zurr. Does the Cup still turn liquors into aphrodisiacs?" Sage asked suddenly.

Alison started. "I don't know. Ask the man who drank from it."

Sage looked across the darkness. "I will. In the morning."

In the morning Rowan came straight to Sage with a question of his own. "You are a mistress of herbs, old woman," he began uneasily.

"I know you despise such things," Sage returned.

"Yes. But have you ever found a potion that will—"

Sage's bushy yellow-white eyebrows lifted.

Rowan flushed "—that will discourage certain impulses?" he finished.

"Certain impulses? Of what sort?"

Rowan gritted his teeth.

"Ah," said Sage.

Rowan turned to leave.

Sage grasped his arm. "Forgive me. I forgot the vow that you have been living with. I am afraid that no herb I have found in Veil will obtain the result you wish. Neither have I found one that will have the opposite effect. It appears that we are doomed to handle such matters with our own resources."

"Are you laughing at me, old woman?" Rowan asked with some sharpness.

Sage smiled until her wrinkled face took on the texture of age-softened lace. "Young Rowan, what you believe to be a difficulty would be a boon to most men. I can tell you only one thing: do not drink liquor-laden beverages from the Cup. It is, after all, a Cup of Earth. It will enhance fruitful inclinations."

Rowan stood stock still. "Even Char?"

Sage nodded. "Especially Char."

"That may explain *her* odd behavior a year ago, but no one drank from the Cup when—" He glared at Sage as if she had been eavesdropping. "I will thank you to keep my request to yourself."

"Oh, indeed," she said with a mock-subservient bow.

"And you can keep the Sylvin brew to yourself in the future as well," he added, then left her abruptly.

The airborne glitter of a single etherion corsair arrived before anyone had finished a breakfast of pomma and berries. It dipped low above the meadow, its wings almost brushing the pine tops that fringed the forest.

Barely had the Littlelost thrown themselves upon the anchor line than the Sylvin pilot was shimmying down the tether. She fluted excitedly, and unintelligibly, at the gathering crowd: the Littlelost, Sage, Alison and, lastly, Rowan.

Alison took the mug from her pack, ran to dip it in the running water, and returned it to the flyer, Lenaree. The tiny creature swallowed the contents at one gulp, then turned to address them again. This time her words fell as sharply as cracked ice, in syllables all could understand.

"Takers. Massing on the next mountain. Halflings, gathering by the score. Even we Sylvins had no notion that Veil hosted so many wandering Halflings. Our flyers report Crux-fire circling the peaks until the night sky is rent to shreds." She panted from her urgency. "We cannot understand why—"

Rowan and Alison exchanged a grim, knowing glance. The Crux had the talisman and was mobilizing its powers.

Sage spoke slowly. "The Littlelost have found a gigantic etherion pit—"

"Taker-harvested, no doubt," Lenaree said.

Sage's venerable head shook. "No. Untouched."

The Sylvin woman straightened, seeming to gain in stature. "Untouched? How . . . gigantic?"

Plume, a shy presence at her side, tugged on a scarf. "I will show."

The two went off together: tiny woman and tiny childlike woman.

"They don't seem real," Alison mused.

Sage eyed her. "Does Veil?"

Alison glanced at Rowan, then looked away. He had seemed quite real yesterday.

The Sylvin and the Littlelost returned at bounding, exuberant speed. "Untouched!" confirmed the Sylvin flyer. "I must tell the others. The Hammerhands are already coming to help you against the Takers and Halflings, so all will be ready—" She sprang up the metal tether as lightly as a grasshopper.

"Ready for what?" Alison asked.

Smiling, the tiny woman sped up the swaying chain. The Littlelost dropped away and the corsair rose, its fragile metallic wing joints working like the sails of a China clipper.

"We must stay here," Sage declared, and would say no more.

Alison ached to tell her of the loss of Rowan's talisman—but to do so would reveal the awkward facts about how and when it had vanished, and came to be off of Rowan's neck. No wonder Rowan had acted so prickly, since. To have lost something he had literally defended with his own neck, while doing something he was sworn not to do. . . .

Alison sat down on a rock amid swaying grass and brooded. Maybe Rowan was disturbed over what had happened for other than heroic reasons. Maybe she didn't measure up to the pampered Loftladies. She flinched again, reminded of Darnellyne's rotting face. She had stolen Dar's own true love-to-be, though Rowan hadn't been enthusiastic about that role lately. Well, he didn't act too enthusiastic about his new role, either.

Something grabbed her foot, shook it, and bit down.

"Ow!"

A wolf-Samoyed pup braced its tiny fluffy feet and pulled back, growling fiercely.

She pried its clamped jaws apart and lifted it onto her lap, a pound of fuzzy, wriggling wonder. "Hey, you want to play rough?" But of course it did, because it would grow up in a rough world. Maybe a world controlled by the Crux. Why? To what end? She had seen enough career jockeying at the newspaper to know that some people just have to control situations and other people for the heck of it, but where did the Crux get its electric-blue power? Who lay behind those spooky manifestations? What did "they" really want?

She had come a far way from her usual life in Minnesota. Here, she had to puzzle out questions of worldwide control and personal relations at the same time. Lucky girl. And lucky that a promising but slow-developing love affair three years ago had persuaded her to get a contraceptive implant. Alison smiled, remembering Rowan's face when he had touched the device. Whether he had looked relieved or horrified was a dead heat.

The pup lay on her lap, happily gnawing her forefinger with its sharp white teeth.

Unless— Didn't she know by now that things didn't work in Veil the way they should? Rambeau, the neutered dog, had fathered pups here. Proof positive gamboled in her lap. Maybe she could— Alison began counting backwards, but time did not run in tune here. Golly, she could be in for more than she thought. If the Veilians were dismayed by a female Talis-woman, what would they think of a *pregnant* one? And if she got back to Minnesota—when, *when* she got back—how could she explain? Ouch.

The pup was gnawing fiercely, as if its little life depended on it, and of course it did. Alison's life depended on other, less primal things. One of them, she began to see, had red hair and an attitude.

19

THUMP, thump, thump. The ground trembled slightly; perhaps even the grasses leaned away from the oncoming thrum.

At first the sound was a dull, rhythmic growl that set the Slinkers keening in the broad daylight. Then it grew louder. Finally it became the relentless drumming of a headache.

Rowan rose and paced, uneasy at a threat he could hear but not see. Equally puzzled, the Slinkers roamed the camp perimeter, growling to themselves like cranky old men. The two women and the Littlelost took the noise in better stride: wait and see, they thought. Surely these were the promised Hammerhands coming. Alison figured that anybody called "Hammerhands" was good to have on their side.

The Hammerhands sang as they came. And not so much sang as chanted, chanted deep, like earthquakes and bass electric guitars, chanted like running water underneath the ground, like pulsing power lines.

Alison also rose and began to pace, but she and Rowan paced in different directions, and they did not look at one another.

The oncomers' heads became visible first: haystack hummocks the colors of rock—gray and browns—jostling over the horizon of grass and vagrant wind. Rambeau flashed toward them, a weaving white form nipping at sound and motion, and barking. Silent Slinkers followed him.

The Hammerhands' shoulders were as wide as rivers, their thighs as thick as trees. Onward they marched, not in formation, but in unity: as an elemental force, as mountains move, unseen but effective.

Rowan retrieved his staff. Alison kept her joints loose, her muscles flexed. Pups hid behind the Littlelost, who in turn massed behind Sage.

Hammerhands crested the last rise and marched down the hill, trampling grass with the indifference of steamrollers. Men muscled like mastodons, leather-kilted, booted; otherwise bare. Hairy and hard and about eight feet tall. Men of steel in a world without Kryptonite.

Alison edged nearer to Sage. "What controls these people? They could stomp all over us."

Sage watched them with a rueful nostalgia. "They are the last of their kind, and the only ones who control them are the Sylvins."

"Those airborne pipsqueaks influence these guys?"

"Sheer power is often harnessed by finesse. You might bear that in mind in your own circumstances." Sage looked slyly at Alison, then advanced to meet that muscular wall of monotone chanting.

The Hammerhands stopped in a mass. They stood quivering with the very tension of their arrested motion, stolid and potent and waiting. At each of their belts, like six-guns, hung enormous hammers, the hafts long enough to brush the sides of their knees.

Sage shuffled forward, a humble and frail figure to confront the massed presence. She spoke to the Hammerhands, at too great a distance to be overheard.

Alison counted only fifteen of the giants, but they seemed like fifty. Rowan came to her side, his eyes on these newcomers as alien to him as to her.

"What undreamed-of beings dwell in Veil—" he began.

"Sage says they're friendly."

"Why have they never stepped forward to compete for the Cup at a Wellsunging?"

"Perhaps they are too remote, both from that custom and in distance. The Sylvins fly hither and yon in a wink, but these, er, men must have marched for a long time if their lands are near the Rookeries and the Quarter of the Four Winds."

"How vast is Veil then?" Rowan spoke in awestruck inquiry.

"Bigger than we think." She found herself smiling into the earth-brown eyes that had turned to her.

"I begin to feel as you must have felt on first finding yourself here," he admitted, "but this is my land."

"No, Rowan, it isn't."

He was about to debate her, but then looked again at the Hammerhands.

"This land isn't my land, either," she added gently, "and it's vaster and stranger than either of us ever imagined."

One huge man stepped forward from the rest and accompanied Sage toward Alison and the others, slowing his stride to baby steps so he wouldn't outwalk the old wisewoman.

Alison recognized the grave, unsmiling courtesy of such an adjustment. "Gentle giants," she murmured.

Rowan was not won over. "Gentle giants will do us no good against the Crux."

"Perhaps you can practice your *taekwondo* on them. Facing a larger opponent might do you good."

"This *taekwondo* of yours will be useless against the Crux."

"But it would work against Takers and these Halflings we hear of."

He shrugged, dubious, and moved a stride away from her, as if irked to be reminded of their practice sessions by the fateful waterfall.

Alison shook her head. Rowan was apparently going to make *not* being celibate as big an issue as he had his celibacy. That was his business; she knew better than to apologize for having hormones.

The ill-matched pair, Sage and the Hammerhand, now approached not Alison and Rowan, but the Littlelost, who stirred uneasily at the arrival of one so like the brutal Takers, only bigger.

Sage reached a hand for one Littlelost in particular: Plume.

The other Littlelost shrank back. Plume, however, came forward in perfect trust. The Hammerhand went carefully down on one knee and held out a hand on which she could have ridden. Like a fairy considering alighting on a particularly large and perhaps loathsome toadstool, Plume hesitated before the giant man.

He spoke to her, not in a language Alison recognized, except that the syllables seemed the guttural equivalent of the Sylvins' native fluting. Plume frowned and looked down at the massive foot in front of her. When she looked up again, calmly, she replied with a Sylvin trill.

More of the slender Sylvin Littlelost edged forward from their safe distance, listening. One lifted a head to the sky and warbled a single Sylvin syllable. The others gathered closer, making a small mob of twelve, warbling eagerly in soprano excitement. Then some of the Littlelost moved closer, sturdy-limbed lads who reminded Alison of chunky, preteen twelve-year-olds who needed to watch their hot-dog consumption.

She reached for Rowan's arm to attract his attention. "Hammerhands!" she told him excitedly. "Hammerhands number among the Littlelost you freed most recently. As well as Sylvins. Only older, of course, than they look."

"Much older." Rowan frowned. "They are indeed minia-tures of the adults of their kind.

"But how did their children become Littlelost?" Rowan asked. "I have noticed no birth-banes among them."

"Would you recognize the birth-banes of a foreign kind? What may be a birth-bane to one people may be a birth-benefit to another. Surely any child could wander into an earthgall pit."

Littlelost now surrounded the kneeling Hammerhand. Syl-vins perched on his knee and shoulder, small Hammerhands pulled on his elbows and beard. The other Littlelost, sharing the quaver of recognition and reunion, gathered around as if to warm themselves at the others' joy.

Sage left the jubilant circle and hobbled over to Rowan and Alison. The old woman was grinning so widely she looked like a wizened child herself.

"Old puzzles solved; new puzzles presented. But we need

not worry. The Hammerhands will work with us to defeat the Crux, and we will work with them."

"We?" Alison inquired.

Sage nodded. "Yes, Taliswoman. And work it will be. The Sylvins and Hammerhands report that the Crux has harvested all the etherion to be found, forcing the craft that need repair to the ground. Without Sylvins aloft to watch our world, the Crux can keep its activities even more secret."

The ground vibrated as the waiting Hammerhands, drawn at last to the strange assembly, joined their brother. In moments the Hammerhands and a swarm of excited Littlelost were thundering down the hill toward the woods . . . and the sinister etherion pit.

"Sage!" Alison regarded the wisewoman's beaming face with disbelief. "You can't mean that the Littlelost will skim etherion off that foul pit!"

Rowan tensed beside her. "What of my quest to the Axletree? We will be mired here for days. And I did not free the Littlelost for more servitude."

"Your quest will keep." Sage spoke swiftly, her words reining Rowan more effectively than physical force. "You need Sylvin and Hammerhand aid on the long journey to their lands—and beyond. Nothing will earn their gratitude more than your patience now, given this vast supply of the etherion they crave as much as air. As for the Littlelost, their servitude will be utter if the Crux prevails. They want to help the Hammerhands, and only the Hammerhands can help them harvest the metal without being borne away by handling so much of it."

"A perfect partnership," Alison said slowly, "of opposite types and needs." She turned to Rowan. "Like Rowan and myself."

Even he heard the laughter in her voice, and his fists unclenched. "I hate to think of them laboring over that stink, even willingly." He looked at Sage, curious. "Why did they accept the Hammerhands so quickly? Don't they have a horror of large men? And the Hammerhands are the largest men I have ever seen."

"People larger than they have not been kind," Sage agreed, "but they accepted the Hammerhands because the Hammerhands accepted them. Felard, the first to step forward, used the Hammerhand-Sylvin tongue of concordance. Some of the Sylvin and Hammerhand Littlelost found their earliest memories of the language returning. Once they saw that they had those few words in common, cooperation banished fear and old hatreds." Sage moved toward the woods. "I will see how their plans come."

As the old woman moved away, Rowan turned slowly toward Alison. "That kind of cooperation is what you hoped to accomplish by insisting that my father meet with the Earth-Eaters?"

She nodded. "If Dusk and the Firemayne discover so much as one common memory, that will go far to reconcile their kinds."

"She was, according to the story you forced from my mother, a mere infant at the time of her . . . loss. What would she remember?"

Alison sighed and shook her head simultaneously, a gesture meant to banish mental weariness. "I don't know. Maybe your father will recognize something of himself in her."

"You dream," Rowan said.

"Don't you?"

"Once I dreamed of winning the Cup and wedding Darnellyne. Now I have nightmares of losing the amulet and watching Lorn die."

"Rowan, you have the Cup. Perhaps you should concentrate on what you have rather than on what you don't have."

"You have said this before."

She nodded. "It's called positive thinking."

"Then, by that philosophy, I should better direct my attention to you than in the direction of Desmeyne." A gleam warmed his eyes, part tease, and part challenge.

This time Alison glanced away. She did not want to cause anyone a bad conscience, most of all, Rowan. But if he could begin to laugh at their mutual indiscretion, that would be a big step toward forgiving himself. And her.

* * *

At sunset, a fleet of etherion corsairs appeared like swallows in the notch of the mountains.

Alison watched the flotilla's swift, silhouetted approach, admiring the efficiencies of nature, human beings, or possibly magic. From this distance, the flyers appeared as delicate as their pilots.

Soon the gliding shadows hovered directly above the darkening mountain meadow. A single Hammerhand could hold the cast tethers of two corsairs and, standing with his arms flung wide, keep the craft from butting their wide, fragile wings.

Sylvins slid down the supple chains, each greeting an individual Hammerhand. The Hammerhand and Sylvin Littlelost gravitated to the arriving flyers, lending the resulting scene the look of a family reunion.

The watchers smiled: Sage, Alison, Rowan, the other Littlelost. Obviously, the Sylvins and Hammerhands thought much of each other, and their joy at having reclaimed their own Littlelost was so transparent that Rowan looked thoughtful through his smile. Such a successful reunion seemed unlikely for Desmeyne and the Earth-Eaters, even for Desmeyne and its alienated Littlelost.

Reunited Hammerhands grew hearty as such massive men can, eagerly telling the women of the rich pit-skim of etherion at their command.

The evening meal involved much passing around of foreign food; the Hammerhands traveled with waist-hung sacks of what Alison welcomed as real food and Rowan tried with customary Desmeynian caution. There was bread with a tough, unbreakable crust, and pungent cheese. Sylvin Zurr—which, like its makers, seemed to go a long way with a little bit—washed down the bread and cheese delightfully.

Then the Slinkers emerged from the woods, where they had been guarding the etherion pit, all except Rambeau, who had been gone for several hours.

Alison was relieved to see his familiar form among the Slinkers ghosting through the twilight toward the fire. She whistled, and Beau threaded through the sprawling ranks of Littlelost to her side.

"Spirit Slinker!" The words came deep and loud, full of angry distrust. A horrified Hammerhand was standing backlit by the firelight, his silhouetted hammer raised to strike.

Beau stopped and growled a soft warning.

"Mine!" Alison said quickly, standing to identify herself.

The Hammerhand brandished his weapon. "Slinkers steal souls."

Rambeau growled at the hostility hitting him like a wave, growled and advanced, barking.

The Hammerhand had never heard a Slinker bark. He sprang forward. Even as Alison darted after Beau, she heard someone scrabbling swiftly behind her, and then Rowan hurled himself between the advancing Hammerhand and Rambeau, his back to the dog, no staff in his hand. He had set his one weapon aside before supper.

Alison watched, horrified. Rowan had struck her as a tall man until she'd seen a Hammerhand. He had never been bulky, and Rambeau in full defensive stance was too much dog to trust one's back to. Rambeau smelled threat; he had no particular obligation to defend this man who stood between him and the object of his fury. Moreover, the dog's bristling ruff showed an aura of Crux-blue.

But Rowan was ignoring the dog. He swayed back and forth before the Hammerhand in a hypnotic way meant to confuse an opponent. Alison winced to remember her jest that Rowan should practice his new knowledge on an opponent bigger than himself. She hadn't meant a superstitious giant armed with the world's—any world's—biggest sledgehammer.

She started forward, trying to decide if she should insert herself between Rowan and the Hammerhand, or between Rowan and Rambeau.

A hand clutched her wrist. "You have taught him; now let him learn that you taught true."

"Sage, he's not ready for this. And I can't answer for Rambeau—"

"Dog will not hurt him. He defends Dog, as he has come to

defend Littlelost. Do not deny him. If you want him to believe you on other matters, you must let him test the truth of your *taekwondo*."

"Other matters? Sage, do you know—"

The wisewoman released her grip. "It is my lot to know more than I tell. A most unpleasant position to be in. You are the Taliswoman, but he is the Talisman. Let him be."

Alison threw up her hands. What was one misplaced dog, one quest-hero, to the indiscriminatory fury of a crazed Hammerhand? But both Rambeau and Rowan were equipped to defend themselves. Still, even if Rowan had forgotten about the revolver he had taken from her and stowed in his pack so long ago, it might yet be there. One shot in the dark would grab everybody's attention.

In a strange, slightly warped way, the scene repeated the Takers' attack in the Island woods. Then Rambeau had sprung to her defense at great risk. Now Rambeau was threatened, and Rowan leaped to his aid. Odd.

Sage's tug on her arm pulled Alison back into a sitting position. At least she had brought that tube of cortisone cream along; man and dog might need it.

The Hammerhand swayed stolidly to match Rowan's hypnotic movements. His eyes were confused, but his hammer never lowered. This man was used to hitting what he aimed at.

"Spirit Slinker," the Hammerhand repeated. Strange to hear fear in the voice of a man so huge. That made him all the more dangerous. "Stand aside."

"No. The animal is tame, like mildwater."

"Tame? It spits Crux-fire and death. A Spirit Slinker can steal your soul; you will dwell forever with the People of the Horizon."

Rowan kept his arms wide, his gestures calming, poised to leap in any direction, fling out any limb, hit any opportune part of his adversary. So far, so good, Alison thought, feeling a flicker of pride. Oh, but one hammer stroke . . .

The men circled in the light thrown by the fire, Rowan looking like a Littlelost compared to the Hammerhand. Alison heard distressed murmurs: the Littlelost, rooting for Rowan but not wanting the Hammerhand injured, and they loved Beau as Alison did. They wanted no one hurt.

Alison's fingers intertwined prayerfully. She hated being on the sidelines, but Sage was right. Rowan had a right to fight for what he believed in, and right now that was Alison's dog, itself become one of the Slinkers that he, too, had feared and despised.

"The animal is one of us," Rowan said, watching the Hammerhand.

The Hammerhand frowned. Once stirred to action, it seemed he had little facility for changing his mind. Rambeau was an anomaly, and he feared anything different. And . . . the Crux was everywhere. He lifted his massive hammer and brought it down in a powerful swoop toward Rowan's head.

A blur of scarlet. The hammer blow had hit air, separating flying strands of long red hair as the wind does. Rowan was behind the Hammerhand, and dancing closer. His leg struck out in a kick that connected with the Hammerhand's elbow.

The strike shook the mighty form but did not dislodge the Hammerhand's grip upon his namesake weapon.

Rowan was dancing before the dazed, suspicious eyes again. "This is not a Slinker, but a dog," he said, parroting Alison's party line. "There is a difference."

As if to argue, Rambeau growled fiercely, shaking his ruff until the blue sparks flew. Alison moaned and buried her face in her hands again. Would neither Dog nor Man modify his nature to common sense?

A thin fluting wafted over the contested clearing, a Sylvin urging reason. She was as impalpable as if she had been one of the Horizon-weft. When two strong men stand face to face, et cetera . . . Alison cursed the biological destiny of testosterone.

A sudden inrushing, a pewter-pale hammer head slicing the fire-lit darkness, a flash of flying red hair. Rowan dancing behind, spinning, kicking the Hammerhand in the kidneys. Even a Hammerhand could feel that. He did. He lurched, fell to one knee. Rowan catapulted by with a karate chop (okay, she wasn't a purist; what works, works) to a forearm the size of a leg of beef. The hammer dropped free from nerveless fingers, dashing itself into Mother Earth with a *thump* that made every ear within hearing ring.

Rambeau skittered backward, barking. His ruff no longer radiated unearthly light. A Sylvin woman ran to the fallen Hammerhand. Rowan straightened in the clearing . . . and sought Alison's eyes. She nodded. An insufficient gesture, but all she had left in her.

There were "Oohs" and "Ahs" from the watching Littlelost, a twittering among the massed Sylvin flyers, a bass grumble from the other Hammerhands. All had one thing in common: stunned respect for a power so seemingly out of proportion to its wielder. A warm wave of satisfaction washed over Alison. She had never taught anyone anything before, had never watched a pupil startle and impress an audience, however inadvertently.

Beau came waggle-tailing over, sorry for having had to establish his territory, his dogness . . . and for something else less definable, something that could be dangerous. Littlelost surrounded them both, Rime clasping her arms around Beau's neck and silently laying her pale head on his paler ruff.

No one comforted Rowan, because he had won, after all, and wasn't that enough? It wasn't, but the only one who knew that was Alison. Her eyes met his. This time he nodded.

20

ODDLY enough, Rowan's defeat of the Hammerhand acted as a kind of social glue for the patchwork party. Hammerhands were not used to being vanquished with such apparent ease. Rowan now served as a focus for everyone's awe. Even the Littlelost, who had reason to be grateful to him, regarded Rowan with new respect.

He had performed as a quest-heir should—quickly and decisively—without the aid of even the most modest weapon. After leveling the Hammerhand, he explained slowly and firmly that the Slinker pack were also members of the alliance; that they would not attack those they had chosen to guide and guard; that Rambeau was the Taliswoman's personal Slinker, and no soul-thief from the People of the Horizon.

Heavy Hammerhand heads nodded soberly, accepting reproof. They had been impulsive and—Alison smiled to hear Rowan say it—prejudiced unjustly against those they did not know.

As a parting shot, Rowan pointed grandly to Beau, basking in the firelight next to Alison and panting amiably.

Hammerhands were easy to abash. The Sylvins, being aerial creatures, had always had little fear of ground-runners like Slinkers. Peace was renewed, and the group had a clear leader in Rowan. Alison wondered what would have happened if she had beat him to Beau's defense. Would she have defeated the Hammerhand? Rowan's larger size could have been an advantage against so huge an opponent. She would never know, because it hadn't happened that way. That was history for you.

Sage passed the Sylvin Zurr again as the action of the evening turned to talk.

"By what magic did you defeat Thorm?" one of the Hammerhands asked Rowan.

Alison saw Rowan wrestle with honesty and the urge to bedazzle a willing audience. Then he turned toward her. "The Taliswoman taught me such tricks," he said. "Perhaps she can instruct you as well."

"Ah, they're a bit oversized for one-on-one practice rounds," she responded. "Perhaps a class—"

" 'Class'?" the Hammerhands droned in a chorus.

"All at once," she explained.

Their bushy eyebrows rose. "She must be a true Taliswoman to contemplate such a mission."

"They say"—Thorm nodded to the Sylvins—"that you bear the marks of a quest-heir, though you come from another place. No woman of Veil has ever been so honored."

"I am not of Veil," Alison said in public for the first time.

She stood. Since the unpremeditated interlude with Rowan, she had covered her scars again. Rightly or wrongly, she felt that they had instigated that rash and regrettable union, but she would bare them now.

She undid her top three shirt buttons. The Hammerhands shambled upright and came to bend their huge heads down and peer at her collarbones. Alison felt like a tattooed lady on parade.

The Sylvins and Littlelost crowded around, gazing up raptly, nodding in mute solemnity. Few in Veil beyond Rowan and Sage knew of her singular status.

When everyone sat down again, they radiated the air of people who had glimpsed a vague purpose and were ready to dedicate themselves to it. In that way they were no different from the Slinkers, who had escorted Rowan and Alison and the Littlelost for no more apparent reason than to be ready if needed.

Rowan was still standing. "The need will come," he said, "for all willing to align themselves against the Crux. What more can the Sylvins and Hammerhands tell of that foul influence? We in Desmeyne have learned that the Crux has delved beneath our very foundations, engaging in trade with the Earth-Eaters who live below."

"The Crux has lifted its ambitions aloft as well," said Lenaree. "Alien skimmers we had seen in the distance now draw near to strike us with the cold fire of their blue bolts."

"What of the Littlelost?" Rowan asked. "You have labored in the etherion pits. Have the Crux-masters shown themselves there?"

Small heads shook.

"Never?" Rowan repeated.

"Never," Twist answered. "We have seen only T-t-takers."

"And Halflings," Wisp, a recently released Littlelost, added ominously.

At those words, frowns of pain passed over the faces of Hammerhand and Sylvin alike.

Alison found it timely to ask questions of her own, hoping that Rowan would not resent the intrusion. "You warn us against these Halflings, yet they are part of you. And these Littlelost Sylvins and Hammerhands . . . you were astounded to find them, yet you have not asked one question about the Littlelost, or why your long-lost children are among them."

Lenaree rose and walked over to Alison. Standing, she could look down on her. She dropped her eyes to the quest-scars. "You never told us you were the Taliswoman. Some things we keep hidden near our hearts. The Halflings are our sorrow. That they have apparently been Crux-corrupted is an even greater heartbreak."

"How has this happened?" Alison asked with puzzled sympathy. "When? Why?"

"You must go back many tens of years, almost beyond memory, to our first uniting with the Hammerhands. I cannot even tell you how our kind discovered etherion and sought to fly with it. Nor how we learned that the Hammerhands were the only people with the strength to handle it, to hold it down and pound it into the shapes that sustain we Sylvins in the air."

"Why did you wish to fly?" Rowan asked, sounding amazed.

Lenaree's answer sounded equally surprised. "Because we

saw that we could. Sylvins are small and light. Although etherion is buoyant, the size of a corsair required to lift a Hammerhand's weight would be immense. We enjoy it, Rowan
Firemayne, as you may enjoy some pleasure known only
to you."

Alison held her breath. That comment cut too close to
Rowan's recent fall from grace. She leaped into the awkward
pause with a reporter's brash need to know. "You see things,
don't you, from aloft? You monitor your world, unbeknownst
to most. Why, then, were the first Littlelost I found so frightened of the etherion coursers we saw near the woods? And
those craft dove at us."

"Those could not have been Sylvin flyers," a Hammerhand
announced angrily in a voice as deep as a bass drum, "but
Crux-craft magically made from this very etherion and used to
hunt renegade Littlelost, and to transport the stolen etherion
far away, where Sylvin flyers can never find it."

Alison nodded. The story was not so unusual for all its
exotic trappings: forbidden traffic in a fabulous substance that
gave its possessors the power to fly. She considered cocaine,
and saw that the Crux was an outside power, motivated by
greed to engage in a war of supply and demand with a far less
sophisticated native population.

"What of their magic?" she asked next. "The way they come
and go in rods of light, the blue lightning they hurl? Is there
anything in Veil like it?"

Lenaree did not answer her, but Felard the Hammerhand
did. "Nothing," he said in tones so ringing that some of the
Littlelost clapped hands to ears. "Only the People of the Horizon are that insubstantial, but they always keep to the cloudy
circle on the rim of things. These Crux-vermin come amongst
us like Spirit Slinkers. They hide behind their wands of light,
pervert the mindless dwellers of deep and remote places to
their purposes, how I cannot say."

To Alison's surprise, Rowan answered the Hammerhand.
"We have long lived with the despised Earth-Eaters beneath
Desmeyne controlling our supply of precious metals and min-
erals, forcing us to bargain with them. We did it, and we

learned to our dismay only recently that the Crux-masters, too, trade with these same Earth-Eaters, and more, make themselves at home in their vile subterranean realm. Crux-masters! At the very roots of Desmeyne!"

His outrage drew sympathetic murmurs from the Sylvins and Hammerhands; given their opposite vocal ranges, the effect was much like an a cappella chorus, melodic and impressive.

"But—" Rowan's voice—and he had a fine, expressive one; Alison had always granted him that—rang above the chorus. "Our weakness was in ourselves, in Desmeynians. Some believe that the Earth-Eaters were our own unwanted, driven below to live interminable lives of slow dissolution, hating us, hating themselves. Whatever the case, when the Crux-masters came, they had ready-made allies."

Alison almost applauded. The moment when Rowan finished was stretched out on a rack of silence.

"It is true," a Hammerhand said gruffly, no music in his voice but mourning. "We, too, created our own outcasts. Though the Halflings declared themselves separate, they should never have been, would never have been had not Sylvins and Hammerhands come together despite the rules of their kind."

"The Halflings combined elements of both parents. Why hate their creators?" Alison wondered.

Rowan answered for the others. "I think I see. The Halflings were neither one nor the other. They were useless. Too heavy to soar, too light to shape ringing metal. Bitterness was their only portion. That the Crux found, and used."

The Sylvins and Hammerhands murmured sad agreement.

"So." Alison turned to the Littlelost faces shining in the firelight. "These . . . miniaturized Hammerhands and Sylvins we have found. Ancient children who . . . what? Were lost to the earthgall pits? They can fly, both male and female. They are small and light enough to gather etherion for the Crux, after all. That's why you were so excited to find them. They were frozen in size."

"But can they . . . breed?" Rowan turned to Alison for an

answer without realizing it. "That is something we have never asked the Littlelost themselves."

"No." Twist's small voice spoke firmly. "That is one boon we Littlelost have. We need not pass on our misery. We are n-n-neither child nor adult, but we are not p-p-parents. We live long, like the Earth-Eaters, but we d-d-do not d-d-duplicate our own unhappiness."

"Hmm." Alison shivered in the fire-glow. "So many on Veil have come to a dead end. And more will. . . ."

"What do you mean?" Rowan demanded.

She paused. He had been too quick to read her own despair; she had been thinking of Darnellyne's perfect face rotting beneath the shimmering veil of skinsilk she had applied so dutifully, and daily.

"I mean that the Crux has tapped into Veil's deepest wrongs to use them against the inhabitants. The Crux is poisoning your world, your people, bit by bit. What is wildwater? Poison. The earthgall pits? A lure that freezes your children in an eternally unproductive state, useful only as captive workers. They have turned the Halflings against both their kinds and to their own Crux purposes, just as they have exploited the Littlelost. Who are these entities? Why are they attacking your weakest points?"

"They are the Crux," a Hammerhand said in a voice of iron. "They exist, like wind, like etherion. Perhaps they have always been there, like the People of the Horizon."

"Clouds!" Alison interrupted. "The Crux is real. And what of that abomination, Dearth, who led me from the dance floor of Desmeyne to a blasted plain?"

A shuddersome silence held the assembly for a moment.

"Dearth takes all," a Hammerhand said, "and has always been there, with the wind and the water. Before the Crux, there was Dearth and the darkness of Dearth."

"And the People of the Horizon," Alison added in frustration. "Me, I'd give anything to get my hands on an actual Crux-master instead of a sliver of neon light. Cowardly Las Vegas charlatans, hiding behind special effects!"

"Oh, Taliswoman, do not." Sage spoke for the first time in

so long that her voice cracked. "Do not wish for things you do not wish to see in reality. Your alien battle-dance may instruct a Firemayne, but it will not stand against a Crux-master, and the Master of the Crux-masters is empty-eyed Dearth. Do not dance with Dearth."

"Maybe we have more weapons than we know," Alison retorted stubbornly, then she remembered the stolen amulet and cringed internally. She had never credited Rowan's quests with anything but a ritual role. What if he had been right, and the amulet was far more potent than the Cup, or could be?

She turned to Rowan and saw his eyes regarding her with the same soul-cankering questions.

What had they unwittingly done? Could they undo it? And how?

21

EVEN in the next morning's sunlight, Alison could not bring herself to approach the etherion pit, not after that disorienting experience on its brink. The others had no such restraint.

The previous evening's tales of Hammerhands, Sylvins, and Halflings, the urgent news that Crux-allies were on the march, had united the travelers.

Since the Crux wanted etherion, no one doubted that the best course was to make sure that Crux-opponents such as the Sylvins had the etherion they needed. No one feared the dark, deep, watery depths of the pit as Alison did.

At the crack of dawn, Hammerhands had cleared a path through the woods by the sheer force of their passage down the slope, pushing bushes aside and pulling saplings free. Alison watched them from atop the rise leading down to the pit. A few rays of pallid sunlight now played over the pit's mordant dark water, illuminating the etherion slick floating on its surface.

Littlelost willingly stripped the foliage from stunted willows drooping over the oily liquid, then wove the wiry, whip-thin branches into thick mats. Among the Littlelost moved the airy figures of Sylvin women, who had never seen so much etherion before. They marveled at the lambent layer coating the dark water and gleaming like snakeskin in the piebald light.

To Alison, it was like watching people preparing to pan for gold in Love Canal.

"They now do eagerly what was bitter slavery to them," a voice said beside her, sounding as dubious as she felt.

She turned to see that Rowan was watching the industrious activity below with a slightly curdled expression. "You must find it ironic, the Littlelost now rush to do the very thing you rescued them from not long ago," she told him.

"I don't know the meaning of this word 'ironic,' but I doubt whether skies full of etherion will save them from the Crux-fire when it strikes full-force."

She nodded.

"Still . . ." Rowan sounded particularly thoughtful. "At least they work for a common cause against a common enemy."

She nodded again.

"You dislike the pit. Their plan makes you uneasy."

"Yes," she said, "this pit returned me to Dearth's lonely place of death and darkness."

"You have not seen a fruitful etherion pit before?"

"No, I have not. If this site is fruitful, it spawns a rotten growth."

"Yet the Crux plucks all such bad fruit it can find."

"Yes. Then why not this one?"

He shrugged. "Even the Crux may miss some advantage, may make a mistake. Are the Crux-masters perfect because you say they are evil?"

"*I* say?" Alison's mouth dropped open.

"They may work toward some purpose they regard as good."

Rowan? Speculating that the Crux's evil might stem from its own perception of good?

"You are becoming very sophisticated," she said.

"Is this good?"

"I don't know yet."

He sighed and crossed his arms. "Is it 'sophisticated' to admit that your *taekwondo* did indeed work?" He eyed her questioningly. "Could you have felled a Hammerhand?"

"I don't know. I'd like to think that if I had to, I could."

His eyes flashed. "Could you still fell me?"

Should she encourage her promising pupil, or discourage the overweening male arrogance of Desmeyne? She struck a middle ground and told him the truth instead. "Yes. Maybe not every time I wanted to, but most of the time."

He nodded. "Then I have learned only enough to dazzle the utterly ignorant. Of course, in Veil that means everybody . . . except you." He grinned.

She accepted his jibe without retaliating. Who could argue with Rowan's new sense of humor, and his budding humility? "Didn't you really believe that it would work?"

"No. You might have let me win to encourage me to continue. Besides, you are a woman and not a true test."

"I take back 'sophisticated'."

"What? I only meant that a man must be measured against a man of similar strength, or greater."

"Felling a Hammerhand makes you King of the Hill."

He took her meaning instantly. He was getting alarmingly better at that. "Exactly. I have chafed because I must go unarmed save by common wood. You have railed against my celibacy, but I am also sworn to abjure edged steel." A sideways glance. "I wonder why you do not also urge me to seize the nearest sword."

Why *had* his ritual celibacy irritated her so much, Alison wondered. Because she had a personal interest in it that did not extend to his sword-bearing limitations, as Rowan had just rather slyly implied? She shook herself to clear her thoughts. Rowan was beginning to play the word games exchanged underneath hanging ferns in singles bars. He was beginning, she thought with horror, to understand her.

"In my world," she answered, "we gave up swords decades ago for nastier weapons. And, as you have seen, a sword can be countered with things other than swords, with . . . nothing."

"Perhaps. But these nastier weapons . . . was the metal artifact you carried before in Veil, the one that spat blue smoke, one of these?"

"Yes! You *do* still have it!"

"In my pack. It seemed more dangerous to abandon a foreign artifact than to keep it. It is steel, but not edged. I . . . used it once, at your direction, you recall, and nothing happened."

"The weapon fired."

"Yes, but I was not struck by Crux-fire; thus, it is not truly edged. A sword is something else again. Yet as I stood before the Hammerhand last night, and as he fell before me, I realized that I perhaps had . . . wasted . . . my time and my heart in aching for a sword. You have shown me the sword that is myself. It occurs to me that if you are right in this matter, you may be right in others."

"Such as?"

"The need for the people of Veil to reconcile in the face of a common danger. The need for Desmeynians to see the Earth-Eater that is in themselves, and for Earth-Eaters to admit the Desmeynian in themselves."

She nodded, a bit leery of where this might be leading. "And?"

Rowan smiled ruefully. "It has occurred to me that you may be right in yet other matters."

"Matters?" Alison swallowed. If Rowan was heading where she thought he was, she was not sure that she was ready to follow. One impulsive encounter did not make a relationship.

"The Cup," he said. He sounded irritated with her slowness.

"The Cup?"

"Of course. You suggested that I might use it to trace the amulet, to perhaps even seize it back. I suggest that we experiment with it."

"Do you need me for this . . . experimentation?"

"Who are better prepared to exploit its power—such power as it harbors—than you and I?"

"No one," she agreed cautiously. Rowan was being so sweetly reasonable that she suspected an ulterior motive. "When do you—"

"Now."

"Er, where do you—"

He gestured down the cleared slope, where Hammerhands, Sylvins, and Littlelost bustled about, now making bridges of the willow mats. "We must not kindle the others' hopes unnecessarily. We must go where few will come. Beyond the waterfall, perhaps."

"We have never been beyond the waterfall."

"Then no one will look for us there."

Alison could think of no ready argument against this plan, other than that she did not want to be part of it. She did not want to be alone with him, did not want to be blamed for his future failures, or to blame herself for them. Glumly she set off at his side.

Was it possible that Rowan *wanted* to be alone with her? Unlikely. He was a virile young man, artificially constrained, who had slipped the bonds of custom. Alison had not caused this; she'd just happened to have been there. The thought was a bit deflating.

Sage greeted them as they walked back into camp. Rambeau was sitting beside her with the pups, watching alertly as she crushed herbs to powder and funneled them into vials. Amazing what a plentitude of supplies her many pockets yielded. Alison suspected that much of Sage's supposed bulk was the equivalent of a beast of burden's packs, which swelled the creature's normally trim presence to that of a full-sailed galleon's.

Beau rose and trotted over to Alison, his nose nudging her hand.

"Good boy!" She patted the short, silky hair on his head, remembering how Eli had always called Rambeau "Dog." Lately, Beau had not been acting much like a dog at all, much less her beloved companion. She knelt and put her arms around the sturdy shoulders, looking deep into those almond-shaped eyes the color of bitter coffee. So intelligent, so loyal, so alien at heart.

Alison sighed and rose. If she could get back to her world, could she somehow take Rambeau with her? Or was he mired here forever, like the Littlelost?

The dog fell back as she and Rowan passed the pile of ashes that marked the evening's fire. Rowan picked up his staff and pack, and she her backpack.

They walked in silence past a few rocks outcropped like frozen sheep grazing in the long grasses, and passed beyond an escarpment. The waterfall's crystalline call echoed off the en-

222

croaching stones. A perfect place for an ambush, Alison thought, but now they had two *taekwondo* practitioners, one battle-scarred staff, one compromised Cup of Earth, and one possibly loaded revolver.

The waterfall tumbled only seven yards or so to the bubbling pool at its base. Alison and Rowan climbed the grassy slope at its side until they reached the streambed above.

This rocky higher ground brought an unexpected vastness of view: one hundred and eighty degrees from circling mountain to mountain, a fluffy tonsure of clouds visible between the highest peaks.

"Do Desmeynians share the Hammerhand belief that people dwell in those distant clouds?" Alison asked.

"We have glimpsed their forms, as well as those of fabulous beasts."

"My world populates the clouds with imagination, too. But the notions drift away with the clouds, shifting shape, dissolving in the wind."

"These clouds do not move but in a circle," Rowan said stubbornly. "Their images do not change, although they are many, and one may see different things from different places. They never draw nearer or move farther away."

"Perhaps that's because you never go close enough to see them better. What is this place you seek, to which you want to bring the amulet?"

Rowan waved an arm at the empty sky. "There . . . somewhere. As Heart of Earth lay beneath my own feet, and those of every Desmeynian—I think you would call that 'ironic'—the Quarter of the Four Winds by nature must be distant and difficult to find."

"Where would winds meet?" Alison asked aloud, approaching the matter as she would a puzzle.

"Where many elements join."

"Where water joins fire and earth and air . . . that could be almost anywhere."

Rowan shook his head, his hair radiating its red color like heat in the bright sunlight. "Only one place will do. The one decreed."

He opened his pack to rummage for the Cup. Alison shrugged off her own backpack, remembering then that Rowan carried the Cup. She felt a momentary stab of loss, like that caused by the sight of Rambeau among the Slinkers, both with them and absent from her. She was leaving a lot of herself in Veil.

The path led upward again, into a swatch of the meandering treeline. She pointed. "The shadow of the woods would be more private. If our experiments fail, no one need know."

Rowan grunted. He had taken out the Cup, as well as a flask, and he unwrapped the worn flannel and held up the Cup to catch the sunlight.

For a moment, with his flowing hair and antique-looking dress, he resembled an illustration from the saga of the Grail. Then he was simply a young man carrying two vessels into the shade.

"If we use the Cup properly, too much success may call the Crux," Alison warned.

"Why do you think so?" He found a fallen log and sat down on the rough bark.

"Because I inadvertently called Dearth at the banquet in Desmeyne. I had been drinking from the Cup, and growing half-tipsy on Char. And I was getting angry with . . . with . . ."

"With who? Me?"

"You. And Desmeyne. With the way the men ruled the roost and the women just perched there like placid chickens."

"Chickens?"

"Dumb, useful birds."

Rowan shook his head. Alison remembered that she had seen few—no—birds in Veil.

"Anyway," she went on, sitting beside him, "I stood and declared myself to be a word I'd never heard before, nor had you or anyone else in Desmeyne."

"Taliswoman." He savored the title, which had once been heresy to him, with a kind of nostalgia. "I remember."

Alison regarded him uneasily. He had done exactly as she had urged. He had changed. The result was . . . unsettling.

"Then Dearth was beside me in the guise of a black prince,"

she said. "Mute. Elegant. The dance seemed so inevitable that I did not think to refuse."

Rowan unstoppered a flask Alison recognized; it held the Sylvin liquor. He poured some Zurr into the Cup. She had never seen the brew in daylight; it was slightly blue and as thick as honey.

"So," he said, "what called the Crux? Your using the Cup? Or your declaring yourself the Taliswoman?"

"Or my anger," Alison said softly. She remembered the rage bubbling in her chest: rage at a world so self-satisfied that it could not see the seeds of its own destruction, sown everywhere around it.

"Strong emotion." Rowan sounded like a scientist computing experimental possibilities.

"What are you up to?" she asked.

"Almost to the brim," he answered promptly, handing her the full Cup in order to stopper the flask.

Alison glanced into the Cup and saw a waterlike expanse as thick and smooth as blue curaçao liqueur. Her own face fleeted over the surface.

"What are you doing?" she demanded, returning the Cup as soon as his hands were again free.

"The Cup is filled to overflowing, but it is lighter than when I took it from the pack," he said, lifting it as for a toast.

"It does that, changes weight for some reason. I have felt that myself."

"Then drink. See if it lightens even more. Or grows heavier."

"I can't. Rowan, we're playing with fire. The Cup has . . . special effects when filled with heady libations."

"That is what we seek, is it not? Special effects. Enough to release the power of the Cup, to call the Crux, to draw me into a state of second-seeing again, so that I may be in two places at once: here, and where the Crux is. Here, and where the amulet abides."

"You want to duplicate the circumstances that called Dearth to Desmeyne? Rowan, I took an insane risk, but only because I didn't know it. If you hadn't . . . seen . . . the shadow of Dearth when no one else did, hadn't seen me walking away into a blasted land, and hadn't managed to come there and give me the Cup I had left behind—"

"If I had not, you would have been gone for good," he mused. He took a long swallow from the Cup. "And I would have had the Cup anyway."

"Exactly. So you don't need me now." She began to rise, but his hand gripped her arm.

"But I do. If my speculations are correct, everything you did that night called Dearth and showed both of us the empty land beyond Veil. Everything you felt was important to what happened."

Alison pulled away. "I've told you everything I felt. It was hardly significant."

"You have *not* told me everything you felt." He handed her the Cup with such a piercing look that she nervously sipped from it. Sylvin liquor crawled down her throat like molasses, like sweet, heady fire.

The Cup felt heavier as she handed it back.

He swirled the thick liquid, then drank, his eyes focusing on memory. "Nor have I told you everything I felt."

"Well, people don't. Do that, I mean. If everybody told everybody everything they felt, we'd have a mess. We all feel unacceptable things, or unworthy things."

"I, too, was angry," Rowan mused. "Angry with you for winning and for flaunting the Cup, for scorning Desmeynian proprieties by speaking and even making a toast; for adopting our women's dress and baring your quest-scars; for being so strong and defiant, so unfeminine; for making me look foolish."

"That wasn't hard," she retorted. "You were very foolish in those days."

"You were angry with more than Desmeyne and its men; you were furious with me."

"Of course. You were all too willing to let your father turn me into an inconvenience rather than letting me be a real person. You acted as if you had won the Cup, after all, in all but name. That's why I was goaded to declare my right to it.

It meant nothing to me then, a mysterious trinket! But it is so unfair to win a prize of any kind and then be disparaged for it. Must we go into all this? It will only revive unhappy feelings."

For answer, Rowan thrust the Cup at her mouth, tipped it until the liquor coated her lips and slithered between her teeth.

Recklessly, he seized the Cup back and drank in turn. Alison was reminded of a cross between a fraternity drinking dare and a couple sharing a bridal toast. . . .

Alison's head began to thicken. The waterfall sounded farther away. She could almost place herself in the great Arcade of Desmeyne again, see the scene, feel the emotions.

Rowan was right, of course. She had not told everything she had felt that night; she never would. How daring it had been for her to don the low-necked Loftlady gown and bare her scars, and yet how exciting to find a place where there was value in what to her had always been a birth-bane. How well the Desmeynian term put it! Excited, too, by the alien environment and her isolation in it even as she played a central role. And the soothing offices of Char and the dancing, elegant ladies and gentlemen; Rowan, her bane, looking suave and sleek as well, even attractive. Oh, that Char. Even now, Alison blushed over her Char-abetted thoughts that night while she had observed Rowan, admired Rowan from head to toe, wondered about being with Rowan . . .

He was staring at her over the Cup rim, as if reading her mind. He did not look displeased.

Alison clapped a hand to her mouth, too late.

He set the Cup carefully on the log between them, balancing the foot on the rugged surface, still holding the stem and the bowl.

"I also was angry," he said meditatively, sounding far too mellow for such emotion. "Angry at losing the Cup to a stranger, a strange female; angry at disappointing my parents and Darnellyne. Angry that you could walk through Veil and be taken for a young man, then don the Loftladies' dress, which left no doubt that you were not a man, and speak out of place, in the place that should have been mine."

"You believe, then, that anger called the Crux rather than

my strong words? That our conjoined pride and anger did it?"

Rowan lifted the Cup to her mouth again, holding it with both hands. The gesture was erotic. Alison lowered her eyes while she put her lips to the rim, warm now and sweetly slick. She drank almost nothing, but it didn't matter. She had left a kiss within the Cup.

Rowan drank, too, his eyes never leaving hers over the Cup rim as it rose, then set, a cool white curve of stone. A sheen of liquor lingered on his lips, like a kiss, when he spoke again.

"Later," he said, "when I brought you the Cup and it banished Dearth, we found ourselves looking foolish on the Arcade floor. My father accused me of drunkenness, because I was dizzy from second-seeing. You brought me to your Loft rooms, a great violation of Desmeynian custom, but I was too ill to protest."

Alison would have squirmed at the memory she saw coming, except that certain aspects of it struck her as enormously pleasurable if she cared to dwell on them.

"I was also influenced then," she managed to put in, "by drinking Char from the Cup. I was not aware of the side effects."

"Nor I. But you gave me Char and then kissed me. I fled, angered that you should trifle with my vow of celibacy, but frightened, because no one had so much shaken my resolve, and you not even a real woman."

"I see. I'm sorry. I shouldn't have violated your integrity that way. It was the Char, and the Cup. I've never done such a thing in my world."

Rowan frowned. "I had only sipped the merest bit of Char, yet I fled because I felt forbidden things. No woman of Veil had kissed me in such a fashion. The village girls are bold, they cling and they tease, but they do not know how to take, only to receive. I fled, as we had fled Dearth, realizing that my courtship dance with Darnellyne was merely that, a pleasant exercise; that my . . . youthful exuberance with Triss was tolerated only because she saw pride of place in being manhood-mate to a quest-heir."

"Rowan, I'm sorry I did it. That kiss came from the Char,

and from anger as much as lust. I wanted to show you that you didn't know everything. And . . . I was hurt by how unfeminine you found me, compared to a Loftlady. I wanted to prove to you that I was a woman."

"It worked," he said. "That is why what happened by the waterfall was fated."

"What are you saying?"

"That I see that you may be right, may always have been right: the condition of celibacy may have helped quest-heirs concentrate on their tasks, but it hampered them at the same time. The quest for the Cup is not simply to possess it, but to learn that old laws must sometimes be broken. You saw yourself; the Cup warmed and glowed after we came together; it seemed to be invigorated, not betrayed. The Cup of Earth is just that: a thing of fruition, of energy—not of denial and icy retreat."

"Then you're saying that the Cup is empowered not by anger, but—"

"—by desire," he said, reaching for her, returning the kiss she had begun a year ago, drawing her toward him. She gasped as her lips met his through an invisible veil of sweet Zurr. The pressure of Rowan's hand on her back pulled her deeper into a whirlpool of sensation and emotion. Nothing held them back, no wrong on either part. But . . . where was the Cup?

Alison tried to pull away from the warm cyclone that embraced her, to murmur "The Cup" against his lips. Cool, indifferent air expanded between them; the world widened to encompass the woods, the log, the grass, the waterfall again.

"The Cup," she said.

They both looked down.

The Cup had tumbled a few inches to the grass-cushioned ground, but it was whole, and lit by a light from within. Zurr had spilled into a gelid puddle as clear as water, even now widening at their feet into the symmetrical oval of a mirror.

Alison stared into the pale, aqua depths and saw the amulet.

22

ROWAN reached for the amulet without thinking.

His fingers broke the mirror's surface, which shattered like glass. The image dispersed into a hundred pieces.

Alison picked one up, a brittle shard with the transparent quality of hard candy. She touched it to her tongue and tasted the strong flavor of Zurr. Magical rock candy.

"Why did the vision vanish?" Rowan asked wearily. He had just seen his brother Lorn snatched from him yet again.

"Perhaps you touched what was meant only to be seen." Alison picked up the Cup. The stone was as smooth and warm as living flesh. Rowan reached for it, and she felt oddly reluctant to part with it. She watched him take it, then glance at her with fervid eyes.

"The stone feels like the richest velvet, like—"

"I know," she said quickly. "It proves your point; my point, actually."

Rowan's fingers turned the Cup as a blind man's would, the very tips absorbing the essence of the object. "What point?" He spoke dreamily, then looked at her again.

"The Cup responds to . . . amplifies notions and emotions of attraction. Feeling these things, sharing them, strengthens the Cup."

"Why did it show us the amulet?"

"I think because—" Alison regarded Rowan ruefully "—because that is your strongest desire."

He shook his head to throw off the dreamy, sensual spell cast by both Cup and Zurr, then set the seductive vessel, empty, on the log. As they watched, it refilled itself.

"Each . . . occasion . . . intensifies the Cup's powers," Rowan said in the slow way of one piecing together a puzzle. "If the Cup can show us the amulet, could it now show us where the amulet lies?"

Alison nodded. "I still don't know how it works. Surely you don't have to half-seduce a willing maiden every time to create the effect. If so, I bow out, and I doubt Sage is willing to substitute for me."

"The effect would not work with Sage," Rowan said with a touch of his old disdain.

"You forget her Loftlady guise."

"But I know now what lies beneath it." He frowned, perhaps thinking of another Loftlady—Darnellyne—who once might have encouraged his warmest thoughts.

Alison frowned, too. Did Darnellyne still bear the skinsilk disfigurements? Or had the Cup-blessed water Alison had left behind worked?

As if reflecting their separate worries, the Cup's glow dimmed, and the stone had cooled to Alison's touch. She started when Rowan's fingers brushed the scarred skin below her throat.

"Why do you wish to urge another on me for this experiment?" he asked. "Has it not worked with us from the beginning?"

"I don't want our relationship to depend upon making an inanimate object blow hot or cold. How can we be sure of true feelings, or of acting according to our true wishes, when another motive influences our every touch?"

He nodded, withdrew his hand, then brushed his fingers along the rim of the Cup. "Cooler, harder. There must be a way to employ the Cup as a key to my second-seeing. If I saw the amulet again, perhaps I could . . . go to it."

"Wherever that may be," Alison warned, "the Crux would not keep such a prize undefended."

"Without it, I can complete none of the remaining quests."

"What is the significance of these quests? Where do they come from?"

Rowan smiled. "The significance, I am finding, is in the doing and the figuring out. The quests appear in the rimes of Desmeyne, verses that the children scratch into the rock-crystal panes. That is the only comfort I take in Lorn's death: it was foretold in one rime's third line: 'The heart that is human, born to Dearth, will beat for all time in an armor of earth'."

"All this"—Alison's open hands indicated woodland and waterfall, the Cup, and Rowan himself—"depends on the rhymes of *children*?"

He flushed. "Who else remembers the old things so well? And our children grow up together in the Webbings, so there is much opportunity to pass on arcane matters."

"What is the meaning or object of this quest, then?"

Rowan shrugged. "I can but tell you the appropriate rime:

" 'Where Axletree reaches roots to the sky,
Where four winds clash and moan and die,
A hero shall hang his heart on a tree
And will bind himself who once was free.' "

Alison shivered in the forest shadows. The late Lorn Fire-mayne, better known as Pickle, had already paid the price of the first rime. Would Rowan pay it for the second?

They returned a bit sheepishly to the campsite, like children who had been up to mischief, the Cup safe in Rowan's pack. Alison was surprised to find that much of the day had slipped away. Sage grinned at them as if correctly suspecting what they had been up to.

A series of loose-knit bags filled with etherion scales bounced like balloons a few feet above the ground at the forest's edge. As the two approached, a Hammerhand trudged up the path from below, bearing more such oddities.

"Etherion!" Lenaree shrilled triumphantly, joining Rowan and Alison in watching.

With tethers of twisted mesh, the Hammerhand lashed the new nets to a slender birch trunk, where they joined their fellows in rocking at anchor in the invisible wind. Sage joined Rowan and Alison in walking over to inspect the catch, if that was what one called gathered etherion.

The weightless metal gleamed in the dappled light beneath the trees. Whatever shape it assumed atop the water, it kept: conjoined curving sections of mottled metal. Copper—in both its bright metallic hue and its soft viridian patina—and bright blue and red hues danced over the gleaming surfaces. Each etherion "scale," as irregular as a jigsaw-puzzle piece, was a foot or two square, and pierced with holes, like lace candy.

Alison touched the etherion: it was slightly rough, very tough, and neither cold nor warm from the random rays of the sun. The surface had shed pit water and scum like Teflon. Its neutral temperature matched the eternally comfortable climate of Veil.

Rowan, too, was dazzled by the harvest, and fingered the metal through the mesh. "I have seen etherion bits before, which Desmeyne acquired from trading with the Earth-Eaters, but so much at once! This amazes even more than the Sylvins' corsairs."

"You have not known amazement," Lenaree boasted enthusiastically, "until you have watched the Hammerhands beat etherion into a corsair. Tomorrow," she promised, her piquant face alight with anticipation, "we will build the first one for Plume."

"Plume!" Alison tried to hide her dismay. "But she is untrained in piloting."

"She will take to it as if liquid etherion ran in her veins. Our first new pilot in generations." Concern crossed Lenaree's joyous face. "A pity she must first sample the sky when the Crux itself has taken on wings."

"A greater pity that the Crux-craft are armed with blue lightning and the Sylvin flyers have no weapons," Alison reminded her. The real world respected weapons with wings.

"The Sylvins have superior skill," said Sage, who had come up behind the group. "That is a weapon in itself."

"Our corsairs are better-made," Lenaree added. "Apparently the Crux relies upon Halflings to construct their coursers; the resulting vessels are cobbled together from disparate parts."

"Still," Alison said, "a year ago, no one but a few Littlelost had ever seen a Crux-courser. Now an entire audience at the Wellsunging saw several of them. The Crux-craft numbers increase, as well as their pilots' audacity."

Lenaree's sigh was so soft that one saw rather than heard it. "Is she always so discouraging?" she asked Rowan.

"No," he answered quickly, laughing unrestrainedly for the first time in days. "Usually the Taliswoman is much more dire in her complaints and predictions. She is being exceptionally optimistic today."

Alison could have pointed out that her "complaints and predictions" were also usually justified, but she didn't. Rowan's spirits had lifted since viewing the amulet in the woods. Hope was a thing with feathers, even if Veil seemed bereft of birds. She wouldn't clip the fragile wings of Rowan's fledgling confidence.

Lenaree looked amused. "I cannot tell you, my friends, how much we appreciate your aid, or how much it has meant to find our own lost young-old ones among the Littlelost, to have all the Littlelost help us with the etherion when they have only recently escaped such weary work—"

Heavy, running footsteps thudded up the pathway, and a Hammerhand's head wobbled into sight, stride by pounding stride.

"A Littlelost!" the huge man named Gelmar panted as he ran. "A Littlelost adrift on the pit."

Rowan and Alison were racing for the path before the others could even blink.

At the oily water's edge, a few Littlelost waited anxiously, eyes on the pit. One of the willow mats—an end one—had slipped the dried vines that bound the mats into a long, floating pier. Littlelost dangerously crowded the farthest attached mat, watching the helpless figure float atop the orphan mat in slow, sweeping semicircles on the still pond-top, drawn along

234

by some unseen force below. The smooth, controlled motion reminded Alison of little metal figures that can be moved about a tabletop by a magnet held on the underside. Surely nothing could live in this muck?

"Who is it?" Rowan asked.

"Twist," Rime answered dolefully.

"Of course. Twist." Alison's stomach spasmed with anxiety. A natural leader, Twist would be the first and farthest out.

She studied those onshore. How could they be of best use: the massive Hammerhands; the tiny Sylvins, and the tinier Littlelost; Sage, Rowan, herself?

Twist's willow raft floated in and out among the sinister objects—the half-floating fins, the mysterious, submerged things—breaking the water at the pit's center.

"It's growing dark already," Rowan announced in a tight voice.

The notion of leaving Twist to circle endlessly on that black tarn in the dark was clearly intolerable. But what were they to do? The Hammerhands would sink any rescue effort they contributed to. Ditto Rowan with these willow rafts the only transportation available. The Littlelost risked joining Twist's predicament if they cut their sections loose. There was no way to pilot them; early attempts to thrust wooden poles into the gooey black liquid had proven disconcertingly useless. The pit appeared to have no bottom, not even near the shoreline.

"Great. One big drop-off," Alison murmured. She imagined herself adrift on such foul water and clenched frustrated fists, only then noticing her damp palms. Twilight was now descending fast in this shaded woodland, as Rowan said. Twist's face was becoming an indistinct, chalky blot on a darkening slate.

Alison looked up. Beyond the dispirited willows overhanging the pit, tall, elmlike growths with alien leaves created an arched cathedral-ceiling of leaves over the clearing the Hammerhands had made.

Alison turned to Gelmar. His large-featured face watched Twist with helpless worry. "The tethered etherion bundles! Bring them," she ordered.

"How many?" he asked.

"All you can." She lifted a foot and tugged at her boot, then sat down and kicked at the heel to force it off.

"What are you doing?" Rowan bent down to watch her in some amazement.

"Trying to get my boot—uh!—off. Don't just stand there. Pull."

He did as she suggested, wrenching off one boot and then the other, so efficiently that he jerked her body two feet forward on the twig-strewn ground. She leaped up to greet the returning Hammerhand.

The obedient giant had unfastened four of the etherion bundles and now held them two to a fist by their tethers. They bumped each other and bounced off the lower limbs of trees. Gelmar stood rooted, his legs as thick as birch trunks braced, his heels lifting from the ground. . . .

Alison smiled—maybe her wild plan would work—then grabbed one tether. As she had hoped, her body lifted up, almost leaving the ground.

Rowan caught her arms, both to anchor her and to demand her attention. "What do you mean to do?"

"Balloons. Etherion balloons." The word "balloons" obviously meant nothing to him, but she had no time to explain. "I mean to float over the pit above Twist, pick him up, and return."

"Over the vile water?" He well knew her terror of the element. "Too dangerous. It burns! Impossible!"

"Not if you'd just let go of me. Don't you remember? The Littlelost spoke once about trying to escape the Takers by hoarding enough etherion, hiding it in their clothes, to simply float away?"

"If you float high enough to reach Twist, how will you lower yourself to collect him, then rise again, much less return to shore?" Rowan was dishing out admirable Desmeynian logic. "Unshaped and untethered etherion knows no direction but its own inclinations."

She nodded at the coiled vine used to link the mats. "Tie the vine to the tether, so you can pull us back." Alison eyed

Gelmar. "Take some etherion pieces from one bundle. I'll hang a few over my arm; when I'm above Twist, I'll drop them on the mat. With less etherion, my body will sink enough for Twist to grab on."

"Then how will you rise again?"

Blank. Good question. Then: "Twist! Twist will grab the fallen pieces and we'll rise again together."

"This is madness!" Rowan shouted. "You can't calculate how much etherion to carry and drop. At least a Sylvin would have some knowledge of flying. Let one of them do it."

"They're too light. If Twist grabbed on, he'd overwhelm the poor woman and drag her down like a stone."

"Then I will go."

"Might as well send a Hammerhand. Rowan, it has to be someone light enough to float out there and strong enough to handle Twist. I'm the only one who's just right for the job."

She held out an arm. "Etherion."

The Sylvins wrestled etherion scales from one mesh bag, fighting the buoyant metal's upward pull with all their might, and pushed them over Alison's extended arm like feather-weight, oversized bracelets. Luckily, the holes were perfect: big enough to slide over her hand, small enough to catch on her forearm and not float back off.

With each piece of metal added, Alison lifted farther, until her toes cleared Mother Earth and she hovered inches above the ground. This unfortunately put her on eye-level with Rowan, who glared wordlessly at her before he tied the vine to the top of the tether, as she had suggested.

With three more etherion bracelets, Alison hovered as high as a Hammerhand, and drifted toward the pit. Apparently some current of air did stir the gelid surface. She studied the glistening opaque black depths. This perverted water underlay the floating etherion, and supposedly the Mother of all Drop-offs, and she hated it. She hated not being able to see through it, hated the beautiful swirls of etherion that formed its decep-tively lovely skin. From above, the pit resembled a caldron of Easter-egg dye and oil.

She hated hanging over that unhealthy stew, kept aloft only

by alien metal in a mesh bag and her grip on a twisted mesh chain. It was too late for regrets. Rowan, the Hammerhands and the Littlelost, the pixie-faced Sylvins, all of them as sober as Hanging Judges, were growing far and wee. No, she was growing far and wee to them.

She glanced down. A foot or two below her feet the water shone like wet, jet-black linoleum, for all the etherion had been harvested beneath her. She saw only that grudgingly reflective surface, saw herself from below: a Clementine-sized pair of stocking-clad, dangling feet, a grotesquely swollen arm, a dwindling body, and a bloated jellyfish shape above her.

Below her, upturned Littlelost faces floated into sudden focus, like a bed of pensive flowers. The Littlelost at the end of the pier. Then she was passing over them and nearing the middle of the pit! They cheered, but her blood was pounding in her ears too loudly for the sound to fully reach her.

Glancing up again, she saw the people on the shoreline blurring into the circle of elmlike trees, except for the extravagance of Rowan's red hair and the umbilical cord of vine stretching long and thin toward him.

The trick would be to find Twist. Targeting his small raft would be like playing an airborne version of "Pin the Tail on the Donkey" on an oil slick.

She craned her neck, trying to look past her own body, her trailing feet, and saw a sharp black object cutting the greasy surface like a lethal fin . . . and another! Only the edges of cylindrical containers, she told herself, but massed like a school of sharks.

Now she thought she could see into the viscous depths. Could see the dim outline of barrels under the water's thick skin. Another fin—much larger—posed frozen like the flukes of a whale. Were they sea creatures trapped here, forever preserved and paralyzed? Not likely, but how many Littlelost had plunged from their fragile rafts into this rich and deadly broth of decay?

She felt a tug from above. The vine stretched taut. Had she come to the end of her leash, too short to reach Twist?

No! She made out motion on the dimming shore, motion

topped by a beacon of red hair. Rowan was *towing* her'. . . . over to Twist, she hoped.

And then a slice of raft gleamed gray in the corner of her eye. Below her, the pit's surface stirred as if riffled by a wind, but she felt no breeze. Her sweating palms clung to the chain, her hair streaked her damp face and neck, her clothes felt like wet rags. She was turning now, spinning with the etherion balloon in reaction to the vine's tugging. The black oil slick that was so near, so pungent—like gasoline and brake fluid—spun, too.

More raft, and then a glimpse of Twist standing, his head almost reaching her knees. A hand grabbed her ankle, and she screamed slightly at the shock of the contact. The warmth of those tight, circling fingers reassured her. Clever Twist, to anchor her!

Now if she could toss off enough bangles to lower herself. She released one bracelet-laden hand from the chain above her head. Oh, Lord; now she really felt vulnerable, like a pull-chain on an overhead light. She shook her arm, trying to dislodge the sheets of etherion, to slide them down toward her wrist and off, one at a time. They shifted sideways at an angle and stuck. She crooked her arm, amazed by the sweat that ran down her face and back, then rattled the metal scales until they shimmied downward.

Two fell off at once, hitting the raft without a sound. Twist's foot clamped them down. Alison dropped five inches, leaving her innards behind for a sinking moment.

Twist's fist was now screwed into the baggy denim at her knee. Better. Closer. How much more? She managed to shake off another etherion scale. Dropped a bit more. Threw off another, sank further. As she sank, the black water seemed to rise subtly around her. It had become her horizon. Nothing was visible beyond it. At this level, the bone-like protrusions of sunken objects projected higher, some as much as a foot or two. Proportion had altered; everything was bigger, except for herself and Twist and the raft.

"Twist, listen." Her voice drifted out and away over the still, waiting water. She repeated the words, louder. She couldn't look down to speak directly to him. "Grab onto me. Grab my

239

waist with both arms as tight as you can, and at the same time, push the etherion pieces over your arm so they'll lift you upward. Any questions?"

A thin voice floated up from below. "What is a 'w-w-waist?' "

Alison almost laughed, but saved her energy for slapping her hand to her side. "Here. Grab here."

Cautiously she lifted her arm back to the rope, not wanting to lose her position over the raft. She could feel Twist moving beneath her, and braced for the sudden pull of his weight as he leaped up.

When it came, the impact still startled her, and pushed her away from the raft. Under Twist's weight, she sank rapidly, and it seemed that the wet horizon rushing toward her was rising up like a tidal wave. Her breath rushed inward in preparation, not for a scream, but for the moment when the horrible, cold, dark liquid swallowed her and closed like a melting seam above her.

A jerk. She stopped sinking, then sank again. Another jerk. Then, gradually, a lifting. The pit was not overwhelming her; she had barely broken its surface. Only her toes felt stuck in tar . . . icy, congealing tar. She flexed her ankles in horror.

The things beneath the surface of the water, the things that played dead—only their twisted limbs and fins and tails protruding above the slick—moved slowly, like reviving dinosaurs. The water seemed to circle around her like a great black slug, undulating, yet not raising waves.

On the pit's surface, a small bubble fattened and spread, rising like a submerged limb or a head. The thick liquid coated it with the semblance of features . . . of streaming long hair . . . of reaching, twisted limbs, as if an Earth-Eater had dug up through the bottom muck.

The water's surface coiled tighter and tighter, creating a whirlpool. Around and around it spun, a fluid boa constrictor of muscle and appetite. A living thing that scented prey and stirred.

A jerk on the vine pulled Alison almost sideways, so that she floated facedown over the awful pit, Twist dangling from her waist, the water so close to his feet that he yelped and quickly threw his legs around hers.

Then they were being reeled in like a flying fish. The seething surface sped beneath them, only a narrow, wet, asphalt-slick ribbon of it visible. They were skimming toward the shoreline, toward smiling faces. Hammerhands pulled on the vine, hand over hand, while Rowan teetered on the verge of the corrosive liquid, reaching to catch Twist and pull him ashore.

Once the Littlelost's ballast was gone, Alison shot straight up, brushing her head against the overarching branches. She felt that she had downed one of Alice's growth potions in Wonderland, but her spirits lifted with her body as she looked below.

Twist stood on solid ground, gazing up at her with the rest of the group. She felt suddenly free, liberated from the pull of the black water and her own past and fears, and laughed. They lowered the "Balloon Lady" inch by inch, Rowan finally hooking his fingers in the waistband of her jeans to drag her down and clasp her tightly against himself. Her arms and shoulders were still thrust upward, frozen in position. Gelmar's huge hands gently unpeeled her grip finger by finger.

Even when her stiff shoulders finally relaxed enough to let her arms fall, Rowan did not release her. Alison felt embarrassed, whether by the others' admiration or by Rowan's close custody, she didn't know, but she didn't try to stand on her own two feet. For once, her ankles were weaker than her best intentions.

23

THE next day the Big People had a hard time keeping the Little People from hitching rides on the etherion "balloons," as they called them now.

Alison watched a Hammerhand patiently extricate a gaggle of Littlelost from the twined tethers of three balloons.

"The Hammerhands are patient and gentle," she remarked to Mesula, who had stopped beside her to watch.

"They are not so much gentle and patient as large and clumsy. Thus they must move cautiously."

Alison often found herself struggling to explain her meaning to the Sylvins. "Still, they are patient to tolerate such active creatures underfoot. I know the Littlelost are old beyond their seeming, yet they act like children as well as resemble them."

The Sylvin's strange, wide-open eyes flicked toward Alison. "Most of them have endured a hard, forced life of endless labor. Play is small reward for such a plight. We will better entertain them by taking them aloft on our corsairs."

"That's a great idea! It will distract them from the Hammerhands, who have work to do. You do realize"—Alison went on, because she could not let the Sylvins embrace their Littlelost flyers without knowing—"that however the Littlelost may frolic, they're adult in all other respects."

Again the unblinking stare. "You mean that they sleep together as man and woman."

Alison nodded, astounded by this simple acceptance.

Sylvins never smiled; their entire dainty appearance was a

242

smile. This one's stare merely lowered for a moment, then regarded Alison again.

"Why should they not?" she asked. "They are what they are, not what we think they ought to be. At least no children spring from their unions. They curse their world with no Halflings."

"Can the Halflings be so unredeemable?"

"This means?"

"Can't you get together with them, find some way for the Halflings to contribute to your work and world?"

"Why should we wish to? They are cruel because they are unhappy with themselves."

Alison's only answer was, "Perhaps if you were happier with them—"

"You have not seen them at their worst." The woman moved away.

But Alison had seen them attacking, and had not been as intimidated by them as she was by the notion of seeing a Hammerhand hammering, which she was about to do. Something soft brushed her hand. She started, looking down to find Beau settling onto his haunches beside her. He eyed her with the careful patience of a Hammerhand.

Her hand, lifted to stroke the top of his head, paused. Was petting patronizing? Probably. She glanced at the dog again. Neutered at ten months to make him an acceptable pet, a reliable city dog, he'd had no voice in the matter. Yet he had remained behind in Veil—of his own choice?—to father a litter of half-breeds. Was this a disaster in Veil's natural order? Or was it a miracle?

That idea brought Alison's thoughts uneasily back to herself. From the apparent time she had spent in Veil on this occasion, she ought to be having a period. If Veil could reverse Beau's earthly alteration, could it sabotage her up-to-the-minute implant also? Something in the water? The notion of being pregnant, of being pregnant by Rowan, a man out of a fairy tale, caused gooseflesh to ripple over her arms.

Rowan came walking toward her now, up the path from the pit, the pine trees' shade painting his exotic hair dark maroon. Then he burst into full sunlight, like a comet tail trailing a human body that could not compete with its own fiery head. Alison couldn't help but smile.

He came toward her, his eyes moving from her face to her body, pausing on her scars, half-visible behind her open-necked shirt. No other man had ever been able to cross that bridge between her head and her heart so naturally. He joined her, unaware of the worries she harbored.

"The Hammerhands will soon begin to work the etherion by these trees," he said. "I am told that it is fascinating to watch them but that we should keep at a distance for our ears' sake."

Rambeau rose, growled softly and backed away, his normally perked ears flattened with canine distrust. Alison laughed as she followed in the dog's retreat until she came to a small hill and sat down. Rowan joined her, his long legs jackknifed between his linked arms. They could have been guests at some civic picnic, waiting for the fireworks to begin.

Beau settled on Alison's other side, soon attracting a complement of pups. Even Madonna belly-crawled almost near enough to be touched—but not quite.

A squirming dynamo of white-and-cream fur burrowed across Alison's lap, tiny nails windmilling. Then it tumbled to the ground and hurtled itself up the hill of Rowan's thigh and onto his lap. He stiffened, holding still while Alison retrieved the animal. Slinkers were feared and despised in Veil; even though Rowan accepted them now as necessary allies, he wasn't quite ready to dance cheek-to-cheek with them, for sure.

Alison held the furry mass against her cheek, remembering Beau's short, soft puppy fur: a silken crew cut. Rowan watched with such polite horror that Alison could not resist. She thrust the warm, wriggling bundle against his now-bare face.

"It can't hurt you, Rowan. See? It just wants to be friends."

Rowan froze in predictable surprise, but the puppy did not disappoint her. Despite its wolfish heritage, its wet black nose began snuffling along Rowan's jaw and probing into his hair. A pink tongue was soon lashing out in damp enthusiasm.

Like anyone who is phobic about anything, Rowan had stiffened at this gentle assault, as if holding himself still would end it. Just as the puppy's tongue-lashing threatened to tickle, Alison pulled the animal back onto her lap and gave it a fore-finger to chew on.

"It will someday grow large and dangerous," Rowan said uneasily, watching it.

"So did you."

He thought about that for a moment. "In Veil, it is unheard of for people to frolic with beasts."

"It is also unheard of for the Littlelost to join forces with those who cast them out. Your world can change, Rowan; you have."

"I have changed too much!" he burst out. "What was once strange to me seems familiar now, and what was familiar—"

She saw the fear in his eyes, his sense of growing alien in his own world, and she understood it. Wasn't she a Halfling now, too? Unable to fade comfortably back into Swan Lake and St. Paul, not while she remembered Veil and the Littlelost and Rowan . . . and she feared she always would.

With both hands, she offered him the puppy again in all its innocent, helpless charm. He touched a fingertip to its head, gingerly, as he had first touched her scars.

For a moment no one—and nothing—moved. Then the puppy's head twisted to nip Rowan's finger. He jerked his hand away as if it had touched Crux-fire.

At that instant, a sound of shaken sheet metal shivered the air. Sheepishly, Rowan pretended that the sound rather than the feeble puppy had startled him.

"The etherion-working has begun," he said, standing up and moving in the direction of the activity. As the puppy whimpered in fear, its mother rose growling to her feet.

Alison freed the pup to placate Madonna and turned her attention to the source of the sound: Hammerhands, their formidable weapons free of their belts. She followed Rowan to watch the giants at work. The Hammerhands stood in pairs like human pillars, keeping raw scales of etherion level and anchored between them. Then their brothers lifted their awe-some hammers, held them high and rang them like drumsticks on the pliant metal.

Beneath this barrage, the flat etherion sheets quivered and bent. New scales of etherion from mesh bags were added to the formation. Soon they, too, were pounded into a three-dimensional shape. Hammerheads ricocheted from the metal, sheer force and speed warming the sheets to a coppery-yellow heat. The sheets virtually oozed like melted ore into dimensional shape, scale after scale hammer-merged with the others.

And while the hammers struck the etherion like huge, high-pitched gongs, the Hammerhands sang their thunderous bass chorus.

Nearby Slinkers, ears flexed at offended angles, scattered into the woods. Rapt Littlelost sat or stood, unsure as to whether the sound enchanted or assaulted them, but the Sylvins gathered into a dainty cluster, a flock of sound-frozen, seduced fairies.

Alison eyed Rowan, the ground vibrating beneath her, her bones thrilling to the sound more than to the sight.

The display ended as abruptly as it had begun. A last hammer lifted, swung, and fell back without touching anything. Between the Hammerhands, lofting slightly despite the pressure of their conjoined hands, there finally floated the thirty-foot articulated length of a corsair wing. So fragile, so magnificent. As beautiful as the limb of a living thing.

With the same fine and flexible chain that tethered the corsairs acting as a leash, the wing was tethered to a pair of tree trunks. Sylvins darted to put cushioning cloths between its burnished contours and the trees at the points where, even though gently, they would collide.

The hammers again lifted, etherion was laid between the gathered Hammerhands, and the ritual, the creation, the craft, began again to the same stirring sound and fury.

Alison soon found it hard to endure the shrill singing of the metal and the deep chanting of the Hammerhands, although she loved seeing the captive etherion brighten to fire-breathing intensity before it faded into new, domesticated shapes.

The process was so swift and skilled that she could not resist watching from a safer distance. Even the Slinkers slunk back, belly-down in the long grass, their ears flattening and pricking as the song of the Hammerhands and their tools rang out through the afternoon.

By the brink of twilight, all the parts of an unassembled Sylvin corsair were hitched to the line of trees, its wings and body bobbing in buoyant single file. The Sylvins swarmed over the bouncing surfaces. They worked in a silence equal to the clamor of their heavy-handed mates, reminding Alison of pixies and brownies attending to some human-annoying mischief. But that image came from her own world's notions and prejudices. She ventured nearer to see what was really happening.

Sylvins were stringing the frame, as if it were an instrument, with the thin, strong, silver-white wires she had seen on other corsairs. This wire, as thin and strong as nylon fish line, was drawn from the Hammerhands' packs.

Alison approached a coiled wire and lifted one end. Another eerily lightweight material, recalling spun fiberglass, Christmas angel hair, the albino color of a Hollywood starlet's platinum locks.

"What is this?" she asked Mesula, who was passing by.

Mesula paused, her gauzy garments filming the shape of her figure, speed personified while yet still, even her eyes tilting back as though eager to flee her piquant face.

"Horizon-hair," the Sylvin said, as if everyone knew, and rushed on.

Alison slid the wire through her fingers. It felt like human hair, wiry and white and ancient, but incredibly strong. She had read somewhere that a head of human hair could lift a horse—could the strands grow long enough, that is. This "horizon-hair" did.

"Where do you get this?" she asked the next bustling Sylvin to pass.

"From the clouds," this Sylvin said, leaping atop a burnished wing like an elegant, scarf-clad grasshopper.

"But the clouds are at the very edge of your world. Can you fly that far?"

The Sylvin went on stringing, knotting and twisting. "We fly to the verge and spin the horizon-hair from the breath of the storm."

The breath of the *storm?* Alison had never experienced any bad weather in Veil. Neither rain, nor snow, nor hail. Not even a heavy wind. Except for dark of night, it was a vacationer's paradise.

"Lenaree," she pleaded as her one-time pilot bowed as low as a ballerina to gather a great length of line and snip it with a tiny clipper attached to her belt.

The Sylvin smiled at Alison, a trifle impatiently. In an odd way, Alison thought, creating a corsair resembled giving birth. The Hammerhands and Sylvins were so many midwives prodding their clumsy newborn into the world, and then into the sky, where it would turn suddenly graceful.

"Lenaree," Alison repeated. "When, where, do you harvest this horizon-hair?"

"Out beyond the Littlelost Rookeries. Almost to where Rowan must go to find the Quarter of the Four Winds. There the People of the Horizon bury their dead, and the featherthings of the air flock. There." Her airy wrist indicated a direction both up and away, and distant beyond seeing.

Rowan had joined Alison in time to hear the last comments. "You can take me there?" he asked eagerly.

The Sylvin looked him up and down. "You are Hammerhand size, not Sylvin. And the season is not right. The winds divide and are dangerous now. Her perhaps." She nodded at Alison and darted off.

Rowan's lips tightened, but he said nothing. Alison guessed that he was tired of hearing that she could better do what he was obligated to do himself.

"Hair." She lifted her hand, a piece of line wound around it. "How can human hair grow this long?"

"Perhaps it is not human," he answered, watching the Sylvins work on their infant, their masterpiece, their corsair that could not take him.

"I wonder." Alison lifted her eyes to the mountain peaks set like jagged jewels against the eternally blue sky. Between them, she glimpsed the barest shred of cloud, remote and insubstantial. "I wonder."

24

A NEW and strange variety of pomma was the featured item on the evening menu.

"We found it," Rime confessed rather than boasted to Alison. She glanced deferentially at Plume. "*She* found it, on the very top pine bough, higher than we other Littlelost dare climb."

Plume blushed as Twist eyed her admiringly. "I am only lighter, not wiser," she said. "I had no hint that such a thing awaited."

Alison weighed their bounty in her hand: a dense, heavy pomma colored like persimmon. Dare they eat this untried foodstuff?

Sage said, "It is unknown to me."

"Give it to Beau," Faun suggested.

The dog sniffed the pomma with his big black nose, but seemed no more ready to taste the item than they did.

"Here," said a new voice. A deep, rumbling voice.

Felard's giant fingers plucked the sample from Alison's palm. She looked up, then raised her own voice to make sure it carried as far as a Hammerhand's ears. He didn't loom more than eight feet tall, but even a man of a mere six feet does not always hear a shorter woman when she speaks.

"It might be tainted," she warned.

Felard tossed the pomma down his throat like a crumb, shaking his head. "Even if it is, this morsel is too small to do more than make me burp."

Alison and the Littlelost exchanged a glance, part worry,

part hilarity. If a Hammerhand burped, would the earth move?

"Tasty," he declared. "Have you more, little one?"

Plume and Rime pointed to the towering pine tops. The Hammerhand bent to lift the Littlelost onto each of his broad shoulders, and into the wood the trio went.

"We'll have more than we need," Sage predicted.

"Had you ever seen a Hammerhand before?" Alison asked.

Sage shook her head. "Not even in my most far-flung travels, though I had heard of them."

Alison frowned. "I wonder how much else in Veil you have not seen, how much more there is to it."

Sage smiled. "More than we guess, or it would not be a whole wide world, but a village in which one knows everyone else, as Desmeyne has attempted to insist that it is. Young Rowan seems downcast," she added.

Alison turned to see Rowan pensively poking the evening fire into lethargic life with a charred stick. The lank line of his untied hair, the slump of his shoulders, announced his uncertainty.

"He . . . has troubles unguessed at," she answered.

Sage nodded. "He pines for the fair Darnellyne."

"No!" Alison immediately backed off from her impetuously vehement denial. "That is, I imagine he does, but his mind turns more on his quests, and he is balked there."

Sage nodded at the Sylvins still scampering over the tethered flyer even as dusk crept upon the camp. "These airborne women are a strange folk. Close of mouth and happier aloft than on earth. Their ways are hard to understand, but may have mercy in them."

What an odd remark. "Sage, are you trying to tell me something?"

"Only that Rowan's fate may not be as sealed as he thinks." The wisewoman's eyes glittered from the bezel of wrinkles in which they rested like timeworn rubies. "So if he does not pine for Desmeyne and Darnellyne, perhaps he has developed more exotic tastes on his travels."

"No!" Alison answered even more fervently than before. She could not tell Sage of the amulet's loss, although she longed to. But that tragedy was embedded in other, more awkward confidences she could share with no one—God help her—but Rowan.

Sage nodded in the fading daylight, turned, and limped back to the fire and Rowan. Alison noticed that one hip rode higher than the other. Sage, despite her occasional Loftlady guise, would be termed "old" in any world. Alison was reminded suddenly of Eli Ravenhare, of the loss she felt over his vanishing from the Island.

Beau came to her, as he had done frequently of late, an albino shadow with eyes so patient, so intelligent, so dark, so wise, so . . . sad. She crouched beside him and put her arms around his neck.

"Oh, Beau, I wish we could go back, but we can't. Not one hour, not one wish or thought or deed can be undone. Everything I've done here has been wrong."

Like any dog, he could neither agree nor disagree. That response was both a comfort and an accusation.

By dinnertime, the Hammerhands and Littlelost had returned with bags full of the new pomma, as Sage had foreseen, and Alison had tallied Rowan's woes and come to a staggering conclusion: they were all her doing!

Because of her, he no longer believed himself Darnellyne's chosen deliverer, and no longer wanted her in a personal sense.

Because of Alison, he no longer saw himself as the impervious hero of his people, born to win every quest.

Because of her, he no longer saw his fellow Desmeynians as wise, or even as good.

Because of her, he had gained—only to lose immediately—an unknown brother.

Because of her, the treasured tablet containing Lorn's remains had been snatched by the dreaded Crux.

Because of her, Rowan was glumly ignoring his pomma at a camp fire shared by many strange folk, Alison perhaps the most alien among them.

She did not eat her pomma, either.

Then, after the Sylvin liquor had been passed—and bypassed by Rowan—one of the tiny women stood: Ystar. The fire-flicker buffeted her airy drapery like a breeze. Its light licked around her translucent scarves, painting her into a delicate idol carved from fire-opal.

So pale and hot, so cold and passionate. So alien. When Ystar spoke, her words were notes to Alison's ears, modulated flutings that made no sense.

Alison began to see that she understood the folk of Veil only to the extent that she understood her own heart. Now she felt guilty and confused, and every word that fell on her ears was garbled.

"Felliken. Scree mnoot flyer."

Alison blinked. The words circled like corsairs above the bright fire, irritating gnats that never stayed long enough to name.

"Rowan," Ystar said.

He sat a third of the way around the circle from Alison, his hair drawing fire-bright highlights as a mirror draws the sun.

The Sylvin's tiny arms spread to embrace the night-dark sky. "Etherion," she said.

Rowan stood, his face transformed. He turned to Alison and saw her confusion, and its other face, wonder.

"A flyer," he said. "The Hammerhands have forged a flyer large enough to carry me to the Quarter of the Four Winds, or near enough to do."

"A flyer?" Alison swiveled to see the anchored forms bobbing in the dark. "This one?"

"This one." A Hammerhand spoke like a bass drum, in two equally accented beats.

Alison turned accusing eyes on Lenaree. "Why didn't you say so earlier today?"

The flimsy scarves shrugged with her dainty shoulders. "Surprise," she trilled, perfectly understandable.

"But—" Alison turned again to find Rowan striding up to her. He lifted her as if she were a Sylvin and he a Hammerhand, spun her around until her head swam.

"It *is* oversize," he crowed. "I see that now. Large enough for me and a Sylvin pilot."

"But you don't like the notion of being airborne."

"I like the notion of giving up even less."

"But—" she said for one last time. He understood and answered her unspoken objection as mutely.

His face sobered as he released her to the ground again. "I will have to attend to . . . my other errand before morning."

"How?"

He shook his head to silence further questions, which might raise curiosity around them. "I will find a way."

The others scattered after the announcement and the meal. The Littlelost crept into dormant piles; the Sylvins and Hammerhands paired off to seek their own private sleeping places. Sage remained on watch, a rock-stable gray lump by the dying fire.

When Rowan began to leave, Alison caught up with him before he could melt from the fire-glow. "Where are you going?"

"Away."

She felt for his hands like a blind woman and found them clutched around the Cup. "What are you going to do?"

"Find the amulet."

"Again? What if this time you actually reach the place where the amulet hangs?"

"Then I shall be closer to it."

"That place is Dearth's."

"The amulet is mine."

"The Crux helped form it, Rowan, as much as you did."

He was silent, his hands unmoving under the warm persuasion of hers.

"Let me help," she urged.

"You cannot."

"But I can."

He did not ask how.

"Where are you going?" she asked again.

He sighed. "To the waterfall."

She nodded, but it was dark now, and he could not see the gesture. Still, he did not object as the occasional crunch of her boots trailed his through the night.

Alison had no idea of how they would recover the amulet, or

even of how they would reach the place the Cup's shattered contents had shown them.

Soon, a pallid glow lit the ground ahead. She came alongside Rowan to find him bracing the Cup against his chest. Light radiated through the chinks between his fingers and poured upward from the Cup's mouth, a flashlight-bright beam that gave his face the up-lit look of a Halloween demon and painted his chest scars blood-red against his paler skin.

Even the stem of the Cup beamed light and illuminated the ground.

"The Cup has never been so potent," Rowan admitted.

"It thrives on our alliance," she murmured.

He said nothing. She guessed that he was already walking into the gray land of second-seeing, moving into the murky mental haze between present and future past.

"It helps," Rowan said then.

"What does?"

"The concentration you taught me during my lessons in *taekwondo*. It aids my sense of second-seeing."

She nodded, not surprised. When she had first encountered Rowan Firemayne, he had been closed to much of his world: the lands, people and possibilities beyond Desmeyne, the value of anyone older or younger or other than male. Closed even to the exercise of his deepest emotions and desires. Now that he knew better, he could tap more of his potential and— she winced inwardly to realize it—take greater risks.

The waterfall's eternal plinking broke through Alison's thoughts as they approached it. Sheets of falling water now glimmered before them, reflecting the Cup's lavish glow.

"Do you have any notion of what you're going to do?" she asked. "How will you reach there, and how will you return?"

"I have more notion than you did when you walked into the dance of Dearth."

"That's not enough now. Dearth and the Crux know you to be a greater danger than before. They will be forearmed."

"They were always forearmed." He lifted the Cup as if to toast the darkness. "If the liquid within the Cup reflected the place where the amulet hangs, perhaps I must use liquid from the Cup to create a larger image."

With that, he walked to the falling water and thrust the Cup under its spray. The force could have ripped the stem from his hands. It didn't, but neither did it fill the Cup, since the current flowed so fast that water poured out as fast as it poured in.

"May I?" Alison stepped into a chill mist of water-drops and tilted the Cup in Rowan's hands so that the flowing water struck the bowl edgewise. The Cup drank up the water so quickly that Alison had to level the vessel as they stepped back from the falls.

"What magic was that?" Rowan wondered, gazing into a water-filled Cup.

"Domestic variety, common in my world," Alison said with a grin. "And not normally one of my talents. Now what?"

Rowan smiled slightly at her modesty, but the deeps of his eyes remained haunted by the absent talisman. "You agree that our . . . oneness empowers the Cup?"

She nodded soberly.

"Then be with me in this enterprise, uncertain as it is."

She nodded again.

Rowan took a deep breath, his eyes bent upon the water trembling in the Cup. "I see a larger scene. I see again that same blasted place we visited before with Dearth, the same stark tree. And the amulet is there!"

He raised his eyes from the vision within the Cup to hers. His expression sought help, advice, guidance from his *taekwondo* teacher. She had little to offer but equal desperation.

"Rowan, remember how the water worked when I threw it at Dearth? It banished him. And in the Harrow-worm trenches, I threw it in an arc and it healed the earth it touched. Water the earth at your feet with the Cup. Turn in a circle; encompass yourself with the Cup-touched water."

She stepped back even as the first drops fell to the ground. They hissed like acid and gave off great veils of steam that rose up between Rowan and Alison, high enough to enclose Rowan in a white curtain of mist.

A stray drop struck Alison on the chest, where it clung to her scars like a globule of hot honey.

The Cup's light radiated through the fog engulfing Rowan to illuminate the area around Alison. Her eyes searched the vague whiteness, anxiety gripping her. She had last encountered a similar wall of fog in the tunnel at the Heart of Earth, and that fog had whisked her from Veil and back to the Island. Was Rowan beyond reach? Had he possibly—unreal thought—been transported to her world? The Cup had resided there, after all. Lord, if they should experiment with unreliable forces and change places for good!

Her gaze probed the mists, trying so hard to force sight that she made herself dizzy. The smoke, bodiless and odorless, swirled around her. Her breathing grew rough with fear. Just as she had convinced herself of the worst, the mists thinned. And she saw what Rowan saw: the vacant landscape in which Dearth had once trapped her. Yet the dark scene had a disturbing, soft focus, like an old movie, as if she were looking through smudged plate glass.

Seeing it with even partial clarity was almost as bad as being there herself—and then Rowan walked into view like an actor onto a set, the Cup still clasped to his chest. Now the vessel's searching light revealed the surrounding emptiness, the gray-toned despair that shaped the uneven rocks beneath Rowan's boots and hovered over the barren hills undulating into the distance.

Rowan's figure had taken on that same icy neutrality, that same absence of life and color. Even his hair seemed tinged with gray, as if he were his father the Firemayne. He resembled a man who had sleepwalked into a vast spiderweb, to be veiled for eternity in its gray shroud.

Yet he moved in this dead world, crossed that ungiving ground too barren to be called earth. Alison saw then what he was headed toward: a twisted, ashen, leaf-bare tree clinging by claws rather than by roots to a huge coal-black stone.

From one bone-pale, broken upper limb hung the amulet on its braided cord of flame-red human hair. She remembered a line from a Desmeynian rime: "A hero shall hang his heart on a tree." Was *this* the Axletree where the Four Winds met? Certainly this bitter, empty place gave no welcome to any element but wind, and even wind would have trouble making an impression on it. There was nothing here to stir, nothing to lift and run off with, nothing alive to drive to its knees.

Except Rowan.

Alison, suddenly panicked, thrust a hand through the last faint shrouds of mist. Unseen tendrils seared her skin. She snatched her fingers back undamaged, though the flesh still stung. She looked down to where the water had fallen and saw a thin, fiery-red line scarring the earth, marking a division both unreal and inarguable.

So, she was not to pass where Rowan had gone. Still, she saw him, saw what he saw. That bespoke a certain participation in his quest, even if only as an eyewitness. That boon could also become a curse, she realized, if Rowan were to get into trouble. What was she thinking of, *if?*

He was moving there, in Dearth's dead lair. Once this place had almost ensnared Alison; now it had a Firemayne and the Cup to itself. What if the amulet was a lure and Rowan had second-seen his way right into the Crux's trap?

Rowan moved painstakingly over the same slick, frozen waves where Alison had once slipped in her Desmeynian gown. It seemed to take him forever to reach the great stone crowned by the distorted tree; another half-eon elapsed while he struggled upward, an unarmored knight tackling an obsidian mountain.

The tree itself was not formidable, only ugly. Perhaps no more than twenty feet tall, it loomed over Rowan like a praying mantis, its bone-white upper limbs still.

Rags of fog drifted in the black sky, starless, except for the glowing moons paired like eyes, one red, one green.

Rowan climbed on toward the tree, the Cup still clutched in one hand. How tiny it looked from this distance! How tiny Rowan was becoming, climbing farther into this world, half-veiled by a curtain of sizzling mist.

And then the moons blinked.

Alison gasped.

Tree limbs flexed and closed, snatching the amulet from Rowan's reach even as he stretched an empty hand for it. The scene shrank, becoming a pattern scribed on the black velvet of a robe that covered some immense chest.

Rowan slid down the dark velvet, an insect brushed from a sleeve, until he met the jagged waves of stone below.

"Rowan!" Alison could not see him at all now. She heard no sound, for not even wind came to Dearth's dark desert, but Rowan must have cried out.

The tree still stood on its hill, but its limbs were twisted into a new shape, and now a Rowan-sized figure stood beside it, velvet-black robes hanging motionless around it, eyes gleaming faintly red and green in turn within the endless black of its face and form.

"Dearth," Alison breathed. "Playing games with Rowan."

She lifted her hands and brought both fists down on the miasma of mist. The barrier hissed like hot steam, and burned as much. She jumped back, panting in pain that melted away as contact ended. Alison raised her booted foot and kicked hard against the gauze of fog. The boot plunged through unharmed, but a thin red rope of pain clamped her calf where the leather ended and tightened up her thigh as her leg straightened. She withdrew her foot, defeated.

On the last occasion they had visited the land of Dearth, Rowan had come to Alison's defense with the Cup. Now he carried the Cup with him. Would it suffice to keep Dearth at bay? The Cup had grown, but so had the Crux's power.

Rowan began trudging over the uneven surface again, began climbing once more the slippery silicon hill. This time success would bring him to the feet of Dearth.

In that concealed dark figure only one thing could be perceived: the thin noose of braided red hair from which the amulet pouch dangled. The pouch hung motionless, unstirred by wind or breath, not even Dearth's breath. Perhaps Dearth did not breathe.

Rowan drew even with the crest and looked up to the black pillar that was Dearth.

Then he climbed over the top and stood up.

The Cup he held blazed, casting liquid yellow light into every crevice of the dread landscape, even bathing the barkless tree in an amber gleam. The blackness of Dearth remained impervious, but in the Cup-light, the amulet pouch and its crimson cord shone in stark contrast to the darkness that possessed them.

For a moment they stood face-to-facelessness, Rowan and the figure, now oddly human size.

The darkness spread its wings, widened and curved to encompass Rowan like the maw of some massive fish.

Alison screamed "No!" as Rowan thrust the glowing Cup into Dearth's black heart.

For a moment the creature's twisted hands appeared, one empty, one twined with the thin red braid of Rowan's hair. Into the empty hand Rowan pushed the Cup, even as he wrenched the talismanic pouch from the other.

Then light was pouring through Dearth like a blood-bright X ray, illuminating bones and muscles and veins, revealing his essence in a lightning flash.

The outline of Dearth quivered, shook, and Rowan fell down the sharp slope, clasping the deadened Cup in one hand, the other hand a clenched fist.

The Dearth-form winked to solid black again, a length of red unraveling in its bony hands and graying into ashy flakes.

Alison once more charged the barrier, boots kicking at the writhing red line marking the circle that held Rowan in and her out as if it were so much smoldering dirt to dampen with fresh earth.

Dust rose, and smoky fog, and heat. She coughed and stamped, trying to obliterate what did not exist, a magical line written in water on earth.

Then a hand thrust the Cup at her through the swirl of cloud and mist. She took it without thought, her flesh chilling at the touch of frozen stone.

As she drew the Cup to herself, the cloud congealed into a comet tail. Rowan unspun from its midst, emerged from the airy cocoon. Nothing remained of Dearth's small and deadly world but a shallow furrow in the ground.

Slowly the Cup warmed, thawing against Alison's hands.

When Rowan spoke, his voice cracked as if he had not used it in many days. "The Cup is yours as well as mine. Whoever holds it can cross the barrier to the other."

"Figured that out before you went, did you?" she asked.

He had the grace to look uneasy. "No. Nor did I know that the Cup was now strong enough to weaken Dearth. Neither did Dearth."

"But the amulet, he kept it. I saw!"

"He kept the cord."

Rowan opened his clenched fist. The pouch lay across his palm. He teased the puckered folds open to lift out the clay tablet formed of earth and his brother's ashes.

Alison sighed her relief to see it again, to see Rowan again. She looked up to his face, but her glance was deflected to his hair. Among the blazing red, a single lock lay gray and sere, robbed of all color by Dearth's last, vengeful grip.

25

"WHAT is it?" he asked.

"Nothing," Alison said.

The seared streak in Rowan's hair struck her as another telling omen of encroaching decay. Still, Rowan would hardly begrudge a few bright hairs sacrificed to recover his brother's ashes. He laughed at her long face and clasped the pouch more tightly.

"I am back, safe! What was mine is mine again." He noticed her quietness. "And you have helped. You were the link between first- and second-seeing. Did you truly view all that happened?"

She nodded.

"Then you, too, have second-seen! The more we test our unguessed powers, the more new possibilities will show themselves."

"As do old enemies, like Dearth," she reminded him. "Rowan, I'm happy that you reclaimed your talisman, but it doesn't mean that Dearth and the Crux-masters are defeated." She tried not to stare at the pale swath through his hair. How much it disquieted her! How much she hated to see any part of that flagrant banner of youthful fire dampened. "You'll need a new cord," she added.

"I've no time now to braid another lock. Sage will dig something serviceable from her many pockets. Come, we've earned another draught of the Sylvins' Zurr."

He took the Cup and threw an arm companionably over her shoulders, leading her toward the woods and the camp fire.

The Cup's mellow glow that lit their path, and Rowan's long, springy strides drew her along as much as his good mood.

And still she felt an unnameable dread.

Rowan radiated a pleased disbelief that he had escaped a dread opponent so easily. Alison shared the joy and the disbelief, and none of his new confidence.

He sensed her reservations and stopped, turning to face her.

"Alison, I have recovered the tablet." His tone softened. "Do you not see? Now I am free again. Free to—" His voice faded as his face lowered to hers. His arms drew her near, until they made a closed circle of breath and body heat and expectation.

The Cup pressed warmly into her back where his hand rested. Never in her life had a moment so begged for consummation; never had rightness and rapture promised so meekly to play partners . . . .

She pushed away from Rowan's innocent hunger, bitterly remembering how the Char-fed Cup had first teased her with this very possibility, and how she had imagined reveling in it.

He had become exactly what she had advocated, so how could she explain her sudden lack of faith in her otherworldly mechanisms, in her right to taste the change she had helped wreak? Because of the secret she carried?

His lips sought her throat to quell the uncertainty he felt rising from her deeps, from the well beneath her scars. Their touch seared her conscience like Crux-fire. In a moment his ardor would persuade her, and she would hate herself in the morning. Again.

"Rowan, what about Darnellyne?"

Like an almost invisible rein, like fine, white horizon-hair, the name gave him pause.

"I will give her the Cup when I return to Desmeyne," he said. "She can then choose whatever man she wishes to hold it, and herself."

"Darnellyne knows no other man but you."

"When she is no longer locked to me, she may find one well worth knowing."

Not with . . . her face as it is, Alison thought. If Rowan knew

of the Loftlady's predicament, he would regret becoming ir-
revocably interwined with Alison. It would seem a betrayal of
Dar when the Cup-maiden needed him most.

"Rowan, I may not be here for very much longer."

His tone grew aggrieved. "You told me that in your world,
men and women do not bind each other with their needs. Was
that a lie?"

"No, only it's not so simple."

"You said that it was." He still held her, and she still had not
the strength in any sense to pull away.

"It is, and it isn't."

"Then your world is like Desmeyne, and things are both
true and untrue at the same moment."

"Sometimes."

"Then what is the difference between them?"

"Not much, I'm learning. Except that I belong there, and
you belong in Veil."

"And we . . . are here." His grip tightened enough to let her
feel the undercurrent of their attraction.

She didn't deny it, but her silence released her. The cool
night—aloof and isolating—rushed in to claim her.

Rowan kept a light hand on her shoulder, but said nothing
more. Soon the crimson blur of the camp fire punched a hole
in the darkness. They walked until they felt its warmth, and
stopped.

Sage still kept vigil by the fire, and lifted her pale head.
Rowan went down on one knee beside her.

"Wisewoman, have you some sturdy cord in your bottomless pockets for my pouch?"

"Have you lost your own?" Sage's face stilled as her eyes
met the blighted strand of hair.

"The cord, only the cord," he answered, triumph edging his
voice.

Sage nodded and began excavating her many pockets. Alison found a flask of Zurr, took the Cup from Rowan's hand
and filled it for him. One drink wouldn't undo her resolve,
or his.

Sage flourished a slender length of leather, then wove it

through the holes in the pouch. Rowan tugged Alison down beside him and offered her the Cup. She paused only briefly before drinking the sweet power it contained.

"You will change your mind," he told her intently, taking the Cup in turn.

Her eyes kept fast on his. "Probably."

Sage watched them, her fingers swiftly threading cord through eye after eye.

"Tomorrow," said Rowan after drinking from the bright Cup, drinking down light and optimism, "tomorrow the Sylvins will take me to the Quarter of the Four Winds and I will find the true Axletree."

"Have you found a false one, young man?" Sage asked.

"Indeed. But it returned what was lost to me. How false can that be?"

"False enough." Sage lifted the pouch by its new cord and drew it shut. "And true enough to serve your purpose." She eyed Alison. "You will not go on this airborne quest?"

"I will serve by sitting and waiting." She kept herself from adding, "like Darnellyne."

"Hmm," Sage responded acidly.

Only Sage could imbue a noncommital "hmm" with editorial comment, Alison decided. The bright old eyes shifted from Rowan to herself with sharp speculation. Gossip, Alison thought at Sage, does not become you.

Rowan was calming from his expedition into second seeing. He stared possessively at the unassembled corsair bobbing against the trees, its pieces shimmering in the fire-flicker.

His expression had grown pensive, which made him look more romantically handsome than ever, like Hamlet or Heathcliff, Alison thought. How unfair that he had won the token free of the dragon, Dearth, and yet did not have a maiden to reward him. How unfair that this maiden had a conscience and could not exploit a hero's hunger!

Alison's sigh attracted Rowan and Sage's attention. "I am tired—" she began, groping for the classic excuse to buttress her noninvolvement. Next she would be saying that she had a headache . . . instead of a heartache.

Rambeau bounded into their midst, a white, bristling form illuminated by the twin radiances of the Cup and the fire. Red and yellow silhouetted him on either side—and then a zigzag of snapping blue light outlined his electrified ruff.

"The Crux!" Sage warned.

A sound like tearing paper, as if the sky had become ripping onion skin, hissed above them. They were on their feet at once, all three, looking upward.

Alison saw nothing but night—night as impenetrable as a blackboard, but a blackboard against which someone had drawn long, invisible fingernails . . . . Chills zippered down her spine. She felt as if her clothes had been wrenched away, leaving her exposed to the elements.

Rowan's hair had lifted like a wolf's ruff, the pale streak showing as white as bone.

Sage started to cry a warning, but a new sound outshrieked her: the ringing rip of sheer metal.

Against the black backdrop of the forest, the corsair parts were writhing as if alive, like howling tin cans caught in a berserk opener. They peeled back piece by piece, airy metal rent and cast down bereft of buoyancy, spit out by the night.

Rowan ran off, leaving the Cup to spill its contents, and Sage to seize it. He returned in an instant with his staff and charged past them to the corsair, Rambeau barking at his heels.

Thuds hit the ground behind him: aroused Hammerhands followed, and Sylvins flew by on bare feet. Alison ran with them. Behind her, the Littlelost milled and Beau barked.

By the trees, splinters of the glorious corsair lay like iron filings. Ystar bent to gather the shards. "Dead. I have never seen etherion in any form afraid to fly. This is dead."

"Slain," Rowan corrected in a deadly monotone. "By the Crux."

A Sylvin keened, then another, in a ghastly soprano chorus. At the top of the sky, lightning jagged in blue brilliance.

Rowan shook his simple wooden staff at the night's dark malevolence. The pouch hung around his neck again, his brother regained at the cost of a more intimate piece of himself lost to the Crux's unholy grip.

And now this last gift in the face of hopelessness—a corsair to fly him to a distant quest-site—lay crushed at his feet.

The Crux knew only its own losses, knew only that another cherished prize of its enemy's had been wrested away. Wild, angry, cruel, the Crux washed down on those below in lightning strokes.

"The other corsairs!" a Sylvin cried in sudden warning. Sylvin forms scattered beneath the sizzling entrails of blue light that veined the night, each pilot rushing to her beloved corsair tethered with its fellows, bobbing helplessly under the naked sky.

Blue wands hissed into sight above the trees . . . narrow, medieval windows opening on unearthly light. In the harsh illumination, Slinkers gathered behind Beau, baying not at the moon, but at the wands and at the evil lightning dancing like an aurora borealis between earth and sky.

A tree glowed in a blue haze, then crashed to earth with a smell of charred sulfur. Another tree lit up, a brain stem with many branches. Bright blue tendrils snapped off, then limbs splintered; at last only a violet-blue trunk stood, burning like a candle down to utter darkness.

Tree after tree flared and guttered. Still the blue wands hovered, slicing with laser precision straight for the forest's dark heart, for the etherion pit.

Rowan darted down that awful path as it opened, Alison and the others behind him. Alongside them, dying trees hissed and snapped, their embers burning blue in rotting cores.

Rowan arrived first. His silhouette was haloed in a lurid glare, standing on the pit's brink, motionless. Fireflies of blue light danced over his head, turning his red hair purple, except for one pale, aqua strand.

Alison pounded to his side, breathless, armed with nothing but *taekwondo*. No one had taught her how to duel light.

Still the trees exploded and fell. Rowan thrust his staff at the lightning strikes as if to engage the lucent barbs in a fencing match and some took up the challenge. Lethal nettles of snapping light wreathed the staff and sizzled down its length to lick at Rowan's fingers.

He drew back, burned by that cold blue light.

Alison cursed her uselessness. Or was being Taliswoman the same as being Talisman? Had she helped Rowan come to this place, as he had drawn her to it? Were they were both more than they had been now, and a match for the Crux?

Five floating wands hovered above the trees, then joined into a single devastating bolt, sizzled in a gigantic, jagged line straight for Rowan, for his heart, for the pouch that both shielded and targeted the scars upon his chest. Rowan swept the staff into its path, the sturdy wood glowing in the bolt's reflected fury.

Crackling, the line of light wreathed the staff, electric-blue barbed wire. Yet inexplicably, as more force charged down its thorny length, the humble wood sprouted branches and limbs of light that curled *away* from Rowan's hands.

Like an artificially lit tree, the staff blossomed with clusters of frustrated energy, glittering and snapping. Rowan held it aloft like a torch. The attack was at an impasse. The Crux-fire could not sear to earth, and Rowan could not lower his now-lethal staff without giving the Crux's fury a bridge to its enemies.

Then the blossoms and the lightning vanished as if a switch had been turned. Gone was the droning buzz and crackle so bizarre to Veilian ears. The Crux-master's wands, five upright bands of blue light, shot up into the dark and vanished.

Rowan lowered the staff, inspecting it. His fingertips fleetingly touched the wood, but must have sensed no heat or cold, for he looked at the others, shaking his head.

"The Cup," Alison suggested. "You are Cup-bearer now, and the Cup doesn't permit unfruitful energy. The power it has given you made the Crux-fire flower rather than destroy."

"I felt no power," Rowan objected. "Only desperation."

"Remember how, when I healed the broken earth, the Cup overflowed my hands and made green growth spring from my very flesh?"

Rowan frowned. "Only you saw such a wonder."

"We all saw your staff turn wild Crux-fire into broken embroidery threads."

"Then we are safe from the Crux?" he asked.

"Only you, perhaps," Alison answered. "But it's you and what you bear that the Crux wants."

"Then the Crux is baffled," he said.

"Not yet!" said a third voice.

They turned to Sage, who pointed up at the great black well of sky overhead. Sparks were sparking to sapphire life above the etherion pit, etching alien constellations on the firmament. Some congregated into clusters. Others fell into intersecting lines and dipped like starry nets toward the water's surface.

"The etherion!" a Hammerhand basso roared. "The light will sweep up the remaining etherion!"

Indeed, the pinpoints of blue light pulled down into a pattern. Drawing between the dots, and Alison envisioned a gigantic mesh hovering above the black water. The mesh's reflection glimmered beneath it. Then the two images met in an explosion of high, hissing whines and sizzling protest, like fat hitting a red-hot skillet.

The onshore watchers drew back, arms lifted to shield their faces from the fireworks, those faces painted a Pictish blue in the strange light.

Something *was* being drawn from the surface of the pit. Bits of etherion, once free of the water, lifted like flocks of birds. A high-pitched wail from the Sylvins joined the Crux-fire's ever-present drone. Unhindered, the etherion floated up to catch against the treetops.

But something more came rising from beneath the water: vast, clumsy forms, distorted shadows against the blue-diamond mesh, lumbering upward like sleeping giants heeding the call of an escaping harp.

The Crux-fire's keening sharpened to a whine. In the lurid neon blitzkrieg, Alison could make out nightmarish shapes, massive, half-seen forms resurrected from the pit's black bottom. One object seemed to be a thirty-foot-long whale's flipper; Alison could think of no other description for that vestigial, blunt-ended shape.

And there—a curving fluke as big as a double garage. What remnants were these? From what world yet unfound? Stiff, unforgiving, the objects of this supernatural salvage operation lifted into the air above the pit, and higher—through the Crux-fire-torn treetops and into the starless night.

"What manner of things are these?" Rowan watched the mighty silhouettes lever slowly through the air, a skin of ether-ion clinging to their massive bodies.

Alison shook her head. She could not name every phenomenon in Veil, though she had rashly tried to when she first arrived, before she knew better.

But now . . . she had few answers.

Except. She had glimpsed these shapes before. Their familiarity tickled her memory as they rose into the air, as she tilted her head to watch them.

Thirty-foot flippers. Fifteen-foot tails. Dinosaur remnants? Explain that to a Desmeynian. Or—Alison blinked, her eyes seeing blue spots even when she closed her lids.

The notion was unthinkable. Incredible. Impossible. But she had seen shapes like this suspended somewhere before . . . from a ceiling. A natural history museum? Eli's cabin, maybe? No! Her brother Peter's bedroom.

"Flyers!" she breathed.

"Flyers?" Rowan repeated.

"*Real* Corsairs. And Mustangs, and Spitfires. See the faded star painted on the flipper? It's a *wing!* But these can't be here. Can't be."

"They are from your world." Rowan's statement rang in her ears like an accusation. Was it possible that she wasn't the only earthly thing to slip through to Veil, the only *person?* But World War II airplanes? How? Some Bermuda Triangle, Twilight Zone conspiracy?

The silhouette of one complete plane took shape against the blue lights: a Corsair, all right. A literal Corsair. Did the Sylvins even guess where their terminology had come from?

As the craft lifted high above the trees, Crux-fire ran berserk over its frame, turning it into a bright, neon-blue kite. This sudden flash revealed the object for what it was: the hulk of an alien flying machine.

Gasps all around Alison competed with the sizzling Crux-fire for a few moments. Her own gasp came latest, longest, and loudest.

Before the Crux-fire dampened and the Corsair became one with the night into which it was assumed, the blue light had coursed through a skeletal pilot, illuminating every bone from toe to skull.

26

MORNING came at last, with no other manifestation of the Crux, though only the wolf cubs had slept.

Signs of Crux fury lay all around.

The freshly hammered corsair intended to convey Rowan and a Sylvin pilot to the Quarter of the Four Winds had been reduced to literal smithereens. Even the wind would not deign to loft these deadened remnants, these slivers of themselves.

The etherion pit's sleeping dead no longer thrust above the murky surface, but their spectacular resurrection had stripped the water of nearly all remaining etherion. Only a few floating scales caught the early sunlight.

During the set-to, the gathered balloons of etherion had been slashed free of their moorings and had drifted up to who-knew-where. No one cared to voice the notion that the Crux had snagged all the fruits of Littlelost labor again.

But the trees were the greatest casualty. Along the path the Crux-fire had carved, blackened trunks stood stripped of all leaves and limbs. Some had toppled askew, leaning against each other like a forest of burnt matchsticks.

Many of the tallest pines had lost their lofty tops. Raw scars streaked down their immense lengths, as if whittled by the lightning.

Sylvins drifted ghostlike through this dark, wasted wood. Littlelost stared up at the shattered pine tops, where the bounty of pomma had been destroyed.

Hammerhands wandered the wood's edge, large men with

little to do, their fingers hanging empty and loose, the tools at their belts a mockery.

Rowan found Alison by the waterfall, staring at the foaming water at its base.

He set his pack down—the Cup had never been so heavy—and settled on a nearby rock.

"The Slinkers are gone," he said.

"I saw the pups."

"The cubs and their mother stayed. The rest left."

"Even—"

"Yes."

She nodded listlessly, neither surprised nor alarmed. She seemed beyond either emotion, any emotion.

He began to search for flotsam among the rubble of their dreams. "No one was hurt, by good fortune."

"The Crux got what it wanted without having to hurt anyone."

"Not this."

His tone forced her to look at the pouch he held away from his quest-scars. It no longer hung from Sage's leather cord, but from a braided length of ash-white hair.

Alison shivered a little, though the sun, as usual, shone warmly and made diamonds dance among the waterfall spray.

"You've removed all Crux-signs from your body," she said. "Didn't it . . . hurt?"

"Yes, but not as much as the Cutting."

She winced to be reminded of that ritual, of her own painfully engraved scars.

"Why have you lost heart?" he asked.

"You haven't?"

He considered that, then sighed. "No. I have the amulet still. Perhaps I was not meant to fly like a Sylvin. I can still walk."

"Oh, what good will walking do? The Crux *can* fly, and now they have air-borne coursers made not only to fly, but to kill. Didn't you see what manner of monster the Crux-net raised from the pit waters?"

"I saw."

"But you don't understand. Otherwise you wouldn't be so calm."

He was slow to answer, unlike Rowan. "Perhaps I would understand if you would explain it to me."

"I'm tired of being the messenger, the bearer of bad news!" she burst out. "I was wrong. No one can do anything about the ills of Veil. They stem not from within, but from without."

"No, you were right, in part. Some ills we have brought on ourselves, through our suspicion of each other."

"A drop in the bucket compared to what you have massing against you."

"Perhaps. But you do not explain what."

"Rowan, the things the Crux raised from the etherion pit are from my world. They were deadly there, though not by nature, and they were literally dead here. Dead in the water. Now the Crux has raised the dead machines of another world to battle you. What can you fight them with? You and the Littlelost? The unarmed Sylvin corsairs? Sage and a few herbs?"

He stretched his long legs. "Did you not teach me that I could fight without a weapon, that my own self was my best defense?"

"Yes! But that's hand-to-hand stuff. The things from the pit are *machines* designed to *spew* death. The skeletons of their pilots went with them. If the Crux can reanimate their weapons somehow, no one in Veil will stand a chance."

"Machines." Rowan nodded. "I have seen the remnants of such devices before. I didn't understand that they came from your world."

"Neither did I." She looked over to him, her eyes almost colorless with despair. "You still have the revolver I left behind."

He nodded soberly. "In my pack. I sensed it was too dangerous a thing to leave to its own fate."

"You'd better give it back to me. Maybe if the people of Veil can somehow remain untainted by technology, they'll be protected. Maybe that's what your rituals and quests are for. And I tried to tell you that they were empty superstitions. They kept you clear of the arms race, didn't they?"

Rowan frowned. "Have you taken ill again, as from the pit-water? You speak of unclear things—tecknowledgey, and arms racing each other."

He finally made her laugh, although the sound was empty.

"Oh, Rowan, I know I speak gibberish sometimes. You don't know how lucky you and your world are that my gibberish means nothing to you."

"You are the Taliswoman. All that you say has some meaning, in some way."

"Oh, I hope not. Because I don't like what I see, and what I might have to say."

He reached into his pack and withdrew a small, flannel-wrapped bundle. "Here is your weapon-machine. It is almost as heavy as the Cup."

"Yeah." Alison balanced it on her palm, then pushed the chamber open and spun it. Four bullets left. Still a loaded weapon. "All I know is that I had better take this. The only signs of my world that I've seen in yours are contaminants."

"Contaminants?"

"A big word for harmful things. I wonder if even the ether-ion . . ." She snapped the weapon closed and sat brooding.

Rowan watched her, more disturbed than he would show. He realized that he had come to expect the Taliswoman's jibes and goads, to depend upon her unexpected opinions, and to welcome her solutions to problems. If she surrendered, he would lose by it—and so would his world.

Her alien ways had seduced him despite himself. She was a world in herself. No woman he had seen in Veil could take the various and unpremeditated directions that Alison took by her very nature. He had grown accustomed to being challenged by her rather than acquiesced to, and not the least in the intimate arena. Even their brief encounters there had revealed actions and reactions he had never dreamed of and that he would now be unwilling to do without.

But this was not the time for such talk, he decided. He understood Alison's state, he thought. He had felt mired in this same deadening mood of self-disgust not many days before, when the Crux had wrested the amulet from him.

Now that he had won it back, perhaps he valued both it and himself even more for the almost-loss. But Alison had lost something she could not reclaim so easily: she came from a world that put its faith in machines, and she could not envision a world with any future that could withstand their power.

Rowan lifted the Cup from his pack as she stood to rejoin the others. It trembled subtly in his hands, like an instrument, gravid and strange, its song not yet sung. No machine could offer that kind of potential.

They returned to camp to find the fire ashes scattered, the Hammerhands massed for marching, and the Sylvins straining at their tethers to be off.

"Nothing for them here now," Sage said to the returning couple. "Lenaree says that if Rowan wishes to walk to the Quarter of the Four Winds, the Hammerhands will guard the march as far as their lands. The Sylvins will fly ahead to hunt for signs of the Crux."

Alison eyed the buoyant corsairs, toys in comparison to the risen planes from Earth's wars. "The Sylvins may be better off here on the ground," she warned. "Their presence aloft may attract the Crux."

Felard, overhearing, turned quickly. "Sylvins are made to fly; you can no more hold them down than you could leash etherion."

"But they may risk their craft, their lives."

The Hammerhand nodded. "So do we all. Enemies of Veil have more often been known to walk than to fly."

Alison looked around. She had wanted the people of Veil to cooperate, and now they stood as a solid mass against her.

"You, too, still wish to accompany Rowan?" she asked the Littlelost. There were unanimous nods, except for the odd head here and there.

Plume spoke from their midst. "We of the Hammerhand and Sylvin kind will go only as far as those people's lands."

Rowan turned to Alison, his eyes brooding with an emotion she had never before detected in his youthful certainty: regret.

"I must always wonder if Pickle would have cared to return to Desmeyne had I been wise enough to offer such a choice."

"All creatures yearn for the place where they began, for home," she answered.

"As you do?" His expression remained oddly intense.

She felt herself color guiltily. Her mind had scarcely been on Minnesota, not with Rambeau here, and the Littlelost and Sage and . . . all right, Rowan.

"I haven't thought about home much," Alison admitted.

He waited. She realized that he had expected a deprecating remark, a joke, some forced lightness that would deflect heavy-handed emotion into laughter. She had none of that now. She had seen the future of Veil, and it was the past of Earth. She knew how the story ended. A reporter did not make a good time traveler.

She managed a rueful shrug. "If everyone wants to forge ahead, I might as well come along. I wish Rambeau were back. And the other Slinkers."

"Perhaps they form a vanguard," Sage suggested, patting her full pockets. "Have you need of your staff?" she asked Rowan. "I could use a cane. I even begin to long for the swaddled comfort of the Lofts."

"My staff has been Crux-touched," he said. "I dare not lend it. But—"

Gelmar stepped to the woods, bent to uproot a sapling and peel it of branches and bark. In mere minutes, Sage's need was answered.

Alison recognized an undeniable democratic upswelling of opinion when she saw it. The majority wished to forge on, so she bent to tuck away the revolver, hefted her now heavier pack with a sigh, and joined the moving throng.

Hammerhands began their Wagnerian chorus. The Lit-tlelost held the tethers while the Sylvin women climbed up and fitted themselves to their corsairs. Then the aircraft were up one after another, an armada of metallic kites bouncing against the sun.

Alison momentarily envied the Sylvins their romantic but efficient craft . . . until she remembered the carrion Corsairs the Crux had raised from the etherion pit. Even Veil's once-pure air was now infected with cruising sharks.

First tainted water, then toxic earth, then polluted air. Veil was following in very familiar footsteps.

She had her own footsteps to follow. Her musings had given the others a head start. Alison trotted after them.

The farther the etherion pit vanished behind the party, the less haunted Veil appeared. They tramped over regular swells of rumpled meadow, treading the thin line between the forests' edge and the upper areas where the mountains' bones broke through their grassy skin to show sharp defiles among cliffs of treacherous shale.

Their path took them north, according to the sun's position. The Hammerhands said that it would take a nine-day march—at Littlelost pace—to reach the lands they shared with the Sylvins, and four more days to the Rookeries where the wild Littlelost dwelled.

Flowers rippled along the crags' rocky bottom line—cheerful flags of nature at a safe distance, rank or scentless when the party's path ventured too near.

Nothing flew overhead save the quick, cruising shadows of etherion corsairs. Once Alison would have taken such fleeting shadows for wispy clouds. But Veil's clouds crouched cowed at the horizon, as always. Perhaps even clouds had a reason for avoiding the open airways.

A chorus of trailing Littlelost echoed the Hammerhands' drone, their higher-pitched voices sounding far, wee, and a trifle off-key.

Rowan walked ahead, talking with Sage, slowing his long strides to her hesitant gait, bending now and then to hear her reply. He could have been the courtly hunter of the fairy tale warning the grandmother of wolves.

If the sinister changes Alison had seen in Veil disquieted, Alison reminded herself that she had seen equally drastic changes for the better in the people of Veil. Perhaps the two forces would balance out.

And thinking of wolves, where were hers? All right, they

weren't "hers," but the wolf pack was the first creatures of Veil she had glimpsed on the Island, even before she saw the Takers, and later, their captive Littlelost. Or were the wolves truly creatures of Veil, any more than she was? Interesting thought.

Madonna walked nearby amid her rambling pups, her head lifting now and then so that nose and ears could do their guard duty. The wolf did not act particularly alarmed, but she remained alert. Alison admitted that she must accept Beau's absence with the unfettered pack members. It was not unusual. And he would hardly desert his family if they were in danger.

Now she walked alone behind them all: new friends, old friends, old enemy and on-again, off-again lover. She knew more about them now, and about some unsuspected parts of herself, but she still did not know why Veil was Crux-plagued and why this seemingly unreal land's ills stemmed so directly from the undeniably real ills of her own world.

A little later, Rowan slowed to join her. Alison tried hard not to feel too pleased.

His unbearded face now held the gauntness of hard decisions rather than the leanness of youth. His hair was no less red, but it no longer struck her as so extravagant that she blinked every time she saw it.

"Would you sense it if the animal had perished?" he asked abruptly.

"Beau? We were close, but not that close. Not psychically so. Why do you—"

"I only speculate." He eyed the inhospitable mountain passes to their left with a frown. "The creature has kept himself from you often on this journey."

"The marvel is that he came back. Before, he stayed here, while I returned to my world alone."

"How could he even know of your departure? He was not in the Earth-Eater tunnels with us."

"Oh, yes he was! He came in the white mist that swept me up the tunnel from Heart of Earth: Rambeau and the whole pack, with the Bone Buffalo and his herd. You had to have seen Beau there! He charged the blue Crux-light first."

Rowan shook his head. "Nothing came with the white mist but obscurity. It swallowed you first. The Littlelost wailed and gave chase. I was busy with the amulet until the fog enveloped me as well. Then I wandered within the fog for a while." He looked confused. "At times I heard Lorn wailing, crying 'No.' I followed the call and finally found myself in the open air again, above-ground, along with the surviving Littlelost. We were . . . surprised that you were not there."

"You never saw Beau and the wolves charge into the Cruxlight, break it with their bodies?"

"Had I seen that they were so talented, I would have paid them more attention during our current travels. Are you saying that these creatures are gifted to fight the Crux without the services of Cup or amulet?"

"I'm telling you what I thought I saw. Maybe I saw only what I needed to. We were both under a dire strain."

"Yes." His hand covered the amulet pouch. "Do you accept the necessity of this now?"

She nodded. "As you now accept the necessity of my having won the Cup, which violated your beliefs as much as your making the amulet from Lorn's ashes challenged mine."

He was silent, then said, "Only one thing troubles me as much as the Slinkers' absence. The Hammerhands' singing will bring the allies of the Crux down upon us."

"You're right."

"But what can I do about this danger?"

"Ask them to stop."

He ceased walking, aghast. "I had not thought of a solution so simple."

Alison chuckled. "You mean that you don't relish the notion of asking such big bruisers to pipe down. I will, then. Their courtesy toward small women will permit them to desist without losing face."

"You are not small," Rowan objected.

"To them I am." She increased her pace to reach the party's forefront.

"Maybe," Rowan shouted as an afterthought, "you should use Rime to do the asking."

Alison shook her head and trotted on without answering. Rowan was becoming a politician worthy of Mother Earth.

The head Hammerhand, Felard, listened gravely to Alison's request, stopping in mid-stride and thereby forcing a rear-end collision behind him that resembled the collapse of a house of cards.

Amid complaints and jostlings, Felard nodded and frowned, the first simultaneous acts he had ever attempted. He bent down to make sure that his ringing voice didn't inform the mountaintops as well as Alison.

"Song comes as easily to us as breathing," he said, "whether we pound the etherion with our hammers or the ground with our feet. But we will try to be silent."

Alison smiled her thanks and let the large men resume the lead. She could see how these deliberate beings had won the trust of the erratic Sylvins.

By midday, the Hammerhands' unnatural quiet had begun to grate on everyone, but then the party came upon a sight that sobered and silenced all of them.

First the Hammerhands stopped, as they always did, en masse, becoming a hairy, muscular, ungiving wall. No one could see past them except the bold Littlelost, who pushed themselves between their legs. Alison felt like a child at church: something awesome was obviously going on up front, but a solid wall of impenetrable backs made the whole thing a mystery.

She tried to push first one way, then another, to no avail. Then hands under her elbows lifted her up, high. She glimpsed the world falling away beyond the Hammerhands, and turned to thank her kindly lifter, expecting perhaps to see Felard.

It was Rowan raising her, his face grimacing with effort.

"You can't keep this up," she objected.

"Just tell me what you see. I can better lift you than the other way around."

The Hammerhands, poised six feet from a last lip of high ground and oblivious to the obstacle their massive bodies made, gazed in utter stillness on the land below.

"Empty space," she reported to Rowan's face beside her

hip. "Like the land itself fell off a tremendous cliff. And flat, flat plains far below as far as the eye can see, with dark water puddling in the low spots—not water—earthgalls! The terrain is pocked with earthgall!"

Rowan lowered her with a jolt. "The Hammerhands lead because they know the way. Have they lost it?"

Thorm deigned to hear him and turned to thunder over his leather-garbed shoulder, "The way has lost us. This land was rolling meadow when we came." And then the man knelt so that the formerly "Big People" in the party could see past him. Other Hammerhands followed slow, polite suit. Sage, Rowan, and Alison crowded forward to observe what the Littlelost had seen from knee level.

Beyond the Hammerhands' heads and shoulders lay a vast, pancake-flat land charred with spots of black earthgall and shining damp patches of swampy water.

The Sylvins' corsairs wheeled in the bland blue sky above this devastation like a confused swarm of bees, too disoriented to land, too shocked to sail away elsewhere.

"Where can we go, then?" Alison asked.

Hammerhand heads jerked toward the frowning escarpment of shale to their right.

"Up," said Felard with no pleasure. "Through the mountain passes, where it is cold and bare."

"But no snow," Alison added hopefully. She had seen little snow frosting the mountaintops so far.

"No snow," Felard agreed tonelessly, thrusting himself up to his feet. He and his fellows rose like moving rocks and plodded across the remaining meadow grasses, aiming for the line of malodorous flowers that divided grasslands from rock-lands.

Rowan eyed Sage's slow-following steps with some concern. "She is tiring from keeping pace," he said.

Alison was startled to notice that the wisewoman's limp had become pronounced. "Twist," she called, "and Faun!"

The two Littlelost weaseled free of the mob and scurried back to Alison, their faces sober.

"Walk with Sage," Rowan instructed them. "One on either side, so she does not fall."

"And don't tell her what you are doing," Alison added.

The pair exchanged glances. They would rather be accompanying the Hammerhands than trailing the party with an old woman, but they nodded and did as they were bid.

Alison looked above. "I don't like being forced into the uplands."

"The walk will be less cushioned," Rowan agreed, "but once we pass the foul flowers—"

"—we will be on higher, barer ground. We will make a better target from above."

"Ah, you mean the vile contrivances the Crux lifted from the pit. You expect them to attack."

Alison nodded.

"But the Sylvins—"

"—are not equipped to deal with the destruction those once-dead flyers carry, believe me. And on high ground, we will be defenseless targets."

"You speak as if you know these things for fact. They have not happened."

"But they have! In my world."

With this he could not argue, but walked on in weighty silence. Alison measured the length of his stride and reflected on how he walked with her as if by choice, by custom. She glanced to the pouch upon his collarbones and the scars glimpsed beneath, feeling a surge of rage. He was a walking target, the Firemayne's red-haired son. And the Crux would come for him.

27

THE very air grew thinner the higher they climbed.

And they were climbing now, not walking. The Hammerhands had resumed their chorus: not so much song as a rhythmic convocation of grunts. Monotonous movement drained these massive men. They toiled up the rock-strewn slopes and through tight defiles, and music made the motions easier.

Agile Littlelost scrambled upward, unhampered by anything, but Alison felt the burdens of her doubts and her pack. She tried not to show her distress, especially when Rowan's hands eased her over boulders the size of Plymouth Rock.

Poor Sage hobbled along the most circuitous route, drawn forward by the Littlelost on either side.

Whenever the party members looked back, they saw a barren land measles-spotted with ruin. The stark view sobered Rowan further, made Sage wince, and Alison bite her lip.

For they had left the Veil that Alison had first encountered: bucolic, wondrous, shot through with exotica, even if blotched with danger. Now the very fabric of Veil was rotting from the inside out.

Rowan's staff struck solid rock each time it reached for earth. Its dull clunk seemed a passing knell for Veil.

The route had angled sharply upward again. Alison no longer yearned for Beau. She would not wish this trek on anyone or anything. She watched the Sylvin corsairs soar higher aloft to keep sight of the party. How fragile they were. They teased the sun, as if soon their metal wings might melt to molten wax.

While still they climbed, that sun softened and sank, reddening the horizon clouds with the maddeningly immoderate colors of Rowan's hair. If the People of the Horizon truly existed, they took a twice-daily bath of fire.

"Where will we settle for the night?" Alison turned to ask Rowan.

The answer was grim. "Perhaps we won't."

The mountains went on and on. Ridge after ridge rippled to the horizon, to the foaming mist of shy clouds clinging to the visible end of things.

The higher clouds faded to palest pink with the sinking sun. Still the Sylvins soared, free and effortless on the invisible upper air, skating on the metal edges of tilted wings.

"If only the Crux hadn't destroyed your corsair," Alison noted between her teeth as she climbed a rough stair of rock.

"I was not made to fly," was Rowan's stoic answer.

And then the sun's rays dipped back into its blood-red inkwell and it sank behind the resulting smear. The sky's last blushes died along the long, healing wound of a horizon line, while rosy clouds clustered like timid sheep on the far edges of the world, both wild and safe in their withdrawal.

Crux-fire rose above the mountaintops in the east. One starry, blue-white sparkle followed another. Icy fireflies clustered, the flashes of Crux-craft still far off. At opposite ends of the visible spectrum, Sylvin corsairs and Crux-coursers lifted and dropped without sound. The last rays of the sun, or the far, unseen stars of Earth, glinted off their wings.

"If the Crux-craft draw near, no one can help the Sylvins." Alison said, watching the corsairs gleam ruddily in the sunset, while the cold, pale fire of the Crux flashed on the opposite horizon.

Rowan's hands were warm on her waist, pushing her upward, farther from the earth, into the unsupporting air.

"We are out of our element," she warned. "One fall and we are lost."

Yet up they went, because down had become back, because dark had become light. For the higher they climbed, the longer the last faint shred of daylight clung to the distant horizon and made Crux-light pale, forced weary body and soul onward and upward.

"They clash!" Sage's aged voice cried faintly from behind.

Alison stared upward. A bolt of aquamarine lightning stitched the distant sky to the land. Sylvin corsairs reeled away from it. Brighter bolts followed, falling stars of swift attack glancing off etherion wings still basking in the warm withdrawal of sunlight.

The Hammerhands' chanting stopped suddenly, then burst out anew as shouts of alarm. Littlelost squealed. At the rear, Rowan and Alison exchanged a startled glance, then looked toward the Hammerhands, up the mountain. The very cliff-face was fracturing and collapsing on the party. Rocks the size of sheep were thundering down the slope . . . not just falling, they were being pushed!

Nimble Littlelost scattered, while the Hammerhands hugged the bottom of the breaking cliff-face. Alison and Rowan, the most exposed, began to dash over the rough rocks, seeking shelter.

"Sage!" Alison screamed.

"I saw the Littlelost steer her to safety," Rowan shouted, prodding her onward. "Run!"

His words spurred her. She leaped from rock to rock, Rowan echoing her frantic dash behind her. At last Alison embraced the cliff, which trembled faintly under her hands.

Small stones hailed past, nicking her boot heels, flailing her elbows, shoulder, and hips. Rowan had flattened himself against the rock wall, facing outward.

Alison was just catching her breath when she felt a passing onrush of large, rock-sized shapes again. "The avalanche hasn't stopped yet?" she asked incredulously. The hail of stone should have signaled diminution.

"It has only begun." Rowan pulled his staff to his chest.

She turned to demand an explanation when she saw it for herself. Figures hurtled down after the rocks and stones: Takers and Halflings come to see what damage their artificial avalanche had done.

A Taker hurled by, screaming, and plunged into the darkening wrinkle of the valley below. Their party's lofty position had one advantage: fallen opponents would literally lose position and nose-dive out of the conflict. And one disadvantage: their own side was equally susceptible to such overthrowing.

For now the Hammerhands up ahead—formidable weapons still slung in their belts—were tossing the first wave of attackers over the cliff-edge before their opponents could even challenge the back ranks of the Littlelost.

Takers rained past Rowan and Alison, while more of them made deeper progress against the Littlelost.

"The Hammerhands fail to deal as harshly with the Half-lings." Rowan's staff gestured.

It was true, Alison saw. The first Halflings, taller than Takers, were dropping down in shock-absorbing crouches to confront the Hammerhands.

Kin still called to kin; the Hammerhands reached instead for the many Takers near at hand. The untouched Halflings plowed forward into the morass of Littlelost, ignoring thigh-high blows as they came straight for Rowan. Or for Alison. Or for both of them.

Alison looked around for a weapon that would extend her reach—a fallen branch, anything—as Rowan hefted his staff to meet the oncoming Halflings.

"Wait!" she warned, following him over the unsteady rocks.

He turned, ready to chivalrously order her back, when he saw her stomping the edge of the drop-off as if smashing a bug.

A large, well-haired hand groped up over the edge and grabbed Alison's ankle. Rowan's staff skewered it with a smashing blow, and it vanished with a howl.

Alison tugged at Rowan's arm. "We've got to climb. Takers who survived the fall are coming back up the cliff. We'll be trapped between them and the Halflings."

Rowan gave the approaching Halflings a regretful look. Alison suspected that he was eager to test his new *taekwondo* skills on Halflings, male or female. But her urgent logic was undeniable.

The pair veered up a makeshift high road to the right, choked with boulders. Battle din dimmed as twilight approached, but shadowy Taker forms still followed them, climbing grimly.

Crux-fire flashed brighter against the now darkening sky. Alison glimpsed, closer than before, Sylvin corsairs darting among the lethal strikes, like the insects called darning needles, basting the sky on the bias with their daring maneuvers. They had no other weapons, only the slim possibility of luring a Crux-courser into a rockface or the ground.

One Sylvin corsair spiraled by as fast as a falling Taker, its unwound tether trailing it like an umbilical cord. Alison turned her face to the rock she struggled to climb, expecting sound and fury, the smash of metal on ground, a cloud of fiery death.

Nothing. She looked down anxiously, leaned so far out over the cliff that Rowan snatched her back against the rock.

"The corsair? It was destroyed?" she asked.

"Perhaps." He eyed the bobbing shapes climbing up behind them. "Faster!" he said.

They clawed their way on up, Rowan hard pressed to keep hold of his staff. She often took and thrust it ahead of them, then climbed, then used the staff to give him a hold to reach her position.

The long, slow death of light that was dusk in Veil aided their effort, even as it revealed them to their enemies. It also showed the forces clashing below them on the mountain and beyond them in the sky.

Alison tried not to think of the Littlelost making the same plunge that the Takers had, of where Sage was, or of Lenaree. She and Rowan had their own skins to save, presumably because two Cup-bearers were worth more than mere life and breath, but served in some symbolic sense. A slim reason for retreat.

"We draw Halflings, too." Rowan spoke between climbing grunts behind her.

It was true. The shadowy mountainside was moving subtly below them, rising like a reversed avalanche on a newsreel film. Alison was not sure that she liked the role of decoy any better than that of escapee.

She glanced out over the valley, trying not to let the vastness of the space unhinge her climbing balance. They had climbed to a level with the dueling Crux-coursers and Sylvin corsairs. The light at the top of the sky etched the rapidly nearing flyers in the soft black-and-white contrast of twilight.

"Good Lord!" she called out.

Rowan paused in prodding her upward and turned to look.

A Crux-courser hung aloft not a hundred feet away, and nearly abreast of them, radiating neon-blue and slowly flapping its wings.

"By the wrath of wildwater!" Rowan swore.

A monstrous hybrid, not only of machine and magically endowed metal, but of times and places grafted onto one another, hovered there, watching them.

Alison knew the mechanical lineage of what she saw. Rowan would not know, but his impression of monstrosity would be as accurate as hers.

"This should not *be*," she muttered.

But it was. There. Before her very eyes, and his. A crude patchwork, Frankensteinian machine. Etherion bandaged the broken wings, the torn tail and battle-eaten nose of a World War II vintage airplane. The object less resembled its component parts than a misshapen third incarnation. The warplane's canopy had half torn off; a corpse still wearing bits of cloth and leather shared the pilot's seat with a skeletal figure bathed in the same blue light that haloed the entire craft. Alison had never seen a Crux-master this close, without the dazzling shield of a specific wand. Of the two macabre figures sitting in that single seat, the Crux-master repelled her the most. Flesh still shaped its bones as clothing clung to the corpse. And yet the Crux-master lived, moved, lifted flared bony fingers over the dead instruments and made them stir as if to invisible strings. The craft wheeled away, back into the conflict.

"Where do they get their power? From the blue light?" Alison asked herself as much as anyone.

"I have never seen such a thing in Veil," Rowan said. "What unhallowed alien machine is this, and what is that creature with the Crux-master?"

"Both are things of my world, I'm afraid. Things dead in my world."

"Your dead live on here?" He sounded truly shocked. "And yet you know no Crux? What can you call such madness, if not Crux-made?"

"Zombies," Alison answered. "We call them zombies." The term was not accurate; from what she saw, the dead pilot was only along for the ride. She risked a glance back and down at Rowan.

He nodded, satisfied by the foreign name. "Zombies. And curses that kill those who mate. No wonder you returned to Veil from your world."

Once she would have argued, even under these circumstances. Instead, she just resumed climbing. Sight of that hybrid flyer had motivated her all the more to stay out of the Crux's hands, especially shuddersome, shrunken hands so touched with death. Were Crux-masters even alive? Had her choice of terms been more appropriate than she guessed? Zombies?

Then she was thinking only of cleaving to the rock, of scraping up, over and across it, and listening for the sounds of Rowan behind her, following. Air fought them now for every breath, the niggardly upper air of mountain passes, cool on the face, burning in the chest as lungs sought to squeeze more oxygen from it.

"Is there no end to this?" Rowan panted.

"None in sight."

He saved his breath by remaining silent. They scrabbled on upward, trying to ignore scrapes and bruises. At least there was no wind to comb them from their perch, Alison thought. And she shared Rowan's anxiety. If they did not crest the ledge above them by dark-fall, they would either be trapped where they were or would misstep in the dark and fall to certain death. Fortunately, the light was dimming slowly.

Contending flyers swooped below them now, and few Sylvins remained aloft. Alison was glad she had not seen them fall. As for the others . . . Rowan pushed her boot, forcing her upward another notch. Luckily, it got no colder higher up.

Their faces, fingers, and feet would have been numb by now on any normal mountain.

The Takers were invisible in the lower dark, and no immediate threat. A kind of peace came from climbing silently to the top of the world, the only wind the gasp of their own breath in their ears.

And then something swept out of the darkening blue, creating an artificial draft, something so large it momentarily blocked the last light.

"Hurry!" Rowan urged from below, his voice hoarse.

She hurried. She, too, had glimpsed the odd-eyed Crux-master perched like a ghoulish puppet on the ruined nose of the hybrid flyer that had brushed so close above them. She shuddered to recall its eyes—one shining red, the other green in the dying light, like a berserk traffic semaphore sending mixed messages to Alison's own survival instincts: Stop. *Go!* Fall. *Climb!* Slower. *Faster!*

Then, silently, without the rush of wind or noise she expected, the entire armada of a dozen Crux-coursers swarmed around them. Silhouettes shot past overhead against the dim blue sky, dipped beside them and hovered there unnervingly.

Pellets of blue light jackhammered into the mountainside, an avalanche of attack spraying them with instant gravel. Left, right, below, above—the courser hissed out a Morse-code pattern of staccato fire.

"What new madness—" Rowan had twisted around to look.

Alison hardly needed to. The resurrected corsair carrying the odd-eyed Crux-master was swaying near again, clumsily flapping its wings. Three thin barrels at the front of each wing sprayed lightning-fast ellipses of light at the mountain.

"What black rods can break Crux-fire into a hail of sparks?" Rowan shouted.

"What I feared," Alison shouted back. "Crux-fire filtering through weapons from my world. Machine guns."

A blast of blue swept underneath their feet, forcing them up farther from the ground, from aid, from any surviving allies.

Before Alison could resume climbing, she glimpsed another sinister shape: a yard-long, finned bullet-shape tucked under the Corsair's intact metal belly. A fighter plane couldn't carry a nuclear bomb, she told herself, but what else might it harbor?

Further gawking would risk their balance and their upward momentum. They climbed, dodging spitting Crux-fire and crushed rock. Alison caught battle images from the corner of her eye: the upward burst of several all-etherion craft, shining dragonflies of the dusk, whining triumphantly.

Swirling past came more ugly hybrid Crux-craft, grinning death's heads painted on once-earthly airplane skins by once-live crews, the grinning death's heads of long-gone pilots lurking behind the hazy light that swathed the airborne Crux-masters.

The rapid-fire rain of blue light swerved from the mountainside to the Sylvin corsairs, which swept close to unbalance the cumbersome Crux-craft. Like large insects, the dueling craft circled and dove, the hum of their near-collisions whining in the lofty quiet. Almost benign, rays of blue light still sizzled against the mountainside, washing Alison and Rowan in the merciless revelation of a spotlight for sickening seconds.

In that lurid light, Alison looked up and saw only further heights ahead. Her muscles had tightened into protesting knots of fire and ice. Worse, her mind had deadened to the hope of escape, even if they should crest the cliff.

Then the blue light died as quickly as it had sprung to life. She blinked helplessly in the too-sudden dark, unable to see or to move. Below her, Rowan was caught in the same pincer of bright and dark.

Another explosion. Alison squinted toward its edges to see a Crux-craft bearing straight for them, the Crux-master's extended rod slicing layers from the rockface ahead. She felt like a gnat on the Rock of Gibraltar, and clung dumbly.

The tilted wing of a Sylvin flyer swept into the laserlike rays, blocking them, but Alison's eyes recovered from the sudden dark in time to spot the Sylvin pilot, a tiny, grim figure, working the fine lines of flight like a mad harpist.

Crux-light hissed into the etherion barrier, and a dark projectile shot from under one slowly sawing wing, exploding in blue glitter as it touched the Sylvin craft. The poised corsair wing simply . . . melted . . . dispersed into a thousand motes. One-winged, the corsair tilted sideways and dropped from sight.

Alison actually began to lift her hands from the rock to cover her eyes. She couldn't bear to witness another Sylvin loss to the Crux, when carnage unknown lurked below.

Then the Crux corsair dropped the bomb. She watched the missile's dark form plummet and diminish, vanish . . . until, only seconds later, a lake of blue fire burst into being on the plain of darkness below. Against it, the tiny black silhouette of a one-winged corsair was falling toward the light, a moth to the flame.

No, Alison thought. What old earth weapon from World War II would do that? Not nuclear, thank God. No. But . . . she had seen the landscape incinerate like that before. On news footage. From 'Nam.

"Napalm," she whispered. "The Crux has napalm!"

Rowan scrambled up behind her in the dark, pressing her to the rock.

"What?" she gasped.

"Something is coming up behind us, fast. Hurry!"

"Rowan, I can't—"

"Hurry!" He pushed her forward, hard.

For a moment she flailed to locate holds, any holds. From behind them, she now heard the hot rhythm of many laboring breaths, increasing at a supernatural speed that no Takers possessed. Now what? Alison wailed to herself, using her last strength to pull herself up the dark rocks toward the final bit of daylight, shining like a beacon atop the mountain.

Crux-light hissed below them now. Stones fell behind them, scraping and then chinking fainter and fainter as they bounced off lower and lower abutments.

"I think," Alison announced, "there's a ledge—"

Rowan didn't waste breath in answering. He lifted her legs while her arms swam forward in a vertical Australian crawl, trying to cut through rock as a swimmer would water.

The pursuers were a din now of dislodged stones and heaving breaths. Alison flung her arms over the ledge and was struggling to pull herself atop it when something bounded past, using her for a stepping-stone. Cut off at the pass, she thought. Beaten by the baddies.

Rowan still pushed from below—at least she hoped it was Rowan. She worked her legs up even harder and then crawled forward until all of her rested on solid, relatively flat ground.

Crux-fire rose with her, blasting at the mountain, lashing her with light and noise. Something smacked to the rock beside her. In the strobe-light flashes she could see Rowan crawling over the edge, his staff already thrust onto the level ground.

She reached to help him up, only then aware that her fingernails were ragged and bleeding.

They both sat on the ledge, panting furiously, the valley below a black quilt lit by the lurid acrobatics of coursers and corsairs. Many coursers, perhaps twenty. Few corsairs, say six.

Several Crux-coursers gravitated to their ledge, their slender refuge in the face of chaos. The craft danced before them, a cruel light-show, beams of Crux-fire admonishing the mountain around them, above them, behind them.

The Crux-master wing-walker, he whose eyes gleamed opposite colors, aimed a surgically thin rapier of light at Rowan. The beam cut the stone at his shoulder, outlined his head, and stopped at the opposite shoulder, all the while showering his face with gravel.

Alison understood: it was Lorn all over again. Rowan was to surrender the amulet or take the consequences.

Rowan understood perfectly, too. "No," he said.

No, Alison thought. Not again. "We can get it back," she urged him. "We did it once."

As if understanding, the Crux-master turned toward her. His pitiless rod outlined her form, sizzled alongside her shoulder, over her head and along her other shoulder.

Rowan said nothing.

The light darted between them, striking near his thigh, her cheek, his neck. It teased a lock of Rowan's hair from his head, and the evil odor of burnt hair clung like incense.

Then the light fell to Alison's left, a dentist's drill of precise attack, and began to chip away at her side of the ledge where they sat.

In the flicker of blue, Rowan's hand went to his throat.

"No!" she said. "I won't be responsible for your losing it twice."

Before he could answer, another sound came into the air-thin dark.

A cry. A whimper. A wail. A hum. A croon. A howl. A holy, inarticulate chant. Beginning. Single. A note struck and held, a note swelling and knelling like a bell. Endless. Beginningless. Another note joined. A mournful calling. A suffering. A celebrating. Another whimper-wail. And another.

The sound was demonic, hypnotic, chilling, inspiring. Wolves in mountaintop chorus, unseen but heard from horizon to horizon.

That was what had rushed up and overtaken them: sure-footed wolves speeding for high ground to create a chorus that would shatter the night. But what could a wolf call do against the Crux?

The Crux-master's light had paused at the sound's beginning, but now it bored drill-like into the rock at Alison's side. Her thigh felt a haze of heat, almost pleasant, even as her mind recognized her imminent danger.

Rowan sighed and lifted his hands to the back of his neck, where the pouch cords were tied.

"Not yet!" she insisted. "Give them a chance."

"What can Slinker howls do?"

"I don't know. But they're doing something."

"They are beasts, mute unless some unreason takes them and they howl."

"Maybe more reason guides them than you think," Alison said, edging closer to Rowan as the rock under her crumbled away.

"I will not let the Crux toy with us." He reached for the knot beneath the frill of hair covering the back of his neck.

"And if you give it the amulet, why should the Crux let us go? We'll be killed anyway."

Rowan hesitated.

The Crux-light sliced a lock of hair from her head, grazed her ear. Ice-fire hitting a nerve. Alison screamed despite herself, adding her cry to the unearthly chorus.

Something bounded onto their ledge from above. Rambeau! Gleaming blue in the brilliant Crux-light, his bristling ruff drawing the lethal beam to itself. He too howled as the Crux-light outlined his form, yet could not touch it.

"The Slinker is giving us a chance," Rowan shouted to Alison. "We must head for higher ground."

She nodded. They could not withstand the dueling light and sound at such close quarters much longer. She pushed with her feet until her backpack inched up the rockface behind her, Rowan doing likewise. Rambeau and the Crux-master, locked in eerie confrontation, paid their attempt no attention.

The Crux-master stood tall, his blue rod aimed, utter darkness except when his Crux-light illuminated the dreadful eyes of red and green. Rambeau braced his feet, head lowered into his neck, his ruff a magnificent white aura burning blue at the edges, his dark eyes winking yellow as the blue light ebbed and flowed, his snout thrust skyward, white fangs glinting. Uncanny howls poured from his throat, aimed straight for the stars.

Above Alison and Rowan, the other Slinkers howled. Finally standing, the two scrambled over a small rockslide and hit surprisingly level ground. They turned to stare at the ledge below, a mere lip on the edge of the greater dark.

"Beau can't hold off the light forever," Alison said.

"We must go. Now. While the Crux-master is distracted." Rowan pulled at her arm.

She resisted. Deserting Rambeau was unthinkable.

"We are fortunate that the beast has the power and the will to draw the Crux-light away from us. Perhaps he can save himself as well. He would not want us to linger, his act in vain."

Alison shook off Rowan's hand. "He's *my* dog! I can't just leave him like this."

Rowan grabbed her, in the old way, like a man accustomed to making up women's minds for them.

295

No way. She was tensing to fight when a band of luminous gray light swept across the northern horizon and the Slinker howls climaxed with a frenzy of pitch and prolongation.

Alison and Rowan froze as if caught in Crux-light. The horizon light swelled, leaking to the east and west. It had no color, only a cold, pearly brightness, like a Minnesota winter dawn. Somehow the wolf howls echoed it, sent chills down Alison's spine and froze her expectations. The animals' ululations grew ghastly, quickening with the light.

Behind the Crux-master perched on the courser wing, the other Crux-craft stirred uneasily in the air.

At the horizon, the steel-gray light rose, lifted into a mushroom cloud, a thunderhead centered in the north. Higher and higher it swelled, until it was halfway up the hemisphere and spawned great gray wings, stretching along the skyline to either side.

"He is making the sun reverse its course!" Rowan's voice was awe-stricken.

Alison shook her head. "I think the Slinkers called something." Hadn't the people of Veil always called Rambeau a "Spirit Slinker"? She had assumed that it was because his white coat looked so ghostly. Now she wondered if there was another reason, forgotten but valid.

And then the thing at the horizon—a cloud, or a light—gathered itself and rushed, leaping off of the earth's edge and fully into the sky.

It barreled toward them like a water bullet: all impact, though immaterial in a solid sense. At its massed front there began to emerge a huge head, with empty whirlwinds for eyes, beneath them a vast maw blacker than a starless night sky.

Beside the head beat wings. Wide gray wings of cloud and dust and twilight trapped for millennia.

"A true Spirit Slinker," Rowan breathed beside her.

She watched it come, a werewolf of wind, a thing of insubstantial fury. Ravening, mindless, its forerunners had already reached them: sudden, slapping shafts of icy, invisible currents. Crux-craft trembled in their uncanny anchorage on air.

The Crux-master turned to look back at his cohort, revealing an almost-human figure in profile.

Cold, flat grayness swept the world into a bizarre daylight brightness bereft of all warmth, color, life. The great-winged sky wolf took fifty-mile strides with legs that had coalesced from clouds, hurtling trees and stones in its wake, churning flotsam into the maelstroms of its night-empty eyes.

It pounced on the Crux-craft, took them up in its icy teeth and shook them until wings broke and tails cracked off. Wands of blue light struck at the white, snarling face and were lost in the gray immensity of its devouring nothingness.

A stench of old corruption exhaled over the mountain, old corruption panting for new prey.

While Crux-craft rocked as if tossed on a stormy sea, while Rowan and Alison stood frozen into their mock-battle poses, Rambeau suddenly lofted over the cliff-top toward them. He landed, watching them, his intelligent eyes alert and expectant, ears flicking back.

"They've stopped," Alison noticed belatedly.

True, a howling persisted, a faint, echoing caterwauling as sharp as a blizzard wind, but the wolves had quieted long before, perhaps at the moment the grayness had grown into a beast.

The Crux armada spun like toys in the wind-wolf's destructive, disembodied grip. Alison suddenly knew the creature's name, had heard it spoken long ago in Eli Ravenhare's cabin on the Island.

She clutched Rowan's arm. "We must leave."

"That is what I was saying," he answered with exasperation.

At Alison's words, Rambeau trotted toward the crest. He paused, looking as impatient as only a dog can look.

"Right," she said. "That thing . . . I know what it is. The Wendigo!"

"Wendigo?" Rowan repeated the word gingerly. "What is that?"

"An Indian Wind Spirit. The Wendigo has no discrimination, no sense of right or wrong, or of good or bad. It's just plain bad news. Bad medicine. Very bad medicine. Somehow the howling awoke it. Rambeau!" She turned to the dog, like a parent confronting a naughty child, as though to demand that he defend his recent action.

Rowan grabbed her arm and stepped in the direction the dog indicated. "You are right. We had best leave—now! If your Slinker called this force, he knows best."

Alison could not argue. Rowan tugged her into the unnaturally lit dark. One by one the Slinkers deserted their separate perches to loosely ring the two people.

Rambeau trotted several paces beyond them, stopped, sniffed, looked up. He crouched and growled, then sped behind them to nip at their heels.

They stumbled onward with the Slinker pack despite their fatigue, with no questions. At their back, a mordant wind licked its chops and dined on Crux-craft.

28

OUTSIDE the mountain cavern, the prowling Wendigo huffed and puffed at the tiny nostril of dark that opened into the odd gray twilight only the Wendigo commanded. The Wind Spirit's breath snorted inward, a blast of icy white mist that dissipated in the serpentine tunnels riddling the inner mountain. Its shrill, frustrated howls echoed through the rock-hewn corridors.

Inside, the two people and the five animals huddled in separate groups, listening to the Wendigo's great claws digging at the cavern entrance, to its hungry wails.

Rowan bent, reached into his knapsack in the dark, and fumbled inside to retrieve some items. In moments, light sparked between his hands. A bit of Sage's incendiary moss had ignited the flannel that wrapped the Cup. He dropped the burning cloth atop the pile of dried sticks before them.

"Good idea." Alison dug in her own pack, found an extra shirt and ripped off a sleeve. The fire feasted slowly on the slender fare, illuminating a golden glitter of Slinker eyes.

Alison offered Rowan some trail mix. This time he took it more enthusiastically, chewing with relish as his teeth bit into raisins and chocolate morsels.

"This is good!"

"Thanks. And thanks for getting me up the mountain."

He shrugged. "I had the Takers at my back, and then those hounds of deepest earth." He nodded almost affectionately at the Slinkers.

Rambeau edged into the faint firelight, then lay down, sighing.

Why did dogs sigh? Alison wondered. It was their most human gesture. Sighs said: It has been hard. I am tired. I don't know what to do. Sighs said: I wish and I want.

She knew what she wished and wanted: the Sylvins to fly again unchallenged, to be safe. And safety for the Littlelost and the Hammerhands. Now she and Rowan were secure—momentarily—but they knew nothing of what ruin may have come to their companions. Were only he and she so precious that they deserved to be spared?

Rowan might have read her thoughts. He reached behind his neck, worked out the knot that tied the pouch, and held the burden on his palm, studying it by the meager light.

"You were ready to surrender it," Alison commented.

"Cold clay seems a high price to pay for warm flesh."

She sighed. That was exactly how she had felt in the Deeps at the Heart of Earth when Pickle died. "Still, that very price was paid nearly a year ago; it would be a shame not to take this quest to its ultimate end."

"The Axletree is no ultimate end, only the next task. Other quests remain."

"I wonder if their costs will be as high."

He nodded soberly, not wondering at all.

Rambeau rose and came to sit at Rowan's left.

The old, one-eared gray Slinker pushed himself upright and went to sit beside Alison, his long nails clicking on the stone floor as he approached. His feral breath reached her before he did, and she stiffened. But the Slinker sat on his haunches, doglike, and paid her no mind, a lax tongue draping his yellowed teeth.

One of the black-furred youngsters stirred and skittered over beside Rambeau. The other black Slinker settled next to the gray wolf. Last was the female, who regarded the bracketing blacks in turn, then completed the circle by arranging herself between them.

Such behavior did not seem odd; the small fire offered a

fickle, fleeting warmth they all might enjoy. "Look," Rowan said suddenly.

The animals' ears were flicking up and down, as if heeding an unheard voice, and their eyes darted around the cavern. In the fire-light tremor, the rock walls glimmered with figures, some human, some animal.

"Drawings like these appeared in the cave Sage led us to," Alison said softly.

"I saw no such figments there."

"You weren't awake." She shot him a fondly accusing glance, remembering the snores of that night and her cranky hope that Rowan was their source, instead of Sage. "But Sage and I awoke and saw the figures dance. At least that's what they appeared to do. Perhaps it was a kind of illusion."

"So," Rowan pointed out, "is this."

And indeed the frieze of figures on the wall did seem to dance, around and around the fire and those circling it. Around and around, until Alison's head grew weary on her neck, and even Rowan's chin nodded sharply toward his chest.

They tried to shake off the lethargy, but the fire's warmth flared to envelop them and make them drowsy.

A scent wafted into the air, potent and rich. They inhaled it amid all the dancing, heaving light. Motes of iridescent yellow glinted from the walls, reflected from the midnight-black wolf eyes circling the fire. Then Alison and Rowan saw no more, but simply sat, heavy and motionless.

Rambeau stretched. Not so much stretched as grew, without moving. The luxuriant white ruff surmounting his shoulders broadened. Rambeau's proud canine head hung limp as his thick neck lengthened. His plume of a tail shrank and crawled up his spine vertebra by vertebra. When his head lifted again, Dog had become no more than a handsome skin covering the head and shoulders of a young, muscular, earth-skinned man with black, glittering eyes.

Those eyes looked to his left. The black-furred youngster had vanished, having given birth to a young, brown-skinned man who crouched on naked haunches.

Rambeau looked to the being on Alison's left. The old gray wolf was only a pelt now, crowning a venerable sage whose mahogany skin glittered like a wrinkled elephant's.

The second black wolf had become a ceremonial skin bedecking another young warrior. And when Rambeau looked last to the lone female, she wore a pale-haired wolfskin like a shawl. Twin black braids shone brighter than wet bark as they snaked across the soft fur.

"Wendigo," the ancient one said, his voice cracking.

Black-haired braves nodded, the wolf heads atop their faces joining in the agreement.

The young woman shot a bright, rebellious glance to the cavern entrance, which glowed with the gray-white fog of northern winters. "Why have you called such a brute to the very doors of our lodges?"

Rambeau sighed, his smooth-skinned face impassive. "It was necessary, children. A worse-than-Wendigo has oozed into this, our last refuge, from our once and only place. Wendigo alone would answer the need. Wendigo of the North is the First of the Four."

"Wendigo will devour us, and these your charges," the warrior sage said flatly. "Once called, Wendigo will come, but none can make Wendigo go."

"It was necessary," Rambeau said again. Before their very eyes, their dark, woodland eyes, he aged into middle youth. "When Wendigo has feasted, he will withdraw. If the other winds come, he will be tamed. We face a more formidable foe."

"Blue men with lightning rods!" one young warrior snorted, the wolfish face atop his head assuming a snarl.

"Men with other lightning rods took our world," he who had been Rambeau reminded them. "Men with such rods beat the very land into submission, ate us as snake does hare.

Brought down buffalo and groundhog. Beat wild rice into swamp mush, and wild swans into pillows for their heads. Beat Mother Earth bloody, and filled Father Sky with flying thunder-claps and poisonous smoke."

"What do you want of us, you who have evoked us in our living semblance?" the maiden asked. "You may command the four-footed servants of the woods and the old world, but who are you to call the White Wolf of the North? Who are you to call Wendigo? Who are you to dare call us from our dead peace?"

"I am," he said, "your son Eli Ravenhare, and your father Blue Sky, and your mother Red Earth. And your father weeps and your mother bleeds. You have faded, children, into a memory, but memory rides between one world and another, one time and another, and I am keeper of this phantom beast. I am Spirit Slinker, neither wholly beast nor wholly human. In some ways, it is better than being either."

They were still, the beads upon their deerskin garments lifting and falling with their airless breaths.

Outside the cave, Wendigo roared.

"What do you wish of us?" the ancient warrior asked, his voice quavering, but his look unshaken.

"You must whirl this world around. You must wind time and distance upon your roof-tree. You must desert your aloof cloud country and take these worlds by the shoulders and shake them until they bruise each other. You must bring my charges to Axletree, where the Four Winds meet to divide up air and fire, earth and water."

"And what will one puny human quest do to stanch blood or tears?" one young warrior demanded with a growl. His brother nodded agreement, black eyes darkening with anger.

The skin of the one named Eli puckered as they watched, and the eyes sank into swamps of failing flesh. "Something. Each one can do something. I call upon you, sister and brothers, to do what has become alien to you. I call upon you to show yourselves for what you were, and are, and may be again."

"When?" the old man barked.

"Morning," said Eli, sinking into oncoming old age as the dog likeness swelled into a sudden furry cloud and swallowed him whole. Great white-fanged jaws yawned wide and ate his Indian face. Tail flared into a spume of powder snow and devoured his spine. "Morning will come soon—or late—enough." Eli's voice animated the Samoyed head in which wise, dark-brown eyes simmered, no matter the semblance.

The fire faded into scattered ruby embers. Wolves and Dog settled onto the cold rock floor, pointed faces lowering to rest upon their slim, furred forelegs.

Alison and Rowan dreamed by the fire, upright in sleep, feeling the Wendigo's long tongue lashing out at them and then retreating. Feeling warmth fade and all sound silence.

In the morning, the wolves rose stiffly from the cold rock floor and trotted from the cave to scout the terrain. The old gray one limped last to the cave mouth.

Alison watched with sympathy. She wondered how long he would lead the pack. Rambeau might well overthrow such a venerable leader; wolf protocol was merciless.

Rowan awoke stiff, and grumpy besides. "I have never slept sitting up before. It is hard upon the tailbone."

"The Wendigo would have been harder upon the tailbone," she reminded him. But her hip ached, and she sparred with bad memories at the fringes of her mind.

After a quick breakfast on their favorite things—turkey jerky for him, trail mix for her—they donned their packs and joined the old Slinker to peer out the cavern entrance.

Gray was gone. In its place, white blanketed the world. The Wendigo's searing, frosty breath had scribed its feathery signature over every inch of rock, even on the now-ivory plains far below. Nothing stirred, but their perch was high, too distant for them to see survivors or those who had perished, or to tell the difference.

"What now?" Alison wondered.

Rowan nodded at Beau, who was waiting impatiently at the

bottom of yet another rocky climb toward the top of the mountain. "Your Slinker seems to know."

"I told you, he's no Slinker, only a dog."

Rowan shrugged. "He got us here, to safety."

"It's temporary, I'm sure." She paused. "Did you have odd . . . dreams last night?"

For some reason, her question irritated him. At least he reddened. "None," he said shortly. "And it's none of your affair in any case."

He started up the frost-slicked rocks Rambeau indicated. Alison eyed the gathered Slinkers, who looked as reluctant as she felt. "Stubborn," she said. "Both of them, man and dog. But what would they do without us wild things to keep them honest?"

She scrambled up the slippery rocks behind the two, hearing wolf nails scrabbling for purchase behind her.

They had climbed only twenty feet before Alison halted. "Wait! Listen."

Up here the eerie silence was pierced by the thin whistle of wind drilling through the chinks and chimneys.

"I heard nothing," Rowan said.

"Nothing but wind," she answered. "Wind! It almost sounds like the Wendigo."

"You think it lurks?"

"I'm sure it lurks, but not here. Not now. We're climbing into a more natural wind."

He touched his amulet pouch. "No trees grow this high upon the mountain."

"I suspect that the Axletree is like no tree we've ever seen. Well, you wanted to climb. Climb!"

They labored upward, Alison's fingers growing white and numb from clinging to frost-coated rocks. Sunlight as weak as chamomile tea sifted through the morning ring of clouds, illuminating but too frail to melt the frost.

With the sun, clouds eased up the horizon, a golden band of fluff. Rambeau paused on an outcropping—as wolves, or even dogs, will—his breath clouding out of his pointed muzzle like gunsmoke.

305

CAROLE NELSON DOUGLAS

"We must be really high," Alison said, looking down.

She could not see the valley below. The clouds had crowded in like morning mist steaming off the meadows, circling them, rising, lazy smoke rings drifting up the mountain slopes.

"Rowan!"

He sensed her alarm and reached down a hand to draw her up another two feet. Wind gentled the hair back from her face, from his; wind stirred Rambeau's fur into peaked whipped cream.

"The clouds—" She looked below, feeling claustrophobic, admittedly ridiculous on such a high, open prow of land.

The clouds were following them softly up the mountain, flowing into their footsteps, covering over their traces, forcing them onto a narrower and higher spit of land, a needle of rock that caught the sunlight in its single eye, the very peak.

Alison was suddenly afraid, for there was no way back. If Rowan was truly right, if there was a particular place where four winds quarreled endlessly, they were heading into the very teeth of that contention. Four counter-blowing winds might make the Wendigo look tame.

As if answering her thoughts, a gust snapped her against the rocks, then weaseled between her and the stone, seeking to pry her loose.

Below them, the clouds had closed like the mouth of a pouch drawing shut. Now the mists swirled smokily, turning the whole slow-rotating earth into a vortex, into the eye of a whirlwind.

She climbed because she needed a more secure purchase, because she sought to avoid the ghostly clouds choking tight upon the mountain. Because she was forced to.

Ahead of her, Rowan toiled upward, sniffing the breeze like Rambeau, an expression of unholy excitement on his face. His hair whipped in the brisk wind, a pennant indicating the strength of the element that buffeted him. Them.

Then two winds met, with Alison in the middle, and the only way to escape the conflict was to heft herself farther up the mountain, now slick with sun-melted frost.

She strained upward, aware of Rowan's booted heels doing

the same above her. A whine made her glance below. Rambeau stood there, neck stretched up as if he were about to break into a howl. Behind him massed the Slinkers, silenced by the thin air, by the wind that snatched the voices from their throats, by the clouds in which their disembodied heads floated.

"Oh, God," Alison said with a shudder. "We're trapped up here alone."

Wind whistled agreement. Wind wove in and out of their hair, their eyelashes, their fingers. Wind teased their grip from the stone. Wind flattened them against rock. Wind keened and wrestled and shrieked and mourned.

"Almost there." Rowan's voice came like a shot of sanity through the rising chorus of piercing sound. "Hold on to my ankle."

She grabbed that circle of reality and let its rhythmic tug pull her body into a vertical crawl. Cheek on rock, hand on niche, foot on notch. Right. Left. Right. Left. Wind was an icicle stabbing her extremities with cold force. *Let go-o-o-o*, it teased. *For-go-o-o-o*, it urged. *We rule he-e-e-re. We tear. We twist. We shimmy. We shiver. We shake loose. Let go-o-o-o.*

Was it the voice of the winds? Or of the Crux? And did it matter?

Alison climbed blindly, every intake of breath a triumph against nature. Then she edged horizontally around a rock and found the winds momentarily at her back.

She opened her eyes to see Rowan motionless ahead of her, though wind combed his hair into a scarlet tangle and wrinkled his clothes against his body.

Beyond them, on a white rock, like a bonsai tree posed for a competition, stood a tree, scoured bare until its pale wood shone like satin bone.

Its upright limbs reached in supplication to the sky. Little dirt sheltered its gnarled, aged roots. What was a tree stripped clean of all life—of leaves and insects and birds—but a contradiction rooted in the cruelest stone of old earth?

No salvation could await at such a site. Alison longed to warn Rowan about that, but the muffling wind still stirred around her. A chill gripped her lower legs and sifted upward.

She looked down: the clouds were consuming her torso, their tumultuous billows bearing the likenesses of faces, some of them human, many of them animal. They were swirling around her waist, their sad eyes as white and dead as dawn. Ghostly birds flocked, shrieking amid snowstorms of falling feathers. Swans and sparrows, bleached to mist, fluttered in a blizzard of beating wings. Whips of dead-white hair entoiled her; the Bone Buffalo thundered noiselessly around her in a frantic circle. Rambeau—*Rambeau!*—lifted a ghostly muzzle to howl at the spectral moon.

She looked up. The sun was halfway up the horizon, now bereft of clouds, but the planet's face was moon-pale. The world had been washed white with wind and pain. She felt a spirit herself, an uncertain accumulation of atoms shaking apart into sand.

She struggled to dig in her pack. The Cup! The Cup of Earth. A thing of solidity and silence, of stillness and ripe possibility. But . . . no! Rowan carried the Cup now.

He was still ahead of her, moving into the teeth of the raucous winds, struggling toward the tree. His amulet pouch was in his hands, wind-forced against his chest even as he strove to bring it to the tree, to give the amulet to the tree. To the Axletree.

Indeed, the entire world turned around the tree, the crowding clouds spinning like albino cotton candy in some cosmic circus. Would Rowan's gesture serve any purpose, accomplish anything?

It must. It *must.*

In her pack, her hand encountered the only concrete thing she had brought from earth.

Rowan lifted his hands in slow motion, every inch of movement a victory over the mindless, milling winds, now howling like a thousand banshees, howling to make wolves wail in frustration.

The pouch swung like a wild bell. Painfully, slowly, Rowan lifted it to a bare branch, ready to release it to the tree, the hanging tree, where it would swing to fulfill a rime.

Out of the swirling mist spurted vast jets of wind so powerful they were as visible as streams of water. Gray, rose, violet, and amber, the arrowed gusts assaulted the fragile amulet. Maws of wind flared open like the mouths of ravening wolves; bright, sharp fangs slashed at the suspended ash and clay.

Then something even more macabre slashed through the roiling air like a sword. A Crux-master's rod!

Unwavering blue fire, upright against the coiling winds, it widened into a window to silhouette a familiar and hellish form against its heavenly light. Eyes gleamed in opposite array: red and green.

Fingers as slender as bone needles, wrapped in a neon-blue aura, reached to pluck the amulet from Rowan's hand.

The winds' force carved Rowan into a statue. To reach for the tree against the four-way tussle of the winds, he had paralyzed himself. In that moment of stasis, of frozen action, the Crux reached forth again to take.

Not this time, Alison vowed, remembering Lorn disintegrating to ashes. Not again. Her hand clutched the weapon that had waited here. She wrested it free of the pack hanging from one shoulder, pulled it around, locked her elbows against the wind, and fired the revolver once, dead into the blue light, and again into the shadowy heart of the blue light.

This attempt to act in a situation that arrested all action but that of the manic winds had no apparent effect. Even the impact of the gun's recoil was countered by the winds.

But the blue portal trembled, and the hand retracted. The dark shadow at the blue flame's heart winked out.

Rowan reached to hang the cord woven of his own hair on the lifeless tree. And the pouch hung motionless. The winds' concentrated colors melted into the airy white of the surrounding clouds. Wild air stilled.

Alison sought Rowan's eyes in wonder.

At that instant, a new, negative wind howled into life, tightened into a funnel and sucked her free of the mountain, lifted her into an expanding blur of light. She felt herself siphoned into the straw of a thin blue wand, flowing into the Crux-master's medium with no more will than liquid.

"No!" she shouted, as poor Lorn had cried at the Heart of Earth.

Rowan turned to her, his horrified expression echoing her one word. No!

A noose of cold wind jerked her farther into the blue light, nearer to the Crux-master's clasp.

"No!" she cried again.

She reached for Rowan with her free hand, but he was a man moving like molasses in a tableau that was fading from sight. A blue aura spread around her, as if rising water and sinking sky merged into one element. Alison could not breathe, feeling herself falling into endless cool brightness. Clouds and daylight, even the wind, grew farther and farther away, until the distance itself became an enclosing sarcophagus of ice sealing her into a weightless plummet through pallid blue liquid.

This, she understood, is what it feels like to drown. No wonder she had always feared water.

29

BLUE wind spiraled Alison down a rabbit hole, deeper and deeper into the dark earth.

Then she plunged into the one substance she dreaded more than death: cold, dark, bottomless water. She flailed with the wild arms of someone who has never known how to swim.

The cold, wet sensation drained away. She stood on a solid something and flapped her arms in dank air. In the dark distance, a blue wand burned like an upright fluorescent tube.

The place she occupied was utterly still, the floor as smooth and hard as marble. Dark blanketed everything; she had no choice but to move toward the Crux-master's rod.

Her hand ached from clenching the revolver, but two bullets yet remained. No matter how disastrous firing into the rod had already proven, she needed some defense.

Her footsteps clicked on the floor, but the wand never wavered as she neared it. Holding her breath, she walked up to it.

Empty.

True-blue, unoccupied light. No shadow, only an azure candle glowing in the dark.

Holding the gun before her, Alison used her other hand to brush the blurred edge of light. She felt nothing, saw no change. She edged a boot toe into the luminescence. Nothing. No cold, no heat. No Crux-master leaping from behind the brilliance.

She edged sideways into the wand, poised to jump back should something threaten. Nothing did. She was halfway consumed by the light, and oddly unafraid.

She plunged into it wholly, through it.

For a moment a blinding brightness dazzled her, and then she was in a dimly lit room, boxlike, with a door at one end.

Looking back, she saw no wand, no light, only the room's far wall. She moved toward the door—it had a knob—and opened it.

A well-lit hall before her ended with a short flight of stairs. The ceiling lights were banks of fluorescents behind a plastic shell, the kind used in every public building on earth.

But not in Veil.

She climbed the stairs, hearing only her own echoes. Another door. Another flight of stairs, ending at yet another door. Another hall.

She went quickly, glancing aside where closed doors suggested other rooms. One door had a glass window in its upper half. Alison glimpsed something vaguely familiar bobbing in the interior dimness. She hurried past, afraid to look.

The last door resisted opening. She tucked the revolver in her pack and hurled her full weight against the aluminum bar that operated it. The door swung ajar, pulling her with it. Cold, white winter light slapped her in the face. Snowdrifts bracketed the path ahead: a narrow white ribbon of hard-packed snow.

Frigid air drifted around her body. She had walked perhaps five feet down the path when she heard the door behind her *whoosh* shut.

Turning, she saw no exterior handle. She saw no door, only drifted snow. The cold wound closer, absorbed her heat and shook her in its icy grip.

Alison shivered and wrapped her arms around herself. Ahead, tree branches encased in a shining carapace of ice bowed low to the ground, forming glittering miniature cathedral naves everywhere. Ice coated every bare branch and each brown leaf. Ice glazed even the snow with a clear, sleek crust. Beneath her boots, snow squeaked as she minced carefully over the slippery surface, her teeth chattering.

She went up the path as fast as she could without falling. The cold was unrepentant. It would cling to her, drain her of

heat and circulation, then of life. Keep moving, she told herself. Don't stop to ask yourself where, or why. Or what or
when. Just keep moving.

Yet the Saran-wrapped woods around her glittered in
beauty to the breaking point. Heavy branches hung to the
snow-covered ground. If the sun didn't melt the ice soon, the
boughs would snap. Sun. But the sky was smooth and chalky.

She hurried through the frozen fairyland, a madhouse of an
ice place that could freeze the smitten gawker. Was this where
the Crux-masters hid? Why was it deserted, then? Was this
where the inclement weather was confined, keeping the rest of
Veil sunny and mild? Maybe wildwater welled from here. Or
earthgall and all of the latter-day curses of Veil. So where
exactly was this place?

Maybe she had destroyed the Crux-master with her shots,
and had used his portal into this strange, inhospitable, yes,
cold and cruel world, the icy, unsunny side of Veil.

There must be a way back. Rowan had succeeded in his
quest; she had seen that, the last sight visible to her at the
Quarter of the Four Winds. She needed to get out of here
before she froze to death, or met any Crux-masters.

She suddenly realized that she didn't know where she had
entered this icy landscape. She looked back down the path and
saw no structure, no door to retreat to. She wriggled out of her
backpack—already her shoulders were stiffening—and pulled
out a spare shirt. Her fingers fought the buttonholes, but she
finally boxed her way into it. She found the cloths that had
covered the gun and wrapped them like bandages around her
palms. There was nothing for her to cover her head.

She hurried forward on numbing toes, plowing from the
neat path that could lead to some place sinister into fresh,
untraveled snow among the trees. Cold turned her jeans to
steel-blue pipes encasing her legs.

She forged ahead, ducking the icy whips of encased saplings.
Each bare tree was a dark skeleton sheathed in a gelatinous
skin; yet that sparkling icy glove could strangle the sleeping life
within.

At last! A structure was visible ahead. Alison stumbled into a hobbling run, her breath huffing white ahead of her. She was too desperate to be cautious, so she ran straight up to the place.

A cabin? The weathered wood was dusted with drifting snow, polished here and there with ice. From the one-story eaves, icicles dribbled to the ground like the elders' thin, dwindling beards. The back of a . . . cabin.

Alison ran around front, trampling ice-laden bushes, hearing their bones crack under her unfeeling feet. Then she gasped out loud. Not *any* cabin. Eli's cabin on the Island! This was it, no doubt about that.

She doubted everything else, including her sanity, as she climbed the snow-shrouded steps she knew were there. One, two, three, four. Her feet lifted the appropriate amount for each well-remembered step.

She crossed the porch to the door. It opened in, so she wouldn't have to fight the snowdrift heaped thigh-high against it. She shook the latch, pushed inward. The door cracked with cold and protest, but inched ajar. Bucking and resisting, it finally fell open; she fell in after it, over the snowdrift.

Eli's cabin. She studied the walls, the simple furnishings, seeing no signs of life . . . or of death. The place was perfectly preserved. That observation stirred her cold-slowed mind.

She clumped over to the big iron stove, clods of packed snow melting in her wake. The old mayonnaise jar still held a fat shock of farmer's matches. Alison's shivering fingers, white to the knuckles, managed to shake some of them out. She opened the cast-iron door and found a half-burned mound of kindling ready for lighting. The first match fizzled. The second struck against the table's deep-down damp wood. The third scratched on cast iron and caught.

She stood before the open stove for minutes after the fire took, letting heat creep down to her toes and up to her frozen nose.

Then she went to work. She found Eli's bottle of Old Crow and drank a shot from it. She went into the adjoining room that she had never seen. There was a cot for a bed, covered in an army-green blanket, and some clothes hung in a tiny closet built into the slanted ceiling.

She donned a worn wool jacket and found some wooly socks that she pulled on over her boots—if she took the boots off now, she would never get them on again. Despite a look of long abandonment, the things, the setting, seemed oddly well-ordered. From orange-crates along one wall she dug out a muffler that she swaddled around her head, and sheepskin gloves about four sizes too big. She jammed her hands into another pair of socks and pulled the gloves on over them.

"Look like Bigfoot," she grumbled, thumping back into the other room.

She stood before the stove to think. All right. This wasn't a Crux-master's hideaway, but her own Island home. Her bullets must have . . . emptied the blue rod. The resulting absence drew her into the Crux-masters' place. So the light wands served as a . . . not as a time machine, but as some sort of travel machine.

And had her bullet banished, or killed, a Crux-master? A chill more mental than physical gripped her mind like numbing ice. Why had it done so? Because the gun was an artifact of earth, and the Crux-masters also were, like Alison, things of earth? And was their headquarters perhaps the hidden building Alison had lost sight of as soon as she left it?

Why had she seen none here on the Island then? And, worse, why was it so cold? It's winter, silly, she admonished herself. You've seen the Island under ice as well as under water when the lake rises in the spring. Everything is normal here but you. The Island is exactly as it should be on a near-zero winter's day in, say, November or January.

And she had come up to the Island in June.

Alison felt her stomach lurch. It couldn't be winter. That would mean she had been . . . away for at least five *months!*

Her head ached, and her nose was running. She wiped the nose on a glove—the cabin was still chilly—and tried to install order in the head, her head.

If this was the Island, and if it was winter, she needed to get off, to some real warmth, fast. She would have to hike across the snowdrifted ice to shore, get the Blazer— No, the Blazer wouldn't be there after five months. Some vacationer would have found it, stolen it, or reported it. In any case, she would have been declared missing.

She sighed, tucked the match jar in her pack and checked to see if the cabin contained anything else she could use, anything she should take.

The rifle was no longer on the table, but it wouldn't be. Alison had taken the rifle to fight the Takers on her first visit to Veil. At least she hadn't been thrust back in time to a point predating her second visit. What was she thinking of? Not very much, and not very clearly.

She felt a crude sense of having been wronged. Once again she had been dislocated against her will. This time she had not renounced Veil, but had tried to protect it, and Rowan, from the Crux. For that she was unceremoniously tossed out without a chance to say good-bye, or even "Hey, what happened?" She had been defrauded.

Well, there was no arguing with a reality as cold as this one. Alison eyed the cabin again, struck by something out of place. Not the fishhooks in the bottles, not the Old Crow, not the chair or the stove. Yet something nagged at her. Something was missing.

At the door, she turned back one more time, needing a last sense of shelter before she braved the cold alone. If only Eli were here, or Rambeau.

And then she realized what was lacking here, what she should have seen, would have seen, had she not been so confused by the sudden loss of a world and by the white-washed cruelty of winter.

The white dogskin no longer decorated the cabin wall.

Snow softened the scenery into a smooth Dairy Queen landscape into which a human being could sink and stay lost until spring. She had to get to civilization.

Where was the land bridge to the mainland? Snowdrifts blurred the difference between frozen earth and icebound water. And was the ice solid, or was a soft underbelly waiting to collapse under the slightest weight?

Alison slid her stocking-covered boots onto the treeless white plain closest to the thick mainland trees. Snow ruffled around her ankles and calves, was blown thin in some places, drifted knee-deep in others.

Beneath her numbed feet, the surface felt rough, but lakes did not always freeze into a smooth, glassy skating rink. Halfway to the mainland pines, she found the snow brushed away from a five-foot-square surface. The cold, white, opaque face of the ice lay a little distance ahead.

Walking on water in any form was not her favorite activity. She glanced back to the Island, considering retreat. But she was past the point of no return; the icy wind made a retreat too taxing. The Island might as well have been Veil, it was so remote.

She sighed and skated forward, then froze again.

A hole gaped in the ice, a thin black slit at this distance, but every step forward would swell it like a dark-absorbing iris, until it became an eye big enough for a fish to pass through: a mighty northern pike, or a muskie.

If the ice was thick enough to support ice-fishers, Alison told herself, it would hold her. Still, she eased past the opening in the ice on virtual tiptoe. The hole, neither round nor square, looked like a Hammerhand's fist had punched it. No signs of an ice-house or its occupants remained.

The ice itself was thick, cloudy.

Alison decided to conquer her irrational fear. She edged nearer, leaned over the icy crater until she glimpsed the water below. Safe water. Trapped by an adamant roof of cold, white marble . . . .

Black water, liquid, moving. Deadly. Wildwater.

She wanted to jump back, but something held her there. The water, so dark under the ice and snow, made a shiny black mirror. Her own face floated on its half-hidden surface—no, not her face, simply a female face. A familiar female face.

She remembered bending over a similar familiarity reflected in the contents of the Cup—and forced herself back. Seeing strange faces was one thing in Veil. This was the Island's hard, cold winter reality, and Veil was behind her.

What face would follow her here? Darnellyne's? Her own, transformed? And why?

Alison stumbled into the rumpled snow bordering the ice hole and began running through the uneven drifts in no coherent direction, seeing only white. Better than black, swallowing water. Better than dead faces.

Wind and cold forced her head down. She tried to rebreathe her own warm breath as it tangled in the muffler swathing her chin and mouth. Her feet hit the hard surface beneath the snow like half-numb stumps.

Ahead now, a dark figure sat on the ice, squatting like a small hill of humanity amid the blinding, bright whiteness. She staggered toward it, seeing iron-gray hair above the bundled dark body. A fisherman huddled, without even the protection of a shack, over the naked ice.

Somewhere a bird was calling, and somewhere a shotgun fired. White feathers—snow, arrows—swirled over the ice. The figure did not move, only became bigger and blacker as she approached.

She expected it to turn, to be—

"Eli?" she shouted.

But it didn't turn, only enlarged, rose, kept on rising, flew past and through her like a giant blackbird. For the blink of an eye, encompassing darkness blacked out the deadly white. And then she squinted her eyes against bright white again. Ahead lay the ice, swept clean in a large circle.

No black hole played bull's-eye on that pristine target, but at its center a large bird lay still, its blood-soaked white feathers smearing the pale canvas of ice like fingerpaint, its long neck scribing an awkward S.

Alison stopped dead, looked around wildly, blinking and squinting.

Two black dots waddled toward her from the shoreline, shouting and lifting empty hands: men in winter parkas and boots, would-be ice fishers turned rescuers. A red Jeep Cherokee posed like a toy truck within the white-shrouded woods.

Alison clapped her cold-deadened hands together in their makeshift mittens and began flailing toward the men like a wounded bird. According to the notions of her world, she was safe at last.

SF AND FANTASY BY
CAROLE NELSON DOUGLAS

☐ 53587-1 PROBE   **$3.50**
                                         Canada **$4.50**

☐ 53596-0 COUNTERPROBE   **$3.95**
                                         Canada **$4.95**

☐ 51248-0 CUP OF CLAY   **$4.99**
                                         Canada **$5.99**

☐ 53594-4 KEEPERS OF EDANVANT: **$3.95**
            SWORD AND CIRCLET I   Canada **$4.95**

☐ 50046-6 HEIR OF RENGARTH   **$4.50**
            SWORD AND CIRCLET II   Canada **$5.50**

☐ 50324-4 SEVEN OF SWORDS: **$4.95**
            SWORD AND CIRCLET III   Canada **$5.95**

Buy them at your local bookstore or use this handy coupon:
Clip and mail this page with your order.

Publishers Book and Audio Mailing Service
P.O. Box 120159, Staten Island, NY 10312-0004

Please send me the book(s) I have checked above. I am enclosing $ _____
(Please add $1.25 for the first book, and $.25 for each additional book to cover postage and handling.
Send check or money order only—no CODs.)

Name _____
Address _____
City _____ State/Zip _____
Please allow six weeks for delivery. Prices subject to change without notice.